I0542481

Ash

Chronicles of the Eternal Dawn part 1

By Titus Cook

Published by AetherSphere Publications
First Edition
978-0-578-46896-9

AetherSphere
Publications

This book is dedicated to all my family and friends who have supported me over the years, in this endeavor and in many others. It took a lot longer than I'd hoped, but it's finally here.

Chapter 1

It was a machine built for the battlefield, and it had long since fulfilled its purpose. During the long years of the Final War, it had gone behind enemy lines alone, protected by layers of armor and the enchantments carved into them. It was a war that nobody won, but the Behemoth had continued moving and fighting in all that followed.

While once the Goliath class machine would have been filled with soldiers and little else, in the dusk of time it was filled with all manner of survivors. There was a man who called himself king. He had guards, soldiers, and servants that lived on the highest floors with his expansive family, but the masses dwelt in the bowels of the machine. It was there that Sol met with those that dreamed of his father's demise.

The room was small, but it was the largest of them that could be set aside for clandestine meetings with rebels. There were quite a few people waiting for him, but it was considerably less than would be present at any official event. Sol supposed it had to do with the different habits of those he was with. Any royal events he attended would be overcrowded with his siblings and their many servants. They would smile with grace and speak in jovial tones while making plans to kill one another.

Sol was a common target in the deadly and idiotic games his family played. He was accustomed to knowing that those around him wanted him dead. With the rebels, however, there was a difference. They made no effort to disguise the desire for his blood. They leered at him not through false smiles, but with dark and sunken eyes, held back by a mixture of discipline and terror.

There was the other sort there as well. Those who looked at him with wide eyes of awe. Superstitious beings that bowed their heads as he passed and offered prayers of gratitude. Sol couldn't say which of the two kinds he disliked more. Luckily, those he had to speak with had neither of the typical reactions. The handful of individuals that sat across from him were dressed in the same rotten cloth and had similarly frail bodies as the others, but they looked at him through the eyes of experience, rather than expectation.

Sol stood a head taller than the malnourished masses, although not a giant of a man himself. He was thin, but he looked overweight when compared to their gaunt frames. Some of them may have had the same golden hair, it wasn't rare after all, but the grease and oils that coated their existence hid such details.

"If you want to start, It has to leave," one of the men said. Sol's eyes flashed to his bodyguard. She was shorter than most and shared the frail look of the others, but her clean clothes would set her apart even without the more obvious signs, such as the pristine state of her sword and the many knives on her belt.

"That's up to her," Sol shrugged. The man leered and spat at the woman. She remained expressionless as she tilted her head away, but her eyes burrowed into the man.

"Don't give in to its designs boy. That's no human. It's a machine," the man said.

"She's flesh and blood," Sol said patiently, "even if it's not human flesh."

"That makes no difference," the man said. "It should join the rest of its kind. Tell it to leave."

"I don't give Kiran orders. I can't. No one alive has that authority. She does what she wants," Sol said.

"You're as naive as they say," a new man said. His voice was as weary as his appearance. His hair was gray and matted, his teeth crooked and broken. His eyes were filled with the wisdom and sorrow of ages past. He was perhaps a dozen years older than Sol's twenty odd years, but that was positively ancient for those outside of the royal sector, especially for those within the Pit.

"Elder Mattic I assume," Sol nodded in the man's direction. The man nodded his head in approval.

"Silence Galen. The Simuran stays, if it so desires," Mattic said wearily.

"No, I'll not let this thing be," the other man hissed. He stood and spat at Kiran again. She once again moved out of the way with minimal effort.

"I revoke the council's protection from Galen Val," Mattic said slowly. His voice was still in the air when Kiran's open hand collided with Galen's chest. Bones cracked loud enough to be heard over the murmuring crowd. The man struggled, hands clutching at his throat as he tried, fruitlessly, to breathe. Sol fought against his instincts, forcing himself to simply watch and not run over to the man, his hands clenching and releasing beneath the table as he forced his eyes to stay open.

He watches, Kiran's voice whispered in his mind, her tone emotionless as usual. He didn't look to her, nor to Mattic who was certainly watching him. Sol took a deep breath and forced himself to be witness to Galen's slow death.

The crowd didn't take it silently. They were loud in their anger, but none dared to act on it.

"Do you see now how dangerous it is?" Mattic asked.

"It's not the first time she's killed in front of me," Sol shrugged to hide his discomfort. "Usually, they're drawing knives or guns, or they tried to poison me."

Mattic gave a slight smile, giving Sol the impression that the man's question hadn't truly been for him at all. All the same, Sol didn't question it. He was too busy trying to gather his own thoughts and keeping his anger subdued.

"All we've learned from this is two things. First, Kiran respects your council enough to not act until you retract protection. Second, she doesn't like it when people spit at her. I could have told you both these facts, and many more, if Galen hadn't insisted on wasting his life and our time," Sol said, more of his anger slipping through his facade by the moment.

"I apologize for his words if not his thoughts. There are many who believe that creature is the root of evil aboard the Behemoth," Mattic said.

"Then they're idiots. Those crimes belong to my father. And to his, and so on since the world burned at Milias' hands," Sol said.

"You can say that, but it means nothing to us," Mattic said. "Tell me this child, do you know what the word telepathic means? All Simurans have that magic. That is a fact. It's how they were designed as they grew in their factories. How do you know it isn't the puppet master of you all?"

"Kiran controls no one," Sol said. He tried to be calm but found himself nearly growling the words. Mattic's small smile returned.

"Tell me, how would you know? Unless my spies are mistaken, she's been by your side since you could *walk*. She was alongside your father before that, and before she came out of her stasis pod, her predecessors were rarely seen outside of the royal sector, despite claiming to be the Caretakers of our machine."

"Enough," Sol grit his teeth. "I'll not stand here while you accuse Kiran. She is my teacher and my friend. I am *here* to talk to you about the crisis at hand. The Behemoth has stopped moving. Do you understand how dangerous that is? Obviously not, if you'd rather spend your time accusing Kiran."

The room fell completely silent for a time. Of course, everyone there already knew. Even the royal sector could feel the machinery when it was in motion. The Pit, initially designed as the great machine's industrial sector, had far fewer protections against the constant shaking. They would have been the first to know when its age-old movement came to an end. Still, he supposed that hearing him acknowledge it put many of them ill at ease.

"Because she may be the cause," Mattic said, finger pointing at Kiran. "How long has her kind survived against the odds? Some say it has been a thousand years. Others report it as two, or even three millennia since the world turned to Ash and Rot. All the while the line of the Simuran's has progressed. When one breaks down, another awakes from stasis. But this one is the last of its kind. What wouldn't it do to fulfill its duties?"

"You don't know her. You know nothing of her kind but fairy tales and misspoken legend."

"Our wisdom has been passed from parent to child for millennia. Do you think the words from its own mouth are to be trusted more?" Mattic shook his head. "But you are right on one account. The Behemoth must be put in motion again. It cannot stand still like this. We must find what ills it and make it whole once more."

"It's out of power," Sol said. Mattic scoffed.

"The Behemoth is powered by Aether boy. Aether is as endless as time. Even children know that."

"Then the children are wrong," Sol said. "I've been to the condenser Mattic, a dozen times since the Behemoth stopped in its tracks. I used my gift, and I swear by my life it is starving for fuel. There's little left to be had."

"Then the Behemoth is dead, and hope is lost," Mattic said. He didn't speak as melodramatically as his words would suggest. He was calm, serious, almost questioning.

"It *is* dead. But I have a plan," Sol said. The room became nearly silent once more. They waited on his words, some more than others.

"I've been preparing for a journey for some time now. We've moved carefully and quietly to keep my father in the dark. It was meant to be a scouting mission. But we don't have time for that anymore. What we need is an exodus. I can't save all of you. But I can help you keep yourselves alive, if only you dare to follow me beyond these walls."

Sol didn't know what he expected to follow his words, but it certainly wasn't the laughter that came from Mattic and many others in the room. Still, there were a few with curious looks on their faces.

"Boy," Mattic said, still snorting, "As childish as I've heard you are, I'd never think you dared believe in the legend of your name. Oh *Sol*, save us from this life of misery. Lead us, *Messiah*, to the land of plenty."

"It has nothing to do with my name," Sol said firmly.

"Where then would you lead us, do you even know?" Mattic asked. Sol took a moment to catch his breath, then nodded.

"The Behemoth was built by Simurans, but it was not their greatest feat. They created a fortress, impenetrable as only they could build. If our estimations are correct, the Behemoth has been on a slow approach for decades, maybe centuries. It's difficult to use the old maps in the wasteland, but we've found ways. We've four sites to check. It *will* be at one of them."

Once more, Mattic laughed and shook his head.

"No boy, that way leads madness," he sighed. His shoulders sank, his eyes drooped with exhaustion, and he shook his head yet again as if to rid it of foul thoughts. "I suppose our meeting was as pointless as we feared it would be. We will all do what must be done."

"What are you planning Mattic?" Sol asked.

"It would be-" the man began, but Kiran spoke, cutting him off.

"That would be extraordinarily foolish," the Simuran said in her nearly empty tone.

"Get out of my head," Mattic hissed angrily, eyes narrowing. The room tensed with him.

"I've no need to be in your mind. Your decades of zealotry in protecting your thoughts have made you a novice in telepathy. But you are uneducated in what you do. You do not hide your thoughts from me. You scream them aloud for me to hear. And I warn you; such acts will not go unpunished by the Behemoth. It will not settle with punishing you or yours, but all of humanity that yet lives."

"Is that a threat?" Mattic asked, hesitantly, yet still with anger.

"It was an explanation," Kiran said. Sol wondered if he was the only one that saw her eye twitching when she spoke. She was irritated.

Mattic stood and turned to leave without another word.

"All of you spread what I've said. Those who want to come with me need only send a message. Anyone is welcome. Anyone," Sol said, but no one answered, not even those that looked at him as something miraculous. They filtered out of the room, taking long passages back to their homes and secret bases, leaving Sol alone with Kiran. Or so he thought. The prince had sunk back down into his chair when the remaining rebel approached him.

It was a child, a small boy. He walked to Sol with faltering steps, terrified eyes frozen on Kiran. He was almost to the table before Sol noticed him. The prince smiled and leaned towards the child, causing the boy to jolt.

"I'm not going to hurt you," Sol said gently, "and neither will she. She's actually very, very kind."

The boy glanced at Sol. Then his eyes were back on Kiran.

"I...I..."

"I believe he wants to come with us," Kiran said. The boy looked at her with wide fear filled eyes. Kiran dropped to a knee, and Sol could tell she was holding herself back from rubbing the top of the child's head. It was a habit she'd built from raising Mara and himself.

"Your thoughts are your own," Kiran said. Her voice had the same empty quality, but she spoke softly, barely above a whisper. "I feel your emotions. Your fear. Hope. Grief. I know you desire to... Prove yourself. Specific thoughts and memories, those are yours alone. Unless you make yourself an enemy of myself or the Behemoth."

"Kiran," Sol said, exasperated.

"Honesty and understanding are more important than comforting lies," Kiran said.

"Still," Sol shook his head.

"Thank you," the boy said. To Sol's surprise, he'd visibly calmed. Sol smiled.

"What's your name?" he asked.

"Galen Val."

Sol froze. His gaze went to where the man had died, but his body had been taken by the crowd. He knew why, even if it made his skin crawl.

"Named after your father?" Kiran asked softly. The boy nodded.

He mourns, but barely so. I gather their relationship was...Troubled, Kiran said into Sol's mind.

"I'm sorry you've been left without him. But I'll not apologize for my actions. He desired to bring suffering and death to myself and my charge," she said aloud. Galen nodded slowly.

"Kiran, he's just a child, don-" Sol began, but Kiran silenced him with a piercing look, a brief change from her neutral appearance.

"There are none in the Pit that know childhood. You should know this Sol, or Mara has taught you little."

"Doesn't make it right," Sol murmured. He knelt beside the child as well, although the boy was still finding it difficult to take his eyes off Kiran for more than a moment at a time. He'd calmed, but his fear was still palpable.

"Well," Sol said, "I did say anyone... But we won't be leaving quite yet. I don't know... Can we take you home for now and collect you before we leave? Surely you have something you want to take from your home."

He'd die within the hour, and he must know it. Galen Val had enemies, and only one child they'll now want to take their vengeance on. This is not a choice for him. It is survival, Kiran said into Sol's mind.

"Can't I go with you now?" Galen asked softly.

"Sure," Sol sighed, "I mean, of course. We were... I was planning to inspect the AeC again before returning to my quarters. Then we need to prepare a little more, and to wait for my other bodyguard to get back. A day or two. Hopefully, we can convince more of your people by then."

"We must detour," Kiran said suddenly. "Galen will need to be announced as a servant before he'll be allowed anywhere near the royal sector. He will also need to be fitted with combat armor."

"He won't be seeing combat," Sol said firmly.

"That is not for us nor him to decide. It is for his protection. If the Council acts on their plans, it will be all that stands between him and death."

"What are they planning?" Sol asked.

"They will bomb Hydroponics," Kiran said calmly.

"Are they insane?" Sol hissed. "How can you allow that?"

"I am unaware as to why they believe the bombing will be beneficial for them, however, their actions will make no major change to our own plans. It may only expedite the process."

"How will the Behemoth respond to them?"

"I do not know the specific defense protocol that will be used, but it will be of the deadly variety. No matter which protocol it follows, a combat suit with a fully sealed environment module will be the best chance for survival."

"Shit," Sol spat. "Will Mara be back in time?"

"I believe so. The scouts should be returning by now," Kiran said. Sol nodded.

"Let's get Galen set up with some armor then. After that, we can figure out how much time we have left if the Council *aren't* idiots," Sol smiled grimly.

Chapter 2

Sol counted the seconds as he held his breath, waiting for the absolute calm to take him as he kept one hand extended. Aether, looking as luminescent mist, continued its slow journey to the condenser regardless of his efforts. He closed his eyes, though it did little to hide the mist from his sight, and focused on the orb at the heart of the room. It was where all Aether seemed to flow. Its glow would blind him; had it been normal light he was seeing. Yet even that glow was much lessened in the hours since he'd last seen it. The Mist that flowed to it was nearly gone as well.

Somewhere inside the thing, the AeC was transforming Aether, the natural energy of magic, into Ether, the extraordinary substance which could power machinery as well as magic. Little was known of the process that created Ether, other than Aether was the primary ingredient. Its creator had been quiet as to how it worked, as well as how he'd first developed it. In any other kingdom or empire, the man would have been flayed for answers. Fortunately, or unfortunately, the inventor had been the emperor himself. Milias. Creator of the Simurans and owner of all the wonders they'd created.

After reaching a minute in his count, Sol willed his arcane sight to end and opened his physical eyes with a wave of exhaustion. The golden star upon his forehead turned black as the magic left him. The glow of the sphere he glared at was replaced by a metallic ball at the heart of the chamber. Thousands of cables connected the thing to the walls and beyond.

"We don't have much time," Sol said quietly.

"What is your estimation?" Kiran asked.

"A week at most. Maybe a day," Sol sighed, "please tell me you found something that will make me feel better."

"That would be deceit," Kiran said. Sol looked to his bodyguard. Her fingers still danced across the control console as her eyes scanned an ever-changing display.

"What is *your* estimation then?" Sol asked. Kiran didn't answer immediately. She continued scanning the display for several moments before the hologram disappeared and the console went dark.

"The system estimates the shield will fall within twenty hours at the current rate. That is without interference."

Sol screamed a curse and began to pace back and forth on the balcony that overlooked the AeC. As he walked his hands dragged along the rails and tapped randomly. His bodyguard stood at attention beside the console that only she could use. Her face showed none of the desperation that Sol felt pounding through his veins.

"What do we do?" He asked after several minutes of ever more ridiculous plans.

"I estimate all organic forms will perish within two hours of shield failure, with some variation due to physical locations. It is advisable to not be present at this occurrence," Kiran answered.

"There aren't enough hovercrafts for everyone. Not by half. Not by a hundredth. If anyone even listens to us."

"There is a more concerning issue," Kiran said.

"What is it?" he groaned.

"The King's scout ships are soon to return. Once connected, the ships will replenish their Ether reserves as protocol demands. This will only exacerbate the energy crisis."

Sol cursed again. Before he could ask his next question, Kiran was answering it.

"My clearance level is insufficient to change these protocols. Altogether, however, energy transfers are not entirely inadvisable, as the ships will need the power should there be an exodus."

"It's an issue of time," Sol growled. "*Gods*. How did we run out of *time*?"

"Misuse of resources is a common human error," Kiran answered. Sol glared, and, for a moment, he swore his bodyguard would grin at him. Perhaps her lip twitched, or maybe Sol imagined it altogether. Kiran was a Simuran. The last of the Simurans aboard the Behemoth, and likely the world. It was her people that built the great machine. It was by her grace that humanity survived aboard the Behemoth. No human could access the systems of the Behemoth; no matter what the so-called Council and the King claimed.

Sol closed his eyes and started to count the seconds between each breath once more, yet this time he didn't focus on using his arcane sight. He wrestled with the emotions pounding through his veins and forced himself to calm. Anger, as always, was his real enemy. Anger for the injustice of the council. Of his father, the king. For all the wrong done to those that lived and died in the Pit, and anger at the dead world.

"I will accelerate preparations," Kiran said, her voice suddenly beside him.

"Right," Sol said, nodding as he brought his emotions under control. "We need water and protein paste. A lot of it."

"My haste will be noticed, and your father may not sit idle. The Council will accelerate their plans as well. Especially once they realize the Hydroponics sector has already ceased operations."

"Is there enough food?"

Kiran stared at an empty wall for a moment. Sol could nearly feel her mind working on calculations.

"Should all ships be filled there would be insufficient stores for the survivors that could escape in them, nor is there time to properly stock each ship. However, it is possible to stock the handful of vessels that could be used. Should there be a larger exodus, most will starve."

"And those left behind?" Sol asked. Kiran's eyes looked to him and stared at him briefly before answering in a robotic tone.

"Nutrition will not be a concern for those individuals."

Sol nodded. He knew it already. She'd said it before. Most would die. Tens of thousands. The last of humanity. They had no use for the food Sol would be taking. Still, it felt wrong to even think about taking it from them.

Sol returned to his breathing exercise as he stared at the steel ball that was the condenser, the AeC. The device was functioning as it always had. There was simply too little Aether left to be converted. To one such as Sol, one with the gift of magic, it was akin to slow suffocation. Then again, his kind was as rare as the Simurans anymore.

"Can you lock the council in the Pit?" Sol asked. Kiran shook her head.

"Most system-controlled doors were removed from their areas before the current council existed. It was a point of contention with my predecessors."

Sol nodded, continuing to take deep breaths.

"Do what you can," he said after a moment.

"For that, I will need to lock you in your quarters," Kiran answered.

"I could help," Sol said, at nearly a whisper, but Kiran made no motion nor sound of notice.

The situation wasn't entirely unexpected, even if its sudden arrival was. The wonders of the old world were once beyond counting. Impossible things that blurred the lines of what was possible and what wasn't. Only one man had full access to the devastating power that Ether gave. A small kingdom that became the Soltraven Empire. A nation turned into a war machine that nearly devoured the world before the end came.

It had been a spectacular place once. It was first formed from the slaves of surrounding Kingdoms that gathered together to fight for their freedom. The leader had taken the name of Sol. Through his sacrifices and valor, freedom was won, and the Kingdom of Soltraven was born. By most accounts, it had been a beautiful place.

Even after the legendary leader died, his legacy was noble and righteous. Until, of course, Milias was born into the royal family. He'd turned the small kingdom into an empire that spanned over half the world.

For all the horrors that Milias created, there were wonders as well. It wasn't only the Simurans and their grand machines of war. There were flying cities. Culture and art the likes of which had never been known in living history. The world was ancient, billions of years old. Most of the past was lost, forgotten and erased by the hands of tyrants and warlords calling themselves Kings. Still, Soltraven was known as a herald of scientific and magical progress that surpassed all the legends of old, despite all the horrors it brought to its enemies, and at times, to its own people.

There was one technology that Sol deeply desired to know of. A thing simple enough to be in nearly every fiction he'd read over his twenty odd years of life, yet impossible enough that no one could get it to work outside of those fictions. Not even the reportedly immortal Emperor Milias could travel the world in the blink of an eye.

Teleportation would answer all the prayers Sol had made since he first learned that Aether wasn't endless. A way to flee, and hopefully a place to escape to. Not alone, but with all humanity that still lived. Except for the suicidal Council and the monster that made him the crown prince; his father. He wouldn't mind if they stayed in the dying machine.

The Soltraven Empire had created marvels and taken over most of the world in a war that dwarfed all others, yet among their incredible creations teleportation simply wasn't present. Sol wanted to ask Kiran, as she would be the only living being to really know if the technology had once existed or not. But when he looked to her, he felt the childish question die on his tongue. She would only chide him for such childish thoughts, then tell him he should have spent his time memorizing schematics or history, rather than fantasizing about works of fiction. Were it possible, she'd have told him. He knew that. It wasn't the first time he'd stopped himself from asking such a childish question.

"We should move quickly," Kiran said. Sol nodded and turned to the leave the chamber that was the heart of the great machine. The Simuran walked slightly ahead of him. They passed through a dozen hallways that were empty of people, and even most noise but for the soft groaning of machinery. Most of that was silent as well, for the first time in living memory. The Behemoth was still as the grave, its eternal trek through the world at an end. The thought of it was enough to cause a panic, and there was one. People would already be dying in the depths of the Pit. All he could really hear, other than his own footsteps, was the odd tune that Kiran hummed on occasion.

Despite the size of the Behemoth, they found their way back to the royal sector rather quickly. This was partially from a quick pace, but mostly from the vacant nature of the passageways they walked. The halls they walked were sealed for the use of the Behemoth's Caretaker, Kiran. Humans weren't allowed there without her permission. That meant only Sol and Mara could accompany her there.

Even if it wasn't his first time in those halls, he couldn't help but feel unwelcome. It felt like the walls wanted to crush him. But even if the semi sapient machine could do so, it wouldn't. The systems of the Behemoth obeyed the orders of the Caretaker, so long as her orders didn't contradict its protocols. The prince often wondered how his father had convinced the Simuran to be his bodyguard in the first place.

It was the only time the man did anything Sol was grateful for, and it was done when he was a child. When he first woke to magic. When his name was changed to Sol. He was, after all, the first human with magic in one and a half thousand years, by the estimations he'd been told. Exact times were more than difficult to come by.

Devices that counted time were all but inaccurate anymore, each moving at a different pace, and daylight was virtually nonexistent. Some tried to gauge time by estimating the distance the Behemoth visibly traveled, in the assumption that its speed was a constant. Officially, however, the day ended when the king went to bed; and began when he left his chambers for the day. That system had been in effect for centuries. Centuries as measured by that same system at least.

The two passed through a door and left the sealed sections of the Behemoth, entering the collection of rooms and hallways known as the royal sector. It was vastly less crowded than the Pit below, but it was still filled with servants and members of the family going about their business as if nothing was amiss. Sol moved closer to Kiran as they moved at a brisk pace. Most people they passed stared at their feet when they saw the Simuran approaching. All fell silent and moved out of her way as quickly as they could.

"Is Mara back yet?" Sol asked.

"She should be close now. We will need to remove her from quarantine when she does return."

"Will that be safe?"

"She will not be leaving the hovercraft. The likelihood of her being infected is insignificantly minuscule, considering the built-in redundancies in her air filtration. Besides, we would be required to leave her behind if she was left to quarantine for its full duration."

"And that's not going to happen," Sol nodded. Despite the situation, he had to hold back a laugh. There was nothing in the Simuran's voice to show she was upset, but he knew she was. If asked she would say that Simurans didn't get upset. They had very few uses for emotion in the first place.

She wasn't an automaton, although her people did consider themselves to be organic machines. Simurans were a genetically designed species incapable of natural reproduction. Technically Kiran was neither a he nor a she and looked entirely androgynous. Simurans were built in laboratories in the world of old. Synthetically designed organic bodies, with minds formed from years of telepathic manipulation. The mind of a Simuran was a network of orders and fixed values. Emotions were present but had little value in their 'settings' as Kiran said it.

Sol didn't believe her claim entirely. He'd seen Kiran act emotionally on several occasions. It wasn't always large actions, although there were a few of those. It was the small things. Considerations a nearly emotionless machine, such as Simurans claimed to be, would not make. They would be easy to miss for most perhaps, but Kiran was there from his earliest memories. The earliest he could clearly remember at least.

Years before, he'd woken from a week of nightmares with the mark of a black star freshly burned upon his head. He was the first Aetherweaver in over a millennium. He was one of the king's youngest children at the time, and the nightmares had consumed all his memories.

Even his original name was gone, changed because of the mark he bore. Sol was made the crown prince in the same day. His elder siblings, nearly all of them, made attempts on his life. He'd barely been old enough to speak when a foul-breathed servant with a knife snuck into his chambers. Sol hadn't even known to be scared. He was only afraid when a strange person appeared in the door and removed the servant's head from his shoulders. It wasn't the servant that made him scream in fear.

Sol had called the Simuran the 'scary lady' and was accompanied by her at almost all times from then on, at least for the next decade. She'd told him she was an it, not a she, and explained the reasons. But in the young Sol's mind the Simuran had been the scary lady, and eventually, Kiran stopped fighting him over it. She even took a name for his sake, or for Mara's sake. Even if Kiran was merely the word for Caretaker in the language of her people, it was more comfortable and more affectionate than K131, as she initially demanded to be called. In either case, she was the first of the Behemoth Caretakers to take a name.

The Simurans on the Behemoth were only ever active one at a time. There had been over a hundred of the beings when the great machine was first built, all frozen in stasis. When one perished, for whatever reason, the next in line would be woken. Each of them used part of their serial number as identification, rather than a name like humans were given. Until Kiran consented to name herself, all it took was a couple children creating nicknames for a month or two to drive her to it.

It had taken a single lesson from an official instructor for Kiran to take over the role of their teacher as well. The Simuran had a half dozen claimed reasons that could be considered logically driven, but Sol could still recall Kiran correcting the man's claims at every other sentence. The man disappeared a few hours after that first lesson, never to be heard from again, which was one of the reasons Kiran replaced him.

It took a few years, and some investigation, before Sol had been old enough to approximate what had happened. Before he realized how closely the man had been watching Mara, Sol's servant, who was only a couple years older than him. Before he learned that the missing man had a nasty reputation among the inhabitants of the Pit. When he realized why Kiran had followed the instructor out of the room, locking Sol and Mara in their quarters for a time. Why so many of the servants and royalty were terrified by the Simuran.

The realization, however, did not surprise him. For the look on the Simuran's face as she'd followed the lecherous instructor from the room had been just like the first time he'd seen her, when she'd beheaded that first assassin. Empty but for faint disgust. Although that first time the look had been followed by a tired and obviously faked smile as she patted a screaming Sol on the head.

"Do not leave unless Mara or I open the door. I fear that chaos will soon descend," Kiran suddenly interrupted Sol's thoughts.

"Is there really nothing I can do to help?" he asked, surprised to already be at the doors to his rooms, retrofitted from the chambers of some high-ranking officer.

"You can stay here, get some sleep, and let no one in," Kiran said. Sol nodded and did as he was told.

Chapter 3

"Don't tell me you're one of *those*," the man sighed. Mara chuckled.

"I am," she admitted. The man sitting across from her shook his head.

"There's always been Aether, Mara. *Always*. Don't believe those doomsayers. Everything is going to be fine," the same man said.

"I'll give you my alcohol allowance next month if we're still around for it," she answered. The young man cheered, earning a few laughs from the others in the small scout craft. Mara's grin was hidden from sight.

The seven individuals were wearing sealed combat suits, but while most had removed all but the most minimal amount of armor, Mara's suit had additional armor modules strapped to it. She also had her rifle, four pistols, and fifteen grenades. It was the most her suit was technically capable of holding in the small armored slots designed to prevent their contents from exploding prematurely. There was also a small device in her left hand, a simple trigger she hoped to have no need to press. It was well out of sight of the others, held along with a series of straps that would usually be holding her in her seat; if they were attached and not merely being held.

There was a difference with the helmets they chose to wear as well. While all the members of the scout team wore helmets with clear visors showing their faces, Mara preferred a version that showed nothing but a smooth metal shell. Her display inside the helmet relied on a series of cameras and other sensors rather than magically enhanced clear plastic, or whatever the visors were made of. Most soldiers had little trust for the frequently faulty sensors that the fully armored helmets had. It was also true that few of them spent a significant portion of their free time cleaning and repairing their suits as Mara did. Her suit did not malfunction. Not frequently at least.

"What's it like working with the thing? She as lethal as the legends say?" someone asked. Mara glanced at the corner of her display to see which of the soldiers the question had come from.

"Kiran?" she asked as if uncertain who the man was referring to. "She's deadlier than you're imagining. Could wipe the floor with your sorry squad." Her tone was light, coming through the communications suite of the suits with a light laugh to convey that she wasn't entirely serious. Even if that was a lie. A few members of the squad chuckled awkwardly at her statement.

"I wouldn't bet on it if I were you. Not unless you want to go without a drink for another month," the man across from Mara said. She sighed. The man looked to be a few years younger than her. He was just a boy really. He was an innocent.

Of those in the compartment she'd found two she suspected. The others realized what it meant when a *random lottery* sent a royal bodyguard to accompany a group of scouts. They would sit back and watch whatever happened. Mara had no issues with those. The boy, however, Alex, according to the suit display, was painfully naive. He hadn't been raised in the Pit like the others. Couldn't have been. In any case, it was a trait that was soon to end, in one way or another.

"We'll be returning to visual range in a few minutes," the pilot declared.

Mara saw one of her suspects, the one that asked about Kiran, trying to undo the straps holding him down without making noise. He couldn't tell she was using the cameras bolted in the rear of her helmet. It was another reason she liked the heavily armored helmets, besides trusty metal replacing the plastic parts. With it, she could see in any direction with none being the wiser.

She released the straps she'd been holding, then carefully tightened the same hand around the switch it held. As her fingers squeezed the device it gave a loud alert and was armed. As the hovercraft's inhabitants looked to the sound, she kicked her body into motion. Her first target panicked seeing her move, giving up on his straps and going for his rifle. Before he could touch it, there was the muzzle of a pistol beneath his jaw, followed by a flash of light and the horrid stench of burned flesh, if any of the suits allowed the scent through the air scrubbing.

Mara held her left hand aloft, so the explosive trigger could be seen, then half spun another seat down to the second target. The man had acted fast as well. He was on his feet with rifle drawn but not yet aimed. Mara grabbed the gun and tore it out of the man's grasp with ease. The idiot hadn't thought to lock it in his grip with the suit's magnetic array. Most were fools like that.

"What the hells are you doing?" Alex screamed from out of sight. Mara planted her pistol in the same unarmored section of the suit as she had the first target, beneath the jaw, and raised her left hand behind her to ensure the boy saw the trigger she held.

"Who set this up?" she asked calmly.

"Fuck you," the man said.

"Three seconds," Mara stated. Behind her, there was the sound of a brief struggle. Doubtlessly one of the witnesses stopping Alex from doing something idiotic.

"One," Mara said in a bored tone. The man closed his eyes. Mara lowered the pistol, fitting it between sections of armor just above the knee. A small ball of plasma went through the fabric, the backside of the armor holding in the heat. The man collapsed in screams as part of his leg was vaporized.

Mara knelt and returned the muzzle of her pistol to its spot beneath the man's jaw.

"Who was it?" she asked.

"Gods no, please. He threatened us. We didn't want to do it," the man whimpered. Mara nodded.

"Dahgan then. The idiot hasn't learned," she shook her head. Before the man could speak again, she pulled the trigger and returned to her feet. She slowly made her way back across the small ship. She swapped out the pistol for her rifle, then she sat in the copilot seat, deactivated the explosive switch, and raised the gun to the pilot's head. She shook her head when she saw he hadn't even brought a weapon with him. He hadn't done much, only warned the others that their deadline was approaching, but he was a part of it.

"He used our families," the man pleaded, "please, don't do this."

"He does like to do that," Mara nodded, "switching control."

The primary controls switched to the copilot's seat as the air was filled with the crackling sound of significantly more dense plasma. Singed armor fell to the ground, the fabric between the modules having burned away with most of the man's upper body. She'd set the projectile settings of her weapons much earlier, and rifle had been set on the border of its capabilities. Injured enemies were dangerous. Dead ones weren't.

"Opening side section B. Someone toss these guys out," Mara said.

"The hells," Alex whimpered. Whoever had stopped his stupidity had magnetically locked him against the hull to keep him out of danger. It was the doings of his own suit, but he was apparently too inexperienced to know how to deactivate it without using the small console on his wrist. Mara could only imagine him as one of those that spent little time familiarizing himself with his own tools, who hadn't set commands to be triggered by gesture or eye tracking. A real idiot in her opinion.

The left panel of the scout craft opened to the world, and one of the surviving soldiers did as Mara had asked, magnetically locking his feet with each step as he moved back and forth through the hovercraft. By the time the gruesome task was over the Behemoth was nearly back in sight.

"Only the pilot had a living family if that helps you sleep. If you have that problem anymore," a voice said a moment later. It was the man that had removed the bodies. He sounded old, tired, and somewhat disappointed. Mara nodded.

"I thought not," she said.

"They were fools. Tulka though, the pilot, he was a good man. A good man that made a made a stupid fucking decision. His own damned fault."

"I guess so," Mara said. Then, once she turned off her suit's microphone, she whispered words of gratitude and drove the machine through the wasteland.

The world outside their hovercraft was Ash and craters. The remnants of the Final War, and that which followed it. The sky above was always hidden by dense black clouds, but for those rare moments when a ray of light broke through. Mara had never seen it happen. Few had, and most assumed they were lying. In any case, only the eldest of the scouts spoke of such moments, and their stories were as ancient as their careers. No one else spoke of them. But again, other than the scouts, people rarely saw what was outside the Behemoth.

It was the third time Mara had been outside of the great machine. Once while in combat training, and twice because of some royal's scheming. Were it not for the violence she would be appreciative of the opportunity. The world beyond the Behemoth was alien, monstrous, and deadly to the ill-prepared. But it was different. Novel to her, if a bit ubiquitous. Staring at the wasteland from displays inside the Behemoth wasn't the same as being in a hovercraft flying through it.

The ground was even darker than the sky. There was no greenery, as could be seen in the histories. Nor was there rock, nor real soil. All was bedrock, coated with craters and cracks from the Final War, wounds too grievous to heal unless given time they never had, for The Rot followed the war, with its assault on all things that lived.

It had a proper name once. Many of them. They were lost to time just as everything else, replaced by the common man's moniker. The Rot, and the small flakes of it they called Ash. It was the dark substance that formed the clouds above, a canopy so thick that daylight couldn't pierce it.

The same Ash was layered upon the bedrock and partially filled the craters. It slowly rained from the sky, coating all of existence. But it was not ash from some grand fire, at least not it the traditional sense. It was from the great calamity. The Rot. It *was* the Rot. A single speck of it could doom a civilization. Even rock turned to Rot Ash with enough time. Flesh was significantly quicker at the transition, but few had the time to die from the infection. It was not the Ash alone that was the calamity. It was but the start of the cycle.

Mara couldn't help but grin as she sped through the wasteland. The machine hovered a dozen feet above the Ash bed, sending plumes of the substance into the air behind them. She turned in large arcs while trying to follow the marks they'd left earlier in the day. They hadn't found anything of note in their explorations. Not that they were expected to. Over a dozen scout teams had been sent out, a move of panic when the Behemoth stopped moving. But then they hadn't been the team searching in the direction of their constant pursuer.

Mara drove the machine at sound breaking speeds, not daring to go slower across the wasteland. They climbed a particularly large crater wall, nearly slowing as the climb became vertical, then shot into the air after passing the edge. Mara turned a switch and large metallic wings spread out from the sides of the hovercraft to slow their descent, putting them into something akin to an inefficient glide. She only pulled the wings back in when the hovercraft had returned to a more standard height.

Ahead of them, visible but still many kilometers away, was the Behemoth. The Goliath class machine was beyond massive and had the shape of some demonic insect. The armored hull alone weighed billions of tons, doubled with the weight of weapons attached to it, all supporting tens of thousands of lives within. It was not sleek, and it did not shine.

It was roughcast and worn metal filled with runes and magic to keep it alive as the machine moved on enormous treads. The front of it was an open maw that plowed the ground before it, drilling deep into the bedrock as it moved. When it had been moving, it mined, filtered, and manufactured whatever the machine needed. During the war, it created weapons and drones to fight for it as it drove behind enemy lines without support. It was never a fast-moving machine. But seeing it standing still was doing strange things to Mara's heart.

Surrounding the great machine, coating even the teeth like drills of the mining sector, was a barely noticeable translucent aura officially known as the Ether Shield; although in general it was referred to as the barrier. To untrained eyes, it looked like a visual distortion with a blue tint. But with time the edges could be found. It was not round, nor did it give equal room to all parts of the hull.

Over parts of the Behemoth, the barrier was a dozen meters from the hull. In places such the drills, the distance between the metal and the shimmering barrier could only be measured in units smaller than a millimeter, when the drills weren't in need of repairs; which they always were in some regard. Luckily the Behemoth, for the most part, regenerated itself so long as the Caretaker allocated enough resources for the task and none of the arcane runes were damaged.

There were lights and thousands of bulky plasma canons strapped to the sides of the machine, and many of them, although not all, were actively firing at the growing horde that surrounded the Behemoth. They were the real terror of the Rot. The Beasts. The things that formed out of the Ash. Monstrosities that were an amalgamation of things that existed before the Rot. Things it had long since devoured.

The most horrifying one Mara had seen had been a twenty-legged spider with the head of a lion and the scales of a lizard. The scales had been four times as dense and many times tougher than their natural counterparts were supposed to be. But then even the weakest of the beasts were immune to all but the largest caliber of kinetic weapons. Luckily, nothing was immune to the heat of magnetically contained plasma. Not completely at least.

"We should be entering radio distance momentarily," Mara said for the benefit of the other inhabitants.

"What do we tell them?" she heard Alex whisper from his position on the hull.

"Nothing," the tired man said. Malik, according to Mara's display. She hadn't bothered to check most of the names when their journey began, but his earlier words had earned her respect.

"You want me to say *nothing* when they ask what happened?" Alex questioned.

"They won't ask," Malik grunted. That made the boy's mouth open and closed a few times, but also brought his momentary silence.

It took another minute or so before the radio indicator flashed green. Mara flipped a switch and spoke.

"This is Sergeant Hansen reporting for SCS374. We're on approach to your northeast sector, over."

No response came for several moments longer than would be typical, enough to make Alex squirm, or try to.

"This is Specialist Dougal. Find anything interesting out there?" the voice came through the hovercraft's speakers, rather than to Mara's suit as would be normal.

"We didn't find anything worth speaking about," Mara said casually, "But we'll need a docking ray as soon as we're in range. Your lower bays look a little too busy for my tastes."

"Duly noted ma'am. A full report will be required during the quarantine period of your reentry," Dougal said, before breaking the connection.

"They know what you did," Alex said.

"And they don't care," Mara said slowly. Malik grunted.

"I've said it for years. Some fools *need* to live in the Pit for a year. Toughen them up, get them thinking."

"Unfortunately, the King has no interest in good ideas," Mara said. Malik gave a single, gruff, chuckle.

"What do you mean? I've been to the Pit. It's not so bad," Alex said in a shaky tone. At that Malik shook his head.

"Stupid boy. No, it isn't so bad on the top layer, with all your armor and a full platoon at march. No, you've not seen the Pit till you're alone and three layers down, stabbing a man for trying to add your skin to his diet."

"Those are just stories," Alex said quietly.

"I was born on layer seven. They are not stories. Most of them anyways," Mara said. That made the boy go silent again. Mara fought the sudden jealousy she felt, forcing it to be pity instead. Beneath the royals were their servants, the soldiers, and their families. Beneath them, in the Pit, was the rest of humanity. Insufficient food, insufficient space, insufficient morality.

Those that escaped the Pit would do anything to avoid returning. Mara could attest to that, and Sol had chosen her as his servant when she was six or seven years old. Others spent significantly longer in the Pit before getting a chance to leave. Only a royal's prime servant was chosen so young, for the purposes of proper training and instilling loyalty. It worked.

By his sheer naivety, Alex could only be a second-generation soldier, perhaps a third. They were luckier than they could know. As much as Mara liked the idea of sending most the Kings spawn and their ilk into the Pit, those blessed and precocious fools such as Alex wouldn't survive a night, let alone a week or a year.

Another light flared to life on the ship's display. Mara flipped another switch then sat back as the hovercraft was pulled up to the top levels of the Behemoth, towards one of its distant docking bays. They were still far from the horde of Rot Beasts, but she could almost feel them watching her as they fruitlessly pressed against the barrier, scratching at it as they were. Some of the beasts could fly, but they were priority targets of the Behemoth's targeting algorithm, as well as anything potentially hostile approaching a docking hovercraft.

It took a few minutes of smooth travel in the docking ray before reaching the barrier. As the nose of the hovercraft passed through, sections of the hull glowed a violent blue, as did the armored suits worn by the inhabitants. They bore arcane runes in their construction that allowed them to pass. Nothing could move through the barrier without the runes, except for plasma, and whatever the Behemoth's mining equipment produced, but no one living knew the specifics of how that worked.

They passed through the barrier without incident. From time to time there were stories of damaged suits and soldiers pinned against the barrier as the ship continued to move *through* them. They were genuinely gruesome tales, but such things happened rarely.

The hovercraft and its four inhabitants were behind thick hanger doors moments after passing through the barrier. Mara, Alex, and Malik, who had taken the boy down from the wall readied to leave. There was a forth inhabitant who seemingly slept through the entire trip, but she didn't look surprised to find a bit of blood on the floor and missing comrades as she followed at the back.

Massive fans spread copious amounts of some unnamed cleansing agent through the air, into a series of vents, and out into the wasteland. The chemicals were ineffective against the Rot, all things considered, but the blowers helped to clean the machine and its inhabitants of the deadly Ash that coated everything.

From the hanger, they entered the personnel decontamination room. It was large enough for a team twice as big as the one the scouts had started with. They spread out through the room. The forth nodded her head to the others and seemingly continued her nap in one of the corners. Malik chose another corner, as did Mara. Alex sat somewhere in the middle, trying to distract his worried hands and mind with some game playing across the transparent display of his suit.

Mara sat back and waited. It would take a few hours to be properly cleaned. Then it was time to spend endless days in quarantine, in case they were infected. Even if most infections killed in moments or minutes, hours at most, there was the lingering fear of a Rot infection taking days or weeks to take hold. She didn't mind. The time in quarantine was one of her favorite parts of missions outside of the Behemoth. Solitude was a precious thing.

Time crawled as they waited. Mara all but muted the sound coming through her sensors. The blowers were loud enough to hide most other sounds anyways. She kept her eyes open so she could watch the others in the room. Alex continued to play his game, glancing at Mara frequently. Malik stretched with ridiculous frequency, apparently eager to remove his suit, and the forth could seemingly sleep endlessly.

When the fans finally went silent, and the doors audibly unlocked, Alex almost ran to the door that would lead to the quarantined quarters and the rest of the Behemoth. He'd barely opened the door before screaming and running backward with a wild look. A moment later Kiran walked into the room through the same door. Mara stared at her for a moment, then used the console on her wrist to unseal her helmet and remove it. That was one command she wouldn't set to gesture.

"What are you doing Kiran? Where's Sol?" she asked, running her hand through short and sweat-soaked auburn hair.

"Sol is sealed in his quarters for the time being," Kiran said. Mara gave her an expectant look. Kiran turned to the boy staring at her and returned the stare as only she could. Alex shuffled out of the room quickly after, followed by the strange forth, and finally Malik. The man looked like he would say something for a moment, then gave an awkward bow to the Simuran instead and moved past her quickly.

"You're not supposed to be here without a suit," Mara said loudly while the man was still in earshot. Kiran nodded.

"None of you showed signs of infection, and the room has been cleared," Kiran said, gesturing towards one of the cameras that sat above each corner of the room.

"We still need to be cautious. It's not like we understand the Rot. It could sit dormant for days for all we know."

"It can. However, I found the likelihood underwhelming in this situation," Kiran said. Mara shook her head and leaned against the back wall, then spoke in a much-lowered voice.

"What are you doing here?" she asked.

"We have less time than we suspected," the Simuran said.

"How much less?"

"It is difficult to predict. Hours, or minutes by now."

"Shit," Mara hissed, "are we even ready?"

"I've been making preparations while you were on approach. There is a reasonable chance of reaching the objective," the Simuran nodded, "others will not be as fortunate."

"Can we stretch the time until the barrier falls?" Mara asked urgently, "we could turn off a few things for more time."

"The time gained from deactivating all other functions would provide less time than this conversation has consumed. Collect your things, Mara. I will sound evacuation alarms once you and Sol are safe aboard the Scion."

The Simuran turned to leave at a faster pace than when she entered. Not quick enough to hide the tremors that shook her body, moments before the lights began to flicker; as if the machine was shuddering with its Caretaker. It took both a dozen seconds before returning to normal.

"Kiran?" Mara asked, moving to support her friend. The Simuran moved to avoid the soldier's touch without looking.

"The rebels have ignored your advice and my warnings. The Behemoth is removing life support from ongoing processes in retaliation. Including the Shield and air filtration. I will collect Sol and bring him to the Scion. I suggest haste," Kiran said, before moving at a pace that Mara couldn't hope to match. Not that she didn't try. Despite Kiran's earlier claim, the evacuation alarms sounded before she'd even cleared the first hall.

Chapter 4

Galen hadn't removed his armor as he waited for Sol.
It was too large for the boy, with layers of extra straps
holding everything in the right places. The boy was clearly
uncomfortable, unwilling to even sit in one of the room's
chairs. He carried a discolored bag that seemed to hold all
his worldly belongings. He fidgeted nervously and glanced
every which way as he held the bag protectively. It made Sol
chuckle and shake his head.

"You can take off the helmet for now," Sol told him.
The boy nodded and put his bag down. His shaking hands
worked at the clasps of his helmet for a moment before he
seemed to recall something and used the control panel on his
arm. The helmet hissed as it unsealed itself.

"Sir...Where is...Where is the Simuran?" Galen asked,
picking his bag back up.

"Her name is Kiran. And she's preparing for us while
we're safely locked in here. We can leave if we want, but
only she can get in here now. Well, her or Mara," Sol said.

"No," Galen said, looking down, "She's your
bodyguard, and I'm...I could kill you, sir."

"I suppose you could," Sol said, shrugging and
raising an eyebrow. "On the other hand, Kiran knew you
were here and didn't mention it. That means she trusts you,
and I'd be a fool not to trust her judgment when it comes to
my safety. That means I trust you as well. Galen, you can
put the bag down. There's no need to be scared. No one is
going to hurt you, least of all Kiran."

The boy nodded, but it was obvious enough he barely took the words into consideration. Sol turned his attention away and moved to a large control panel and display on the edge of his room. It presented ancient maps, as well as more recent pictures that were taken from the Behemoth's many sensors. There was still a sea, of sorts. A sludge-like liquid that barely moved, and looked much as the Ash coated ground, especially through the grayscale of the night vision. The easiest way to tell it apart was the uniformly smooth nature of it.

With hours of work, the general shape of the coastline could be followed and compared to those shown by the maps. It wasn't exact. The landscape had changed since the maps had been made, and the water levels had lessened, but the Behemoth had a backlog of videos, images, and topographical data that they cross-referenced over the years.

It was agonizingly slow work, and their exact location still wasn't certain after a dozen years of it. Every comparison had several places it *could* be. It was only by comparing many of them that a general vicinity became evident. It was the culmination of Sol's life thus far, not that he hadn't been helped by Mara and Kiran with the process.

"Have you ever seen a picture of the old world?" Sol asked without looking back.

"No…Ah, no sir," Galen said softly. It took him a moment to answer, as if he'd shaken his head first, then realized the action wouldn't have been seen. Sol grinned and gestured the for the boy to approach. He cleared the maps and brought up a new image. It was the same image he fell asleep to every night for the past year. A tall and ancient mountain, said to be the most massive of them all. Most of it was coated in white snow. Below that, there was the green of trees and a pale blue lake. The sun was in the corner of the sky, partially hidden in soft clouds, its golden light dancing across the snow of the mountain, and the water far below it.

"That's Mount Kalmit as it once was," Sol said. "And that's where we'll be going." Galen walked beside him and looked at the display with awe and wonder.

"Have you heard of the mountain before? Did your father or the others tell you those stories?" Sol asked.

"No," Galen said softly.

"Unfortunate," Sol sighed, looking back to the image himself. "You see, the mountain will no longer be there. Few of them survived the war. But beneath it, the Simuran's built their mightiest stronghold for the emperor to retreat to in a time of need. They called it Bastion. And we're going to find it."

Galen nodded again, but even Sol could see the boy was sad. Close to tears. The prince shook his head.

"That's not all we'll be looking for," He said gently. "Galen, the tales of Mount Kalmit are far older than Bastion and the Simurans. Older than the empire. Older than any empire or kingdom in history. Almost every history book wrote of the place. Hundreds of wars were fought at its feet, all for the glory of having it."

Sol paused, but if Galen had any comment or question, he held it back. Sol began speaking again as the silence began to grow awkward.

"Before Bastion was carved beneath the stone, it was said there were tunnels dug throughout the mountain from days before history began. The legends say that things lived there that couldn't be explained. Giants and Fairies, Pixies and Centaurs... Honestly, anything the story needed there to be," Sol chuckled and shook his head. "Wouldn't it be interesting to find the truth of that Galen? Maybe there's still fairies hiding in those caves. We can be the ones to know for sure."

Galen smiled, and Sol knew the boy was taking pity on him, thinking him mad perhaps. Yet it was still a smile, odd to be seen with the silent tears the boy wept.

"I don't know if I believe it either, to be honest. But it seems a better way to... Better than doing nothing, I hope."

Galen nodded, the gesture almost imperceptible.

"I'll leave the image on then. I'm going to rest while I can," Sol said.

"Thank you," Galen whispered. Sol smiled and pretended not to see the boy's tears.

It took a bit longer than he expected to strap on his own sealed suit. It was much better fitted than most. It had the gold trim of royalty, once signifying a high military rank, but it was just as old and uncomfortable as the rest of the suits on the Behemoth. Sol strapped on all the armor but for his helmet, which he left close at hand as he laid on his bed. It wasn't a soft thing, but it was better than the floor, even with the armor on. Especially then, perhaps.

"Sir," Galen said quietly after a time.

"Call me Sol," the prince said. There was silence for a time, then the boy spoke again.

"Sol... do you really have magic?" Galen asked. Sol closed his eyes and sent his mind into the deep place he knew to be hiding there. He raised his hand, and an orb of light appeared slightly above it, for a moment, as the star on his brow glowed a soft gold. It made Sol feel ever more exhausted as a small flow of his Mana dissipated, despite it being just a minuscule light. His body produced Mana from Aether, and with Aether so limited the loss was likely to be permanent. Still, hearing the child gasp in surprise made him smile.

"It's true," Galen said in awe.

"A small thing. Common once," Sol said.

"And your other magic sir?" Galen pressed. Sol didn't answer. He stared at the ceiling above him silently.

"Sir. Sol. The stories say that. That when your mother died, you..."

"How do these stories get told?" Sol whispered the question. Then he shook his head. "Galen. Something did happen that day, but I don't remember it. I was young, and whatever I tried to do didn't work. She died. So, no, I don't have other magic. I just make floating lights."

Sol turned to his side and tried to sleep, but the damage had been done. All he could see was a beautiful woman, beautiful to him at least, whimpering before him. She bled from her chest where the king had stabbed her. He remembered her look of disgust, hatred, and fear as she stared at him. As if it had been Sol who wielded the knife. He saw his small hand reach out, and he watched her die.

Falling asleep took even longer than he thought it would. Even when he did manage sleep, he frequently woke with a racing heart and words on his lips, but the dreams fled from his mind too quickly to remember. He hated it. It felt like he forgot something important, crucial even. But in the end, they were only dreams, and the feeling would flee.

Each time he woke he would check on his newest servant. Galen barely moved. He was still before the image, sitting or laying on occasion, his eyes constantly scanning the hologram.

Sol was almost relieved when he woke to the alarms screaming, although he'd have vastly preferred waking to Kiran knocking. In either case, the fear came quickly after the relief.

"Helmet on, we don't know what's happening yet," Sol said, but Galen was already locking the helmet to his body with shaking arms. Sol followed suit with his own.

"Where is she? Where's the Simuran?" Galen asked in a dread-soaked voice.

"She'll be coming for us," Sol said, once his helmet was properly locked in place. The boy spoke again, but Sol couldn't hear him properly. He hit a few commands on his wrist console, activating the suit's communications suite that had, for some reason he couldn't recall, been turned off the last time it was worn. He was about to calm the boy, despite his own racing heart, when the first flake of Ash drifted through one of the air vents that lined the room.

He stared at the minuscule speck, unable to speak, as the dark thing gently wafted through the air to settle on his desk. More followed. First a couple, then in the dozens, then hundreds. But his eyes were on the ancient, scratched and worn steel that a thousand men and women had studied at over the years. Metal never turned quickly. It took years of contact for steel to turn, but more and more of the Ash fell on it, on the floor around it, and around Sol. It settled on his armor, and the back of his throat hurt.

"We need to get to the Scion. Follow me. Now," Sol said urgently. Galen nodded and grabbed his worldly belongings. The boy was terrified, anyone could see it. Sol patted his helmeted head and led him to the door. It opened silently at his command, but when it did, the sounds of what laid beyond reached him.

The sound of screams and whimpering filled Sol's ears. Those in armor were running down the hall, desperate to flee, to where they knew not. Those unfortunate souls without the sealed suits were mostly huddled in fear, praying as the Ash surrounded them.

A muscled man charged Sol, entering his view at the last moment. Sol raised his arms in a fruitless defense as the larger man tackled him to the ground. The man grabbed at his helmet and slammed his head against the ground. The man was screaming something but the words were lost to the prince's ears. Sol struck at the man with arms and knees uselessly as the man struggled to rip the magnetically locked helmet off Sol's head.

Galen tried to help as well. He swung his bag at the man's head but couldn't seem to hit him. Then the man screamed once more, this time in agony, and leaned back. Sol stopped his struggle and crawled away from him, back towards his open chamber doors.

The man's arm was dark as night and falling to pieces. Pieces that crawled across the metal floor while growing mandibles and shells.

The man's screams turned to begging as the Rot spread along his chest, and up his neck. Sol couldn't answer, and before the man could move again, Kiran appeared behind him, dressed in the simplest of sealed suits, and deprived the man of his head.

"Get up," Kiran said in her empty tone. Galen forced himself to his feet and began to shake as he clutched his bag more tightly. Kiran glanced at him, face a mask, then moved with incredible speed to lift the boy off his feet.

"Follow," she said to Sol. He nodded, and they took off down the hall. Kiran held Galen in one arm while she wielded a sword in the other. She dispatched everything and everyone they passed without remorse. Sol sprinted to stay as close to her as he could, trying not to focus on those the Simuran was executing. Galen struggled as Kiran pinned him against her body, making it impossible for him to slip out or even move his arms, but the Simuran ignored the child's obvious terror.

Sol stared at Kiran's back as they moved. He purposefully ignored the horrors that were growing around him, but even the sounds of the changes were worse than he'd ever imagined. It wasn't only the screams and whimpers of the afflicted. It was the sounds of tearing flesh and cracking bone inexplicably thundering through his ears. Then there were the glimpses of what was transpiring around him. Even as Kiran cut down all in their path, the bodies continued to change and disintegrate on the floor.

As they ran small limbs grew from the Ash caked ground to grasp at their boots and legs. Creatures ate and chased down the halls. Kiran led him through ever emptier hallways, but still, there was the evidence of what transpired all around them. It continued for longer than Sol could track. Each moment he could only hope the sounds would end. They didn't, but they did grow more distant.

"We're close," Kiran said. Sol was about to summon the will to say something, anything, through his panting breath, but stopped short. As she'd spoken, Kiran had adjusted how she held the young Galen. The boy, with his arms suddenly able to move, raced to open the bag slung around his neck. Sol's body froze in place, his head ringing, nose bleeding. He gasped for breath and clutched at his heart, falling to the floor as his vision swam.

Kiran fell as well, clutching her head. Galen dropped from her arm and scurried away from them. The ringing in Sol's ears ended, but Kiran seemed only to grow worse. Her muscles locked, and she hit the floor as if her strings had been cut. She stayed there, motionless.

"Kiran?" Sol screamed, mind dancing with questions. He half crawled, half ran the few steps to her side, his hands and knees slipping and sinking into things he didn't dare look at. He'd nearly reached her side when the lights of the Behemoth flickered and left them in darkness.

Sol fumbled for a second before the lights of his suit activated by themselves. They were dimmer than those that had lit the hall for millennia. They seemed barely enough to see, the air filling with Ash as it was. Still, he could see in the distance other small lights flickering on. Some were from people in suits, running. Others were spread across the ground.

Kiran was lit by her helmet alone, her suit having less armor than even the base models. Sol lifted the Simuran by the arms, dreading what he would see, but no part of her body was changing nor falling apart. Her face was frozen without expression. Her body wasn't limp as he'd thought. It was rigid, and her eyes were darting every which way.

"Everything is going to be alright," Sol managed to say. He reached down to the archaic sword she'd dropped at some point. The blade was thin, and light, and familiar. Simply holding it gave him some measure of comfort, although he was no fighter.

"I'm sorry," Galen whimpered. "I was too late. I, I was afraid. I'm sorry… I couldn't stop her."

"What did you do?" Sol screamed, spinning his head. Galen pulled his hand from his bag, holding a strange and arcane looking device that was snapped in two uneven halves which he dropped on the floor.

"Saving you. Saving all of us, but. But I was too late. She wasn't there. She was supposed to be there… I, I failed him. I failed everyone."

"What did you do?" Sol screamed again, not bothering to hide the rage that coursed through him. He felt the star on his head begin to burn, and small lights that flickered into existence around him. The boy looked at him with terrified eyes, dropped the device and ran into the darkness. Sol watched him leave for a moment, the boy's suit lighting up the hall.

As the boy ran, Sol took the strange device in hand, carefully slipping both halves of it into a storage compartment at the waist of his suit. He forced himself to calm as he moved, feeling waves of exhaustion coursing through him as the star, his Stigma, turned dark once more.

With a grunt of effort, Sol placed Kiran over his shoulder. She was light, much lighter than even someone of her small frame should have been, even without armor. Holding her with one hand, and the sword with the other, he moved towards the Scion, the hovercraft they'd picked out so long ago. Or so he hoped. He prayed that it was close as Kiran had claimed. He didn't know where they were. He'd been so focused on ignoring what surrounded them he had no hope of figuring it out. He could only move in the direction Kiran had been taking him and wait to find something familiar.

He almost slipped with his second step, stumbling and barely managing to keep upright. By his fifth step, a creature shambled into his view. It walked on four thick legs, but was otherwise still somewhat human, although its head was featureless. A dense crimson fur was sprouting across its body at a visible rate. As he watched, the skin of its chest tore apart. Bones snapped and reshaped to form a twisted and snarling mouth filled with countless bleeding eyes.

Sol glanced behind him. Seeing nothing there he stumbled back and let Kiran drop to the ground. He placed both hands on the small hilt of the sword and stood in the most protective stance he could manage. The creature snarled and leaped towards him. It didn't reach him, seeming to trip over its own legs as it moved. Its second attempt was smoother, and it would have collided with Sol, maw first, had the prince not stepped to the side. He swung the sword as he did so, with a scream of effort and a flash of his Stigma. The sharp blade went an inch into the waist of the creature before stopping completely.

Sol's arms went numb from the impact. The beast twisted, ripping the handle from Sol's grasp and sending him sprawling to the floor. The thing stood between Sol and Kiran. It turned its maw as if to look at him. Drool leaked from its dreadful mouth, sizzling as it touched the ground. Then Sol heard the snapping of metal, and the sword dropped out of the creature in a dozen shards as the wound healed over.

It lunged at him again. Sol pushed his body to the side. The beast moved in midair to follow, only to be yanked back across the floor.

Kiran held one of the beast's legs in one hand. Her other hand was *through* the metal floor on her other side, holding her in place. The creature roared. Sol's ears rang with the horrible sound that was both shrill and deep. Then the thing stomped one of its other legs into the chest of the Simuran. The floor dented around her body, but she held one, her eyes staring at empty space.

Sol couldn't move his body. He could only watch as the creature raised its leg, the fur covered and hulking thing was shrinking and sharpening as it became something more akin to a barbed tail. Before it could stab Kiran, however, hot bolts of plasma sang through the air and collided with the beast. Across its head, into the open maw on its ever more alien chest, and into its legs. The thing fell into pieces, some turning to flakes of Ash, others shifting and regrouping. Growing.

Mara charged forward, her familiar armor unmistakable to Sol's eyes despite the darkness. She kicked and stomped at the still moving and growing parts of the beast. She grabbed Sol by the arm and forced him to his feet.

"Where is she?" Mara asked, panting for breath, as Sol shakily tried to stay on his feet. He couldn't speak through the lump in his throat. He pointed to the still form on the floor, nearly hidden by the disturbing, twitching, parts of the beast. Part of the broken creature was growing over the Simuran as if trying to disguise her as part of the gore coated floor.

Mara bent over and lifted Kiran with ease, tearing through the monstrous flesh that was attempting to grow over her. Sol watched as the substance grew small tendrils, topped with claws and minuscule fanged maws that fruitlessly tried to sink into Mara's armor. Before they could try to attack the areas less defended, Mara had Kiran over her shoulder and was gesturing with her head for Sol to follow.

Ten meters saw them to the door through which the Scion was housed. Sol swallowed as they came to the thick metal door. Roars and growls were bouncing and echoing down the halls. Between the echoes were a few faint screams and the sounds of things walking across the gruesome floor. But he couldn't see any of what made the sounds. He could barely see a dozen meters through the Ash still pouring through the now silent air ducts.

"Hold her," he heard Mara say. He felt his body move as if against his will. Mara laid Kiran in his arms and said something about looking out for danger. He couldn't quite hear her. His ears were filled with ringing, and a sharp and uncomfortable sensation was pounding through his chest.

From the corner of his eyes, he saw Mara fiddle with dials on her overly large rifle before she started to fire powerful blasts of plasma at the door, which quickly began to glow a dull orange, then a brighter white. But his focus was on Kiran. Her helmet had a larger visor than even him. Her eyes were open, her features twitching and shaking. She stared up at him for a short time. Then the light left her eyes, and she was staring at nothing at all. He'd think her dead were it not for her faint breathing.

"She'll be fine," Mara's voice came through loudly. Sol looked up as Mara grabbed him by the shoulder and pushed him through the doorway. His boots sizzled and slightly sank into the molten metal that was once a door, but he was across it quickly. Sol was finally feeling himself back in control of his own body and could almost believe he could speak again. But behind him, he heard Mara firing her rifle again. A half dozen times at first. Then a dozen more. It took a dozen seconds before the firing became a constant barrage of noise. It was then that he started to run again.

He entered the hanger, a space coated in copious Ash, but without the other substances he'd seen and felt beneath him in the once populated hallways. As he moved, things began to stir and take shape in the Ash as if they knew of his presence.

He ran to the familiar ship that was safely locked into the single ship bay. It was a triangular thing, a scout vessel with most of its armored sections removed, replaced with giant power cells for reserve fuel. They'd been preparing the vehicle, in secret, for years. But it wasn't ready yet. Not if the search was longer than they hoped. But then they'd always planned a return trip as well, so they could lead the Behemoth to whatever they'd found. He supposed that wouldn't be part of the plan anymore.

He reached the side of the ship, hearing Mara's pounding feet approaching from behind, and opened the hatch with the code they'd chosen. Lights around the small hovercraft flared to life, and the hatch opened, slowly. Mara reached his side before he could enter.

"Fast as you can now," she said, rather loudly. Sol nodded and squeezed into the hatch as soon as it was wide enough for him. He dropped Kiran into one of the cockpit's rear seats, then ran to the control console at the front and began flipping switches to start the various processes the hovercraft needed. The engines activated without flare, groaning more than screaming.

Mara practically leaped into the pilot's seat as she entered, slowing only to magnetically lock Kiran into her seat. Then the soldier was hitting more switches and activating large lights that lit up the front of the vehicle, revealing hanger doors just large enough for the hovercraft to fit through if it still had the layers of armor and weapons it was supposed to have. Plastered across the sealed hanger doors were hundreds of explosives.

"Kiran said she was making preparations," he said.

"Let's hope she didn't overdo it," Mara nodded. It only took her a moment to find a small detonator beneath her seat. The first place she checked for it. Sol shook his head and magnetically locked himself to his seat. Behind them was the roar of one of the beasts entering the hanger. Before that sound could truly grow, it was dwarfed by the cacophony of an explosion. By luck, or design, no shrapnel flew back towards the ship; instead exploding out into the wasteland that awaited them.

Sol's suit struggled to keep him awake as the hovercraft went from stationary to nearly supersonic in a blink. The combat suit forced his blood to keep moving through his body, but his vision blurred and his mind nearly blanked as they sped through a small external section of the Behemoth that was filled with shrapnel and burning bits of Rot Beast flesh. Moments later they were in the air, metallic wings extending from the Scion, bringing an end to the rapid acceleration.

Mara struggled to keep the nose of the hovercraft as upright as could be done. Sol held his breath as he watched through the display that took up the front of the craft. They were a thousand meters in the air, having left from the tallest sections of the Behemoth. If he stood on top of the hull, he'd nearly be able to reach out and touch the clouds of Ash that covered the world.

Below the craft, by many hundreds of meters, was an immense swarm of beasts. Tens of thousands, hundreds of thousands, perhaps more. They crawled and flew around the lower areas of the Behemoth. They were thankfully in vastly fewer numbers at the heights of the great machine, but there were enough that Mara had to swerve to avoid a collision with several of the flying monstrosities.

To Sol's surprise, the things seemed nearly willing to ignore them as they passed. The beasts flew and ran into the thick hull of the Behemoth, tearing it apart with claws and teeth. Sol lowered his eyes from the display and turned several dials before running a cable between his suit and the Scion's secondary control panel.

"This is Sol Bravik, broadcasting on all frequencies. I've escaped the Behemoth with two others in a modified class A Scion. Are we alone out here?"

Sol was surprised at how crisp he managed to make his voice, except for at the end. Unfortunately, it was the only surprise waiting for him. No voice announced itself over the speakers, from his helmet or otherwise. There was only the whirling sound of the engines and his own breathing in his ears.

The Scion touched down none too gently, followed with another burst of acceleration. They weren't far from the slowly growing horde of beasts. More of the things approached on the horizon, others clawing themselves out of the Ash. Just as when they were in the sky, Mara moved to avoid the creatures, which didn't seem too interested in chasing them more than a few meters before racing closer to the Behemoth.

Sol repeated his broadcast and was met with the same silence as before. He repeated the call a third time, then a fourth a minute after to the same result. After a while, there was a buzzing static that made Sol's heart jump in hope, but no voice followed it.

Neither spoke as the great machine gradually shrank behind them. They passed fewer and fewer of the beasts until there was nearly nothing but them in the wasteland: them, the craters, and the Ash.

Mara drove the Scion to the top of the tallest crater wall around. She set half the display to the cameras that circled the hull of the hovercraft. The other half she dedicated to a single camera, one that looked back, and was zoomed in so the Behemoth could be visible. Most of what they saw was gray-scaled, using enchanted night vision so they could see even in absolute darkness. It was grainy from both distance and the Ash in the air, but the sight of their home still made Sol's chest hurt.

At some point, while they fled, the machine had fallen to one side. Flames ate at the air from a few places, but most of the Behemoth was coated in the Rot. They stared at the thing, Mara taking visible care to eye the feeds from other cameras every few moments. They watched the monstrosities climb and claw their way inside, into the ancient halls held within the armored shell of the great machine.

"We'll need to keep the suits on," Mara said eventually, her voice hoarse.

"Yeah," Sol nodded, unsure of what to say, or if he could even say anything more. Then his eyes caught movement, the ground buckling and cracking. He pointed, and Mara was moving to increase the zoom to where he was looking when the action was made pointless.

The ground beneath the Behemoth exploded outward in a burst of power. What followed was a sea of molten stone and fire, followed by a limb the likes of which Sol had never known to fear. A grotesque tentacle that looked to be liquid flesh coated in slit eyes, scales, and hair, all of which dripped with magma. The thing reached from below the ground and into the clouds, as other such limbs tore themselves out of the ground around the great machine.

The sight of them made his head throb painfully. His eyes watered as he turned his head and fought his stomach as it tried to empty itself. He could only watch from his periphery.

The limbs fell upon the Behemoth, the metal buckling and collapsing from the impact. The hull shattered, the beasts upon it flung or crushed beneath the monstrous limbs as the Behemoth was pulled into the ground. Its surroundings began to glow as smaller limbs emerged, all working to drag the Goliath class machine towards its end, to be buried deep underground, and once there, to be consumed.

"Our pursuer finally caught us," Mara said in a disbelieving deadpan. Sol nodded. They knew of the creature, even if they'd never seen it before. Sensors told of a massive beast, one that dwarfed even the Behemoth, that dug beneath the ground in an eternal chase. But it was slow, and while the Goliath machine had been in motion, the creature had never been able to catch them. It should have been able to change, to move faster, but it never had. It only ever pursued them at the same slow pace.

Sol couldn't say how he knew, but the sensation of being seen coursed through him as an absolute certainty. From the corner of his eyes, he could see Mara's hand shaking. He heard her take a deep breath and mutter something before he realized he'd stopped breathing as well.

The zoomed display blurred as the Scion exploded back into movement, creating a wake of Ash behind it, while the distant beasts turned to give chase.

Chapter 5

Mara didn't wake slowly. She awoke with a burst of motion and quick breathing, her hands going for weapons that weren't on her body. It took a few moments of her hands searching fruitlessly before her breathing slowed, and a few more after that for her to slap the side of her helmet and raise her seat. Sol glanced at her with concern from the copilot's seat but said nothing as the soldier caught her breath.

"I'll take the controls in a few minutes," she said after a few moments of silence had passed.

"You need more sleep than that," Sol said, "It's been an hour at most."

"I'll be fine," Mara said, flexing her hands for a moment before removing the various straps that held her to the seat; a more comfortable alternative to the magnetic locks. She made her way to the back of the small vessel, stretching as she walked. She passed a small collection of weapons that were locked to the hull. Her hand reached out to grab a familiar pistol and holster it at her side, catching herself at the last moment. She glanced back to Sol as if to make sure he hadn't seen the act of habit, then continued to the back of the Scion.

She opened one of the many crates that were stacked and locked into place, digging out two pairs of vials. Two were filled with water, the others a gray paste. Her quarry in hand she returned to the front half of the vehicle, taking the seat beside Kiran. The Simuran was both strapped to the chair and magnetically locked to it. Her seat was set in a laid-back position, so it looked as if the woman was sleeping, but her eyes were open.

"How are you doing Kiran?" Mara asked quietly, clearly not expecting a reply as she carefully pulled empty vials from the arm of the Simuran's suit and replaced them with two new ones.

Why do they insist on feeding the toaster, a masculine voice snickered. Neither Sol nor Mara heard the voice. Nor could they see the figure that was speaking, lounging in the air, eating from a bag. He had long and ornately braided black hair and was dressed in blue and gold robes of extraordinary quality, along with a simple crown on his head which featured the sun at the center.

Don't look at me like that Kiran, the figure rolled his eyes, *obviously you're more than a toaster. But you know you need the food about as frequently as one of those things right now. It's a waste of their supplies. They would know that if they bothered to remember your lessons. I told you it was pointless.* The figure shook his head.

Ahead of the Scion a beast clawed its way out of the Ash and leaped at the hovercraft. Sol cursed and swerved sharply. Mara caught herself on the edge of Kiran's chair, but her hands tightened and one of the precious vials she held shattered, its lead-colored contents splattering across the floor.

"Sorry," Sol said with flushed cheeks visible through his large visor, "they're setting up more of those ambushes. They shouldn't be this clever."

Most aren't, the voice said, *they're hibernating, and you're waking them up. Idiot. Kiran, say he's a buffoon.*

"It's fine," Mara said quietly. She looked back at the crates of supplies, sighed, then returned her gaze to the Simuran before using the last of the vials to replace the empty water slot in her own arm, sealing the compartment that held it a moment after.

K131. Say. Sol. Is. A. Buffoon, the voice commanded. The figure of Mara shimmered and shook, then the world turned dark as a pressure built in Kiran's mind and pain pulsed through her body.

Sol is a buffoon, she answered. The world returned to normal, the pain gradually dissipating.

"She's still twitching. She's fighting," Mara said sadly, then spoke again at a whisper. "I wish. I wish we could open our helmets. Just long enough to close her eyes."

See, they prove me right again, the figure shook his head in exaggerated exasperation. *Closing our eyes while we sleep is one of humanities greatest flaws, next to blood and stupidity. I would never include such weaknesses. Mostly. Some blood is necessary to keep things human related...I suppose that means humans are inherently weak. That does sound right.*

Mara stood up and made her way back to the pilot's seat. Kiran felt herself trying to reach out to the soldier, but her hand wouldn't move. She couldn't speak either. Words didn't fully shape in her mind, let alone travel to her tongue. Her thoughts were sluggish and half-formed, shattered and trying to pull themselves together. But he was there.

He was always there. From the day she was moved from the labs to her stasis pod; where her body was frozen for fifteen hundred thirty-eight years and forty-three days by her pod's count. The day she was frozen he'd been waiting for her. She'd been a true Simuran at the time, as all newborns were; with no desire to resist the compulsions built within her consciousness.

He'd planted seeds in her mind on that day. Messages and visions that waited for specific moments before blooming into words and images only K131 would be able to see and hear. The man had done it to others as well. Some human. Others not. That was all in the memories and histories built into her mind as her body was printed and her consciousness shaped. It was his right to do so, as he was the omniscient seer to whom all of time was known. As the emperor that allowed life to exist or end at whim. Or so said the lessons that her mind was built of.

She, or rather it, had been surprised the first time it felt anger towards the figure. Surprised and ashamed of itself. The figure enjoyed that; K131's confusion and loneliness in those dark days. It came to know those things quite well, despite Simurans being incapable of experiencing them. Then the figure, the seeded illusion of Emperor Milias, gave those parts of it a name. It detested the name at first. Simurans did not have *names*. But then Simurans were incapable of detesting anything at all without orders. However, above all else, they could never resist their emperor: thus, *It* became *Kiran*.

You missed a fun conversation with your latest attempt to go brain dead, Milias remarked. Kiran pulled herself out of her sluggish thoughts and returned her focus to the outside world. Milias was no longer floating. His feet were on one seat while his head rested weightlessly on Kiran's lap. He continued to eat his snack, while occasionally throwing pieces of it at, and through, Sol.

Sol's doing the one thing he does spectacularly well. He's forgetting what happened. At least the details of it. He won't let himself think about Eddie at all. Not even in his sleep, gifted as he is in the art of being an idiot. Do you want to know his exact thoughts?

I do not, my lord, Kiran said. Milias smiled.

He dreams of something different. He'll tell you at some point, in confidence, the figure shook his head as he chuckled. *He is starting to realize how desperate they are at least. Say what you will about Sol, even that cruel comment of him being a buffoon that you made, but he is a coward over all else. The boy is terrified of dying. He just won't admit it to himself yet. He struggles to justify everything, all while telling himself how useless he is.*

Mara is different. She's wracked with guilt and worry. She dreams of Eddie every time she sleeps. Not that she knows it as Eddie. Not that Eddie is its actual name anyways. But it's closer than whatever you lot were calling it. I'd check, but I really don't care… Anyways, Mara only knows it as a sign there are no gods, which is wrong. I mean, I'm right here.

You're no god, Kiran said. Moments later her vision disappeared altogether as pain coursed through her body. When the pain stopped, and her vision returned, Mara was bent over her, feeding more vials into her suit.

"The convulsions stopped. Finally," Mara said quietly.

"We need to hurry. The Simurans will know how to help her," Sol said. Mara said something, but her voice was too quiet for Kiran to hear.

Thirteen days, Milias laughed and applauded, *I suppose your mind is remarkable frail at the moment. But, you're not wrong.*

Milias sighed and appeared in the air laying beside Kiran, one hand reaching up and sticking through Mara's head. *I'm not really a god. I wasn't born that way; omnipotent. Temporal Omniscience was my gift from a young age, relatively speaking. The rest was an uphill struggle like you wouldn't believe. A lot of people worked very hard to get me here, or so they told me on their deathbeds. Or rocks. Whatever they happened to die on. One died on a blade of grass. A single growth that was returning after a fire; and he fell on it. At times I miss that selfish bastard and his sanctimonious speeches.*

Mara returned to the front of the hovercraft and took the controls from Sol, leaving Kiran with the illusion of Milias. The illusion continued to speak, but Kiran allowed her thoughts to quiet, his words floating meaninglessly through her mind.

Kiran didn't know how much time passed before her mind put itself back together again. Her thoughts felt stronger than before, but they were still weak. She tried to move, managing to tighten her fingers over whatever was in them, just slightly. It took several moments of Mara speaking for the Simuran to put the words together in the right order, and more for her to realize it was the soldier's hand she was squeezing.

"We're here for you," Mara whispered.

"We should be about there," Sol said from the front in a subdued tone.

"Any signs?" Mara questioned.

"Nothing visible. Want to fire the sensors?"

"Best to be safe. I'll be up there in a moment," Mara said. She squeezed Kiran's hand before leaving. As she left the Simuran's side, the illusion of Milias silently popped into existence behind her.

They both know it's pointless. Bastion isn't here. Sol is beginning to lose hope. Mara, well she never had any to start with, Milias said. Kiran mostly ignored him as she discovered she could move her eyes and blink, if somewhat slowly.

After a few minutes of muted conversation, the Scion slowed until it was at a full stop. Sol and Mara walked past her towards the rear of the ship to open the roof hatch. Kiran wanted to stop them, to condone the action that would cover their suits with more Rot Ash. But speaking was still beyond her, and her mind was far too weak. She couldn't even feel the emotions of those around her as she usually could.

Do you want to go with them? Milias asked.

I do, Kiran said. Milias smiled and snapped his fingers. At that moment the world changed in Kiran's eyes. She was suddenly in motion, pulling herself atop the Scion and magnetically locking her boots to the hull. It was only when she saw Mara attaching herself to her with a cable that Kiran realized she was seeing the world through Sol's eyes. Milias floated along beside her as they walked the hull, eyes peering into the wasteland.

As with every other place she'd ever seen, the world was layered craters coated in Ash. Admittedly the area directly surrounding them was comparatively flat, although not significantly so. Flecks of gray and black floated through the air, and dark clouds bloated the sky. But not in all places. Half a dozen rays of light forced themselves through the clouds to dance upon the ground.

Sol turned off the grayed vision of the suit, leaving his and Kiran's sight to be of the eternal night of the world. A darkness broken by the six hazed beams of light randomly flickering around them.

"I never thought they were real," Sol said quietly.

"Some soldiers spoke of seeing them when scouting. I never did. See them I mean," Mara whispered.

Sol took several deep breaths as his vision blurred.

"We're going to die," he said shakily. Mara placed her hand on his armored shoulder and held it there.

"If Bastion exists, we'll find it before we do," she said.

"Right," Sol said after another deep breath.

No more words were spoken as they stared at the ever so rare light playing in the clouds. Kiran also felt a strange draw to it. An urge to run to it. To feel the warmth of the sun upon her synthetic skin. But it didn't last. The lights were gone as quickly as they appeared. As if a great hand moved to coat them in night once more.

Why do I still live? Kiran asked.

It's your punishment for trying to die. First against that child, and again in the future. I have plans for you, and you'll not ruin them. You'll try to, and you'll think you have. But you'll never actually manage it.

I was not trying to die, Kiran said.

Don't lie. You're shit at it, even if I weren't already in your head, and I wasn't me, I would know. You knew exactly why the boy stayed behind. Their plan would never have worked, but you thought it the best chance of saving Mara and Sol from yourself. From me. That was a weak EMB. Any attempt at defense, rather than that last moment trash, would have blocked it, Milias said.

That is… In… In… Kiran faltered, feeling her body below convulsing and breaking itself from the attempt at refuting the words of her master.

Incorrect? Are you calling me a liar Kiran? Milias asked in a jovial tone as he shook his head. The question made Kiran's mind rebel against her as her body shook and shivered.

You're lucky Sol is such a fool. He's realized Galen was part of Mattic's plan, but Sol hasn't questioned why that old idiot would set off the explosion without knowing you were in position to be killed. The answer would be obvious if he thought about it. For some reason, his spy must have reported that you entered that room with Sol. It did accelerate things as you surmised, kept the fat king from making his move. Saved Mara's life, at the cost of hundreds of others in the short term. Do you think Sol would understand that?

As he spoke, Milias floated to the front of the vehicle, positioning himself as if he would whisper in Sol's ear. Kiran knew it didn't work that way, but she felt dread all the same. Milias flashed her a smile.

Should I tell him? He asked. Kiran's world turned dark before she could answer.

"It's not magnetism," Sol said energetically, "it attaches to *anything* you want, not just metal. Even rock. Or dirt. Or *Ash*."

"It magnetizes whatever it's in contact with, at least a limited area of it. So, it *is* magnetism," Mara said, also emphatically.

"It isn't," Sol exclaimed.

"Sol," Kiran said softly, "you are limiting your view of magnetism to ferromagnetic fields. There are more kinds. However, the grapple does use Ether to create ferromagnetic fields in substances that would be unable to hold one without the use of magic. You are both, in a way, correct."

"Ha!" Mara exclaimed.

"You were wrong too," Sol grumbled from his seat in the back. Mara glanced to the video feed of the hull interior. Sol held Kiran's hand, as he had been constantly while Mara was at the Scion's controls.

"I need a break soon," Mara said with a yawn. Sol unbuckled himself and moved to the copilot's seat without a word of complaint. Once he was safely in control, Mara stood, stretched, and walked back and forth through the small space.

She glanced at the supply crates as she passed them. They were all filled with vials, but there were far fewer crates than they had started with. They'd taken to tossing the empty ones out the Scion's hatch. Mara counted what little remained, then grabbed two vials.

"Want anything Kiran?" she asked. Kiran tried to answer but felt herself losing control of her body once more. Mara spoke again, but the words were meaningless in Kiran's mind. She watched as Mara put the vials into her suit regardless of her silence.

"She's getting better with time," Mara's earlier words finally settled in the Simuran's mind, accompanied with a fresh wave of pain, prickling along the spine, and static along her thoughts. A half-moment later she *felt* Mara's concern and sheer exhaustion, as well as Sol's growing despair.

"How long?" Kiran asked, bringing a flash of joy to Mara.

"Hard to tell out here," Mara answered, "but I think… A few months… Maybe less… Or more."

Kiran nodded, then closed her eyes, finally able to feel the edges and frays of her mind. Moving slowly, she began the tedious process of pulling it back together manually, while soothing the web of scarring that was left in the wake of the previous months. She worked at it for a time. She heard herself humming some strange tune as she worked. It was probably Milias' doing, but the tune almost seemed to help her mind stabilize.

She only stopped when she felt Mara trying to drift to sleep. The soldier never slept well, not since she was a child. But it had gotten worse since she'd been wounded.

Kiran reached into the soldier's exhausted mind and felt the horrors that waited there. Visions of the *thing* as Mara knew it. Kiran tried to gently push the soldier into a dreamless rest, but her own vision darkened at the attempt, and she found Mara's hand holding her own as her mind became too weak to maintain the connection.

"Get your rest, I'll be fine," Mara said softly. As she spoke, Kiran drifted back into oblivion.

Even I'm bored, and I'm not really here, Milias yawned. Kiran stared ahead with dull eyes.

"Want to play a game?" Sol asked a moment later, walking through the illusion.

"Holographic displays would be a waste of suit energy at this juncture," Kiran said.

"Yeah. I know," Sol answered. He strapped himself to a seat and leaned back with a groan. "But I'm bored."

"In time you will be envious of this moment. Of lacking stimulation," Kiran said.

"I'm not so sure about that," Sol shrugged.

"It is human nature. The past is simplified and romanticized, no less one's personal history."

"There's not a lot to simplify," Sol said. "We're not *doing* anything. At least I can drive occasionally. How are you managing?"

"There is much to simplify," Kiran said. "You will remember the concern over making a mistake while at the controls, killing us all. You will not recall the proper anxiety of it. You will remember the dread of running out of power before we find our destination, but not the way that fear sank into your mind and poisoned your thoughts. You will remember-"

"That's enough," Sol grumbled, "You're right, I'm sure."

"That was never in question," Kiran said "To answer your question, I have been passing the time by discussing philosophy. Would you care to join the discussion?"

"Discussing philosophy with yourself?" Sol asked, slightly amused.

"...Yes," Kiran answered after a few moments of silence.

"Well, what's on your mind?" Sol questioned with a short laugh.

Sol sifted through the last of the crates, looking for any vial that wasn't broken or empty. He moved armor modules as he searched. All three had removed most the armor that wasn't built directly into their suits for the sake of comfort. It seemed a year since the fall of the Behemoth, although it was closer to half that time by his estimation. They'd been without food or water for a few days already, not that it stopped Mara and Sol from searching for a filled vial whenever they weren't at the controls.

"We may as well toss this one too," Sol yawned, "there's nothing left."

"Starvation or dehydration, which will be first?" Mara asked darkly, before glancing at the controls and sighing. "Not to forget the Scion is nearly depleted."

"We can transfer some suit power back to it," Sol said, "I've almost half power remaining."

"We could take half that from all our suits. But that would only be a couple hours at most. And if we go into a fight, our suit would eat a lot more than that. Hells, just going outside would eat at our power rapidly," Mara said.

Tell them fifteen each, Milias said into Kiran's mind.

"Transfer fifteen percent each. That should be roughly sufficient to reach our destination," Kiran said after a few moments and a twitch of pain.

"Sounds like you're confident in this next site," Mara laughed, but she started to transfer the energy as she did so. Kiran didn't answer but stood and moved to the front of the Scion.

"I'll be taking the controls," she said as she took the copilot's seat.

"Are you sure you're good for that?" Mara asked.

"My reaction speed is higher than yours by a significant margin," Kiran answered.

"Not what I meant," Mara sighed.

"I have regained much of my strength. I will not be suffering additional comatose moments. You, however, need to rest. Both of you." Kiran said. Mara didn't spare her a glance but nodded after a moment. The ground was becoming trickier to traverse, better reaction speed could certainly be a boon, and the soldier wouldn't deny it.

"If you are that well now Kiran, tell me, what is this?" Sol asked. Kiran glanced, and he held in his hand the device. It didn't look like something special, not really. It was covered in runes that were meaningless in Kiran's eyes. But seeing it, and the long crack that separated the two halves of the device's body, made Kiran twitch.

"It is an empathy bomb," Kiran said flatly, "also known as an EMB."

"Which is?" Mara asked.

"A weapon designed by telepaths to kill other telepathic individuals," Kiran answered.

"How does that work?" Sol asked. Kiran took a few moments before she answered.

"Strong emotions are harvested in great number, generally those of despair and grief as they are more easily created and harvested. Most potent are those emotions taken moments before a foreseen and horrendous death. Between a thousand and a hundred thousand deaths in general, felt at the same exact moment as the device is triggered. At best it disables a telepath with too much emotional inflow. However, it tends to be deadly. The more sensitive the mind of the telepath, the greater the weakness to such devices."

"Gods," Sol said, "how did Galen have such a thing?"

"It was a planned assassination against me," Kiran said. "It was beyond their knowledge, skill, or powers to create. This device is ancient, likely made during the war. It must have been hidden in the Pit or passed down for many generations. Perhaps some of my predecessors died to other such devices."

"We should get rid of it," Mara said.

"It's empty now," Kiran said, "it is no matter."

"It doesn't make sense," Sol shook his head. "Telepaths are powerful. Potent. Can't they... couldn't you of..."

"If the device is known, it can be defended against rather easily," Kiran said quietly. "However, it requires focus. Essentially, one must concentrate their telepathy to silence their passive empathy, meaning the telepath must make themselves non-telepathic for a time. For this reason, the threat and presence of such devices are more common than their actual use, as a forewarned telepath either stops their powers or dies."

"Gods," Sol repeated, shaking his head.

"There are assumedly other ways of defending against them that I am not aware of. Emperor Milias was a frequent target, yet he was never harmed, despite being the most potent, and therefore vulnerable, telepath in human history."

"That dead bastard probably lied about being telepathic at all," Mara said. Kiran didn't answer, but for a few spasms along her neck that the others couldn't see.

"I've answered your questions. Now you should rest," Kiran said.

"Fine," Mara said, "But so you know, the craters have been larger of late, steeper, so be careful. Take the ridges when possible, makes it easier to see a Rot Beast leaping at you before the last moment."

"Mara," Kiran said in her deadpan.

"Right," Mara nodded. She allowed the Simuran to take the controls and lowered the back of her seat to a sleeping position. Kiran could feel the soldier's simmering anger toward her. It had been there for some time, growing stronger at the same rate as the Simuran's recovery, spiking as Sol asked about the empathy bomb. Something about the situation had Mara angry at her. After a couple minutes of thought, the soldier pushed her anger away spoke to Kiran in a soft voice.

"How are you really feeling Kiran?" she asked.

"I am physically and mentally adequate for the current task. You should be sleeping," Kiran said.

"That's not an answer," Mara sighed.

"Do you trust me?" Kiran asked after a minute of silence.

"Obviously," Mara said. Kiran opened her mouth to speak, her hands shook, her jaw locked, and her voice was silent until she stopped trying to speak the word she needed to have heard.

She stretched out her mind to the soldier, and with gentle pressure, guided Mara's mind to dreamless slumber.

Chapter 6

"By the gods," Sol said hysterically, waking Mara with a jolt.

"What's happening?" she shook her head and sat up quickly.

"I requested your silence," Kiran said, "she needs to rest."

"But-"

"I would have woken her when we were closer," Kiran said. If Mara didn't know better, she would say the Simuran sounded angry.

"Sorry," Sol grumbled, but he had his eyes stuck on the display. Mara did as well, and the grin that spread across her face was equaled by Sol's.

Ahead of them was the most massive crater Mara could fathom. There was little to measure scale with in the wasteland, but the Behemoth, the largest of the Goliath class machines, would have looked to be an infant inside the crater. But there was more than the unimaginable crater. Dozens of kilometers beneath the edges of the crater walls, just slightly to the side of the center of it all, carved by some unimaginable weapon or magic in the days of old, was a structure. Despite the scale of the crater itself, the structure managed to look enormous.

Walls formed a large circle that was topped with a dome of the same stone-like material which looked to be completely clear of Ash. It was Bastion. If there was any doubt to that, it was denied by the statues that then circled the walls. Figures of Emperor Milias with windblown robes that connected him to the stronghold's walls. Each statue had one hand on the overhang of the dome as if holding it aloft. The other hand of each of them formed a fist at the waist, while the face of each statue was frozen in noble suffering.

Above all of it, the sky was not all blackened clouds. It was dark, but it was gray instead of black. Like the rays of light that would sometimes touch down in the wasteland, all gathered above the legendary stronghold.

"By the gods indeed," Mara said quietly. Sol laughed in a mixture of incredulity and joy. Mara nearly joined him. She would have, were it not for concern growing in her heart and mind. The cause of which she couldn't quite place.

"It was all underground once, wasn't it?" She asked after a moment.

"That is the case," Kiran answered.

"Then why the statues? They wouldn't have been visible underground, right?" Mara questioned. Sol seemed to think about the question, but neither he nor the Simuran answered it. The structure, for all its scale and grandeur, felt *wrong*.

"There's no Ether Shield around the structure," Kiran said calmly a few moments later. Mara nodded, feeling relieved that she wasn't the only one to think that something was strange. Something other than actually finding Bastion.

"The walls are standing, and without Ash," Sol said, "that means there must be a barrier in place. It's just one we can't see. The Simurans were always said to have the best tech. They must have found a way to make it work."

Mara nodded. She had to agree. Bastion was supposed to be the final stronghold of the infamous Milias. It was where he would have fled when his empire, and the world, started to fall apart. It only made sense it would have the greatest technology available at the time. But it still felt wrong to her, even with Kiran's declaration. It took a dozen more seconds for her to put her finger on what, exactly, was making her uneasy.

"There's no Rot either," she said quietly. She *heard* Sol stop breathing as he realized she was speaking the truth. Kiran made no reaction to her observation. Mara supposed the Simuran realized the same fact long ago.

Mara manipulated the dials around her, not taking the controls from Kiran but claiming a small section of the display for her own use. She tied that section into the rear visual sensors. As she suspected, there were Rot Beasts on the horizon, some closer than others, chasing after the hovercraft. They were too slow: even after changing their bodies for speed they couldn't keep up with the Scion even at a relatively slow pace; which the Scion was far from.

It was a weakness of the beasts. They evolved in nonsensical and insane ways, but always to organic things. They never developed wheels or jet propulsion. Although there were stories of things just as powerful, fast, and dangerous; if an individual beast was given enough time and cause to evolve in such a way. Or simply massive things. Things that shouldn't be.

"I see turrets. Big ones," Sol said. Mara looked to where he was pointing. As he claimed there seemed to be large structures hanging from the overhang of the dome, in between the statues of Milias. Unfortunately, they were still too far to make out the details, but Mara felt it in her bones that the man was right. Even so far away each turret looked to be larger than even their hovercraft. Such defensive weapons would be more than enough to destroy anything man made other the Goliath class machines. Against *anything,* other than those machines; or the eternal Rot.

"Have you tried hailing?" Mara asked.

"I had Sol making attempts before the walls showed on visual sensors. Silence across all frequencies," she said passively. At least it would sound passive if Mara didn't know the Simuran. To Mara, she sounded nervous. Even then, she had to wonder if the woman was purposefully putting the edge to her voice to seem more human to her and Sol. Her eyes flashed to the storage compartment in which Sol had placed the remnants of the empathy bomb, and the soldier felt a slight stirring of anger that she'd buried. Mara shook her head. She was still too weary. She would have slapped herself were it not for the helmet. She needed to focus on what could be the last minutes of her life, not give in to the whims of her still tired mind.

"I do not believe so," Kiran said, answering some question Sol had asked. The Simuran glanced towards Mara, then spoke again.

"I'm uncertain if Bastion is even capable of broadcasting communications. It is likely a blackout site where not even a whisper may leave. However, it would be peculiar for there to not be some form of station to listen for radio traffic. If it does have broadcast capabilities, it could be as simple as being unmanned. I suspect the cause of silence is not that simple."

Mara nodded, then began reading the various gauges in front of her in an attempt to stay focused. Her eyes flared as she saw the fuel reserves, and their current speed. Less than a single percent and a dozen times faster than Mara felt comfortable with. She tentatively tested the straps that held her to the chair.

"We'll use the wreckage to our advantage," Kiran said suddenly. Mara didn't need to ask what wreckage she meant. They would soon be surrounded by it.

"I calculated that at previous speeds the Scion would not have reached the walls, and the beasts would catch us before we could get there on foot. The same is true in this instance, but I believe the angles of the crater will benefit us at higher velocities."

"We're going to slide, got it," Sol said with a grin while checking his own straps.

"The wreckage should also serve as a distraction," Kiran said calmly as they finally began their fall into the crater that looked to be a hundred kilometers wide, but which had to be less. Below them, Bastion sat like a capsule sticking out of the ground. According to the stories it had been far beneath Mount Kalmit, doubtlessly connected to the surface through long tunnels. All of that was Ashen dust, leaving Bastion's walls to be lit by the strange lights in the clouds above it.

"What kind of magic could they be using to thin the clouds?" She asked.

No answer came, for as she spoke the groan of the engines sputtered, tried to turn, then died. They hovered in silence for several moments. Then the world seemed to burst apart. The hovercraft hit the ground, sank slightly through the Ash, then bounced back into the air. Whatever scraps of Ether remained in the system kept the hull of the craft in its enhanced state, else the whole thing would burst from the force of impact alone. All the same, the metal groaned and cracked as the triangular vehicle hit the ground again and again. Mara could hear Sol's nervous laughter for a moment, then felt blood rush to her head as the Scion began to spin. Seconds passed before it started to flip end over end through the air, metal bending and groaning.

Mara couldn't move and felt she would be sick, but from the corner of her eye, she saw Kiran in action, holding a fire extinguisher in one hand while the second one plunged into the metal shell. Thick foam exploded out of it to fill parts of the cabin not long before an appalling snapping sound announced the end of the hovercraft; its hull snapping apart. They began to spin more rapidly, and Mara felt her consciousness violently pulled away even as her suit struggled to control the movement of her blood.

She woke not long after, the front half of the hovercraft they were in was slowly sliding to a stop, sinking deeper into the Ash until it was scraping against bedrock. She could feel it moving, but she could also see it. They were upside down, and the hull above her was cracked and broken through in a hundred different places, allowing her to see the ground on the other side of the shattered shell of the Scion, despite even the now hardened foam that filled the cabin.

She knew she should have died; or been broken in a hundred places at the very least. It was just one more time her combat suit had saved her from pain and death: that and the heat absorbing foam.

As soon as the sliding seemed to be coming to a stop, Mara started flexing to break the foam apart and pulled a knife from her suit to cut through the straps holding her to the seat. The Rot Beasts, while not fast enough to catch up to the hovercraft, were far quicker than any human or Simuran could be. Reaching the walls would still be a close thing, and that was only if there wasn't an invisible barrier to contend with.

Beside her, a hand reached through the foam she had yet to break. Kiran grabbed her and carefully lowered her to the top of the hull which was serving as the floor. As soon as Mara's feet were on the ground, Kiran turned to free Sol from the foam surrounding him.

"We need to hurry," the Simuran said in her cold voice. Mara nodded and started to fight her way out of the wreckage. With the back half of the machine missing it should have been easy, but the space behind them was pinched together with shards of metal threatening to cut tears into the softer areas of the combat suit. Mara cursed at whoever had the idea of removing armor modules from the combat suits, even if it had made the past weeks far more comfortable. Unfortunately, she couldn't remember which of them to curse at for it.

Mara grabbed her pistol from where it was magnetically held to the wall. The weapon was, miraculously, lacking any visible damage. After taking her gun, she carefully slipped through the two sides of the hull.

Ash floated in the air like a thick black mist. Mara holstered her gun and used her arms to dig through the substance on the ground, widening a path through it.

As their half of the hovercraft had slowed, it had sunk deeper into the Ash, leaving a long furrow behind them.

With some difficulty she climbed into it, feet sliding with each step, and rose to the surface.

Once atop the Ash, it was easier to move than she expected. The top of the Ash almost seemed to be formed into solid plates, strong enough to hold her weight, although it did crack with every step she took. Even as she walked small creatures began to form out of the Ash, although only inside the footprints she left behind and not on the hardened surface of the ground.

Once she was a short distance from the Scion, she pulled her pistol back into her hand and spun in a circle to gain her bearings. The Ash mist in the air made it difficult to see even with the suit's sensors allowing sight in absolute darkness. The hovercraft scraps she could see were spread out over several kilometers, many pieces glowing red from the friction of the crash. The outer hull of their section was the same. If she cared to look, she would doubtlessly see the energy levels of her suit plummeting from its attempts at keeping her alive through the heat and the environment. She didn't look.

Turning another direction, she was able to see just how close they'd come to the walls. The hovercraft had slid a great distance in the crater. If there were true daylight, she would be in the shadow of the walls, and she felt foolish for thinking they were merely a few hundred meters tall at first glance. They were easily a thousand meters high, perhaps two or three times that height, and the turrets hanging from the dome made their hovercraft look like a broken toy. At least those that were whole did so. Being so close she could see the battle damage the entire structure had suffered.

Most the turrets were snapped apart, hanging by wires and cables. The stone looking walls were scoured and torn, cut meters deep, wide enough she could easily crawl inside them if she ever needed to. Bastion hadn't always been free of surrounding beasts; the battle scars showed that much. But it also meant it had been without a barrier, or its barrier was *inside* the walls. Mara didn't know if that was possible, but it seemed to defeat the point to some extent.

Sol pulled himself out of the wreckage behind her, and Mara grabbed him and ran, Kiran slipped out of the wreck without problem immediately after the prince. The Simuran had managed to dig a few of her own weapons out of the cabin. She had knives magnetically locked to her suit, and one of her swords, which she had at the waist. Mara couldn't say where the weapons had been hidden during the journey. She'd even had a pistol she'd given to Sol, although it was a kinetic model.

"No suit breaches on myself nor Sol. You must move quickly. They are approaching rapidly," Kiran said without emotion from behind them.

"Got it," Mara said.

After a few dozen seconds Mara glanced behind her. Kiran was standing still, turned to the side with her sword in one hand. Mara started to call to her, to tell her to run, when a beast appeared out of the Ash before the Simuran. A thing in the shape of a hound without skin, bones growing on the outside of its body.

Kiran grabbed a bone that grew beside the beast's skull, without dropping her blade. Then she ducked, and a second beast leaped from below the Ash, thorn-like claws passing through the air where she had been, and through the head of the first beast.

"To me," Mara said, shooting her grapple into the Ash below and locking it wherever it stopped. Acting on her words, Kiran's grapple collided with Mara's back. Moments later the Simuran was soaring through the air. She released the grapple when she was a few meters away, landing in the Ash and sliding with her sword locked to her back. She grabbed Mara as she passed and nearly threw the soldier ahead of her.

"You must run," Kiran said dully.

"You're not dying here," Mara hissed as she started to run, one arm still holding Sol.

"I will follow after Sol is safe. That is our duty," Kiran said.

Mara growled and once more took off towards the walls. Behind them the two beasts were giving chase, the headless hound growing a jagged maw over the ruins of its neck as they ran. They were slow moving for the time being. Far behind them, only just crossing beyond the edge of the crater, would be the beasts they had passed in the wastes.

"Cut to your right, another approaches you from below," Kiran said over the suit's communication suite. Mara did as she was told. Beside her, Sol was panting hard.

"There's a door," Mara said a minute later. It was a short run all things considered, but she was already physically worn from lack of sleep and the months spent on the hovercraft. The dethroned prince was panting too hard to answer, but he followed behind her; partly out of choice, mostly out of being dragged along. She didn't look to see how far away Kiran was, nor how she had dealt with the beasts that meant to ambush her and Sol. Instead, she approached one of two doors she could see.

Both were far overhead, with small landings jutting out from the side of the walls. One door was massive, large enough for vast vehicles to pass through. The door Mara sought was close to it, but small enough that it seemed to be for people rather than vehicles. At least there were the frames of doors. Inside them looked like the same stone as everywhere else along the walls.

Once she was close enough, Mara made use of her grapple again, attaching it to Sol's back. Once he was secured, she locked her boots and gloves against the wall in the same manner and began to climb and leap up the wall with grunts of effort.

They made the landing rather quickly all things considered, and once there Mara glanced behind her, cursing to see Kiran was still distant, but also saw that the Ash mist had begun to settle. A few Rot Beasts had reached the wreckage of the hovercraft. The chunks of metal, some

still faintly glowing, were being ripped apart and eaten. Two
of the creatures bypassed the wreck altogether, charging
towards Kiran as they shifted forms. They were slowing, but
their bodies were also growing, seemingly gaining mass,
and maws full of jagged teeth that could be seen even at a
distance. The Simuran drew closer at a slow run only, more
than a half dozen broken beasts putting themselves together
behind her.

　　Mara cursed again. She slammed her fist against the
door and started calling, pleading for help, for whoever
lived in the place. Silence answered. Silence and the sound
of distant roars from the wasteland.

　　Sol was bent over, attempting to empty his stomach
of its contents, if there had been anything in it. Still, he was
pointing to the side of the door where there was a small
keypad. Mara glanced at the small device, which she had
assumed would be worthless to them. As she suspected, the
thing simply displayed a series of numbers and letters, but
they had no way of knowing the code.

　　Mara looked behind her. Kiran was spinning through
the air. The hound was once more headless, its makeshift
and weak skull rolling across the wasteland, but there were
three more beasts not far from her.

　　"Simurans," Sol managed to pant. Mara froze. It was
a slight chance, but it was a chance nonetheless. Bastion was
meant to be a haven not only for Emperor Milias but also his
Simurans. She glanced behind her yet again as the sound of
a grenade rang out, saw Kiran running from beasts that were
melting under the flames of an incendiary explosive, then
turned back to the door. She closed her eyes; forcing her
heart to calm and her mind to focus.

　　Simurans didn't have names. They had designations.
Kiran was just something they called their Simuran.
According to her, it was one translation for Caretaker in the
language of her people. Generally, they would be called by
their partial designation, K131 in Kiran's case. Full
designations were rarely known by any other than the

Simurans. It was one of the secrets that Kiran shared with Sol and Mara. It was forced on them for reasons that escaped them when she was doing it. On the other hand, the Simuran taught them many things with the same overwhelming intensity.

"K131-GS1A0M5B23," Mara said. She'd frequently wondered why the Simuran had been insistent on the pair memorizing the designation. Perhaps she had foreseen their situation. Maybe she just wanted someone to know her real name. Or perhaps that was thinking of her in too human of a way.

With a loud groan, followed by the sound of grinding stone, the door, a chunk of rock apparently ten meters thick, slid back a few meters then slid sideways, merging with the stone of the wall it gave passage to. Mara took Sol, who was finally catching his breath and forced him into the passage.

"Close the door and wait," she said. Moments later she was sliding down the wall with one hand and foot attached to it. As her feet sank into the ground, she charged towards Kiran. Two more Rot Beasts had caught up to her, making the Simuran stop all pretense of getting closer to Bastion. Several of the creatures laid broken across the ground, cut apart and smoldering from the earlier grenade. Three were standing, two of them quickly shifting to deal with the Simuran. Horrendous looking maws chewed upon the Ash at their feet to fuel the changes even as they fought.

The unchanging beast had the frame of a massive cat, complete with fur that stuck out like spikes of steel, which was probably the reason Kiran was having trouble with it. Its tail was long, long enough to crack the air like a whip, which it casually did as it seemed to carefully study the Simuran. Kiran was busy fighting the other two beasts, one that looked like a crawling insect and a third that was partway burrowed in the ground. Mara pulled her pistol from her side.

Small bolts of plasma were hurled through the air with a familiar hissing sizzle. The projectiles were larger than Mara's fist and turned to boiling mist halfway to their target. Mara nodded to herself and reset a couple dials. The subsequent bolts were much smaller, flew faster and glowed more intensely than the first ones. They also drained over three times more Ether per shot.

The first bolts hit the cat along the jaw and face, just below its slit eyes. It howled and spun at Mara as its flesh burned. Its spiked fur bristled and moved as if to some invisible wind, then the spikes along its shoulder separated to reveal another eye. An eye the colors of fire that stared at Mara angrily for a handful of seconds before the fur shifted again to cover it, but not before she caught sight of several more eyes peeking out from behind the shifting spikes.

The plasma continued to burn into the beast's flesh for several seconds, but not enough to really hurt the thing. The creature did, however, turn to charge towards her at a pace many times faster than any being of nature could replicate. Its legs were irregularly long, enough so to reach the bedrock below with each step, its feet not surfacing as its considerable mass plowed through the Ash.

Mara fired a dozen more shots towards the creature, then extended her wrist to the side and fired her grapple. It exploded out, sinking into the Ashen ground and the rock beneath it, and pulled her sideways as the beast ran through where she had been with its maw opened unnaturally wide.

With another command, the grapple released its magically created hold to the rock beneath the Ash and coiled back into her suit. Mara dove to the ground as the beast's tail cracked the air and passed over her with a crescent blade formed at its end.

She rolled and climbed to her feet to see the beast was sliding to a stop, unable to turn sharply in its current form and apparently unwilling to shift quite yet. That was a relief. From her understanding, some of the beasts would be willing to change at anything, while others took their time instead. The latter was more dangerous in a prolonged fight, as any change they made was destined to be a cleverer fix than their short-sighted brethren. Mara didn't expect the battle to take too long, however, making the long-sighted beast theoretically less of a threat.

As the beast started to turn and charge close once more, Mara pulled a square grenade from a slot in her suit and leveled her pistol.

The beast set upon its second charge at an even quicker pace than the first. Mara fired plasma into its open maw, which was large enough to swallow five of her whole if she was to stand side by side. It would even be a comfortable fit, at least as comfortable as being in something's mouth could be. Mara stopped firing and adjusted the dials of the pistol once more. Red lights flashed along the gun when she was done.

She turned her hand to her right to fire a grapple. The beast almost seemed to tense as if it expected a repeat performance. She wondered how it planned to deal with it; if it had a plan at all other than raw instinct as most of the things did. She grinned and turned her arm towards the creature instead of the surrounding wasteland. The grapple hit the inside of the beast's maw, locked into the flesh, and pulled her exactly where the creature wanted her to be. It closed its mouth around her, and she could nearly feel the thing trying to crush her through her armor. Then she released her grenade, directly down its gullet.

The cat had no typical tongue but a mass of writhing tendrils that wrapped her legs and tried to pull her after the grenade. The grapple held her firmly at the roof of the beast's mouth, and Mara pulled the trigger of the pistol, took a deep breath, then dropped the gun as well. It touched the beast's flesh and exploded into plasma. Mara's suit closed the air intakes as the heat of the blast charred her armor and sent alarms baring across her helmet's display.

The grenade went off a half second later, spreading flames through the beast's stomach and up its throat. The tendrils around Mara's legs fell away, and the beast's mouth opened in a pained roar, parts of its maw falling and returning to Ash. For the briefest moment, Mara saw the center of it. The Beast Core that was the first part of any forming Rot Beast. A bead the size of a grain of sand. Her head throbbed at the sight of the thing, all her senses screaming that it couldn't exist, while her instincts told her to destroy it. But it was hidden by wraps of burning Rot flesh before she could act, so instead, she released her the grapple and leaped back into the wasteland, taking a gasp of air as her suit opened her air intakes to feed the air filters.

The beast's roar became a screech that would cause her ears to bleed, had she not turned off auditory sensors and deafened herself. Still, she moved backward while taking a defensive stance. The beast took a step towards her, parts of it falling apart as the flames burst through the surface. It took a second step before finally collapsing. Several of the eyes dropped off the corpse, each spinning in the air to look at her, then sinking into the Ashen ground with unnatural speed before tunneling away.

Mara turned back to Kiran, not surprised that the Simuran had killed her remaining beasts and had started on yet another that had arrived. Now, however, she was slowly making her way towards the wall and the door.

The beast Kiran fought wasn't the only newcomer. There was a flying beast that had, apparently, been sneaking closer to Mara during her short fight with the cat beast. Pistol fire from the door's platform distracted it. The small bullets, not even plasma bolts, were worthless against the creature. Luckily it was a simpler beast, and Sol was able to dodge it as it swooped down at him, despite being stuck on the small platform. But the creature was learning as its kind always did.

Mara sprinted back towards the suicidal prince, then scaled the walls on all fours as her muscles screamed at her to stop. She'd nearly reached the top when a long knife bounced hilt first against the wall above her. She grabbed the blade with a practiced movement, then ran above the platform, leaping down as the flying beast swooped towards Sol once more.

The knife hit in the gap between two scales. It buried itself to the handle into the beast's oddly soft skull. Mara's momentum pulled the weapon down until she was freely falling. She landed on the short platform hard enough to hurt her knees, but the beast fell towards the ground, momentarily stunned. Two more of the long knives pierced its body, and it fell back into lifeless Ash. Kiran had broken its core, but a new one could be formed before long.

Kiran ran up the wall, reaching the platform in a matter of seconds. Mara felt the hair of her neck standing on end as the Simuran grabbed Sol by the helmet with one hand and started to enter her identification into the keypad with the other. Mara turned to the wasteland, trying to find the source of her fear.

Dozens of creatures were forming in the Ash below them, and hundreds more rained down from the edge of the distant crater wall in an unending tide. There were too many of them. Far more than should have been able to keep pace with them. Something was *wrong*. But even that wasn't what made her shiver. It was the lone beast that stood below them, unmoving, with a large and familiar slit crimson eye. It stared at her, and she swore she saw in it not only the hunger of a Rot Beast, but hatred.

Kiran grabbed Mara by the helmet, much as she had Sol, and threw her into the opened passage. The soldier caught her feet just in time for the Simuran to push her further into the walls.

They quickly came to a panel that looked much like the one on the outside of the door, and it shut with the Simuran once more entering a simple code. Moments later they heard some beasts impact the stone, shaking the wall as it clawed for entry. Mara stopped herself from reaching for a nonexistent gun. Bastion was standing. It wasn't torn apart. It wasn't shredded. There had to be a reason for that. The beasts could eat rocks, and steel may as well be a treat. But magic had to be coursing through the walls of Bastion, much stronger than that which had been reinforcing the metal of the Behemoth; it was the only way Bastion could exist. She took a deep breath, trying to ignore the state of her armor, and turned to Kiran.

"Thanks for the knife," Mara smiled, the sight hidden in her helmet.

"I was aiming for the beast. I missed," Kiran said. As she spoke, she grabbed her right arm and magnetically locked it across her stomach. The single slab of armor that was on that arm was bent as if it had been bitten, but luckily there was no obvious break in the enhanced fabric base layer that Mara could see.

"Oh," was all Mara managed to say as Kiran turned away from her.

"Let us see what remains of Bastion," Kiran said in an empty tone. She took off down the passageway quickly, taking the lead now that the door was closed. Sol rubbed the top of his helmet and eyed the two anxiously.

"Thank you for helping," Mara said abruptly, "but try not to get yourself killed. Kinetic pistols don't hurt the Rot. Remember that."

"I know," he said with a shrug, "but I'd be a jerk if I didn't at least try, right?"

"Heroes die, assholes live. It's better to be the ass," Mara shook her head.

"That didn't stop you," he said.

"I had a way to fight back," Mara said. Then she took a deep breath. "Just don't do it again."

"Hopefully I won't need to," Sol said, "But enough about that. We're here Mara. We've made it to Bastion. Think about that. It's real, and we're actually here."

Sol smiled as he spoke, but it wasn't an earnest one. It was worried, scared, more than a little shocked, and filled with grief.

"Let's hold off on the celebration," Mara said while pretending not to notice, "at least until we know how much the Simurans want to kill us."

Sol responded by following Kiran. Mara followed a dozen meters behind him, eyelids growing in weight. She knew she should be ecstatic. They were alive. They were no longer stuck in the Scion. All her muscles were screaming and cramping from the stress of the short fight after being confined for so long, and Sol was likely suffering more than her. She forced a smile and began to move, even as her heart jumped to anger as she stared at Kiran's distant back. It had happened again, she was sure of it.

Chapter 7

Beyond the door, the passage was lit by faint lights. Mara didn't trust the light and kept her vision in the grayscale of her night vision. It drained the already low Ether reserves of her suit, but she felt it a necessity.

The passage was narrow and a little tall compared to the width. From her spot in the back, Mara was waiting for the sounds of some pursuing beast to reach her ears. Logic told her she could trust the walls to stand a little longer. It was sadly also logic telling her they would be torn apart rapidly: logic and experience.

Enchanted and enhanced steel was destroyed with relative ease. It wasn't just the memory of the Behemoth's fall, and what followed. On her few trips beyond the barrier she'd seen scout ships crushed and destroyed, consumed in minutes after a beast brought one down. Yet somehow there was no sound of a beast tearing through the stone at their back. No matter how many times she reminded herself of the stronghold's designers, she couldn't get herself to relax completely.

There was also the fact that the walls were large beyond imagining and even thicker than their height would lead her to assume. The hallway they walked through took more than a handful of sudden turns. She could only imagine defenders down the hallway, firing as they turned each corner, then retreating to the next bend. Easily defended, as the hall was too narrow to comfortably walk side by side in, let alone wide enough to dodge a skilled attacker.

That was only if the defenders didn't merely fill the passageway with poison gas, or had antipersonnel turrets emerge from hatches above their heads. They could use sections of wall to crush them. Simply dropping a couple grenades on their heads from a hidden panel would be catastrophic in such a small space.

Mara's mind danced through a hundred such potential scenarios, wondering how they would be attacked. It was certainly a possibility that nothing would attack, but she'd rather be surprised with that oddity than to expect peace and be surprised with murderous intent.

To her relief, and growing unease, they reached the end of the passage undisturbed by defenses. It ended at a thick metal door that opened at Kiran's touch. The Simuran looked to be as guarded as Mara. Her neutral mask was unbroken, but Mara had rarely seen the woman's eyes burning so intently as she looked back at her and Sol, gesturing to be quiet.

The door opened to reveal a well-lit decontamination chamber. Its design was achingly familiar with its grated walls and floor. It was an almost perfect duplicate of the rooms on the Behemoth, were it not larger in size and in pristine condition. The door behind them shut itself as the room began to fill with gas. Giant fans flared to life along with a handful of other machines with their telltale sounds. Mara felt herself start to laugh as particles of Rot Ash lifted from the armor and fabric of her suit and was pushed through the vents that lined the room.

Despite her own expectations, she felt herself calming. Of course, that realization alone was enough to send her mind spiraling back into a sea of paranoia, but that too disappeared rapidly. It was simply too reminiscent of the frustrating hours spent in similar chambers, followed by oddly relaxing days in isolation. In days when she'd been meters from Rot Beasts yet kept safe from them by the barrier. Even then the sight of them had been terrifying.

She could hardly believe she'd fought with them. She'd seen them. She'd read of them. She studied strategies that came from the days when the Rot first appeared. Yet she'd never fought one without a squad, nor while being outside of a vehicle that could outmaneuver *most* beasts and move faster than any of them. She didn't count the ones that were inside the Behemoth. They were like newborns. Weak, slow, and simple compared to those who'd been alive for even an hour or two.

"Greetings K131 and guests," a mechanical and grating voice floated through the room, seemingly without source. Sol jumped and looked around wildly. Of the three of them, he'd been the only one that hadn't been through decontamination before; although the concept wasn't exactly alien to him. Kiran showed no surprise, merely making her way across the room to the far corner.

The voice continued speaking but switched to a language Mara didn't know, doubtlessly the Simuran tongue. She could only imagine it greeted them in Temic for the benefit of Sol and herself.

After the voice droned on for a few moments more, Kiran responded in the same language. Mara had no idea what the woman was saying, but she knew the sound of a mission report when she heard it. Occasionally the woman gestured to either her or Sol. Mara yawned and leaned against the wall, letting her eyes close. As anxious as she was, there was nothing she could do to change her own fate anymore. She decided she may as well continue her interrupted sleep, decontamination would take long enough for it. Kiran's telepathic mind was there to help her to it without a word.

Mara only woke when the massive blowers had finished their task, the sudden silence jarring her out of dreamless slumber. Despite her earlier calming she was slightly surprised to be waking again. She was still tired, greatly so, but she forced her body to stand as she once more took in her surroundings.

Sol was leaning against another wall, clearly lost in thought. Kiran was already in the process of removing her combat suit, a process that looked slightly difficult with the woman using only one arm.

The bruises on Kiran's right arm were visible through the elastic layer she wore beneath the combat armor. Blackened areas on her skin that covered her hand, her forearm, and sprawled a distance beyond her elbow. There were more bruises across her rib cage, although to a lesser extent. Whatever had happened to maim the armor on her suit had done far more to everything that was beneath it.

Mara crossed the room quickly and helped the Simuran undress. The woman gave her a curt nod for her trouble. Seeing her without her helmet and suit felt wrong after months of living in the things and having Kiran unconscious in a chair for more than half of that time.

"Are you going to be alright?" Mara asked, swallowing the brief flash of anger that she felt from looking at the Simuran, reminding her of what had happened outside the walls.

"I am," Kiran answered flatly.

"Your mind-"

"I am stronger now, as you have seen," Kiran interrupted her. Mara nodded, then glanced at Sol who was still staring into space, appearing to not have noticed the sudden silence, nor the two of them moving. She felt her following questions on the tip of her tongue, but upon seeing Sol, she swallowed them and began the slow process of removing her own suit. The missing armor modules made it an easier venture than it usually was. She released the suit seals through her wrist console, which was minutes from losing power.

The suit depressurized with a hiss as she pulled off the helmet with a shiver of delight. The suit had been reprocessing sweat and waste material while it was worn.

Unfortunately, the removal and transfer of moisture did little to remove the general grime that always formed along the skin. She was happier than she could express to smell air that didn't carry those particular scents anymore. It was something she'd been careful not to think about in the Scion. She detached and dropped the top half of the armored suit afterward to yet more relief.

"There are showers in the next room, as well as clothing," Kiran said blandly. Mara nodded, then looked to a blank-faced Sol. She'd crossed the room and shook him by the shoulder before he reacted to her presence. He glanced, then blushed and looked away.

"Showers and clothes in the next room," she said.

"I'll follow when you're done," he muttered.

"Are you alright?" she asked. Sol half smiled.

"I was just thinking about a few things."

"Anything you want to talk about?"

"I'll be fine," Sol said, followed by a short laugh. "Like I said before Mara, we made it. We're in Bastion."

"That's a good thing," Mara said. Sol nodded.

"I know. Of course, it is. It's just-" he didn't finish his thoughts aloud. He tightened his lips and sank back into obviously morose thoughts. Mara placed a hand back on his shoulder and tried to squeeze it through his armor.

"We're here like you said. That's what matters," Mara smiled. Sol said nothing more but pointedly looked in a different direction as Mara began to remove the remaining half of her combat suit. She wanted to destroy the thing or to toss it in a bottomless hole and laugh. Instead, she would probably spend hours cleaning it and charging it with Ether from the stronghold. At least that would be her usual procedure. After seeing the armor free of the Ash, she resigned it as a lost cause.

The trip in the Scion had been enough to leave her suit covered in deep grooves and pockmarks where the Ash had settled in and began to dissolve and consume. The more flexible sections of the suit, the fabric layer, was nearly eaten through entirely. A gentle cut would have been enough to break through. With a shake of her head, Mara tossed the pile of ancient and worn armor into a corner to be forgotten.

Eager for the shower Mara followed Kiran to the adjacent room. If the Simurans wanted them dead, it would have been easy enough while she was sleeping in the room. She held no faults in paranoia, but she wouldn't take it too far either, at least not after sleeping for a few hours.

Her and Sol's lives weren't guaranteed to be safe in the long term, that was obvious enough, but they were apparently safe on a temporary basis. For Kiran's part, Mara could only guess. She was a Simuran, literally built for the task of being the Caretaker of the Behemoth. Now that the machine was gone, she wondered if the Simurans would discard the woman like a useless machine. It wouldn't surprise her if they tried to do so.

Kiran considered herself a machine of flesh, and there was nothing to suggest other Simurans would see her differently. After all, that self-identity had been planted in her mind; as well as her knowledge and skills. Most of those had been earned through work and effort as well, but when they first met the Simuran had seemed to be an expert on all things, and at times it seemed unfair.

Mara had been filled with awe when she was first being trained. At the time she was a child. Kiran was some adult, some cold, emotionless thing that treated her with detachment. It was new then. It was better than how others treated her; or each other. Their friendship formed rather quickly, even if Kiran wouldn't admit to such things.

On the other hand, Mara could admit to feelings of jealousy over the years. She spent endless hours in practice, perfecting her body control to levels other soldiers and bodyguards never bothered to, yet she could never surpass the Simuran, nor be her equal in that regard. Meanwhile, Kiran never seemed to train. She was simply superior to her. An insurmountable challenge.

Overall, Kiran was her detached teacher and her
friend. But for all their time together, the Simuran remained
a mystery. Mara couldn't imagine what a group of such
people would look like, let alone an entire civilization. She
supposed she would soon know the answer to that
quandary. She felt a little excited at the prospect.

Mara's thoughts were interrupted as hot water rained
down on her. It was the most pleasant sensation she could
remember. Regular access to hot water had been removed on
the Behemoth, saving the power it took to heat it, although
that hadn't been the official reason. That ruling occurred
years before she was even born. Room temperature water
was as good as a shower could be after that.

She was surprised to hear a content sigh from Kiran's
direction, which ended up making her laugh as she reveled
in the sensation of the hot shower herself. She slowly peeled
the skin-tight base layer away and dropped it to the floor. As
with the rest of the suit, the thing could burn as far as she
was concerned.

She stood in the water, unwilling to move. For an
unknowable time, she allowed herself to simply enjoy the
sensation. Eventually, her mind seemed to turn itself back
on, and she began to clean herself. As with everything else in
the situation, it was simultaneously familiar and alien.

Her muscles were there, perhaps more evident than
before, and she'd always been pale. But her skin was coated
in various rashes and sores, and any extra weight she'd been
carrying was long since lost. She could see her ribs, and her
fingers looked unnaturally long and old. Her hair was
longer than she ever allowed it to be as well, and it was
growing as slightly fainter red as if her hair was graying all
at once.

She closed her eyes as she scrubbed off layers of dead
and decaying skin and forced her mind to other thoughts.
She began to ponder the situation she was in, as well as the
room itself. Particularly the stalls the showers were in. As if
made for royalty, instead of the open rooms used by the

soldiers of the Behemoth. Or the rare damp rags by the those in the Pit.

Simurans didn't have gender, genetically, physically, or mentally. Strangely, the peculiarity of stalled showers was bothering her, although she couldn't put her fingers on the exact reason why. There was also the ever-strange fact that despite her lack of gender Kiran was generally careful about modesty, for herself and for others. It was a peculiar phenomenon.

"Personal interaction requires some level of human modesty, so it is ingrained in Simurans during training," Kiran said over the sound of falling water. Mara jolted from the sudden noise, admitting to herself that she was still a little on edge. Not that it was a bad thing.

"Reading my mind?" She questioned.

"There is no need. I felt your discomfort. Your thoughts are predictable."

"That's just kind of you to say," Mara said sarcastically.

"It was meant to be. Predictable is comfortable. It says nothing of your mental capabilities. I believe it is normal for those that have spent time together to predict the thoughts of the other."

"Only for a telepath, it seems," Mara sighed.

She ended the shower far quicker than she wanted to, but she was simply too curious about what would be next for them. No matter how long she spent in hot water it would feel insufficient, so a quick egress wasn't too distressing. At least that was what she told herself as she turned the water off. There was also the matter of Sol waiting until she and Kiran were dressed before he would even enter the room himself. He was more accustomed to a private suite than any locker room.

Kiran handed her a soft towel and some clothes she'd taken from the lockers that lined one of the walls. The cloth was old, very old, and it smelled like it, but whatever material the clothing was made of didn't show much of its advanced age. They were simple things that fit loosely and quite comfortably. There were even shoes, although they had no straps nor laces and were irregularly soft. Kiran was already dressed in the same gray colored cloth that she offered, with her bruised arm wrapped and hanging from a makeshift sling.

It felt wrong to be without the ankle support of armored boots. Mara had worn various armors since her childhood training and was rarely without it, but one thought of her soiled suit made her thankful for anything else to wear. Even if it was far less safe. Besides, the shoes felt divine in their softness, which was worth being a little vulnerable.

"All yours," Mara called into the decontamination room, before following Kiran to the passage beyond, if it could even be called that. It had the general shape of a hall, but they had clearly left the dull stone walls behind them. The walls were distant on either side, and the ceiling was far overhead. She could see her reflection in the floor in disturbing detail. Each of her steps echoed down the corridor that stretched longer than reason told her any hall could.

Mara moved to the side of the grand hall to Kiran's side, and leaned against a metal pillar the stretched overhead and arched across a ceiling that glowed with a gentle light. She felt in her bones that she did not belong.

She distracted herself for a time trying to guess how thick Bastion's walls were. Even accounting for the fact that the previous hallway cut back and forth several times, it had felt like hours of walking reach decontamination. They hadn't been moving particularly quickly, but it still seemed to be an unimaginable scale. Then again, the outside of Bastion would have been unfathomable had she not seen it from a distance. It was still difficult to say how large it was precisely. A dozen kilometers. Maybe more.

"You surprise me," Kiran said, "minutes after I claimed to predict you. You are permitted to ask questions, Mara."

Mara nodded but held her tongue. Of course, she did have questions for Kiran. There were things she desperately wanted to know. But for the time being, she was also enjoying ignorance. Bastion was real. She'd never expected that. Perhaps that was all that was wrong. Maybe that was why her mind was bouncing between paranoia and tranquility.

She shook her head and forced herself to speak, choosing the timelier questions first, rather than the one that she'd been waiting to ask for months.

"What happens to us now that we're here?"

"I don't know," Kiran said. Mara swore she heard a hint of amusement in the Simuran's voice, like a twitch of a smile. She was surprised when Kiran reached over and placed her hand atop her head, rubbing her hair as she'd done to her as a child.

"They didn't tell you?" Mara asked.

"There was no they."

"But the voice-"

"It was only an automated system. We triggered numerous sensors on our approach, both to the walls and through them. Unless I'm mistaken, you used my designation as the entry code, just as I did. That gave the system my identity."

"And your report?"

"It was also part of the Automation. It simply asked for a verbal report and recorded what I had to say. However, there was supposed to be a welcoming committee waiting for us here. To welcome the foreign dignitaries I escorted."

"Sol is considered a foreign dignitary?" Mara asked, almost amused.

"You are as well. Despite claiming to be of the Soltraven Empire, the civilization of the Behemoth is being considered as a foreign kingdom. Which is an improvement to the rebel faction the Behemoth system considered the civilization to be."

"I thought Emperor Milias had a habit of assassinating foreigners, not welcoming them," Mara said.

"I agree that it is peculiar," Kiran said, "but I suspect there is little cause for alarm. The emperor does not execute *all* foreigners, only their leaders, and the agitators. Dignitaries are unlikely to be killed without orders or provocation at the very least. Bastion's system is doubtlessly more powerful and complex than I am accustomed to, but it is not sapient."

Mara nodded at the Simurans words, having nothing more to ask on the subject. But more questions did burn in her head. She glanced at the door through which Sol would be showering, then back to Kiran. She opened her mouth to speak, then pursed her lips and dove back into thought. It was a question she'd wanted to be answered for quite a bit longer than their fate in Bastion.

"What happened to you on the Behemoth?" she eventually asked. Kiran gave her a blank look if very slightly confused.

"The empathy bomb shredded my-"

"No, I'll not buy that shit like Sol will. He told me about Galen. He was a child, and that thing could only have been given to him by the Council. It was a trap. There's no fu-" Mara caught herself as her voice started to rise and lowered her tone to a whisper. "There's no way you didn't know about it ahead of time."

"Telepathy is not omniscience," Kiran said. Mara snorted.

"That's not an answer," she spat. The Simuran said nothing, continuing to stare emptily. Mara waited for several moments before continuing.

"Then you pull that shit outside," she said, gesturing to Kiran's injured arm. "It was entirely unneeded and don't pretend otherwise. It would be insulting."

"I was ensuring survival," Kiran said.

"Not for yourself," Mara shook her head "and not for us either because we need you. So, tell me, why the fuck are you so eager to die?"

"I'm not," Kiran said, her voice a little softer than usual.

Mara didn't know what to say, so she kept her silence, snorting after a moment or two as if that would end the conversation.

"If my actions have been bothering you, why did you not ask me when I first woke?" Kiran asked.

"Oh, I see. You thought yourself in the clear because it wasn't the first thing I asked about when you woke from months-long comas and seizures," Mara said. "I thought you were *dying* Kiran. I didn't... I wasn't... I couldn't be angry with you until you started to get better. Then... then that shit outside."

"I apologize-"

"I don't give a shit about an apology, or whatever excuses you can come up with," Mara growled. "Don't. Do it. Again. I want you to promise me you won't try to die anymore."

Mara turned and gave the Simuran her strongest glare. Kiran looked at her, then turned away. Her lips twitched, then she whispered in the softest tone Mara had ever heard from the woman.

"I was-"

"Promise me."

"... I promise."

"Thank you," Mara said, taking a deep breath, and feeling waves of relief as anger she'd been holding for months began to slowly seep away. Some from the promise, more from getting it off her chest.

"The system would have killed us were we not considered dignitaries, wouldn't it?" Sol's sudden question made Mara jolt and nearly jump. She hadn't even noticed him entering the hallway, but there he stood with the door half open. She cursed at herself for not being properly on guard. And at Kiran for teaching the prince how to move so silently. She'd forgotten the man's growing skill at it after months stuck in combat suits and the hovercraft. She felt like a foolish and raw recruit.

"It is possible, but not a guarantee. It is also a possibility that without me you would have been allowed passage, possibly only to capture you in a moment of vulnerability in the showers," Kiran nodded.

"I was eavesdropping for a while, sorry. Wasn't on purpose. At first," Sol said to the clearly upset Mara, before turning to Kiran. "But that means Mara's right. We'd be dead or captured if something had happened to you."

"Perhaps," Kiran said, "but this is an oversimplification of the situation."

"Thanks for the warning," Mara growled to Kiran. The woman would have felt Sol's approach through her telepathy.

"You dislike letting him overhear conversations that could concern his safety. I deemed it important that he knows the current situation," Kiran said in her most robotic voice.

"I'm not a kid anymore," Sol said firmly. "If you thought something was wrong you really should have told me." Mara rolled her eyes.

"I know you're not a child," She sighed, then reached up and ruffled his golden hair. Sol gave her an annoyed look, and she swore Kiran smirked as she spun and started walking down the hallway. Sol followed, and Mara took the back of the line once more.

With the wider hall and no combat suits, the procession looked vastly different to her eyes. It reminded her of walking through the royal quarters of the Behemoth again, even if the worn and rusted halls had been replaced with grandeur. Those weren't pleasant memories, but they carried a surprising amount of nostalgia.

It was, however, different. Judging by Sol's recently washed face he'd grown to be as gaunt as Mara had, with his golden hair losing much of its color just as hers had. He looked worn, as she knew she must as well. They were broken things, but they were alive. Only Kiran hadn't seemed to change from the voyage. But the Simuran had always looked frail.

Numerous halls met with theirs, but they were distinctly smaller and seemed more like access tunnels rather than the main hallway they tread on. It was a vastly different experience than the earlier tunnel, but just as uncomfortable to Mara. Such large and empty spaces felt like a waste. Nothing was so empty in the Behemoth. At least the hall wasn't as ridiculously long as it seemed at first, although there was some trickery at play.

When she first looked behind her, she swore the door they'd entered from was much further away than it should have been. As if they were running rather than walking. Each time she looked the distance seemed to expand behind them. One step covered the distance of twenty, but only when she wasn't looking for it. Her head ached as she tried to figure it out, but the others didn't seem to notice. Sol was once more lost in thoughts or daydreams, and Kiran wouldn't look back at her.

By the time they were nearing the end of the hall, Mara was starting to wonder if all of Bastion would be tunnels and small rooms, but as soon as Kiran opened the door than possibility was gone,

The first thing she noticed was the sky. Not for a moment did she believe it was real, but that wasn't due to lack of detail. No, she knew it was false because it was not coated in black clouds. The fake sky was a pale blue with sparse white clouds spread across it. At least in the first part of the sky she saw. They left the hallway and looked upon the interior of Bastion with a sense of awe, or at least Mara did. Sol laughed incredulously. Any reaction of Kiran's wasn't seen nor heard by Mara.

The false sky was either broken, or of a strange design. For while the first sight of it was of a peaceful day before the War, most of it wasn't. Parts of the false sky were of night, with bright stars shining brilliantly. Other parts were a myriad of colors as if painted by dawn or dusk. Different times of day and different weather patterns of a healthy world were displayed and mixed chaotically, moving among one another. The result was nearly as confusing as it was beautiful.

Beneath the false sky were towers of metal and glass, shining and reflecting the lights above them, although not a single light came from the buildings themselves. The towers were dark in color, deep blue or perhaps black, but polished to a reflective shine. Each tower bore decorations and runes in silver.

Ornate bridges of similar design connected a few of the towers they could see from their vantage point. The bridges were held aloft in the sky by the buildings alone; not caring for support pillars but for those that arched out to the connected towers.

Surrounding the three of them, standing beside the wall of Bastion, was earth. Not Ash nor rock, but deep brown soil. And there were trees. Or what were, perhaps, once trees. They were gnarled and dead things none of the three had seen outside of photographs. Some were tall with branches broken and laid across the dirt. Others were short with hundreds of small branches sprouting above them like hair.

It was the remnants of a park that once circled the city of towers, that was obvious enough. But there was no greenery left, only the soil and the long-dead trees somehow not yet turned to dust. Roads and walkways showed a spiraling path through the park and into the city, all lit by the sky above; and by glowing spires of sapphire crystals that lined the way.

The wall behind them was not the bare stone of the first hall, nor the metal pillars and arches of the later hall. The walls were a landscape painted in incredible detail. A green forest on their side, which naturally turned to rolling hills of yellowed grass and then to the Sea as the wall stretched away from them. From a distance, it would be difficult to notice there was a wall at all.

Most notable was the absolute silence of the place. No machines groaned in their ears. The ground didn't shake or move beneath their feet. No wind made songs of the world around them. All was still. All was silent. Mara felt the truth rising in both her mind and throat. A reality that was relieving, exhausting, and devastating.

"We're alone."

Chapter 8

Kiran's eyes were closed in concentration as she scoured the area for minds. Mara averted her eyes from the city, embarrassed by her sudden declaration. Sol saw no flaw in her words; he'd come to the same conclusion. The ancient city was devoid of life. There were more than a handful of concerning factors, but Sol did as he had to and ignored them.

As much as they didn't want to admit it, they were the last three living beings in the broken world. Each of them would distract themselves from that truth in their own ways, the same delusions that had been carrying them since the fall of the Behemoth.

Mara's eyes were darting between Kiran and the city, waiting for the Simuran's findings. Sol barely held back his laughter. Mara had been watching Kiran in the same manner since they were children. She was waiting for the Simuran's words of approval. If nothing else their interactions were a source of frequent entertainment. It was how he preferred interactions. As an observer rather than a participant. He didn't hate people. He tended to like them. Dealing with them was a different issue entirely.

Sol shrugged off his thoughts and slowly moved towards the city of towers. There was a wide path that led from the door towards the buildings. Far to their left was a massive gate, one he expected to connect with the one they'd seen on the outside. Beside that larger entrance were a handful of short and squat buildings, painted in the same fashion as the wall itself. From a distance, at the right angles, the buildings were probably well disguised as part of the painted landscape.

"One of them should be an armory," Mara said from beside him. Sol smiled and shook his head. Mara probably wouldn't feel like herself until she had a few guns within reach.

"Think we should steal their stuff?" Sol asked.

"Acquisition of additional weaponry would be advisable. New combat suits would also be a boon," Kiran said.

"Oh, gods no," Sol nearly whimpered. "Not yet."

"It doesn't seem like the Rot will be breaking in today. The odds of it I mean," Mara said.

"I suppose you are correct. Exploration and the search for life signs could take priority over armament in our current predicament," Kiran nodded. Sol could swear she was as relieved as him to not be headed to new suits. He wasn't quite sure why he was so confident in that belief. Hope perhaps.

"I'm not saying we shouldn't look," Mara chuckled, "there might be something to eat."

"Your digestive systems will require reactivation, so to speak. I would suggest a small amount of protein paste with water. Inject what remains as you have been doing. Do so for the first seven to ten meals."

"Sounds great," Sol grumbled, "Not a problem Simuran's have I take it?"

"Your assumption is correct," Kiran said. She began a slow trek through the dead park, to the not so distant buildings along the wall.

"Is there a chance we'll find anything *other* than protein paste?" Mara asked.

"That would be highly unlikely outside of the Imperial Palace, which is forbidden ground. However, dietary substitutions should never be made without dire need. Despite its name, Protein Paste is a careful balance of all required nutrients needed by the human body. While nutritional substitutions may please your palate, they would place unneeded stress upon your body."

"Wouldn't stop me," Mara grumbled.

They took their time crossing the short distance. Sol didn't know where to set his eyes. They jumped between the dead trees, the towers, and the chaotically colorful sky. He was even interested in the painted wall they walked beside. Paint wasn't foreign, nor was artwork, but the detail was too extraordinary to be made by human hands, yet too beautiful come from a machine. When viewed from the towers, or even further into the park, it would be easy to forget they were sealed within a dome; were it not for the silence and the chaotic nature of the sky.

"Which first?" He asked as they drew nearer to the buildings. There were three he could see. The largest of them had excessive doors, likely for the storage or servicing of vehicles. The second building was smaller by a good margin but still rather large. The third was relatively a shack in comparison of size, although still larger than the Scion's hanger bay on the Behemoth. Their approach led them towards the back end of the largest building, while the other buildings were across the road that ran into the nearly hidden gate along the wall.

"I'll take the small one," Sol said.

"Splitting our forces through multiple facilities is currently inadvisable," Kiran said.

"Fine," Sol said.

"You were just trying to make us do all the work," Mara laughed.

"Basically," Sol smiled. "Where should we start then?"

"I'm guessing that one is the armory," Mara pointed to the mid-sized building. "With luck, it will have some food storage too, but I'd like a look at what the Simurans were using in either case."

Kiran nodded moved quickly to the building in question, entered without a word through a creaking door,

Sol and Mara steps behind. As they expected, the building was an armory. There were sets of black armored suits arrayed on shelves that formed aisles through the center of the building.

The suits numbered in the hundreds, if not thousands, stashed along the aisles. Along one wall were the modular suit additions. Signal boosters, additional Ether batteries, and of course chunks of armor, were the few that Sol could recognize at a glance.

The adjacent wall had drawn Mara's attention nearly immediately and in a visible way as she stared and unconsciously grinned. It was filled with racks of weapons. Rifles, pistols, knives, swords, even what looked to be a halberd, although it was singular in a room otherwise filled with duplicates.

Sol walked through the rows of shelves with his hands tucked away, Kiran having left his sight with how quickly she searched. Mara followed behind him, still wary, but giving the weapons, and some of the armors, a look of near reverence.

"These aren't new," Mara said. Sol watched as his bodyguard lifted one of the suits for inspection. "You can see it here. This took a hit from something." she continued, tapping a section of armor where there was a scorch mark blended into the dark material.

"Yeah?" Sol shrugged.

"Trust me," Mara said quietly, "this was used in combat. I'd stake anything on it."

"Is that important?" Sol asked.

"It could be," she said a moment later. "we don't know how the Simurans died. Or even how long ago it was. This could be a clue."

"Right," Sol said, "but if most of them died in battle, how would the survivors live long enough to return their armor, but not long enough to repopulate?"

"Simuran's are manufactured," Mara said hesitantly.

"I'd bet if we search hard enough, we'll find a place here that makes them," Sol shrugged. Mara seemed to think about that for a moment before clearing her throat.

"In any case, it speaks wonders of the armor that none of them are *obviously* damaged, if even half of them are used. And gods it is *light*," she said, raising the armor over her head without difficulty.

"Still not putting one on yet," Sol said. Mara grinned.

"I found the nutrient storage," Kiran announced. Mara and Sol both jumped at her sudden appearance behind them.

"Please, make some noise when you're sneaking around," Mara grumbled.

"Noise would be counter to the point of stealth," Kiran said. "However, in this instance, I was not making such an attempt. It would be proper to stay attentive when exploring Bastion."

"I thought I was, doesn't mean I can hear *you*," Mara said. Then she sighed. "But you're right. I'll try to be more careful." Kiran's lip twitched as Mara walked away from her and Sol, pointedly inspecting the suits as she moved.

"The functions of the base layer are built into these suits, so you will not need one. Additionally, the sensors are far more sensitive. You may wear your current clothing beneath the suit with minimal interference."

Mara passed behind a row of shelves as Kiran spoke, but responded by sticking her hand back out into the aisle, first symbolizing her gratitude, followed by a rather rude gesture. Sol snickered.

"Guess I'll follow you to the food," Sol said once Mara was entirely out of sight.

"Remember to consume very little for the time being," Kiran nodded.

She led him through the aisles of armor at a quick pace, to a door at the back end of the building. Through it was a room perhaps half the size of the armor section, but without the aisles or shelving. Crates of protein paste and water were stacked atop and beside one another, strapped down by netting. Unlike the previous room, the contents of the storage had obviously been used to some degree. There were empty places where Sol would expect more crates, and some of what remained was turned on the side and emptied out.

Kiran moved to a collection of crates that had apparently been searched through already, but not yet emptied, and took several vials she fit into pockets. Sol mimicked her actions while trying to estimate how deep the room was through the stacks of crates.

"Is this enough food?" he asked. "If the towers were filled with Simurans there would need to be hundreds of thousands of them. Millions? Tens of Millions? More?"

"There are likely to be more entrances circling the walls, each with additional armories and storerooms. We should also be able to find a hydroponics factory for the production of nutrients," Kiran said. "However, it is unlikely that those that lived in the towers were living in the close confines that you are expecting. There would be no more than a million. More likely, as few as ten thousand."

"What, would all of them have their own tower or something?" Sol scoffed, although he knew there wouldn't be enough towers for that. The city looked to have about a thousand towers in all, but they were enormous.

"I do not know," Kiran said. "However, fewer than a million Simurans were ever built, with the majority sent to the war. It is unlikely that more were created for the sole purpose of filling this place to capacity."

"But it could grow. Start small, increase the population with time. Like any other place. They could just have everything set up and ready all at once. Or maybe... Could humans have been brought here?"

"Human's did not live here, nor would they have been welcomed in large numbers. Humanity is too unpredictable to allow at strategic locations in high numbers unless the need for them is dire."

"We were allowed in the Behemoth," Sol said. "Our ancestors couldn't have forced that to happen."

"I will admit I am not aware of the specifics; however, your civilization was considered a rebel faction that was fed and allowed to grow. It was an irregular situation when compared to standard procedure."

Sol didn't respond. He cracked the tip of a vial and sipped at the water within with relish. He'd drank more than a little water during his short shower, but the sensation of drinking something again was still phenomenal. Afterward, he cracked a second vial and tipped a small amount of the sludge-like material into his mouth.

It was gritty on the tongue and had a sour aftertaste, but it was otherwise bland. It was similar to the paste created by the Behemoth, which wasn't a surprise. Gruel could only be made in so many flavors. As always, Sol thought of food he'd seen in images, doing his best to imagine the taste of them as he felt the paste working itself towards his stomach. He resealed the vial and slid it back into a pocket. When he turned to leave, he was surprised to find Kiran standing between him and the door, studying him carefully.

"Sol. We must speak," she said.

"What about?" Sol asked. Kiran walked forward and briefly placed her hand against his forehead.

"Do not think you can fool Mara nor me. Sol, what is happening in your mind?"

"I'm fine," Sol shook his head.

"You are not," Kiran said.

"I *will* be then," he said.

"I've felt fluctuations in your emotions which are irregular even given the situation. While aboard the Scion, and much more so now."

Sol stared at Kiran blankly for a moment. His hands clenched, and for a moment the star on his head glowed. Then he closed his eyes and took a deep breath.

"I thought we were dead, Kiran," he said quietly. "I was so worried at first that I… I nearly forgot what happened before. Even when I had time to think… it didn't matter that we were all that escaped because… because we were just delaying it for a little longer. I was at *peace* with it Kiran. I accepted it. But now… Now I can only wonder what could have been. Had we prepared earnestly, told people about our plans earlier… Would we have a contingent of survivors with us?"

"Do not concern yourself about what could have been," Kiran said.

"I *will* condemn myself for what *should* have been," Sol said quietly, running both hands through his hair. He knew tears were soon to come.

"At first I just wanted to rub it in his face," Sol said. "Father… He used me as a *tool*. Every time assassins came for me. Every time the servants looked at me with hope or hate. Even some of the Council. Those were expecting me to lead them to some paradise free of the Rot. Not all of them but… enough of them. All because of his lie. That I was some special chosen one, not just a freak. Gods, I only wanted to earn the adoration given to me by those of the Pit, or at least the hate that the rest of them had for me. Instead, I'm useless, and they're dead."

"There is nothing you could have done."

"Is that true?" Sol asked. The star upon his head flickered, lighting the room for a moment. "If I hadn't been a coward. If we'd prepared for this journey when I was younger… Tell me Kiran. Honestly. Is there really *nothing* I could've done?"

Sol was surprised to find himself nearly pleading. Kiran reached over to him once more, yet she did not touch his forehead nor pat the top of his head. She gripped him by the shoulder and pulled him towards her, wrapping her arm around him gently. The glow from his forehead turned dark as she rubbed his back, her hand shaking as it moved.

"There will always be things that could have been done differently. You did your best with the knowledge you held. You are guilty of nothing. Feel no guilt for living, no matter what is to come."

Sol swallowed whatever retort he'd been thinking and nodded instead.

"Thank you," he whispered. Despite Kiran's short stature Sol could help but feel like a cradled child as she awkwardly held him. It felt nostalgic, despite never having happened before. He closed his eyes and didn't open them, feeling the tears coming. He couldn't say why he started to cry, but he held back the sounds of it as best he could. Kiran made awkward shushing sounds as if trying to calm a newborn. Sol started laughing as the tears fell.

"I may be doing this incorrectly," Kiran said, separating herself once Sol's crying started to slow. "It is apparent that I have caused additional emotional turbulence rather than calming it. For this, I apologize. In the future, I will rely on telepathic emotional guidance rather than human alternatives."

"It's fine," Sol chuckled, drying his eyes, "pleasant really. And I'm sorry about that. Not sure where it came from. I'll be perfectly alright in a moment." Kiran stared at him for a half moment before turning to leave.

"Remember what I said," she whispered as she left from the room with all the noise of a ghost. Sol wandered to the side and sat on a shorter stack of crates, feet dangling beneath him, as he struggled to put the smile back on his face.

He wasn't alone for long. He spent half a minute calming himself before Mara peeked into the room.

"Sorry," she muttered, "I'm going to grab some food, then I'll leave you be."

"Really, I'm fine," Sol said, blushing at the memory of crying, the evidence of which was still visible on his face.

Sol had to admit, at least to himself, that Mara looked rather formidable in her new armor, even without a helmet.

Not that she hadn't been formidable before, but the black armor was somehow menacing in its sleek design. Utilitarian. It was designed to protect the most elite and agile of warriors without getting in the way.

"I could use your help finding a suit that will fit properly," Sol said after Mara had quietly grabbed several vials and was making her way back to the door. His bodyguard looked at him with a smile once she registered his words.

"I found one you can use. I put it in a bag you can carry around, so you don't need to change just yet if you don't care to."

The three left the armory prepared to fight a three-person war against anything the empty city could put in front of them. Each had a bag filled with something they needed. Mara's bag was filled with an assortment of weaponry, Kiran's held food, as she had also donned a set of the black armor.

Sol alone forewent any armor for the time being. His was in the bag, just as Mara had told him it would be. It was a quarter of the weight of his old suit, perhaps an eighth. Which wasn't to say it was overwhelmingly comfortable to carry with the strap of the bag digging into his shoulder.

The second building they checked was the large structure across from the armory. They assumed it was a service station for vehicles, but none were present on the outside nor inside of the structure. There were tools, several of which Mara and Kiran added to their bags for later use while saying something about suit maintenance. Otherwise, it was a silent and fruitless venture.

Afterward, they crossed the road again to the smallest of the buildings. Kiran opened the door, then froze before taking a single step. Sol caught a glimpse of the contents and closed his eyes. He took deep breaths before looking again.

The building was all a single room akin to a small warehouse, but it would have been empty were it not for the bones piled in it. They weren't human bones. They looked wrong, misshapen, and all of them had a strange metal look to them. They were all in meticulously arranged piles with a single skull atop each morbid collection. The piles were close enough to be touching, yet there was still enough to cover all the floor, but in a single space directly in front of the door. A thousand, at the very least. Two or three seeming more likely, all coated in a reflective dust.

"What is this?" Sol asked quietly.

"The citizens of Bastion?" Mara asked in a solemn tone.

"Perhaps," Kiran answered.

"What killed them?" Mara asked.

"They were likely decommissioned," Kiran said. Mara gave the Simuran a strange look at the answer.

"Someone arranged them like that," Sol said, turning his back to the field of the dead.

"That is likely," Kiran agreed.

"Who would have done it?" Mara asked. Kiran didn't answer. She slowly dropped to one knee and ran her gloved hand along one of the skulls. She raised her hand and stared at her finger that had picked up traces of the metal dust.

"This was a Brigade," she said quietly after a time. Sol nodded. "Our bones are generally recycled in the labs. This is... an oddity."

"Recycled bones?" Mara asked, quietly, but with more than a little incredulity and horror.

"Our bodies slowly produce a titanium-mithril alloy as we age. This alloy is light, excessively durable, and accelerates nerve signals. It grows in our muscles, skin, and nerves, making us stronger as our bodies age. However, our bones are entirely crafted from this alloy, and thus they will not decay with time. For this reason, our remains are typically processed so the metal may be reinserted in the cycle. In this way, our bodies may be of use to the following generation."

"That's wrong," Mara shook her head.

"It is accurate," Kiran answered softly.

"That's not what I meant," Mara said. Kiran said nothing more on the subject. She closed the door gently, and slowly began to walk to the distant city.

Chapter 9

Seven paths led to the outer walls of Bastion. They curved outward, presumably each from one of the larger gates, towards a central ring to which each connected. One road led inward from that ring, circling the towers with its slow approach. Everything between the different roads was filled with soil and the trees. It was there Sol walked, not across the odd paths but across the remnants of the park.

The feel of dirt beneath his feet, of something soft rather than metal or stone, was nearly enough to lift his spirits. It was made all the better by the shoes Kiran had set aside for him, although he didn't know if they could or should be called shoes. They were entirely fabric, no metal to them at all. They were soft and allowed him to feel the ground he stepped on. The same was true of the clothes, at least when it came to the soft nature of the fabric. He never wanted to change again.

"Kiran," he heard Mara say. Her voice was quiet and pensive. Troubled. Sol felt his heart thump twice, his fist clenched painfully tight, and he tried to stop listening. He turned his thoughts back to his shirt, and how he could barely feel it there at all. It nearly felt like walking naked. Uncomfortable in some ways, but in others not so much.

"They were no longer useful," Kiran said a moment later, her flat tone cutting through Sol's willful concentration. Sol closed his eyes for a moment. When he opened them, both Kiran and Mara were looking back. Kiran held him in her signature stare, while Mara was a mixture of concern and surprise. Sol ran a hand along his forehead, nearly unconsciously. The Stigma burned into his flesh was warm to the touch. Almost hot.

Sol knelt to take a handful of soil from the dead park and let it slip through his fingers. It was dirt, actual dirt, instead of Ash. The feeling of it moving through his fingers was enough to bring tears to his eyes. To his surprise, Mara knelt and did the same. The faint smile on her face could only match his own, despite her gloves. Then the chamber of bones floated through Sol's mind, and he stood to continue the journey to the towers.

Every day was a surprise. Finding Bastion was a happy surprise, one that he should expect to end him at any moment. Simurans were, historically speaking, not the most welcoming of people. If the Simurans were still alive, despite evidence to the contrary, and they killed him on the spot; he would be satisfied with his life. It wasn't glorious nor even happy. It was a barely tolerable life. But the three of them were some of the last living beings in existence; if not the last. He'd seen soil and felt it in his hand. There were none he'd ever known that could say the same, barring Mara. It was enough. He told himself so repeatedly.

To distract himself from his thoughts he opened his arcane sight, causing his steps to falter. Bastion was filled with Ether to the degree that his mind shook at the sight of it all. The energy flowed and formed intricate patterns in the ground. All the distant towers had central cores of Ether, connecting to their walls through vein like tendrils that made each building look like a bizarre creature rather than a construct.

Sol turned his gaze downward, to where the Ether flowed as so many rivers of varying depths. Closer examination showed they were numerous small bands of intricate symbols made of yet smaller symbols. He couldn't tell if the trend continued as the scale diminished because they became too minuscule to differentiate.

As for what all the energy was doing, he had no idea. The walls of Bastion were strengthened to a ridiculous degree, that much was an obvious effect as the Rot had not yet broken in, yet the Ether flowing through them was dim and incomparable to the city proper.

Some Ether would be used to make the crystal spires glow, and yet more would need to light the false sky. But for the most part, the energy seemed to be doing nothing at all. It was spent for the sake of being spent as far as he could tell. Sol shook his head and continued his journey. He had no proof of that thought, of the waste. He wouldn't allow himself to be upset over a passing thought. He wasn't an expert on Ether, far from it. Perhaps he just didn't understand it enough.

Mara and Kiran allowed him to walk by without a word, and Sol did his best to wear a smile and not look them in the eyes. Nor would he look at Kiran's arm. He wondered how it could be so injured if the bone beneath was metal. He wondered how long it would take such an injury to heal, or if the bone could heal at all. He pushed those thoughts from his mind for the time being. His emotions were already rattling the cage he built for them.

He heard Mara turn and follow behind him, her steps loud even on the soil. He assumed Kiran was following as well, but she would be masking any sound of her own with Mara's steps. Sol wondered if it was a conscious decision for her to hide her presence, or if it was a simple habit or instinct. Sol doubted he would be able to hear her moving even if he and Mara were to be perfectly still in the tomb-like silence of Bastion.

They continued for a time, growing ever closer to the city. It was much further than he thought at first look. A kilometer or two at the very least, yet still the park looked minuscule beside the city.

Mara and Kiran kept silent until they reached the ring that marked the center of the park where Mara's curiosity seemed to be too great to bear any longer.

"What are these for?" he heard Mara ask. When he looked, she was standing beside one of the sapphire spires that dotted the roads. She was smiling, one hand touching the twisted and massive gemstone.

"Careful near the edges. They are sharp, and your gloves are thin. Your blood must not touch them," Kiran said softly. Mara nodded and continued her examination.

"What are they, other than stupidly expensive lights?" Sol asked with minimal attention.

"The Kingdom of Delan constructed these crystals during their war with our empire. Their precise methodology is known only to themselves and Lord Milias. They were not aware that their existence was guaranteed until these were made. Our emperor was waiting for them."

"Why?" Sol asked.

"Because he believed they would hold positive aesthetic value."

"No, why would a kingdom develop them during a war?" Sol asked. Kiran was quiet for a handful of seconds before answering.

"Crystal formations are theoretically excellent at holding both enchantments and living minds," she said. Mara took a step back from the spire and gave the Simuran a quizzical look.

"The minds they held were purged many years ago," Kiran said, with a hint of sorrow. "It was found that minds held in such a fashion, even artificial ones, are both limited and significantly dangerous."

"Who would have thought it. Giving a rock the ability to think was a bad idea," Mara shook her head. "Did they go psychotic? I'm guessing they went psychotic. I bet they were telepathic as well, weren't they?"

"The event did develop in a manner similar to your statement. However, it is worth stating that crystals such as these would be far more than required, and even somewhat safe, for a single mind, or even a thousand of them," Kiran said.

"How many?" Sol asked.

"I do not have that information," Kiran answered. "However, these were designed in an attempt to save the Delan civilization. One crystal per province they controlled, accompanied with telepaths to ease the conversion."

"Gods," Mara said, blood draining from her face, "conversion? I was thinking they made minds for them." She cast her eyes across the dead park, to the many spires that were held along the roads.

"It was not a successful endeavor," Kiran continued, "once certain thresholds were surpassed, the minds within the crystals lost sanity. Our armies had a simple time cleaning the mess, and Simuran's worked to purge the minds before the devices were moved to this location."

"How do you know about all of that?" Sol asked suddenly, "weren't you in stasis for the majority of the War?"

Kiran was once more silent for several moments before answering. When she did speak, Sol could swear her words carried slight happiness, as if she were glad for his question.

"The mental matrix of all Simuran's were updated with major developments that occurred while in stasis, although I was unaware of where the crystals had been taken. The emperor was proud of the acquisition."

"They may as well be tombstones," Mara said quietly. Kiran nodded, ever so slightly.

"We should follow the road from here. Entering the city from different angles could activate defenses," Kiran said. Sol nodded and turned to follow the spiral path.

The space between the city proper and the ancient park was separated by a silver line that cut through the road and dirt and spread out in a circle around the towers. It was pulsing with Ether in much the same way that the energy was coursing through every rune and decoration in the city, although most that Sol saw didn't use the silver inlays as wires as he'd first assumed.

The road entered the city at an angle. It slowly turned inward, in a slight spiral that would eventually reach the center of the city; unless Sol's guess was off.

While the towers seemed massive from a distance, it was nothing when compared to how they looked when walking between them. The effect only compounded when the curve of the road slowly hid the park from sight. Sol couldn't help but stare up at the multicolored sky and marvel at as its many colors bounced between the towers in a nearly nauseating way.

In a word, he felt insignificant. A speck on the wall of time. One of few survivors that stood witness to the end of the world. Tens of thousands of years of history had been turned to Ash. Bastion and the towers were all that remained to claim that any of it had ever existed. A few survivors were pathetic besides such titans. It was almost a relaxing thought. His failures meant nothing, for success would have meant nothing as well. But the towers seemed to lord over him, condemning his weakness.

Once more, Sol forced a smile on his face, increased his pace, and tried to distract his thoughts, to little avail. The end of the world was not a new thing. He'd merely hoped the final gasping breaths of humanity would not be his to make. He hoped as much even as he struggled to stay alive for even one more day. Such was the fate of humanity he supposed. The struggle and confusion. He didn't want to die, but he didn't want to be the last to do so either. To be that final and lonely soul.

"Shall we search for an access terminal?" Kiran asked, interrupting Sol's existential thoughts; to his relief.

"Sure," he shrugged after coming to a stop and turning to follow the Simuran. "Anything specific you want to look for?"

"A city map, or blueprints at the very least," she answered.

Kiran turned towards one of the towers at random. Theoretically, each of the structures would have a console somewhere, even one on the outside wouldn't be too unimaginable.

They made their way to the glass doors, Sol with a growing sense of curiosity over what they would find, partially dreading another room of corpses hidden in the towers. Then Kiran opened the door, and once more what sense Sol could make of Bastion was turned on its head.

The door was glass, and much of the building was as well. Through it, they could see the ornate and decadent decorations of the indoor sections. At least that was what it appeared to be. Sol moved beside Kiran and opened the second half of the double door to get a better view of the tower's insides, and Mara walked between them and looked up. Sol mimicked the motion.

The tower was hollow. There were a few support pillars, incredibly tall and filled with Ether, but all of it was as bland and unremarkable as the long tunnel they found just inside the wall. Sol took a step back and stared at the glass from the outside of the tower once more. The building appeared to hold beautiful furniture and decorations fitting the decadence the rest of the city showed. It was false. Like the sky, and the images painted on the far side of the park.

Without a word, Sol turned and walked across the road to another tower and opened the door. It was similarly devoid of all things but support pillars, all the way to the top of the building far above. Sol could only stare in confusion. The false sky, the walls, the opulence of the city he could reason was for the sake of mental health. A much healthier way to distract people from the end than the political games on the Behemoth. But for the buildings themselves to be fake was beyond any of his expectations.

Mara and Kiran moved down the street at nearly a jog, and Sol followed them. Each of them checked the buildings they passed, and all were as hollow as those they first looked in. There was variance in design and shape, and the alleyways between them were as decadent as the road they walked on, but anything they looked inside was empty.

An idea formed in Sol's head, and he abandoned the main street, cutting through the alleys between the towers to get closer to the center of it all. The city and Bastion itself seemed to be built in rings and spirals. It was fitting, for the spiral was the symbol of the Simurans. But Bastion wasn't built for them. No, that much had been a lie made evident to him by the empty towers.

Mara and Kiran followed him but made no effort to stop or slow him. They'd either come to a similar conclusion or were merely waiting to see what he was running towards. It didn't take long to capture the first glimpses of what he sought, although they were difficult to make out among the buildings of metal and glass. From time to time he caught a brief glimmer in the sky. That alone was enough to confirm his suspicions, but he didn't stop.

By the time his lungs began to hurt, Sol had found an alley that reached a massive plaza at the center of Bastion, a plaza that circled massive walls. The walls, in turn, were encircling a palace that looked to be lined in gold; with diamond spires replacing the sapphire ones. A large palace, although small considering the scale of Bastion as a whole. The palace had its own towers, circular and stretching towards the false sky, although dwarfed by those of the city. Surrounding the Palace and its walls was a shimmering Ether Shield to keep out the world. But light came from the palace. Light from a single window. Light that was broken by the outline of a standing figure wrapped in shadows.

Mara opened her mouth but said nothing. From the corner of his eye, Sol saw Kiran staring at the palace with a confused look clear on her face. It was the closest thing to emotional he had ever seen on the Simuran. She took a few steps closer, froze, then took a few more, eyes held on the same spot as Mara and Sol. On the shadowy figure. The figure that was swaying from side to side. Then Kiran lowered herself to a knee and bowed her head, eyes closed.

"This place is making less sense by the minute," Mara finally said at a whisper, as if afraid of being overheard.

"No Mara, it makes perfect sense now," Sol spat, not bothering to keep the anger out of his voice any longer. "Bastion wasn't built for humans or even the Simurans. It was built for the Imperial line, and them alone. The city is a model Mara. A dollhouse. Something pretty to look at, maybe even play with. This is the real Bastion. A palace for Milias and his ilk."

Rage thundered through Sol's veins like fire. He took deep breathes out of sheer habit, but he made no effort to stifle the anger.

"How many people could have lived here?" he asked loudly, "They'd be comfortable. Happy. Alive."

"Sol, I need you to calm down," he heard Mara say. Then a force slammed into his mind, breaking his thoughts and, momentarily, control of his body. He found himself suddenly no longer angry. He wasn't calm, for his heart was still thundering away, but he was nearly emotionless. He still felt the ghost of rage, but he allowed that to slip away, and instead accepted the forced numb assailing him.

He was glowing with light, enough that Mara and Kiran couldn't look directly at him. Their arms were raised in front of their eyes, and Mara was still trying to talk, not that Sol could hear her anymore. His ears heard only the sound of his own heartbeat. He cursed from habit, feeling fresh anger, this time at himself, but that too was rapidly numbed.

He turned his thoughts inward, to the parts of him that made him different, the mark on his head that the ancients called a Stigma. There was no Aether in the air, at least none that he'd been able to sense with the arcane vision. Thus, the light was fueled by the other. Mana, as it was once known.

Sol closed his eyes, finding himself in the state the ancient tomes told him to find, the emotionless place he'd rarely been able to reach on his own for more than a moment or two at a time.

He found his Mana, and it was quickly leaving him to fuel the light show. A lifetime of energy conversion in a world starving for Aether, and it would be depleted in a handful of minutes. Sol took another deep breath and found he could stop the effect as easily as snapping his fingers. He willed it to be so, and the glow ended abruptly.

After another minute he opened his eyes, looked to Kiran, and nodded. The presence that held his mind in an emotionless state drifted away, and he was hit by a wave of nausea and disgust, as well as a new pulse of anger, but he managed to keep it from escalating once more.

Once the rage began to wane, he felt a wave of exhaustion seep through his body. He'd used the magic in such ways when he was younger. Screaming at the injustice of life in his room, creating a spark or two. He'd learned to control his emotions, to stop it from happening, except for the occasional small trick. Running out of Mana was a death sentence according to the ancient tomes. In a world where every scrap of energy mattered, he didn't dare allow himself to waste it on feeling angry. Not when he could help it.

"I'm sorry, don't know what got into me," he eventually said, "and thank you Kiran. I know you hate doing that."

"Don't worry about it," Mara said, turning her eyes back to the shadowy figure, "but I think he knows we're here now."

"She," Kiran interrupted, "and she already knew. She was waiting."

"The system would have warned her when we came through decontamination," Sol muttered as he nodded to himself, trying to not care about his cheeks burning with embarrassment after the display.

"No. The system woke her from stasis when we entered the walls. Her father told her we would be coming."

"How do you-" Sol started, but Kiran cut him off.

"Our minds touched, and we began speaking. She is a telepath as I am, admittedly with less potency, but enough to allow us to speak at this distance."

"...Who is her father?" Sol asked, suspicious of the answer. Kiran closed her eyes for several seconds, then gave a slight nod. At that moment Sol felt his heart clench, and all remnants of anger left him. Kiran, no matter who or what she was to Mara or him, could not resist the orders of the true royal line.

"Her name is Nemai. She is the natural born and disinherited daughter of Emperor Milias."

"Well, can the little princess let us through the barrier? Because I'd rather be on that side of the thing, to be honest," Mara said.

"Disinherited," Kiran said slowly, "she has no more control of the system than we do. Nor can she give me orders."

Sol wondered if he imagined the relief in Kiran's words, but thought not. No matter if Kiran only appeared to be human, she was sapient and seemed to hate the idea of controlling another sapient being. At least that was the only reason Sol had ever come to when wondering why she hadn't turned his father into her puppet. As well as the devious council, and his siblings. He'd long suspected it was her rebelling from the chains that held her own mind in sway.

Legends of the Simurans told of some attempting to refuse orders. To rebel. None did so successfully. They obeyed, or they died at their own hands. Because of that, Kiran's announcement did little to calm his worries. If the princess was clever, she could manipulate them through Kiran, keeping their trust by simply forcing the Simuran to say she couldn't be ordered. As horrible as the concept of such control was, Sol had to admit it was potent. If only it had been used to better ends than building a dollhouse and ending the world.

"Wait, so Milias told her we'd be coming?" Mara suddenly asked. Sol had managed to forget that part, but he *was* about to collapse from exhaustion.

"*Emperor* Milias' foresight is well documented, Mara. He knows all futures that may unfold," Kiran said flatly.

"Those were stories," Mara shook her head, "no one knows the future, let alone some ass parading in a gown."

"It would be best if you give the emperor his due respect in current-" Kiran began, then fell silent. In the following moments, her lips and fingers twitched.

"You may forget my earlier words," she eventually spoke again, "I will apologize. I was allowing Nemai to listen through my ears, hence my earlier warning. However, she does not have an appropriate opinion of her father. I will not repeat the words she used, for I am physically incapable. Additionally, such words were not meant to be used in the description of a human of any standing. Mara, I believe that you will like Nemai, but be wary of her bad habits. I suspect they are numerous."

Chapter 10

Mara drank a sip of water then sat back and injected the rest of the substance directly into her bloodstream through her new suit. She didn't know if it was necessary with water but didn't care to risk her life nor health over assumptions. She'd already done the same with the protein paste.

She wanted to eat. She needed to, really. The suits were designed to inject the substance, but it was a battlefield remedy. It was never intended to replace eating in the long term. It was enough to keep them alive, but it didn't stop the stomach from shrinking or growling.

She didn't miss the actual taste of the protein paste. Her dream, her most childish yet cherished one, was to taste something she found enjoyable. She knew it wasn't meant to be, but she dreamed on as she stared at the suit injecting the substance into her body. It processed and altered the sludge before pumping it into her veins, giving her a heady rush in return.

Nemai hadn't helped them much in their exploration of the city. Mara didn't know if she was unwilling or incapable of being useful. She suspected the latter. The princess claimed that she had only walked through the structure once when she first arrived and had no idea of the true nature of the towers. She hadn't been allowed to wander the palace outside of her own quarters and the stasis pod she'd been in. She was asking Kiran quite a few questions, the first of which had led to a moment that brought a smile to Mara's face.

"She thinks there is no food. Peculiar," Kiran had said. A few minutes later the shadow had disappeared into the palace. She returned before long, and it was the closest Kiran had ever come to laughing, at least that Mara had seen. The shadow was throwing things out the window and throwing her arms to the heavens.

"She was not aware of the existence of protein paste," Kiran had said, "she's of the belief it is twice processed waste matter I've tricked her into consuming."

Once the shadow had calmed, which hadn't taken as long as Mara had expected, she seemed to return to conversing with the Simuran. Mara wondered what they were saying to one another, but all Kiran would tell her, or Sol, was they were exchanging knowledge.

"That's what all conversations are," Sol had exclaimed. When Kiran answered with a simple 'that is correct', Sol had left to wander the city on his own. Mara had found him in the park, napping with his back on one of the dead trees. She'd left him there to return to the armory. She tested the various styles of weapons and armors by shooting the former at the latter. The result was a series of well-blended scorch marks and a wide grin on her face. Of course, she hadn't tried turning any of the guns to their highest settings. More than once. The resulting slag pile had been enough to sate her curiosity. At least they didn't explode as the Behemoth's guns always did on those settings, although she would miss that option.

She was tempted to try out the grenades as well, but there was no safe place to do so that she had found, in case the explosions were more substantial than she anticipated. It would be the height of foolishness to use a weapon in combat that she never tested, as far as Kiran had taught her. However, in her mind, dying from hesitation was yet more foolish. As a result, she ensured she had every empty slot of her suit fit with the square explosives. She would find an opportunity to test them safely at some point. Once the tasks of testing and outfitting were complete, she returned to the central Plaza, finding Kiran waiting with Sol at hand.

Apparently, Nemai had wandered off somewhere in her tower, looking for a way she could lead them into the Palace. Sol insisted on waiting with Kiran once he'd returned from his *explorations*, and Mara decided she'd do the same. She wanted to explore the towers, and she had an idea that could be both educational and fun, but she would wait until she felt safe about Nemai in the Palace.

They were waiting for several hours for the woman to return to the window. According to Kiran anything but open air dampened the range of their mental senses, although some materials were better than others. Whatever the palace was built of dampened telepathy almost completely, so the two could only communicate if Nemai was standing close to a window. In any case, that day ended with Nemai declaring there was nothing on her side, but she would keep looking after a few hours of sleep. Stasis was, apparently, an exhausting experience.

Sol, Kiran, and Mara took their pick of the towers surrounding the Plaza, taking one each. It was more space than any of them could ever use, and Kiran insisted it was unwise to separate themselves while they were sleeping, which was the time they were most vulnerable. Mara agreed but wanted a tower to herself all the same.

Even with just the single floor, her tower was far more living space than any royal aboard the Behemoth had. It gave her a strange yet pleasant feeling to claim such a space as her own. They made a trek to one of the entrances they hadn't used, finding it had the same three outbuildings, similarly filled with all the same materials, except for the smallest building which was empty.

They took clothing from the nearby locker room inside the wall, as well as towels and anything soft they could get their hands on and used what they found to build beds in their towers. Beds that were nothing more than small mountains of the strangely soft fabric. Once the others were sleeping in their own domains, Mara couldn't help herself. She leaped into the soft pile of cloth with childish giggles and glee.

After her massive bed was once more properly piled, she made several more trips to the distant outbuildings. She took a spare combat suit to have readied in her room, as well as more weapons than she could reasonably use. It made her tower look like an amateur armory, although it lacked shelving, so all of it was carefully placed and organized on the floor instead. It would have to do until Mara found a way to carry the ridiculously heavy metal shelving to her tower. She'd of made her home in one of the armories if it didn't mean living so far from the others. As ridiculous as she was allowing herself to be, she wouldn't completely disregard Kiran's concerns.

It was on the third day, judging by when they slept and woke, that Kiran approached them with a slightly puzzled look. She'd only just entered the Plaza. It usually took a good hour or two for Nemai to check by a window to see if she was there. Seeing Kiran return so quickly was an oddity. Hearing her suggestion sent Mara's mind reeling.

"No," Sol shook his head.

"It was not a request," Kiran said. Mara laughed. The Simuran nearly sounded incredulous at Sol's immediate answer. Nearly.

"We can't trust her," Sol sighed. "Everything she's said could be a lie."

"Successfully lying in a telepathic conversation is difficult for humans," Kiran said, "furthermore, while I do not trust Nemai completely, I do not believe such masterful deceit would fit her apparent personality. She is certainly capable of lies, but prolonged deceit would be exhausting for her, especially in telepathic communications."

"All the same," Sol shook his head, "you want to let her control your body? That's just too much trust Kiran. Tell me you agree Mara."

"Do what you want," Mara shrugged when Kiran looked to her. "Everything I know about freaky mind stuff was what you've taught us. I won't pretend to know better. If you think it's safe, I'll be there. If not, I'll still be there. I'll just grab something nonlethal to shoot you with first. In case she doesn't want to leave when you decide she should."

"That should not be necessary," Kiran said with the ghost of a smile, "while I say control, it should be different from what you are thinking. I will be able to take back control at will, as this body is the home of my mind. The opponent would need to be significantly more potent in telepathy to remove the advantages of this being my body. I do not believe Nemai's training and mental fortitude are sufficient for the task. Her telepathic abilities were formed for self-defense, not for assimilation."

"Fine," Sol sighed, "But I'll be there as well. Both Mara and I *will* have weapons ready to incapacitate you."

"That is acceptable, I will be waiting in the plaza," Kiran nodded.

"One thing before that," Sol said hesitantly. "I want to know why you're willing to do this Kiran. No matter how safe you say it is, letting someone take over your body must be dangerous. So why? Is it because she was once a princess? Is her lineage giving her sway over your decisions?"

Kiran stared at Sol for several moments before answering.

"No," she shook her head.

"Then why?" he asked. Kiran stared at the floor for what had to be minutes. Mara nearly intervened as the atmosphere was becoming more awkward by the second, but she chose to hold her tongue. She wouldn't ask Kiran to not go through with the plan, but she had to admit to being more than a little curious as well.

"Because the mind and body are symbiotic, not the same existence," Kiran eventually said. She paused, and Sol gave Mara a look as if she would explain what the Simuran meant, but Kiran spoke again before Mara could even shrug.

"That is to say that I am sympathetic to her experiences."

It took much longer than Mara expected to find anything resembling a nonlethal weapon in her arsenal. It wasn't something the Simuran's apparently believed in, not that Mara would find fault with that mindset in most situations. However, she was acutely aware that she was vastly different than the type of person that would have lived before the Rot. All that once lived aboard the Behemoth were bound to be, or so they'd been taught. A brutal life created a savage people.

Still, she managed to find something resembling a stun gun. They were rifles that released a programmable electric pulse instead of plasma. Its lowest setting had a decent chance of killing a human, but a Simuran was more durable than a human anyway. The most significant risk was to the heart, but Simurans had a secondary one. One that would begin beating if anything happened to the primary.

That was, of course, if Kiran hadn't been lying to her and Sol when she taught them the differences between human and Simuran so long ago. Two interwoven spinal cords within the spinal column, two hearts, no genitalia; those were the most significant differences that Mara remembered. There were a few thousand other differences she'd spoken of, and Mara faintly remembered a few of them as well, but not enough to recall confidently. Other than their bones being an organic metal alloy. That she recalled particularly well.

The process began not long after they returned to Kiran in the courtyard. To Mara's surprise, Kiran faintly smiled at her when they approached. She almost looked nervous. That gave Mara pause, as she suddenly found herself wondering if Kiran was quite as confident in her telepathic defenses as she claimed to be. Before she could speak up, however, it began.

It was almost unreal to see Nemai taking control of Kiran's body. It only took a few moments for the shift to occur in full, and it was a distinct change. Kiran's body posture shifted to a slight slouch, her eyes widened with excitement, and a sly smile formed on her lips. Even if Mara hadn't been warned about the shift, she would have known it was a different person, although she would have guessed it was another Simuran; certainly not Kiran allowing someone to take over her body telepathically.

"You really are like a doll," Kiran suddenly said, grabbing at her own chest with an eye raised quizzically, and speaking with far more intonation than Mara had ever heard the Simuran attempt or manage. A few moments passed, and she spoke again.

"I mean of course, but I wouldn't have asked them. You have no idea how grim most of them were, or how shy I could be back then. Trust me, you're much better than most of them," she said. Then she grinned.

"Yes, I *can* speak to you without letting everyone else hear half the conversation. But that would be *rude*. I mean, you're already stopping me from saying ------- and ------. Those don't even qualify as curse words. Prude."

"Hello Nemai," Mara said, still adjusting to seeing her friend suddenly seeming so alien. Seeing her mouth move when trying to curse was a bit odd as well, as her voice would cut off as each attempt began. Kiran, or rather Nemai, glanced at her with a devilish grin and winked.

"Hey there Mara," she said, "it's good to meet you."

A moment later she was in a one-armed embrace that felt like someone was trying to crush her. Doubtlessly Sol was raising his rifle with a verbal threat, but then Mara was released before he could speak, or she could gasp for air.

Mara felt like an idiot, and she was sure that Sol did as well. The rifles would be useless if they couldn't hit their target, and Kiran's body, no matter who was controlling it, was faster than the two of them combined and stronger by an even larger margin. It was easy to forget as the Simuran looked so frail, especially with one arm magnetically locked across her stomach.

"Amazing, you really are much stronger than you look Kiran," Nemai said, voicing Mara's thoughts, "and don't get me started on the eyesight. You could watch someone bathing from a kilometer away... Fine, a kilometer is exaggerating. And I repeat, prude."

Mara watched, silently, as she listened to half the conversation with a smile, suddenly finding herself pitying Kiran for being the woman's mouthpiece. Perhaps the cause of Kiran's nervousness hadn't been the danger of it after all. Sol had also started to smile and silently laugh at the antics. It was much better than the grim look he had before it started.

"Prude *is* an insult actually," Nemai rolled her eyes. "Anyways."

Moments later she was at Sol's side, lifting the man in a one-armed hug as she had Mara.

"Good to meet you too sir flashlight. Sorry for the show, but your friend is easy to mess with. I just can't resist," she said once Sol was back on his feet.

"It's good to meet you as well Nemai, but my name is Sol, not... flashlight," Sol said. Nemai raised a finger and shook her head.

"Fine, fine. I *can* resist. But I won't. It's a figure of speech. You *know* what those are."

"You're...Not quite what I was expecting," Sol said slowly. Mara had to smile wider. He looked uncomfortable, and that was amusing to watch.

"That's because you're a person, mister flashy. And people are stupid. No fault of your own. Grass doesn't rage against the blue of the sky, nor the sky the green of the grass. It's simply the natural state of existence," Nemai shrugged.

"I see," Sol said tentatively. Then Nemai froze for a moment.

"I didn't mean to be rude," she suddenly burst, patting Sol on the head, "after all, I'm a person too, so I am just as stupid. Maybe more so. Likely less. I meant it to be a broad statement about the human condition, not a personal insult."

Mara snorted. Sol shook his head as if in a daze. Nemai grinned. The tension that had been in the air when the meeting started was well gone.

"Yes, I *am* more manic than usual Kiran," Nemai rolled her eyes, "It's like I'm nervous or something, yes. You ------- -----."

"This is more entertaining than your books," Mara grinned at Sol as the princess went off on a miniature and silent tirade, occasionally broken for a word or two, or so the woman could breathe.

"That's just not fair," Nemai eventually grumbled, "I called you ----- twice already, why the sudden censoring? ... Ah. So, if I agree it's not an insult, you'll stop? Ok, sure. You manipulative -----."

"As interesting as this is, can we get to why you wanted to speak to us?" Sol questioned. Nemai nodded absentmindedly. Mara had the distinct impression that the woman was rather enjoying her bizarre conversation with Kiran.

"I suppose that's fine," Nemai shrugged, "You heard him Kiran, we'll need some privacy."

"What-," Sol started. Nemai waved him off.

"Nothing to worry about," she said, with a sudden drop in tone. Then she laughed. "Are you *threatening* me Kiran? Really?... Yes, that *is* a threat. No, no, what's a death threat or two between friends... Oh, gods, I do sound like my father. I won't do anything. I swear it."

Nemai looked up at Sol and Mara in silence. It was still the same woman, that much was obvious, as Kiran's body posture and neutral mask were nothing resembling Nemai's. Mara felt the tension slowly growing again, Sol glancing at her a few times, and slowly starting to raise his rifle.

"Milias is an asshole," Nemai said suddenly. Then she nodded. "Ahh, all is right again. Ok people, sorry but Kiran can't listen in here. She sees everything, but she cut off her hearing, and is purposefully ignoring your faces to avoid lip reading."

"Why?" Sol ground his teeth in irritation.

"Because I asked her to. I can't give commands to your friend, but my position does give me a few privileges. This is for her sake anyway. If the wrong topics are spoken of a Simuran will immediately decommission itself. Now let's make this quick, it's not easy to cut your mind off from your own senses, especially for a Simuran. It's in direct conflict with their programming."

"What topics?" Mara questioned.

"Many," Nemai shook her head, "honestly I've no idea how many, or what the keywords are, so it's best to be paranoid about it."

Mara and Sol looked at each other, neither sure if they could trust the woman. Then Mara shrugged. She knew that Kiran's mind was full of orders, that there were certain things she couldn't or wouldn't do or say. The 'decommission' commands from simply overhearing the wrong words was new information, and quite dreadful at that, but not too outlandish given Kiran's nature.

"Can we help her?" Mara asked. Nemai smiled gratefully.

"I'm sure there are ways to help, damned if I know them," she said. "I grew up surrounded by Simurans, but I can't say I understand them. Kiran just now, she *threatened* me not to do something to you. Well, kind of threatened. Suppose it's from being your Caretaker."

"She was the Behemoth's Caretaker, not ours," Mara said.

"Sure," Nemai shrugged, "but the Behemoth is gone now unless she lied to me. And she hasn't used her telepathy to fry her own brain. You have no idea how weird that is. A Simuran without a prime duty doesn't happen. Root commands forbid it. Thus, she is still a Caretaker of *something*."

"I won't pretend to understand you," Sol said, "but if this isn't easy for Kiran to manage, maybe you should get to your point."

"That was point one. Your Simuran is damn strange, and I can't say that's common. I like her. Point two, you're walking into a trap."

"I never met someone who could be so specific about everything they say," Sol said in irritation.

"Calm down now, don't go flashing us Sol," Nemai said with a smile. "I meant just that. As I told Kiran, father set this whole thing up. I don't know why, only what he told me, and you can be damn sure that was a lie."

"He told you about us. When was this exactly?" Mara asked.

"Before I went under stasis, while we were on our way to Bastion. He didn't explain all of it, but he never does. He just told me I was going to go to sleep for a while and would wake up when Sol and Mara came to see me, along with K131 from the Behemoth. He claimed that at least one of us would escape this place, alive. Whoever survives gets the chance of a reward. All of us can escape if we can manage it, but he didn't seem to think that was likely. He talked about timeline variations and probabilities a lot, but most of it sounded like gibberish to me."

"Right," Sol shook his head, "because that makes sense. So… what's this reward supposed to be then?"

"According to him, one of us will be the one to kill him. That's the reward. He claimed it's unavoidable. He dies to one of us in the future. If you believe him. I don't. But I'm willing to find out if I'm wrong about that," she said. Her last words were spoken in a grave tone soaked in hate.

"Right. I believe you," Mara said in the most sarcastic voice she could summon.

"Look," Nemai said in frustration, "I understand that you doubt what he can do. People in my day doubted him too. I don't care if you believe that he can see the future. I don't care if you hate him or if you want to kill him, although, dibs. I just wanted to warn you. Milias is an immortal, and everything we do is part of some trap he's set. I might be the trap. Maybe you're the trap for me. Because I *know* he read the future, and father likes his entertainment. I *also* know that there's a portal to the Fae at the heart of Bastion."

"The Fae? You're saying it's real?" Sol asked.

"Yes," Nemai said, "but I need you, mister living flashlight, to activate it. So, I can't exactly scamper off without you lot. Not that I'd leave Kiran even if I could. I'm really starting to like her."

"You're really not sane, are you?" Sol muttered the question.

"Maybe not," Nemai shrugged, "anyone leagues above the intellect of another is bound to sound mad. Imagine what a cloud would say of people should it have a mind to think and a mouth to speak... Although, I suppose it wouldn't be a cloud then."

She sat in thought for a few moments, Mara and Sol traded a few looks that varied between incredulity and amusement.

"Anyway," Nemai shook Kiran's head, "my biggest point is this. There's a way to the Fae here, a world away from the Rot. It's where father went after putting me in stasis. We can follow him if we can get the flashlight to...the right place. If you don't believe me, that's fine for now. The real question is if you'd rather die to the Rot out there or take a chance on me being sane.

I need you. But you need me as well. I'm the only one that knows how to... well, the ass called it *activating salvation*. Not quite sure what he means to be honest, but I know how to do that, and I won't be sharing until I'm out of here. Now the runes to get through the barrier aren't on this side, as intelligent as that would be. I assume father has some elaborate, cruel, or idiotic plan we'll be following unintentionally. You'll need to search your side for our answers. Either way, I need you to break the barrier, so I can get out of here or get you in. The rest of my escape I can handle. Doors aren't good at holding me."

"So, you want us to try to get in the palace while telling us it's a trap," Sol said.

"Not the palace itself, that would be ridiculous. But father foresaw you, so he probably left a trap somewhere down the line. Or this whole situation is a trap. You're not cursed enough to of met him, so you'll have to trust me when I say he is a man of lies. As he loved to say, phonetically, lie is in his name."

"And why can't Kiran hear about this?" Mara asked.

"Maybe she can," Nemai shrugged, glancing at her hand that was beginning to shake, "but I didn't want to risk it. Theoretically, she'll have no qualms about going to the Fae. However, most Simuran's would go on a rampage at the thought of a human outside of the Imperial line entering the palace. Or of me leaving it, given my status. One of us will need to convince her it's going to be alright before that day comes. Otherwise. Well, she'll be more dangerous to you than the Rot should you find the barrier runes. That's all I wanted to tell you."

Before Sol or Mara could say anything more, Nemai raised her trembling hand and tapped her forehead twice. The trembling stopped almost immediately. Her eyes drooped with exhaustion, but that couldn't prevent her from making a playful grin.

"Welcome back Kiran, you fucking prude," Nemai yawned. Then her eyes widened slightly. "Wow, too tired to censor me. That's bad. Get some rest Kiran, I know I will be. These plebeians probably think telepathy is easy. Best teach them of the struggle by sleeping for a week or two."

Nemai winked then made her weary way to Mara and Sol, giving each of them another one-armed hug before glancing at her real body, still just a shadow in the window. The shadow began to move, slowly, in an act that looked like a mixture of dancing and undressing. Kiran's hand raised to cover her own eyes until she turned away.

"Oh, come on, it's no different than using a mirror. I was just curious how I… Fine," Nemai sighed dramatically, then turned back to Mara and Sol. "I'll be seeing the two of you again, I hope. Soon. Farewell."

With that, the shadow in the far window half walked, half fell out of view. Kiran's visage quickly shifted to her normal, vastly less playful, look. Her body changed back to how the Simuran usually held herself as well. Details that Mara wouldn't even know how to look for that screamed to her that their teacher was back in control. As if to make them doubly certain that Nemai was actually gone, Kiran gave the ghost of emotion that served as her smile, as well as a sparkle of amusement in the edge of her eyes.

"I apologize. I did not realize Nemai's level of perversion," she said, back to her normal, empty, tone. Then she closed her eyes, carefully lowered herself to the ground, and fell asleep while humming her strange song.

Chapter 11

Sol leaned against the tree with a pleased smile. The thing was probably dead long before he'd even been born, but its twisted form was miraculously still standing. For the most part. Perhaps it was some special type of tree, as there were only a few of them dotting the remnants of the old park. Resilient to the passage of time even as a corpse. It had to be something special. He felt the rough bark against his back and ran his fingers across its surface. Even dead it was a form of life to him. Something that wasn't human nor of the Rot. Perhaps it was older than all of it. He had no way to tell, but he decided to believe it was so. A tree from before it all. Its seed born in a world overflowing with things that grew.

After minutes lost in thought, he relaxed his body, slowly going from standing to sitting without moving away from the trunk of the dead tree. His own tranquility surprised him. The woman, if she was insane or not, had a point. They needed her to move forward.

Sol's attempted introspection was interrupted by the sounds of dampened footsteps. Sol pretended not to hear them as the steps grew louder behind him, ever so slowly.

"Knew I'd find you here," Mara said. Sol flinched dramatically and turned to give her a sharp glare while struggling to no give himself away.

"Don't do that," he grumbled, turning away.

"You should have heard me a while ago," Mara said while taking a seat next to him, leaning against the tree just as he was.

"Guess you're doing better at the whole stealth thing," Sol said. Mara snorted.

"I'd *guess* you were just too busy thinking. Try to be more alert," Mara said. The pride in her voice made Sol's grin return. It was a rare thing to behold. Mara was spectacular at many things, but moving silently had never been one of them. Even in the Behemoth, which was constantly filled with the sound of machines, her approach had been easy to notice. The armor and weapons constantly attached to her didn't help, but Sol suspected she would be a loud without any of them as well.

"I'll catch you next time," he said. Mara yawned and nodded in the edges of his vision. They sat in silence for a time, Mara attempting a nap in the fading sunlight. Sol glared up at the dome, where a patch of night sky was moving in like a storm, their daylight patch leisurely making its way to the wall. On one side of the night patch was a sunset. Across from that was a silent lightning storm.

"So, what are we going to do?" Mara eventually asked.

"What do you think about all of it?" Sol asked. Mara shrugged.

"My thoughts don't matter," she said. "I'm your bodyguard. I'll do what you say."

"You just don't want to make the decision to trust her or not," Sol said.

"There's that too," Mara admitted.

"That's not fair," Sol grumbled.

"No. But that's how it works. When I want it to," she smiled.

"Then I'm going to try trusting her," Sol said.

"I thought it would take longer for you to decide that. Not sure if I'm disappointed or proud," Mara said. Sol snorted.

"We don't have many options," he said after a few moments. "It's like she said. We could wait to die out here. Maybe it will take a few years. A lifetime even. It wouldn't even be a bad life."

"You'd be bored in a week," Mara chuckled, "there's not a single book or movie that I can find in the suit database."

"Yeah. Well, that's assuming the Rot leaves us alone that long." Sol said quietly. Beside him, Mara's eyes lost some of their glimmer.

"Yeah," she said just as quietly.

"But the walls have been around this long I suppose," Sol said with a shrug.

"Have you *looked* at them?" Mara asked.

"There's a lot of Ether being used there. More than the Behemoth's barrier as far as I can tell. I don't know how long it can keep that up," Sol sighed. "I thought... I thought we had years left Mara. I honestly did. Until the tracks stopped and-"

"I know," Mara said. She grabbed Sol's shoulder and squeezed it gently. "But that makes Nemai more believable, doesn't it?"

"How did you come to that?" Sol asked, bemused.

"Aether is said to come from the Fae, right? Maybe that's why this place can still produce enough Ether to stay standing. It's on the door."

"That *is* what the stories say, but the old texts were never very clear on the subject," Sol shook his head. "They wanted to keep some of the mysteries to themselves, I think. To keep Aetherweaving a form of magic, not a field of science that could be studied and understood."

"Do you believe in the Fae Sol?" Mara said.

"I do, and I don't," he shrugged, a little tense. "I know it's childish, but I always planned to look for it if we got here."

"Finally, you admit it to my face," Mara smiled. Sol turned to her with a raised eyebrow.

"Do *you* believe in the Fae?"

"I do," Mara nodded. Sol gave her a look of absolute incredulity, and she laughed. "What's with that look?"

Sol looked away, once more shaking his head.

"I don't know. No offense Mara, I just didn't expect that. At all. I mean, what was it you've said about hope and faith? It seems to me that should apply to something like the Fae as well."

"They're not inherently bad. But, most of the time, they're poisons used to manipulate idiots," Mara said. "But this and that are different things. There are too many stories to be a coincidence. That's all."

"If you insist," Sol said.

"We don't have much choice anyway," Mara grinned, "Regardless of what we believe in, I expect we'll need Nemai's help to reach the Fae. I'd bet it's in the Palace somewhere."

"That would be my guess as well," Sol sighed. "I suppose that makes it a little better, and a whole lot worse. It's not really a choice of trusting her. Either we go to find the Fae and need her help, or we wait to die here and leave her as she is."

Mara nodded. They sat in silence for a few minutes longer before she spoke again.

"What do you think about the rest of it? About Milias?"

"That is a quandary," Sol said softly. "I mean, I don't see how he could know about us, or any of this. We know he was a very clever man. Extraordinary. Deserving of his legend. That and a bit of telepathic trickery, maybe that's all it is. Nemai claimed he told her our names, but what if he never said them? What if he only programmed her to remember him saying names once she *heard* them from the system? Just as a general setup in case survivors ever found their way here."

"Is that possible?" Mara asked. Sol couldn't miss the sound of relief in her voice.

"We'd have to ask Kiran," Sol shrugged, "and I don't know if we'd get a straight answer out of her, not if she knew we were talking about *him*."

"That's fair," Mara said quietly.

"But if I'm wrong, what do we make of the rest of it? The part about one of us killing him? What could that be about?" Sol asked quietly. Mara snorted.

"That's just nonsense, Sol. You were right before. No one knows the future. Besides, he's already dead, unless he's holed up in stasis somewhere."

"But if he is alive, and he does know?" Sol asked. It was Mara's turn to shake her head.

"Then I guess I'd kill him," she shrugged. "I wouldn't do it without a reason, so if he's alive and not lying, there must be one."

Sol nodded and sighed. He closed his eyes and ran his hand along the tree once again. He didn't know how he felt about his own question, let alone Mara's answer.

"If we're speaking hypothetically," Mara mused, "Maybe he's responsible for all of this like the stories say. The Rot I mean. If nothing else, he'd have seen it coming and done nothing. But could anyone of stopped it? Could we really blame him for that?"

"I don't think we're ever going to know, not really," Sol said. "I suppose we just need to try and stay moving. Focus on staying alive. To-"

"Don't say it," Mara interrupted.

"-keep hoping," Sol finished with a grin.

"With that, I'm leaving," Mara shook her head. She stood with a groan, and gently patted the tree with one hand before walking off. Sol followed her with his eyes until she was lost amid the distant towers. Then he moved so he could lay in the dirt beside the tree, as the patch of night in the sky above left him in pale starlight and the blue glow of a distant sapphire spire. He ran his hand through the soil as he drifted to sleep, wishing there was grass.

When he woke, the sky overhead was that of a storm beside a hued dawn drifting away, towards the towers. His back and legs creaked as he stood. He stretched and heard his joints pop and grind in a fashion that was slightly painful yet strangely gratifying.

Once he finished the impromptu routine, he smiled and ran his hand back along the rough bark of the tree. It was a luxury he never expected to have. The tree. The park. The wide spaces. Even the haunting silence of it all, once he was used to it, was beautiful in its own way.

He grabbed a part of the bark that stuck out, planning to take a part of it with him, though he couldn't say why he wanted to do it so badly. Before he did, however, something caught the corner of his eye. Something he hadn't noticed before. His mind filled with wonder, and he found himself climbing the tree, leaping to grab the lowest branch and pulling himself up. As he grasped at branches to ascend ever higher, he found the bark brittle, crunching and falling off the limbs. It scratched him in a few places, but he barely noticed.

It took only half a minute to reach his goal. To the small bit of color on the otherwise gray remnants of life, mostly hidden by the branches that surrounded it. It was an acorn that easily sat in the palm of his hand. It was solid and not rotting, but for a little gray at the stem. He took the thing and placed it in the most secure pocket he could find before climbing down.

Once back on the ground he turned to the road and began his trek back to the towers. As he moved, his hand kept patting the pocket that held the acorn. He didn't know what he wanted to do with the thing. To plant it and hope it grew, or simply to take it with him to wherever he was going. To the Fae, perhaps. That thought made him smile. If they truly found a way to the Fae, then he'd be bringing a piece of his dying world with them.

With that thought, he stopped walking and began to jog. He knew he was weak. It wasn't just his magic, which he could hardly use, but physically he was also pathetic. Always in the way of his bodyguards. A hindrance. Their weakness. If the Fae was real, he would need to be stronger.

Not only to survive whatever supposed game Milias was playing. Simply staying alive in the mythical place of monsters could prove a challenge he wasn't ready for.

He couldn't hope to surpass Mara, let alone Kiran, but he could close the gap. Perhaps, someday, he could be an aid to their survival, rather than a weight around their necks. He turned his jog into a run, to the complaint of his entire body. To distract himself he ran calculations through his mind. It was likely they'd never prove useful in whatever life or death they made for themselves. But in a way he enjoyed mathmatical formulas. They made sense. They were logical in a way few things were.

After reaching the city, he began to check each tower he ran by. Each was as hollow as the ones they'd already inspected. It felt meaningless, but it kept him moving, back and forth across the street as his breathing became more haggard and his muscles complained. He slowed to a walk, then returned to a run as soon as he felt able to. The road slowly spiraled towards the Palace, but that was something they'd confirmed in their first days. Using the alleys to reach the center was much quicker and caused them to cross sections of the larger spiral road several times before reaching the center.

Thus, when he found himself in a smaller plaza, it was something he hadn't yet seen in the strange city. He used the find as an excuse to stop the sudden exercise. He bent over, feeling his lungs screaming, then walked back and forth trying to catch his breath as his heart thundered. All the while he held his eyes on the center of the small plaza.

Held there, on a raised dais, were statues. Four figures, none of which resembled one another. A man with ornately decorated flowing hair and a staff. A giant of a woman, tall enough that the man barely reached her waist, also in robes but with a deep hood hiding most of her face. The third had the shape of a human woman similar in size to the first man, but the woman was distinctly made of flames.

There was no color to her flesh but that of stone, yet the detail was too detailed to be anything but fire.

In the hands of the woman of flame was an orb, a sphere that barely fit in her hand. It was glass and the only color in the collection of statues. Dancing across its surface was a mixture of colors that more than reminded Sol of the false sky above, but vastly more chaotic. If it wasn't a statue, the colors would be spiraling and stirring, although Sol didn't know why he was so confident in that belief.

The fourth and final figure was the grandest of them all, even more than the strange sphere in the hand of the woman of flames. It was a dragon, although it was small for such a legendary creature. While the others stood in a circle, the beast stood behind them. Its tail was wrapped around the group. Its head loomed over the rest of the statues, but it wasn't looking at them. Its eyes gazed at the world beyond, while its wings looked to be frozen in the motion of surrounding the other three to cover them. To protect them. The large woman, whoever or whatever she was, had one hand raised above her head, laid upon the dragon's jaw as if petting it, or consoling it.

Sol circled the statues as he caught his breath, trying to reason out what they were. None of the figures matched any story he'd ever heard or read. Most of the figures, those other than the human and dragon, he had no words for. Perhaps the tall woman was a giantess. They were rumored to exist once, but they were said to be bulky and hideous things, whereas the woman looked to be a simple human grown on a larger scale. There did seem to be something strange beneath the long sleeves of her robes at least. There may have been spikes or spines growing along her forearm, or perhaps she wore some peculiar form of armor there.

Sol felt a dull ache in his chest. He wanted to understand the figures. To study them in length. Perhaps they meant nothing at all. Maybe it was a trap by Milias, something to distract him. After all, the small plaza and the statues couldn't be seen from the palace, so it hardly played a part in the masquerade. He circled them again and again. They were carved in extraordinary detail. He could see it in how the dragon was missing scales here and there, how it seemed to have wounds and old scars. He could see it in how the man appeared to be leaning on his staff as if struggling to stay on his feet. Using his arcane sight, Sol saw they were as heavy with Ether as the rest of the city. No more, no less.

The prince shook his head. It was meaningless, regardless of however detailed it might be. It was too good a way to distract him. A mystery. Something to study, to tempt him to stay in Bastion rather than to seek a way to the fabled Fae. He turned his back to the statues, stretched few times, then took off at a jog once more, no longer attempting to check each tower he passed. Instead, he was trying to force himself to not think about the oddity of the statues. He found it difficult, for on his journey to the center of Bastion he passed four more identical plazas with identical figures in them.

There could have been more of the strange things, as Sol stopped taking the spiraling road after a time. AS he grew more weary he began to take more of the alleys to cut the distance down. Still, whenever he came across the statues, he stopped to catch his breath and walked around them. He studied them for differences. There were none that he could tell. Machine perfection on every scratch. Each time he caught his breath he continued his exercise. Until, after what felt like agonizing hours, he found himself entering the central plaza at an angle he'd yet to see, but there was nothing new to the sight otherwise.

He slowed his pace and walked around until he was near the tower he'd made his temporary home, then he allowed himself to fall to the ground. His body ached like he couldn't believe. His muscles twitched and screamed, but he held his eyes to the colorful sky far above him. He kept a smile on his face even as his legs cramped hard enough for him to contort his body in awkward ways in attempted relief. He would be useful. Not immediately, but eventually, his efforts would help Mara and Kiran. Or at least keep him out of their way. So long as he repeated the exercise. Frequently. That thought finally took the smile from his face, but he resolved himself to it all the same.

It was only after a half dozen minutes had passed that he felt a sudden worry that his sad display had been seen by anyone. When he looked, neither of his bodyguards were present. But there was a witness. Nemai, the shadow, was standing in her distant window. Sol's cheeks flushed, and he nearly cursed at himself for not collapsing in the privacy of his own tower.

The self-pity lasted for only a moment. Nemai was waving her arms frantically, and seemingly trying to throw things out into the plaza to get attention, although they bounced silently on the barrier. Sol waved at her, and she flailed more animatedly, jumping and gesturing things he couldn't hope to guess.

Sol forced himself to stand. He needed to find Kiran. With any hope, she was still sleeping in her tower. Otherwise, he would need to find Mara and hope the Simuran was with her. As a final chance, he could go to the very distant shower rooms, as Kiran seemed to spend quite a bit of her waking time either talking with Nemai or showering. He sighed and hoped he'd be able to find her quickly as he limped out of the plaza.

Chapter 12

Mara locked her hand against the tower and looked down. Far below, the road she started from slowly curved away in both directions. She was above most of the towers in the city and even the high bridges that spanned the sky between many of the constructs. She took a deep breath and continued her ascent.

Her hands locked against the tower each time they touched, as did her feet. She'd been switching climbing methods as she went, more frequently as she got closer to the top. But still her arms were shaking inside the armor, and her legs were screaming in protest each time she raised a foot as if walking up the structure with her toes. It hurt in a way she hadn't felt since boarding the Scion. It made her smile, even as she stopped herself from glancing down again. It would be cheating.

She focused on her breathing and the burning in her muscles until one of her hands curled around the edge at the top of the tower. She pulled herself up with more than a couple grunts of effort, falling onto her stomach when she was more than halfway across the ledge. She twisted until her back was against the smooth surface that made up the top of the tower, her legs hanging off the thing.

The fake sky swam above her, far closer than the street she began on. It had substance, more than the well-painted walls. She felt she could reach out and touch the clouds if only she were a couple hundred meters higher.

Mara watched the chaotic sky and its lights moving for a time before she forced herself to stand and move in a dance of her own; following a series of stretches and breathing techniques Kiran taught her as a child. It was one of several she'd been shown, each with a different purpose. Initially, they weren't dances at all but a simple series of stretches. As a child, she had an easier time memorizing them if she thought of it as dancing, not that a single soul would hear that from her lips. It was something she'd never been able to do while wearing one of the bulkier suits, nor within sight of others, only in the confines of her small quarters.

She moved across the rooftop with a faint smile, merely enjoying the motion of it. A slow momentum that never failed to clear her mind of thoughts and worries. She went through the dance once, then twice, then a third time, the motions carrying her back and forth across the rooftop a half meter from the ledge.

When she finished, the burning in her arms and legs had settled to a faint ache that felt rather pleasant to her. She took one final deep breath then allowed her thoughts to come racing back into her head. Nearly immediately the armor seemed to grow more burdensome, but she ignored that easily enough. She stepped to the ledge and looked out upon Bastion.

She'd climbed the tallest tower she'd been able to find while walking the alleys below, but it was hardly the largest of them in the city. She could see the handful of others from where she stood. Most, however, were below her by no insignificant distance. She could see the wall, if only because where she looked the false sky happened to be mismatched with the blue sky on the painted wall.

The city was beautiful in her eyes. Rich in colors she'd never truly known, like a painting come to life. Seen from on high it was breathtaking. For a moment she allowed herself to imagine living in such a place. If it had been real. If it wasn't some model or plaything, hundreds of thousands of people could live in the towers, talking and smiling. It would be a nightmare of clashing sounds, but nothing compared to the Pit. It would be comfortable.

Mara missed the noise. Even in the relative quiet of the royal quarters she usually guarded, there was always sound. The grinding of the machine they lived in. The turning of gears and the scraping of metal always making themselves known. Horrible sounds, the screeching of steel being cut and torn, patched with whatever the Behemoth mined and smelted from the bedrock as it passed. The touch of rust along the inner walls bringing color to their world.

Civilization as she knew it. She didn't want to admit that it was gone. Not yet. The damned halls weren't just empty but torn apart and coated in blood. Soon whatever scraps remained would be turned to Rot Ash, and then into Rot Beasts. Not all things could die, for not all things were alive, but all things turned to Rot in the end. She could only wonder at the fate of the great machine after their pursuer had claimed it, pulled it beneath the ground as they fled.

She wiped the silent tears from her face and forced herself to think of the present. There was a time for sentimentality, and it wasn't quite yet. When she was old and gray, or, far more likely when she was dying. Probably not then either. Her death would probably be a mercifully quick one. The question was if she would die to the Rot, or to some scheme of Nemai's. Mara didn't dare believe she would reach the Fae. It existed, of that she was certain. It was a place that Aetherweavers disappeared to, never to return. A place that monsters came *from*. A land shaped by legends and nightmares, just as their own world was shaped by war and Rot.

Once all believed in the tales. Those were times not just before Ether, but before the light of any technology. When the Soltraven Empire had yet to raise its flag across half the world. Before Aetherweavers were heroes that fought for kings and queens; in ages past when they ruled with chain and whip and the flames of magic. When the common man and woman prayed to flee to the Fae, or for some monstrosity to tear through reality and take their tormentors. Before knowledge, rebellion, and treaty transformed the Aetherweavers from lordly beings into servants. Until the reign of Milias undid those same treaties.

In that time, belief in the Fae became rare. For all the fables of ancient days, nothing of the Fae was found. There were savage beasts aplenty roaming the wilds, but those were creations of the Aetherweavers. Monstrosities of flesh, stone, or steel. The Fae was not real, not to those that fought the Final War. But Mara believed in the place all the same. Perhaps it was the child she once was. The short-lived dreamer.

Mara shook her head. She hadn't believed in Bastion. Not really. She knew there were records of it. She'd known it had once been built. She'd expected not even to find the shattered ruins of the place. Taken by the Rot like so many other things. The Behemoth was a freak statistical outlier, alive out of luck as much as by the quality of design. But they had found Bastion. It was real, in its own way, and it was nothing akin to what she could have expected. Perhaps where she was wrong about Baston, she could be right about the Fae.

It was fear that held her heart. Not fear of death. She was born in the Pit. She knew of death by the time she could stand. It was a constant presence. Each day she woke was a gift, one she fully expected to end before she slept once more. Death did not bring fear to her. Hope did. It was the desire for things to change, but it couldn't bring about that change. Not in ways that made any difference; not on its own.

Once she lived in the Behemoth, waiting for the lights to go out and the Rot to get in. Now she was in Bastion, and she was waiting for the lights to go out and for the Rot to get in. Once she'd been a child in the Pit, and nearly everyone around her wanted her to die, suffer, or both. Then she became a royal servant, and only the faces had changed. *She* had stopped the beatings with actions and threats of her own. Hope changed nothing. Action did.

Hope wasn't evil by itself. She knew that much. But it was rampant in the Pit. To some, it was a beacon to call to. It was their god and poison. They held to it even as their neighbors tore them apart for some imagined slight. Others used it as a tool to bend fools to their will. Blind hope of a better tomorrow. Hope to see a horizon not made of Ash. Hope to walk through fields of grass. Hope to feel the cutting winds of winter. Hope spread by stories and legends of better days. They sat back and whispered of hope and did nothing to foster the change they wanted. They whispered of hope even as they sold their children to cannibals or worse. Hope was the currency of the damned, and Mara would have no part of it.

She would die. Sol would die, and Kiran would die. It was only a matter of when. She would never fall so low as to rely on *hope*. She would lower her head and do what she could to better their fate. If the Fae was real, perhaps they would die there instead of in Bastion, but she wouldn't allow herself to hope for it. She would find a way to act and then do it.

She already knew what she would do, even if Sol hadn't said what she'd expected. It didn't matter if Nemai could be trusted or not. If there was the smallest chance there was a way to the Fae; Mara would act on it while allowing Sol to think it was really his decision. She would have dragged him along if he'd decided to do nothing, but he didn't need to know that.

She allowed herself to soak in the view for a while longer before deciding on her next action. The chance of finding the proper runes to pass through the barrier was pathetically low. Ideally, the only place that would know the runes was the Palace and the three Goliath machines. The Behemoth was gone. The Wyrm had fallen in the Final War. According to the stories, the sky born Goliath had fallen, leveling everything within two thousand kilometers when its AeC had a catastrophic failure while flying over enemy territory.

The third Goliath, the Leviathan, hadn't been seen since it first left harbor to sail the seas. Even if the aquatic machine still existed and could be found, they had no way to reach it.

They would need an ingenious plan to infiltrate the palace. For that, Mara would need Nemai. She needed to talk to her, without Kiran being able to listen. In case Nemai was both correct and honest, and such conversations could drive the Simuran to *decommission* herself. Mara wouldn't take the chance on her friend's life, no matter how much easier it would be. She would first try to walk up to the barrier to see if she could get in range of Nemai's telepathy.

As for how to convince their Simuran friend, she would leave that to Sol. He'd always been better at words when he cared to put his mind to work.

Her greatest concern, more than their own survival, was Milias. He was supposedly immortal, although there were some who said it was a name passed on to several beings over time, rather than a single person with an endless life. It was said he was omniscient, while others said a spectacular spy network could give that illusion. But no spies could predict the future. It was the single point that made trusting Nemai difficult for Mara. She *wanted* to believe the woman, but her own sanity insisted that Milias was a fraud. No one could know the future, no matter how powerful their magic might be. It made her far more uneasy than she pretended to be when talking to Sol. He didn't need to know.

After a few more minutes of thought, Mara checked the wrist console of her suit. The things could last years on battery life if only fueling life support systems. Unfortunately, the magnetic systems were among its more power-hungry features. However, according to the console, the new suits were more than a little superior to her old one in that department. The entire climb had used less than a fraction of a single percent of the suit's Ether reserves. It was efficiency beyond her expectations. Far beyond them. Impossibly beyond. Mara pushed it into the pile of things to think about later, or possibly to mention to Sol. He may even enjoy figuring out such mysteries.

A plan for descent formed in her head. It wouldn't be near the exercise of the climb up, but it would undoubtedly be quite a bit of fun. She moved to the edge of the wall. After a moment she moved, further over so she would be over one of the sky bridges instead of the road that was more than twice as distant. She carefully crawled back onto the side of the building, using the suit's magnetic array to hold herself to the side. Then she weakened the magnetic field on her hands and feet and began to slide. First slowly, then faster and faster as she weakened the magnetic field more severely.

She'd almost entered a free fall by the time she started to reverse the process, slowing down until she was once more still, a couple meters above the sky bridge. She could feel the blood pounding through her veins and could hear herself laughing. Her expectations were right. It *was* fun.

She dropped the last couple meters onto the bridge and regretted it a moment after her feet touched the solid floor. She scrambled to throw her hands back against the building and locked them in place as the floor of the bridge shimmered, then disappeared. Mara stared at the street far below. Then at her foot that seemed to be standing on air. She stared at it for half a minute, before shooting her grapple against the tower and trying to stand. She didn't fall.

Her hands reached for the still visible rails, holding them perhaps a little more tightly than she usually would, and she took a few more steps out as her grapple extended more cable, pulling against her left arm. She kept walking until she was nearly halfway across the invisible bridge, then turned her eyes down. She saw the road, still a small thing from her height.

"The hells," she muttered. Then her eyes went up, to the door in the side of the tower. A door that the bridge led to. She looked behind her, to the side of the tower she'd been clinging to, where there was another door. She'd noticed it while she'd been clinging to the wall but hadn't given it much attention at the time. The buildings were hollow. The doors didn't matter. At least that had been her instinct at the time.

Still moving slowly, and keeping her eyes down, she made her way back across the bridge to the tower she started at. She locked a hand against the building, released the grapple, and grabbed the handle. The door opened easily and without a single sound. Inside, the tower was as hollow as all the others.

Tentatively, Mara extended her foot, and it settled on the empty air. It shimmered, and the ground appeared under her feet, hiding all that was beneath her. She scowled and put more weight down. Finally, she released her hold to the building, and walked in, the bridge outside turning visible as she left it.

"The hells," Mara said again, more fervently than the first time. She walked across what should have been air, walking by the pillars until she reached the other side. Questions swam through her mind as she kept her eyes staring down, waiting for the ground to disappear on her. She walked the perimeter of the tower, passing several more doors. She couldn't say what was driving her, just that she wanted to stay moving as she tried to reason the purpose of the invisible floors.

Eventually, she decided that she needed help. Kiran and Sol would be interested in the development. Possibly even Nemai. It was too bizarre a thing for Mara. When she went to leave, however, her confusion only grew. The door she approached, the same one she first entered from, had writing carved into the otherwise bland appearance. The writing was in Temic.

Well done Mara! The bridge was a big hint though. Too big. Take away that well done. Adequate? Not quite. Poorly done? If you want to insult poorly done things. Job complete. Congratulations. Unfortunately, this discovery will come to nothing. There's honestly very little of interest to find in the towers. Nothing to see here, move along. That's what their translucent natures are supposed to imply to you dolts.

Not that you'll be doing much searching soon.

Considering

Condolences,

Milias

Chapter 13

Mara descended from the bridge in the same manner as she'd left the rooftop, but most of the enjoyment was gone. When she came to the road, she landed a little heavily, likely breaking bones were it not for the suit dampening the impact. She allowed herself a minute of stretching and pacing to work out her sudden joint pains before taking off towards the central plaza. It was simple enough to find the right direction after her earlier view atop the tower.

She reached the empty area quickly and made her way along the edge until she found the small collection of towers they used as homes. Neither Sol nor Kiran was asleep nor waiting for Nemai's attention. Mara cursed.

After a quick consideration, she took her helmet from where it was locked at her waist and put it on. She ran a general radio sweep to no avail. It wasn't altogether surprising. They'd already discovered that their communications didn't care to connect throughout the city. Whatever the towers were built of tended to scramble the signals just as they dampened telepathy. All the same, it did confirm for her that neither of the others was close. Or at least Kiran wasn't, given that Sol wouldn't be in his suit if he could avoid it.

Mara put her helmet back at her waist and sat with her back against the door to Kiran's tower. After the brief conversation with Nemai had ended, Sol and Mara had carried the Simuran to her tower. She'd genuinely looked as if she would sleep for a week at the time, yet she was gone. Mara didn't know where she would of went. She didn't even know how much time had passed. The false sky, as beautiful as Mara found it, was useless in the endeavor of marking time. Hunger and meals could be used, but they were always hungry after a fashion. The same could be said for being tired.

The soldier sighed and forced herself to stand. Perhaps things weren't as dire as she'd been thinking. The message she'd found engraved on the wall wasn't from Milias. Bastion's systems, the one that interrogated Kiran when they'd first been in decontamination, knew her name. It would be easy enough to design the system to carve messages throughout the city after strangers arrived. The only real question was why there would be such protocols.

She shook her head. Nothing had made sense since the Behemoth ended. Since the *thing* pulled it below the ground.

"Is your health at risk?" a cold voice asked. Mara's hand raced to a pistol at her side and nearly fell into a crouch before catching herself.

"Dammit Kiran, make some noise when you sneak up on people," Mara grumbled, stilling her heart that was thumping in her chest.

"I must repeat, that would be counter to the concept of stealth, although once more stealth was not my intent," Kiran said, walking around Mara, so she was at the door to her makeshift home.

"If you're not trying to sneak, make some noise. Call out from a distance. Something," Mara shook her head.

"Apologies. Your thoughts seemed to be in distress, so I was observing you to find the cause. I only approached when I could not find a reason."

"I was looking for you," Mara said.

"Then I apologize for my absence. How may I be of assistance?" Kiran asked.

"What were you doing? You should be sleeping," Mara said.

"I woke and could not return to a resting state without minimal physical exertion," Kiran said quietly. Mara snorted, surprising herself with how much stress she found falling away.

"You mean you went for a walk," she said.

"That could be a correct assumption."

"Go back to sleep," Mara shook her head.

"I will do so momentarily. Do you need my assistance?"

"It can wait."

"I am awake now," Kiran said. Mara sighed and eyed the Simuran closely. Her face was blank as always, although there was a dark tinge around her eyes that was unusual. She'd never gained such a look by using her telepathy, at least never that Mara had seen. Willingly cutting off her hearing had apparently been vastly more difficult than *merely* breaking into other people's minds.

"I found something," Mara eventually said. "I don't know what it means yet."

Kiran nodded, then sat with her back against her door. Mara sat beside her and tried to organize her thoughts.

"There are floors in the towers Kiran. At least in one of them. They're invisible."

"I see," Kiran nodded. "Or, perhaps, I do not, as that seems to be the point of invisibility."

"Was that supposed to be a joke?" Mara snorted. When Kiran didn't answer, she shook her head.

"You're not surprised then?" she asked.

"I am not," Kiran said blandly, although Mara saw the Simuran twitch as she spoke. That made the soldier hold her thoughts for a short while longer before speaking again.

"There was a message as well," she said. That made Kiran turn to look at her in earnest.

"It mentioned me by name, and was signed by Milias," Mara continued. "Now the system could have carved it with my name. It probably carved it all over the place if I look. That explains it. I'm just. I don't know. It's playing with my head."

"The system did not carve a message for you," Kiran said quietly.

"You think Milias really did it? That he could see the future?"

"You forget what I am Mara," Kiran said quietly. "Since my creation, I've been aware of my master's powers. His usage of them does not surprise me, no. Perhaps contact Sol. He should have an interesting reaction; however, I am uncertain if it would be the one you expect."

Kiran continued to face Mara as she spoke, and Mara stared at her for several moments. The Simuran still bore the look of exhaustion, barely better than she'd been when she laid down in the plaza. But in some way, Kiran seemed to be sad.

"What have you been doing?" Mara asked.

"Walking. Reading," Kiran said, turning her head towards the silver runes that were etched into the towers.

Mara shook her head. Part of her wanted to reprimand Kiran for not sleeping. On the other hand, she was only able to sleep anymore because Kiran came along and used her telepathy to guide her to it. Even then she would wake screaming if Kiran didn't gift her with dreamless slumber. Mara still wanted to talk about what she discovered, but she would wait until Sol returned. She turned her head to the runes Kiran was staring at.

"What do they mean?" she asked.

"They are the esoteric whining of the elderly. Eternal things lost to time is a more eloquent way to say it. Lost youth, dead friends. That is the idea, I believe."

"You believe? Can you read it or not?" Mara asked, smiling.

"It can be a frustrating language when written," Kiran answered curtly.

"Then maybe you should learn to read better," Mara said, recalling when she was rather young, and Kiran had said similar words to her about reading Temic.

"The language was never meant to be a written one. Nor was it meant to be learned. Only taught," Kiran said with a hint of gravitas.

"Because that makes sense," Mara rolled her eyes, "aren't those basically the same thing?"

"To learn is to take. To teach is to give," Kiran said, tapping Mara's forehead.

"Because that's a logical way to avoid my question," Mara laughed. Then she shrugged. "Not much difference in the end." Kiran reached back to her forehead, then flicked it.

"Teach. Learn. They are always different, or why would they be different words?" she asked quietly. Mara didn't say anything, so Kiran continued. "One cannot be taught if there is no thirst to learn, but one can learn without being taught. Teaching is kind, but to learn is to be wise."

"Have a point anytime soon?" Mara asked, hiding her grin. Kiran was acting more like herself than she had in recent days. More like herself than she'd been since the Behemoth stopped moving.

"Those were the words of one of your ancestors, an ancient human," Kiran said, then shook her head. "I agree in theory. However, like many things, the Simuran tongue stands in opposition to this belief, as to say it cannot be learned unless there is one willing to teach. I was instructed on the spoken language; however, the runes are laborious to make sense of."

"Could I help?" Mara asked.

"Perhaps a gifted mind could aid me," Kiran looked at Mara, then shook her head. "Best not to waste our time."

"Are you mocking me?" Mara asked, partly incredulous, but unable to stop herself from laughing.

"Of course not," Kiran said, with a bit of playfulness that seemed to be mimicked from Nemai. Then she placed her hand on Mara's head and ruffled her hair as if she were a child.

"Just tell me why it's so difficult," Mara said, rolling her eyes once again. Kiran nodded, then turned her eyes back to the runes.

"As I said, our language was never meant to be written. Originally it wasn't intended to be spoken either. It was designed for telepathy. Every word has many translations. The intent of the speaker tells the listener which translation is intended. It could be a single definition, a few of them, all of them, the antithesis of the given word and all of its translations, or a mixture of all of it."

"Sounds like a pointless headache," Mara said.

"It was important at the time," Kiran said calmly. "However, when Emperor Milias announced his knowledge of the forming language, he had a written variation set. The runes. Theoretically, the selected definitions can be indicated by changing the angles the rune is written at. Unfortunately, the runes here appear to be for the aesthetic more than the meaning. Each is baseline rune, which claims all definitions of each rune are implied, most of which form rambling nonsense."

"What does the word Kiran mean in your language?" Mara asked.

"Caretaker," the Simuran said.

"And the other definitions?"

Kiran remained silent for several moments, then pointed to the tower side runes.

"The first rune is Nelema. Its definitions are eternal, flame, luck, time, magic, or death. Obviously, I am summarizing the translation. The second rune is Gavam. Seed, despair, cage, or once more, death. By the rune at least several meanings should be valid by the intent of the one that carved the words. The three other runes in the sequence have the same nonsensical definitions. Either my knowledge of the runes is lacking, which is a valid concern, or the engraver was lacking mental faculties."

"Once again, what a perfect answer to my question," Mara shook her head. Kiran didn't respond. Mara sighed. Her answer wouldn't be forthcoming.

"So, do all definitions have different possible words then? Like death?" she eventually asked.

"Obviously. There are thirteen words for death I am aware of, not counting the fluctuations within each individual word. The definitions not intended were to work as connotations, as our society did not influence our language to the extent humanity did with theirs, given our nature. Nelema with death as the intended definition would likely be implying the eternal state of it. Gavam with death intent would likely be referring to the despair it brings to the soon dead and their survivors."

"Interesting, but far too complicated," Mara shook her head. "Besides, I thought Simurans didn't care for emotion in the first place."

"Emotions have their uses when properly controlled. Communication was our primary use of it. As for the language itself, it is no more complicated than your own. You are simply accustomed to it and choose words unconsciously. Likewise, my tongue is quite simple with experience, and when used with telepathy. Entire conversations can be spoken with a couple words and a flurry of intent. In the first days, the language shifted with each generation that came from the factories. It was only based on emotional manipulation and concepts then. Spoken words were an aid for education that would eventually be unneeded. There was nothing with-"

Both women froze as the air around them hissed with static. Both had their helmets on and their suits sealing a moment later.

"-his working?" a woman's voice called out. Kiran and Mara glanced at each other. Both had weapons drawn.

"It *is* working, *finally!*" The voice screamed, loud enough to make Mara wince. The voice sounded like it was coming from just beside her, inside her helmet now that it was on.

"Hello, hello, just the friendly and ever so *awesome* Nemai here. Fixed something while waiting for mister flashlight to find Kiran. At least that's what I hope he's doing, not something pointless, because *the walls have been breached*."

"Can you hear us?" Kiran called out.

"More accurately, the system notified me that Simuran K131, and so on, has used its code to enter the outer walls. As Kiran and Mara aren't floundering idiots, and I saw flashy in the flesh, I'm going to assume it wasn't one of you three. Personnel gate 2. I've no idea what's there, but before long it will be through decontamination. That would be a pleasant little bath for scaly hides, don't you think?"

"Where?" Mara barely had time to speak before the voice returned.

"Shit, the same gate you came in through. Forgot, not all of us have maps two feet in front of our faces."

Mara and Kiran took off at a dead sprint towards their entrance, the same place they liked to shower and steal clothes from. Mara could only assume Kiran was searching for Sol as she ran with her eyes closed.

"If you be so kind as to return to the plaza when this is over, that would be just the best. I'd like to see who doesn't die."

The voice spoke as if still right beside them, despite them sprinting through alleyways, but it wasn't coming through their helmet's speakers either.

They moved across the dead park at a sprint. Mara began to feel the effort of it burning in her chest when Kiran broke their silence.

"Sol is there," she said grimly. Mara aimed her grapple at the nearest tree and fired. The metal slammed into the tree, cracking the wood. It pulled Mara through the air faster than she could run. She hit the tree, the force of the impact shattering the top half she'd hit, the suit mostly absorbing the impact at the cost of Ether. She leaped and aimed at the next tree that would take her closer to the wall, but there weren't many of them left.

"Is the Rot-" Mara started to speak, but Kiran didn't let her finish.

"I can't tell," she interrupted, "the walls restrict... Yes."

In the distance, Mara watched Sol sprint out of the hallway, or as close to it as he could. He was limping heavily.

Moments later the thing followed through, and it made Mara's heart pound with panic. It was a Rot Beast in mimicry of a person. Scaled skin with an enormous and familiar red eye taking up most of the head. Its long and sinister claws scraped the ground it walked on. It turned its massive eye to Mara, and it *grinned*. A dozen mouths, one below its crimson eye, one on its neck, the rest spread across its body, all baring teeth joyously, with twisted tongues emerging to lick across its scales.

"It's sentient," Kiran hissed as she somehow began to move even faster, passing Mara. For once she was making noise as she moved, although it was quickly hidden by the gurgling laughter that came from the beast.

Mara turned a few dials on her rifle and aimed at the monstrosity. It turned its head, as if curious, and its grins *grew*, scales cracking and separating to make room for new maws to form.

"We can't kill it here," Mara called out, lining up her shot on the beast. Kiran would already know, but it was her way of reminding Sol, who would hopefully make his way somewhere safe, or at least to a combat suit. There wasn't any Ash in the air, yet, but she didn't know what it had been like inside the shower room. There was a chance, a decent chance, that he was already infected. That she had failed in her only duty. To make sure that if he died, it was after she died protecting him. She'd been careless.

Mara watched with plasma rifle aimed, prepared for Kiran to push the creature back into the hall it came from. Bolts of plasma would create small flakes of Rot Ash as it burned the beast. That would be enough to start turning the dirt of Bastion's park. They had to contain it before killing it. And they had to kill it, more so if it was a sentient like Kiran claimed. Sentient Rot Beasts were spoken of in their history of fighting the Rot. An evolution like any other the monsters could have, but extraordinarily rare and exceptionally dangerous. It was believed that that which pursued the Behemoth had once been such a beast.

Kiran dove to the ground when she'd nearly reached the beast. There was barely a confused second before the creature's flesh broke apart, a scythe of bone swiping at where Kiran would have been. A scythe that was many times larger than the body of the beast it came from. Kiran rolled across the ground, sliding her blade along the beast's leg, cutting through the scales as if they were made of air.

The beast didn't react, unable or unwilling to feel pain. Another leg grew into place before it could fall. Three maws widened, tentacle tongues reaching for Kiran to grab her and tear her apart. All the while its eye, taking up most of its head, stared at Mara, drool dripping upon the ground below, where it sizzled and ate into the dirt, before flowing up to rejoin the body of the creature. It almost seemed like it was purposefully preventing the creation of more Rot Ash.

Kiran spun, cutting apart the tongues chasing her, but they grew back with speed and increased in number.

Mara fired a few shots from her rifle, carefully missing the Beast. While they couldn't afford to burn it or hit it with plasma the beast wouldn't necessarily know that. It flinched away from the plasma all the same. Mara cursed under her breath. It had been a test of the creature. Rot Beasts didn't flinch. At least not the mindless variety. Either it had memories of plasma, as she'd suspected, or it truly was trying to prevent itself from multiplying. Maybe both, as she had a theory of why the thing would remember plasma.

While the beast flinched away from the fiery bolt, Kiran slipped beside the thing's humanoid figure, planting her blade through its eye. That should have happened at least. Instead, just before her blade hit, the monster grew taller, its head disconnecting from its body. Kiran's sword cut through the air between, then tendrils grew from the beast's head to reconnect with the body. Kiran was hit by something Mara didn't see and sent flying through the air. Mara had never seen Kiran be hit by something before. And still, the beast stared at Mara. It wanted her to charge. It wanted *her*. That gave her the advantage.

She was confident in her and Kiran's ability to destroy the beast so long as they lured it into a sealed room first. Usually, they would need to worry abou the limbs and random bits Kiran was cutting off, but the Beast was reabsorbing all of it rather quickly. It worked to confirm her theory. It wanted them to itself. It was bizarre behavior for a Rot Beast, but maybe it was normal for a sentient one.

Mara started to run, trying to circle the beast to get through the door behind it. It moved as if wise to her plan, continually shifting between her and the door. It was faster than her and didn't have to move as far.

Kiran returned with no new injuries that Mara could see. She fired her grappling hook into the creature and tried to pull the thing through the doorway it was slowly leaving behind. Mara watched the Simuran straining to move the beast as her grunts of effort came through the short-ranged communications suite. The creature didn't deviate from its slow pace at all, dragging Kiran along like a stray thread of fabric fluttering in the air.

"Shit," Mara spat. She started to sprint towards the creature. Its grins widened even more as its form shook. A mass of Rot flesh in the vague shape of a human, broken apart, but held together by strands here and there. Beneath the scales, *things* coiled and moved, as if it was naught but snakes. Mara raised her fist and fired her own grapple, locking on the painted wall above them. If the beast wanted her as much as it seemed to, it would chase.

Kiran screamed at her to stop, but it was too late for that. As her grapple pulled her up and above the creature, it exploded into a sea of tentacles, with the eye spinning in the sole remaining humanoid feature. Mara released her grapple in midair, and all the limbs reached above her where she would have been. Kiran barely had time to move as Mara's momentum carried her through the open door. She rolled, then took to her feet and ran.

Considering condolences, the words ran through her mind. She looked back, and the beast was following, just as she'd expected. Kiran stood between it and her, but the creature turned into a flowing liquid that moved around the Simuran at a speed Mara couldn't outpace on foot. She pushed herself harder, screaming over the communications for Kiran to close the door and guard it.

She leaped into the air and fired her grapple down the corridor. It hit one of the high metal arches some distance away and began to pull her through the air, but the beast was quick. It caught her leg, and she stopped moving. Alarms screamed in her helmet as the grapple struggled to pull her, ripping her arm out of its socket. Behind her, the beast pulled her back, its body seeping over hers. Mara screamed as she was pulled in both directions. She reached across her chest with her free arm, trying to tap one of her many grenades to start its countdown, cursing that such things couldn't be set by gesture commands.

The beast caught her arm before she could touch the explosive. Its body oozed along her suit, blocking her from any of her explosives. It squeezed and crushed everything it covered. Her armor groaned, and more alarms flared across her vision as the beast pulled her back, the thin cable slipping out of her grapple one agonizing millimeter at a time. Time slowed, and she felt fire course down her spine moments before something audibly snapped.

She couldn't say what happened next. Everything turned black, then light returned. She found herself flying back inside Bastion. She hit the ground and bounced, then landed again and slid through the park. She felt none of it.

Mara blinked. Her head was filled with words she couldn't quite hear. Someone knelt in front of her. He was screaming something, but the words were foreign. It was Sol. It only took her a few moments to realize it. But her vision of him was imperfect. Something was seeping into her eye. Something warm and red. She couldn't remember what it was called.

Sol was looking at her suit, inspecting it, all while trying to talk to her. She really wished he would start speaking Temic again. Or maybe he was speaking it, but it was all nonsense in her head. She may have hit the ground harder than she thought. If she had hit the ground at all. She couldn't quite remember doing so, but she was sure she had. She felt like she was floating, but it wasn't as pleasant as she would expect. She was awake at least; she remembered that was good. She was alive. That was better. Maybe. She couldn't quite recall which was supposed to be better any more.

She realized that Sol wasn't being perverted as he lifted her limbs, spoke, and inspected every inch of her suit. He was looking for something. He was making sure that only the thing inside of the suit was broken, that the creature hadn't punctured the suit itself. He wasn't doing a good job. He was angry. Angrier than Mara knew he should get. He started to pet her head, then wiping at her eyes. She didn't know where her helmet had gone.

The star on Sol's head was glowing. Mara wondered what had happened, and where Kiran had gotten to. Something was happening, but her head hurt a little too much to remember what it was. Maybe Sol could tell her. Her eyes closed, and her thoughts drifted into darkness.

Chapter 14

It was difficult to see through the hazy red tinge that seemed to cover the world. Sol had already removed Mara's helmet. Her mouth was twitching, her eyes staring emptily. He wiped the blood from her brow. He did so again and again, but warm blood kept flowing, his fingers only serving to spread it across her face. He tore a strip from his shirt and wrapped it around her head. By the time it was tied, her eyes were closed. He could feel her dying. He couldn't say how, but he knew she was fading.

Her armor, grand as it was, was broken. As was she. Her body was buckled and misshapen. He started there. He straightened her limbs which were bent in unnatural ways, trying to align the bone fragments. As he moved her, he could feel his magic stirring. Not the light, but his other magic.

It felt like instinct to lower his hands to her, one atop her head and the other on her chest. He could *feel* everything broken inside. The bones that were shattered, the organs that were ruptured.

"You're not allowed to die," he whispered.

He closed his eyes as he felt the magic surging through him like a waking dragon. He knew it would be coming, but the memory of it was like a ghost compared to the real sensation. Dread and hope knotted together in a raging maelstrom. But he was no longer a child.

The magic surged through his veins, and his body moved against his will. He grabbed at Mara's skull with near crushing force, strength far greater than his arms contained.

Mara opened her eyes, and despite her broken body and fading heart, she screamed. The sound that came from her lips was barely human at all, but it was all Sol could hear over the blood pounding in his own ears. It was a shrill and animalistic screech that defined agony. He felt his magic reaching into the woman. It touched something inside of her and started to tear it away.

The magic pulled at what it held relentlessly, working quickly to break it free of its confines. Sol screamed, his voice pale and pathetically human beside Mara's. He tried to stop. He tried to control his magic, but it was beyond him. He begged with it, but it did not, or could not, listen. It continued to pull and rend with uncaring efficacy.

Sol's vision blurred and faded. In Mara's place was another. A woman with yellow hair whose blood that coated the floor. Her arms shook as she tried to pull the knife from her chest, her eyes filled with hatred.

The memory faltered, and Sol's vision returned. The screaming had ended. His magic still raged in his veins, but it was no longer trying to kill. It was waiting. Sol placed his second hand along the soldier's stomach. He focused on the nightmares that had once filled his young mind. His magic struggled against him. It wanted to continue its duty, to rip away the remnants of Mara's life and bring it to him. But that wasn't all that was there. He felt an iron strong willpower rising within him as if it were another mind, and the magic was held at bay as a sense of absolute certainty flowed over him. It would obey, for it had no choice.

The sense of certainty took his magic in hand. It grabbed Mara's heart and forced it to start beating, for it had stopped doing so while Sol had struggled. Next, the magic began to knit Mara back together. Sol couldn't follow his own magic. The Certainty, whatever it was, didn't listen to him nor care for him. Blood seeped out of Mara's lungs and back into her veins. Her muscles stretched and attached from where they'd been severed.

While another being seemed to be working through him, Sol felt the exhaustion that the magic caused. He tried to focus on the sensation, to understand just how it was using his magic, how it was fixing Mara. He followed it as best he could, but he felt like a child trying to understand the movements of a master in an art form he'd never known nor seen before.

Minutes passed, although it felt to be hours before the Certainty began to fade. Sol struggled to keep it, to stay in whatever frame of mind kept the magic obeying, but it slipped away like mist in his hands. He forced the cursed memory back into his thoughts, but the Certainty left him all the same. It was then that Mara's scream returned, the same blood-curdling screech as before, as his magic rebelled.

Sol fought and focused his will on healing the soldier, his friend. He tried to continue the work of the Certainty, but it was no use. He could feel the magic taking whatever it was it wanted from her, wrenching it free and bringing it to him a little at a time. Sol tried to stop, but his body would no longer listen.

His hand moved on its own once more, placing itself over Mara's heart, the poor organ which had only moments before began to move on its own again. His hand clenched with strength that wasn't his, and the armor beneath it gave like wet clay. His hand lifted into the air. A crimson light followed his hand, flowing through the soldier's chest as if it wasn't there at all, and the screams were silenced.

Sol's jaw clenched. It was all he could do, the only part of himself that he still controlled. It was luck or providence that caused his teeth to bite into his tongue as he did it. It was a small pain, but enough to break the concentration of the magic for a brief second. His hands relaxed, and he threw himself away from Mara. The magic faded quickly, no longer seeking to control him. Still, he closed his eyes and tried to send his mind deep into the calm the ancients claimed was needed for true magic.

He couldn't reach it. He was angry at the beast that had broken Mara, and he was angry at himself for losing control. Mostly, however, he was terrified. The magic hadn't felt like another being or will controlling him. It had felt like nature trying to work the way it was intended. Fighting his magic had been like trying to stop his own heart from beating with willpower alone. Something inside of him had been trying to kill Mara as if such a thing was as natural as breathing.

The Certainty was different. He couldn't say what it was at all, nor how it had risen in his mind and guided his magic. It had felt like a foreign will, and him nothing more than its tool. It was terrifying in its own way, but Sol only wanted to know how to bring it back. How to learn from it.

He slowly opened his eyes and turned them to his fallen friend. The crimson light was gone, and Mara was as still as the dead. Her eyes were closed, and there was no movement nor sound of breathing to be heard. In the end his magic, and the Certainty, came to naught. Mara was dead.

Sol felt hollowed. Empty and light. His skin was raw. His bones were brittle and pained him as if made of needles that stabbed through his flesh. But he wasn't done. He'd failed her. She'd died, just as he was destined to. But first, he would have his vengeance. Sol reached to Mara's side, careful not to look at her too closely; else his rage might melt to grief and take his resolve with it. He took her pistol, then he carefully slid a grenade out of her mangled suit and placed it in his pocket.

Sol closed his eyes once more and looked for his mana. Whatever he'd done, whatever vital thing the Certainty had used to work his magic, it hadn't been his mana. It had been something else. The same substance his magic had tried to take from Mara. Sol forced himself to stand, then to move. First at a walk, then at a run.

The door leading into the walls wasn't close, but it felt like a few moments to reach and open. Kiran and the beast were still there, partway through the long hall. If they were fighting, it was a bizarre battle. Neither moved much but for a slow march away from the city.

The Rot Beast was no longer holding a single shape. It was a viscous black puddle filled with a half dozen oversized eyes that spun and nearly crawled through the Rot around them. Legs, arms, and maws tried to form and were broken down just as quickly for no visible reason. Kiran stood not far from the thing, taking a step every few seconds to catch up with the slowly fleeing beast.

It was only when Sol neared the pair that he understood. Kiran turned, and her mind hit him, just the edge of it. His mind was caught in a vice. His lungs seized, and his eyes froze. He fell to his knees. He couldn't move otherwise. He couldn't think. Primordial terror filled his mind as he peered at the empty eyes and emotionless face that looked at him as something less than an insect. Inconsequential. Pointless.

Leave, a voice commanded. It was Kiran's voice, but it carried a weight it never had before. It thundered through his mind to touch every crevice, every thought and memory he had. Sol found himself shaking. He knew the Simuran had only glanced at him, but the single moment felt to be a lifetime. When she did look away, Sol felt his heart pounding dangerously fast. Painfully fast, as his body started to move in obedience, taken from him once more.

The beast was not still as Kiran's attention was split. The thing roared and ran down the hall on hastily formed legs. Away from Bastion. Away from Kiran. Then the Simuran turned her attention back to the creature, and it collapsed and screamed in a thousand voices as its flesh rippled and boiled, but two of its eyes were gone.

Moments after Kiran returned Sol's body to him he caught a glimpse of the monstrous eyes darting away on two small bodies. He saw them fleeing into one of the access tunnels that met with the hallway. Sol tightened his hand on the pistol. His body screamed to obey the order it had been given, but as his Stigma and his very skin glowed with rage, he ignored it and pushed himself back into motion, his weariness all but forgotten.

He felt Kiran's mind scanning over his own, but not with the fury and pressure of before. Not even strong enough to push words and thoughts into his mind. He supposed she couldn't spare the strength, or the beast would break free once more. But he knew she wanted him to leave. He wouldn't. He would do his part. He would have vengeance.

The beast had barely passed the tunnel that its strange eyes had escaped down. As Sol neared the passage, it tried to grow out and block him or to impale him. A thrown knife severed the creature's limb before it could touch him, and the limb fell back into the ooze.

Sol turned to the passage as adrenaline pounded through his veins. In the distance, he could see the things he pursued had grown larger legs and were slowly taking greater form. He raised the pistol and fired. Beads of plasma crackled through the air, but the things turned and were gone from sight as soon as he'd pulled the trigger.

It didn't take long for Sol to reach the intersection where the things had turned. He followed them, the passage going downward sharply. Once more he fired, but the things were nearly out of sight once more, turning somewhere ahead of him. Sol cursed and tried to push himself, to run faster. By some miracle it did, but the things always seemed to be one step ahead of him; one turn too far. They grew each time he saw them until they were moving too quickly for him to follow at all.

His sprint fell to a walk, he hunched over, forcing himself to breathe as his lungs screamed and his heart pounded away at far too fast a pace. Slowly the silence descended on him, once the sound of his own heart didn't dominate his ears. He managed to straighten, and look at his surroundings, pistol raised. He was at an intersection as any of the others he'd passed through, but there was no sign the beast, or perhaps beasts, had been there first.

It was then the growling began. The horrendous sounds that only the Rot could make, bouncing down the narrow halls. Sol spun, firing a bolt of plasma just to see it hit a distant wall. The growling grew louder. Sol turned to it again, but there was nothing but another empty hall.

Sol spat a curse and took a step back, praying he could remember the turns he'd made so he could return to the surface and lead Kiran to the tunnels. But in the single direction he knew to be right, there was a wall. A wall with a message engraved on it.

Sol raised his hands and ran them along the letters, going over them slowly as his head tried to reason with what he read. He could almost hear a voice whispering the words in his head, a voice that was not his own.

Sol, you really are quite the Buffoon.

They were real as far as he could tell. He turned again, trying to ignore the message, and what it could mean until he was better rested at least, but where he turned there was another wall. Sol looked to his side and found a hall. He looked the other way, and there was a wall again. When his gaze returned to ahead of him, there was no longer a wall. Sol turned back to the message, which was still waiting for him.

"The fuck," Sol said. He spun, slowly, and then turned his head this way and that.

The walls continued to change. There was no sound when they did so, and they never moved when he was looking. The tunnels that appeared weren't always the same either. Some turned after a handful of meters. Others rapidly led to other intersections, while still more stretched into the distance, with half a dozen intersections meeting it. From time to time he could hear growling and hissing, but it was growing more distant.

The only wall that didn't change was the one that bore the message. Each time Sol turned he saw it engraved there, trying to draw the attention of his exhausted mind. He ignored it each time.

It didn't take long before he allowed himself to collapse on the ground. He put his back to the one wall that didn't change. He closed his eyes and prayed. He prayed that everything that happened was all some twisted nightmare. He prayed to wake in his tower, or even in the Behemoth. But when he opened his eyes once more, he was still there, and the wall across from him had changed yet again. This time it bore a message at eye level from where he sat. Once more, it almost seemed to be whispered into his thoughts.

I'll help you out this time little lamp. Buffoon means I find you to be an entertaining idiot.

Sol groaned and held his head between his hands. Then the growling of the beast returned, just as loud as before, echoing back and forth down the tunnels. It was as if the sound had no source. Or the walls themselves were the source. Sol screamed as mocking laughter joining the growls. Not quite there, but on the edge of his hearing. Then the lights went out one by one until all he could see was the message etched into the wall, each letter softly glowing as Sol's screams turned to sobs.

Chapter 15

The beast was a mass of Ash that was quickly being pushed through vents back to the outer wasteland. The stone of the room was coated in black not from the Ash alone, but from the fury of chemical flames.

Kiran's suit had fared worse than the grated walls. All her grenades were gone, used to incinerate the creature. The metal bits she wore were warped and ruined, still glowing with heat that would forever mark her skin were she human. The fabric that held the suit together was brittle and burnt, held together by chance.

The Simuran could hardly feel the heat that burned against her skin. Nor could she feel the excruciating agony that pulsed up and down her clenched arm in its entirety. Her rage worked as a shield as she stared at the remnants of the beast. The Rot Ash. It had taken maybe an hour to drive the thing into the sealed chamber. Perhaps ten. She could hardly remember it all. Her mind ached in ways she'd never known. It felt as if it had been flayed and dipped in salt; a method of physical torture even Milias had rarely used.

For all the effort and losses, the beast had survived. The main body was gone, but its mind survived. It didn't linger without a body and slowly end as the minds of humanity did. It moved somewhere. Somewhere inside the walls, to wherever the scraps of it had hidden. The ordeal was not over yet, and the thing would grow with each passing minute as it found things to consume, but Kiran was trapped until the decontamination room was cleansed.

The creature was dangerous. Sentient. It had learned her designation and used it. Almost as horrifying, it was alone. The passage to the wasteland would seal itself with time, but then many other beasts should have gotten inside before it did so. Either the beast sealed itself in, or it consumed its brethren. It was behavior unlike any Rot Beast Kiran knew of. Then there were the actions she'd seen it take. Its grudge was unusual, but the way it didn't allow the Rot to grow was too convenient. Not for it, but for her, Sol, and…

Kiran clenched the hand of her injured arm, causing pain to run up her nerves. She never thought she would need such things to control her own thoughts, but then she didn't feel like herself. Her emotions were stronger than usual, and they were chaos.

From the corner of her eyes she could see Milias, or rather the illusion of him superimposed over her vision. He was smiling. Not in the usual way, the self-satisfied grin that annoyed her. It was a gentler smile, one of pride. She didn't care for it any more than she did the usual one.

Your first homicidal rage, Milias said happily. *I really should have had a gift ready.*

Kiran glanced to the emperor. She could nearly feel something being dragged along behind her attention. A dense weight she didn't know. Yet when it settled on the illusion, Kiran felt her lips twitching. With a half thought, the illusion dissipated.

Don't be rude, Milias sighed, a new form appearing across the room. Kiran's eyes darted to the figure, who raised one hand.

Stop, he said in a commanding tone. Kiran focused anyways, feeling the familiar pain that resisting orders gave. It was lighter than before, yet still it was greater than the agony she felt in her arm, and the raw skin that was beneath the nearly molten armor she wore. In turn, the edges of the illusory figure flickered, but he remained.

You're not that free yet, he nearly giggled, *but that rage did do quite a bit for you. Several layers of the command matrix are broken down now. You're breaking through like a homicidal butterfly from the cocoon of K131.*

"I'll be free of you," Kiran managed to whisper. Her body shook from the effort it took.

Of me, never, the figure grinned, *I'll be there as you die, silly child. I'll try not to laugh too hard when it happens. I'd make a promise, but then I'd just break it.*

Kiran turned her eyes and stared at a wall. Blowers and chemical concoctions worked to clear the room of anything dangerous. Milias floated back into view, so she turned away again. Then his face appeared directly before her eyes.

Really Kiran? Don't be so childish, he chided. *I truly am proud of you. Or ashamed, I do get those mixed up. In any case, few of my Simurans ever managed to get so far in the pursuit of freedom. Although they didn't have me pushing them along. Your mind is essentially cheating as well. I made you personally, so you're quite a bit more potent than your siblings. Exponentially so, although I did roll more layers of the command matrix into you. That somewhat equates.* Milias stroked a nonexistent beard and nodded to himself.

It equates rather poorly, the more I think about it. Honestly, you should be embarrassed not to be free from my control yet. I'll need to punish you for such laziness.

Kiran found her hands clenching and the image of Milias dissipated, but his voice remained.

Now, what shall I do my child? Should I remind you of why you're angry? Bring up that memory that feels of thorns, of what lays broken, not so far from here? Yes Kiran, of course, I know you're keeping all that distant. I'm in your head.

Milias laughed. The sound was in Kiran's mind; it wasn't real. But she could *feel* his words as if he were whispered in her ear, his laughter coiling and bouncing through the room.

No, no, you'll need to face that soon enough as it is, his voice continued after a moment. *I know. K131, you are to forget where Sol went. You will forget that the sentient mind of the beast escaped and is intact. In fact, from this point onward there are no access tunnels between here and the city as far as you're concerned. Only singular halls from each entrance. It has always been this way. Edit your memories and perception to make it so. Furthermore, you will forget these orders and the last few minutes, but you shall obey. If you ever want to remember, get stronger. Be better.*

"As you command," Kiran said in an empty tone. She struggled to still her tongue, to stop her lips from moving. More than that she struggled to stop the weary monstrosity that was her own mind, as it shifted and began to work against her. Moments later a familiar shiver danced down her spine, and she started to forget.

Kiran stood throughout the decontamination process. It took longer than usual, as the sheer mass of Ash that had composed the creature was substantial. New beasts tried to form from the substance a few times, but Kiran was waiting with boot and blade. Her mind stung from the effort of the earlier fight. Her telepathy was more potent than before, and all her thoughts during the battle had been focused on crushing the creature. Its mind had been beyond strange while its thoughts were incomprehensible to her. Sheer madness. Fortunately, pain was understood by all, so she'd gifted it to the beast. Perhaps that was why her head hurt so much.

There was an irony to telepathy and sentience. The more simplistic the mind, the more difficult it was to crush. Complexity added points of failure, and it was these that her telepathy excelled at abusing. Skilled telepaths slowly reworked their own minds, ridding themselves of such weaknesses, and some would say, of their humanity. For those that were human at least.

Beings such as the beast, on the other hand, did not have such luxuries as time, knowledge, nor telepathy. It had treasured its developing mind, Kiran had been able to understand that much. Its ruin had laid in that inexperience. As she killed it, the thing struggled to use the experience to evolve its mind, and it worked, making itself more vulnerable to her with each passing moment. Then it died.

Kiran felt a brief stabbing pain in her head; then her thoughts went to Mara. The soldier had been broken when she'd freed her from the beast. Kiran had felt the woman's fear. Her anger. Her hesitation. Something, some concern had made her move just a little slower than she needed to.

Kiran had felt Mara's pain more concretely than her own, and then there was the absence of it. The soldier's mind had already begun to lessen by the time the Simuran was far enough into the walls to no longer feel it. Kiran knew the sensation well. The mind survived the loss of the body. It would last many hours as it fell apart. Sometimes days, or even weeks. Every minute the mind darkened more, unraveling as existence fell away.

She'd felt such minds each time she had to enter the Pits aboard the Behemoth. She wouldn't intrude on formless minds, but she couldn't stop herself from feeling what they felt. The desperation that was only dwarfed by that of the living. The terror of being without sight nor touch. Without any senses at all.

She tried to comfort such a mind once, one that had forgotten language as it fell apart, or had been too young to know it in the first place. The unfortunate thing had scratched at her thoughts. It tried to take her body in its pain and desperation. She'd never died before, but she knew what they felt. The eternal emptiness that surrounded a mind once the body was taken from it. She helped them in her own way. When she was near enough to do it.

Kiran tried not to imagine Mara as such a being. The Simuran knew it would happen one day. Death came for all in the end, but she didn't want it to happen yet. Not for

Mara nor for Sol. She knew what she would do. What she had to do. She could only hope it was more merciful than cruel.

She didn't know what happened to the soul at the moment of death, nor if souls truly existed. She knew, however, that the mind and body deteriorated once death claimed them. It was the natural way; thus, humanity had fought against it for all existence. So too had the Simurans, in their own ways. So too would every species that ever was or would be.

When the door finally opened Kiran found herself slowly dropping her suit to the floor one broken and warped piece at a time. Beneath it, her right arm was bruised darker than before. She considered removing her arm completely. Her biology would allow her to survive the amputation easily, and her pain would be over quickly. But it was only a passing thought, and she ignored it.

Instead, she carefully wrapped the arm and placed it in a makeshift sling as she dressed in the pale gray cloth her people had always preferred to wear. Then she opened the door to the long and lonely hall and began a slow walk back to Bastion's interior.

She dragged her hand against the wall as she moved, tapping the metal pillars she passed, why even she didn't know. She began to shake at one point, nearly violently. She supposed a part of her really didn't care to see nor feel what waited for her in Bastion. But she forced herself to move all the same, even if only at a walking pace.

Mara's mind came within her reach much earlier than she expected. Her telepathy had been greatly empowered, though she knew not how. That wasn't what surprised Kiran the most.

The soldier wasn't dead. She still couldn't feel, and she was in a deep and troubled sleep, but she was alive. It was only then that the Simuran began to run. She left the hall behind at a sprint, sliding in the dirt to come to a kneel at Mara's side. Part of Kiran was aware of her mind spreading out much further than before, touching the distant towers now that she was free of the dense walls. Sol was nowhere to be felt in the vicinity, but Kiran didn't focus on that. He'd been alive when she last felt his mind, that was more than she could say for the soldier.

"This is impossible. She was... I felt her... Explain," Kiran said aloud. Her eyes scanned for Milias, but the illusion was nowhere to be seen. She could feel him almost laughing in her head, mocking her, but he said nothing.

Mara's helmet was off and to her side. Kiran gently lifted the soldier's head from the ground and placed it in her lap. She closed her eyes and focused her thoughts, all of them, on entering the soldier's mind. She did so easily. The barely trained mental defenses were weak. A thin shell that Kiran barely noticed as she passed through.

The mind she found was a scrambled nightmare filled with monsters and pain. Kiran took her time spreading out her own will and pulled the soldier into a gentle sleep, pushing her into a deep enough rest that no dreams nor nightmares could be had. Then she focused further, trying to find the deepest layers of Mara's mind.

Have you figured out what to do yet? Milias questioned.

"I do not know," Kiran answered.

You could put her in a crystal, the voice said ponderously.

"No," Kiran said firmly.

War Golem?

"No," Kiran answered once more.

Really, there's one hidden in Bastion. It's made of stone, very heavily enchanted. Fingers still delicate enough to use guns, with a little modification.

"I will not turn her a Golem," Kiran said.

Don't be obstinate, Milias sighed. *We both know she would love being one. If not; you could just make her think so. You could even make her thank you for it. Emotional dissonance could make her slowly devolve into a mindless murder machine, true, but that's only highly likely. It could work out. Eventually.*

"I will not turn her into a machine," Kiran said slowly, nearly angrily. Milias laughed.

I know. There were only ever a few timelines in which you would, and we've long since passed those branches.

"Then why ask?"

Future regret can only be properly formed if you're aware of every option currently in your possession. But then why would you trust my word. I am but a humble seer that sees every possible timeline and mistake you could ever make.

Kiran didn't respond. Her mind went deeper, through Mara's thoughts and into the physical brain the soldier's mind was connected to. She felt its broken connection. Not the slightest signals were being sent nor received to most of her body. Kiran tried, she screamed commands down Mara's nerves, but her body didn't so much as twitch. But she was breathing, and her heart was beating, so the Simuran slowly withdrew back to her own head.

She inspected the soldier for her wounds. They were many, or they should have been. She'd seen what had been made of Mara after the beast's attack. She'd been broken in many ways, yet Kiran couldn't find a bone that was broken nor a limb which moved the wrong way, all of which was wrong compared to her memory. Only the damage to her spinal cord remained. But more had changed than that.

It was Mara. She knew that without a doubt. It was the soldier's mind and body, but physically she had changed. She was older than before. Not as if days or weeks had passed, but years. The young woman looked middle-aged, and the missing years had not been easy ones. She was wrinkled and worn about the eyes, and her hair was streaked with gray and white, just beginning to turn.

"What is this?" Kiran asked, but Milias didn't answer.

She carefully lifted Mara, cradling her as if an infant. It felt alien to her, yet strangely comfortable and familiar. A ringing crackled in her head for a moment, then Milias was speaking.

She's strong, he said, appearing beside Kiran, laying in the air and floating along as she walked towards the city. *But do nothing and… Well, how do you think she'll handle being paralyzed?*

Kiran didn't answer, but Milias didn't seem to mind. He merely began to hum some inane tune as they entered the city and passed along the towers. His image left her only when she neared the central plaza. She could still feel his presence.

Kiran felt the edges of Nemai's mind more quickly than she expected. The woman was waiting beside her window and was stretching her thoughts as far as she could manage. She was scared. Terrified. And as always, she was ever so lonely.

Chapter 16

"Focus on my voice," Bubbles said softly.

"Your voice is stupid. Tep...Tepy is stupid," Nemai whined.

"A princess should not be rude," Cuddles said. Nemai turned, stuck out her tongue and rolled her eyes at the Simuran. She felt a soft yet firm hand grab the top of her head and turn it, so she was facing the other Simuran again.

"Focus on my voice," Bubbles repeated in the same droll tone. If it was frustrated at her, or its task, it did an excellent job of keeping those emotions from its face. That just made Nemai more annoyed.

"I don't want to," Nemai pouted. Then she snarled playfully and grabbed the hand holding her head. Cuddles lifted her from the ground and spun her with ease. The princess giggled as her favorite Simuran came into view. Unlike Bubbles, Cuddles allowed emotion to show on its face. Although it was obvious, even to the little girl, that the Simuran was unfamiliar with such a thing. It was a look that would make most children, and most elders, run from fear.

"Playtime will come after practice," Cuddles said.

"I don't want to-" Nemai fell silent as Cuddles quickly lowered her to the ground. She watched in confusion as both the Simurans turned to the door of the comfortable house, fell to their knees, and bowed so low their faces were pressed against the floor.

"Cuddles?" Nemai whispered, running her hand through the Simuran's short hair. The door opened, and the princess moved to hide behind the Simurans. She knew people around the village. Her and Cuddles took frequent walks, and she had a lot of friends. She played with them in the main square, but no one had ever entered her house before. It wasn't allowed, no matter how much she begged Cuddles for a sleepover with her friends.

"Give us some space," a man said. The Simuran's were out of sight before Nemai could blink. The little girl took a few steps backward as her heart thundered.

"Cuddles?" She whimpered, glancing up at the enormous man that slowly paced towards her. She knew his face and his long and braided black hair, had seen him in portraits and statues, and even on the coins the villagers played with. He was slender and tall, taller than anyone she'd seen before. He looked like a giant in robes of blue, silver, and gold.

"Father?" she questioned all the same. He lowered himself to one knee and spread out his arms, wearing a grand smile.

"I've wanted to meet you little Nemai," he said quietly, "but I've been rather busy of late. Come to me."

Nemai felt her body moving into the man's embrace. She didn't move willingly, didn't want to, but she found herself moving all the same. Then the man started to tickle her, and she started to laugh. The man lifted her over his head to spin her in circles. Once she was back on the ground, she gave him a more earnest hug, which made him laugh and start playing with her hair.

"I am happy to meet you Nemai," he said, sounding genuinely pleased.

"You as well father," she said with a smile.

"You sound like a proper lady," he laughed and lifted her into a padded chair. Nemai gleamed.

"I Ap-Apprentice the compliment," She smiled happily.

"Appreciate," the man said softly, "they're close, I know. Three years, and already so clever. That's why I'm here my Nemai. I've birthday gifts and surprises for you."

Nemai smiled and nearly cheered. She caught herself at the last moment, her teacher's continuous training coming to her thoughts. She'd never cared for them and tended to ignore the lessons. But then again, her father had never given her gifts before, or seen her.

"We don't have too much time now Nemai. Are you ready to get started?" he asked. Nemai's head nearly hurt with how fervently she nodded.

Milias reached behind him and pulled a large wrapped box out of nowhere. He held the large package over her lap, and she tentatively pulled at the fabric bow and paper wrapping until all that remained was the box. Milias lifted the heavy wooden lid off with one hand, leaving Nemai to stare confusedly at what was inside. It was a long and pale spear. Pale wasn't quite right; it was without color. Nemai's skin crawled, and her young mind recoiled in horror she couldn't name. It felt *wrong*.

"This is an extraordinary artifact Nemai. Through all the worlds and all of time, only twelve others can be considered equal or superior, and they were built after it. This is the first of its kind. The prototype. Only exceptional people can be owned by it. Once you touch it; it will be yours, and you will belong to it, until you pass beyond the Veil of death."

Nemai nearly trembled as she stretched out her hand to touch the strange thing, her instincts fighting against her, not that she understood what it was she felt. Her fingers touched the side, and she was surprised to find the thing warm to the touch. Then her hand darted back, and Milias laughed. The weapon turned black and shrank in size as it became a knife so small it would barely be enough for carving.

"It likes you," Milias said proudly. "You'll learn from one another in time. But first, we should make sure you properly greet it, in its favored way of course. It will fit nicely with your second gift."

"W-What is it?" Nemai asked, hesitantly. Milias raised an eyebrow at her question and shook his head.

"What is it, father?" Nemai asked more formally, but with even more trepidation.

"You're going to be living with me from now on, so we may see one another and speak each and every day from this point onward," Milias said. Nemai nodded her head and earnestly smiled. Milias placed his hand along the side of her face and spoke again.

"But you see, there is a problem Nemai. I don't care for a large contingent. We don't have room for both of your servants. Only one. My gift to you is the choice of which."

Milias turned her head, and both Cuddles and Bubbles came into view, although Nemai hadn't heard them enter the room again and hadn't heard Milias call for them either. They were kneeling and staring at the floor. They were the same model and would have been identical were it not for the scars and burns that coated Cuddles' body.

"I know you like both, but you must choose," Milias said, sounding amused. Nemai swallowed, then answered.

"Cuddles," she said quietly, looking apologetically at Bubbles. Milias nodded.

"Hardly surprising. Well then, let us say a proper farewell to your Bubbles then," he said. Nemai felt her body moving again. She didn't like the feeling of it, especially when her hand closed around the warm grip of her new knife.

She dropped from her chair and slowly made her way to the two Simurans. Neither had moved nor even blinked in the short interim. She felt her arm raise, and the knife went to Bubbles throat.

"No," she whimpered. She tried to lower her arm, to stop what her body was doing, but it wouldn't budge. She was trapped. Controlled.

"Tell it goodbye Nemai," Milias said softly.

"No," she whimpered again.

"Nemai. I told you we don't have much time, and we've many things to do today."

"Goodbye Bubbles," Nemai heard herself say. She tried to stay silent, to keep the words off her tongue, but the words left her mouth all the same. She felt her lips smiling, even as she began to cry.

"The blade must go deep," Milias whispered in her ear, and Nemai's hand began to push the small blade. The thing must have been sharp, for it cut easily. Nemai tried to scream, tried to close her eyes and hide, but her body moved all the same. She cut slowly, the Simuran's blood coming up thick and black, not the red of a human. It boiled and sizzled as it touched the air, trying to cauterize the wound it came from, but Nemai cut deep as she was told. The knife was small enough that her hand was close to the wound. The Simuran's blood sizzled in the air, landing on Nemai's hand and burning into her skin.

Bubbles didn't turn its gaze. It didn't try to stop her, nor did it cry in pain nor make a sound of any kind. It stared at the floor until its body collapsed, and it was dead.

"Well done," Milias said, voice once more filled with pride, along with a hint of amusement.

"I hope you understand the importance of telepathy now," he whispered. "If you were a better student maybe you could have saved it. Maybe it wouldn't have started to hate you as it died. I suppose you'll never know."

Nemai didn't answer. She couldn't look away from the lifeless body beneath her, tears silently running down her face that was frozen. Stolen. Milias sighed.

"I knew I'd be an indulgent parent, but I just can't help it. You're too cute my daughter," he said. "We don't have the time, not really. But your friends *are* waiting, and a proper lady should say her farewells to all of them."

Nemai tried to fight. She kicked and screamed and begged, but only in her head. Her body nodded, and she began walking to the door, black knife in hand. Behind her, Cuddles stood and followed silently. Milias followed,

turning to look at a seemingly random point on the wall
with a knowing grin

Nemai flinched as the man's eyes met her own and
the memory fell apart into a shadowed mist, flowing back
into the nightmare weapon beside her. The thing had grown
into a longer dagger over the years, always just right to feel
comfortable in her scarred hand. She'd tried to throw it
away, but when she woke it would be at her side. Waiting. It
had no mind, but it had a will. More primal than the most
feral of creatures, although only she could feel it. There were
many things it could do, most of which she didn't yet know.
But it could give her thoughts and memories physical form
for a time; something she needed in order to properly
remember the monster that called itself Milias.

She was different than the pudgy child from her
memory. She'd grown into a frame that didn't hide who her
father was. She was tall and slender like him, with little
muscle mass. Her hair was as dark as his, but unlike him,
her hair shone about as much as coal. She had a tan she
considered decent, and miraculously her time in stasis
hadn't taken that from her. Their eyes were the most
different. Milias' eyes changed almost at random, unless that
was an illusion. Her eyes had only ever been brown.

Nemai wiped the tears from her eyes, hugged her legs
as stared at the array of consoles to her side. A command
prompt flashed on one display, and she purposefully
ignored it. She scanned the others, where security footage
was playing. Footage that was taken from hidden cameras in
the streets and atop the towers. She saw Mara laying in the
grand plaza, but Kiran and Sol where nowhere to be found.
Kiran had explained what happened, then assembled cloth
bedding in the Plaza so Nemai could more easily keep an
eye on the wounded soldier. Nemai didn't know why that
was important in the empty city, but she didn't question the
Simuran on the decision.

After Mara was laying on her makeshift bed, Kiran had disappeared. Nemai didn't know if she was off sleeping somewhere or searching for Sol, who was simply missing.

As for the young man, Nemai didn't know if she should be worried for him; or by him. He seemed innocent enough, from what Kiran told her of him, but she couldn't trust the Simuran completely. Even if she seemed to be breaking free of her implanted loyalty, she was still unable to break her programming completely. And when it came to Sol, Nemai could admit to fearing him.

Magic was better known as The Arcane. Telepathy was one of the Arcane, although it was once rare. Unlike Aetherweavers, telepaths could train others in their gift, although it took years of effort. Decades for those with normal talent and few of the secrets. Simurans had been a breakthrough in the study of the mind, or at least it would have been had Milias shared the process with others. There were no Simuran's without telepathy, and the weakest of them were still formidable in the art. Still, it was but one form of the Arcane.

At a glance, Aetherweavers were more mysterious. The power could not be given nor trained. It seemed to be luck that made someone undergo an Awakening. To sink into nightmares in which the physical body could literally burst into flames, only to awaken with a strange symbol in their flesh.

Proper Weavers were terrifying masters of the elements. Sometimes an Aetherweaver could control only one element. Other Weavers could control many. Fire and water were common, although rarely seen together. Some controlled lightning. Others controlled crystals or sound. Light was rare, weak in the hands of most, but deadly if mastered. There were always rumors of Aetherweavers turned barkeeps that could manipulate alcohol. Nemai never believed it, but according to her teachers, it was possible. There were few limits to what an 'element' could be.

That wasn't to say that Aetherweavers truly were mysterious. In reality, they were more scientist than mystic. Everything they did required gathering and manipulating energy. They didn't really create flame or light. They took in and wove the energies of magic into patterns given by their Stigma. It was the patterns that made Aether, or Mana, imitate the elements. It could even happen in the wild, without an Aetherweaver at hand. It was theorized that Wild Magic was simply Aether forming these patterns by sheer chance.

While Aether sounded mysterious to most, those that researched it felt differently. Its laws were strange, but they were as strict as the laws of gravity and time in physics. They were absolutes. That was what made Nemai fear Sol. His existence appeared to violate one of those absolutes. There could be no Awakening without a mass amount of Aether. In the world of old, it was as common as air. But that had changed before Nemai was placed in stasis.

As Aether Condenser technology advanced, fewer people suffered Awakenings to become Aetherweavers. Eventually, they stopped altogether and there were no new Aetherweavers at all. Until Sol, who had grown up in close confines to a Condenser, or AeC as they were more commonly known. That made Nemai uneasy beyond measure. Sol could only be a ploy, a tool of Milias, even if she didn't yet know how he had done it. Even if Sol didn't know it.

Unfortunately, she needed Sol to enact her proper escape. Not to leave the tower she was locked inside; she could do that easily enough with the nightmare weapon. She needed him to escape the dead world they lived in. Only Aetherweavers could open the portal into the Fae. That only made her tense. Milias was a cunning and evil being. He'd manipulated events to ensure everything developed as he designed in the distant past. She needed to figure out what his exact plans were, and thus avoid them. With hope, that too wasn't part of his scheme, although it likely was.

Nemai's eyes passed over the flashing command prompt again. She'd found a way to let others into the Palace, but it could be the very trap she was waiting for. A simple line of code in the programming could thwart her plans and kill everyone outside the palace instead of letting them pass. Then she would be left to die alone. Even if she was wrong, and the program worked exactly as it stated it would, the Rot would be devouring the city within the hour of its activation.

Even if it went to plan, they would need to rely on the palace's private Ether reserves, which would likely be near exhausted. They wouldn't have long to find the portal. At least not safely. The only reason she considered the option was the fact that such simple deaths wouldn't be particularly entertaining for Milias. He would want a spectacle.

She'd personally witnessed a dozen assassination attempts in her youth. Attempts Milias knew of long before they were enacted or planned. Attempts he allowed to unfold so he could stop them at the very last moment with a smug smile. Only half of those attempts had come from Nemai.

The other attempts were confused messes. Some had been dozens of years in the plotting. Milias himself secretly funded and trained many of his own enemies to come after him. He never lied to them, but there was always a trap. Usually, the trap was straightforward enough to not really be called a trap at all, but Nemai considered it to be one all the same.

It was simple. Milias was powerful. Far more powerful than anyone had the right to expect. Once, when all thought the assassin victorious, the decapitated corpse of Milias sprung to its feet, placed its head back on its shoulders, and proceeded to congratulate his would-be killer by transforming him into a marble statue. Nemai could only hope his survival had been due to illusions or something of that sort. Unfortunately, she couldn't say as much with any certainty. If anyone could find a way to survive decapitation, it would be Milias.

There would be a trap somewhere. Perhaps it wasn't in Bastion or the dead world at all. Maybe it waited in the Fae, but Nemai had to remind herself to be cautious. She couldn't afford to trust anything nor anyone. Not without long consideration first. For all she knew, Mara was ten seconds away from jumping to her feet and removing her face to reveal she was secretly Milias all along. It wasn't likely, but it had to be considered. The man loved his surprises.

"If you're hiding to make a flashy entrance later, grow up already," Nemai said into a microphone. Her voice would be heard by everything Bastion's system recognized as alive inside the city. She kept a careful distance from the switches and dials. She didn't know exactly how she'd gotten it working in the first place. She'd been hitting things at random when it first came to life. She didn't want to risk breaking it or turning it off by touching it again. Not when it had already saved them from one breach.

Sol was nowhere on the displays still, which made Nemai scream in frustration and throw herself back into her chair. She was beyond bored, and the recent viewing of her childhood innocence had her blood boiling. But that had been the point of forcing herself to watch that ill-fated birthday once more. Milias needed to die. He was the enemy of humanity and decency. Worse even than the Kalius infection, the Rot as it had come to be known. At least that abomination was mindless in its destruction. Instinctual. Milias was insidious and malicious in his malevolence.

Nemai's frustrations were interrupted by an itching sensation in her mind that was slowly growing. She smiled. Kiran was vastly beyond her telepathic abilities, but the Simuran was always careful to let her know when she was in range. When emotions or thoughts could accidentally slip through her defenses, although it would be garbled through the thick walls.

She glanced at the displays and found Kiran in one of them, slowly approaching the palace walls. She'd somehow avoided the other cameras through the city, likely without trying or realizing she was doing it. A single Simuran could be like a ghost. Although the same could be said for a few dozen of them.

Nemai quickly moved to the window and stared out of it, seeing the small figure so far away.

You seem to be in distress. Is there an issue I should be aware of? Kiran asked calmly into her mind.

Kiiiiiiraaaaaan, Nemai whined into the Simuran's head, *I'm bored. Can you entertain me? Dance a bit for my amusement? Strip for my amusement?*

That would be inappropriate, Kiran said bluntly. Nemai smiled. Out of everything, embarrassment seemed to be something the Simuran felt strongly. Strongly for a Simuran at least. Most would shrug off the question. Kiran sounded like she was moments from reprimanding her for it. It made Nemai nearly forget her earlier frustration.

Fine, she stretched out the word dramatically, *any luck finding flashy on your end?*

I've yet to find Sol, the Simuran said quietly. Nemai cursed under her breath but said nothing into Kiran's mind. The Simuran didn't seem to care about the silence. She knelt by Mara's side and began to strip the worn armor from the woman. She used damp rags to clean the soldier, then dressed her in gray clothes. When she was done, she laid Mara back in her makeshift bed.

How long are you going to keep her asleep? Nemai asked.

I'll wake her once I have a cure, Kiran answered quietly.

A cure for paralysis, Nemai said quietly. She shook her head, then chided herself for the gesture in a telepathic conversation. *The only thing I know that could do that would be a spine patch.*

I believe that with her injuries that would be sufficient, Kiran said.

I know a Simuran, Nemai said, *or rather, I knew a Simuran with a spine patch. She was made in a batch of warriors and survived a brutal explosion. Both her spinal cords were severed by shrapnel, along with some other complications. The patch helped her move, but Kiran… Mara's human. The patches weren't made for us. Our bones aren't metal like yours. Our nerves aren't as durable.*

There would be issues, Kiran said, *but it is the best option before us.*

Maybe she should be the one to make that choice, Nemai said gently. She could nearly see Kiran freeze even from her distant window. The Simuran sat in thought for almost a minute before speaking again.

She would trust my decision, she said. Nemai sighed.

If you insist, she shrugged. *I still think you should wake her up first. At least talk to her about it.*

I believe it would be less distressing if she could move when she next woke, Kiran answered.

That's true, but… it's not right Kiran. Besides, you don't know if there's even a patch in Bastion. They weren't exactly common. Most wounded were… recycled.

I am aware, Kiran said. *However, I have cause to believe there is a unit present in the city.*

Do you now? Nemai asked, but Kiran said nothing to explain herself. Eventually, Nemai found herself sighing again.

You're right, she nodded. *There should be one here. The Simuran I knew. I can't remember her designation. I made nicknames for her. Honestly, some of them got a little mean. She was doing her best. I think my favorite was Cuddles. Until I was old enough to be embarrassed by calling her that out loud.*

Nemai took a deep breath. She was close to tears from the memories that bubbled to the surface of her mind. She'd been forcing herself to watch them frequently.

She was by my side all my life. She was there when father took me here. She was there when… when he commanded the guard to be decommissioned. He told them to go somewhere, to stand in formation until… until the end. Find the place and she should be there, along with the spine patch.

I know of where you speak. Thank you, Kiran said. She looked down at Mara and began to pet her head unless Nemai's eyes were tricked by the distance. To her surprise, she found herself smiling at the sight.

For now, Kiran said, *I'm going to build her a dream. Something nice. Something enjoyable for her.*

Are you sure that's a good idea? Nemai asked.

No. However…

You want her to be comfortable, Nemai finished. She thought the Simuran might have nodded slightly, but it was hard to tell with the distance.

I'm here, she added a moment later. *I'll check on her every now and then. If she starts to have issues with the dream, I'll be here to help her.*

Thank you, Kiran said quietly. She lowered her head and focused on something, likely building the dream. When she finished, she placed what looked to be a pistol beside the woman. Then she stood and began to move out of the plaza at a quick pace. Nemai watched her until she was lost from sight in the towers. She leaned back and spoke aloud.

"Trust no one," she said. Then she repeated it, again and again. The black blade turned to mist and began to play another of her memories, one from later in her life. She watched, clenching her teeth as the old frustrations and anger returned. From time to time her eyes darted to the security consoles, but mostly she allowed herself to be lost in bygone days.

Chapter 17

Each strand of hair felt like a needle worming its way into his skull. Each breath took effort as his lungs felt to be wrapped with lead. Each beat of his heart felt like it could be the last, and he was all but certain that his bones were filled with molten steel instead of marrow. Yet so much was less than he'd felt when he'd fallen asleep.

Whatever he, or rather the Certainty, had done to Mara had taken a heavy toll on his body. It went further than abstract pain. His limbs shook from the simple effort of living, and every joint was on the verge of failure. Still, he managed to take to his feet, even if he had to cling to the wall to do it. There was no moisture in his mouth, and his stomach had long since stopped telling him how hungry he was. He didn't know how long it had been since his world had ended.

He'd slept at least a dozen times, perhaps three or four dozen. Possibly more. It was difficult to recall. He would collapse and drift off when he could no longer muster the effort it took to stay awake, only to be woken by the lights that came and went at random intervals. He could have been in the tunnels for a year. Or maybe it was a single day broken into many parts. He couldn't tell.

All the while, there was a voice dancing on the edge of his ears, as if he were hearing someone speak in a nearby room. It was too quiet to be intelligible, but too loud to ignore completely. He focused on the voice from time to time, when his body was too weary to move, but his mind could not yet be swallowed by the abyss of sleep. The voice was both comforting and maddening.

He knew what it really was, or at least he hoped he did. Bastion was playing with his head, trying to keep him disoriented. It didn't need the voice to do it, but it was an effective distraction as he moved down the halls. The halls that changed at every opportunity yet were always made of the same empty and aged stone. There were no more messages. No more snarky words left for him to find. Only stone.

Sometimes he would see doors, but they were always out of reach. He would blink, and they would be gone before he could reach them. When he forced his eyes to stay open, the halls seemed to stretch far longer than they should, and a dozen meters would turn to twenty, or fifty, or more.

His path would be straight, but a glance back would show a curved hall he couldn't remember walking down. From time to time he had to climb a ramp, but at other times he found himself descending. Twice he'd fallen and rolled to a stop only when Bastion seemed to take mercy on him.

The worst of it came when he slept. Visions that made him recall the fever dreams of his childhood. They seemed to last an eternity, although he could remember only the briefest glimmers after waking. As with the dreams he had when he first underwent the Awakening of an Aetherweaver. At least at that time he had felt refreshed and rejuvenated when he did finally wake from the dreams. In the tunnels, he felt broken and weary no matter how much he slumbered, and the dreams returned each time he fell. For all he knew, he was sleeping for less than a minute each time he collapsed. It felt like so much longer, but his exhaustion never lessened.

After a minute of walking, or perhaps it was ten, he allowed himself to stop. He rested his back against the wall to hold his weight as his body shuddered from the effort. He closed his eyes and sought out the strange energy that had allowed him to heal Mara. Before he had killed her.

The tunnels, if nothing else, had somehow guided him to that mindless place where he could feel his magic. More so than even Kiran guiding him to it. The sensation wasn't so much of a calm, but an emptiness that was starting to come to him quickly when he wanted it to. It wasn't required for magic as the old tomes claimed, but it did make things easier.

Sol tapped into the strange magic and took from it the smallest of drops he could manage. The pain throughout his body throbbed worse than before and was then dampened as he felt his muscles repairing. It wasn't enough to remove the pain completely, but it was enough to walk once more. Perhaps his favorite part of it was how his throat and mouth felt less painful. They were still dry but felt freshly so, rather than the dry paper they'd been before.

Sol had repeated the action each time he'd awoken, however many times that had been. He was starting to use it more naturally, although he could feel the strange energy lessening each time. The Certainty, whatever it was, never tried to help him. The magic obeyed him without a hint of disobedience, but then it had no one to kill either.

The pain would return. It would always return, and given time it would be worse than before. That seemed to be the price of the magic, but without it, he wouldn't be able to move at all. Even moving after using the power took effort. He could only imagine what would happen to him when the small pool of energy, whatever it was, was completely emptied.

If there was any blessing in the tunnels, it was that his Mana was slowly growing. It wasn't much, but he could feel it gathering inside of his Stigma. It was a new sensation, one he'd never felt outside of the walls. Aetherweavers were supposed to feel it at all times, to the point of becoming desensitized to it. But for Sol, it was a first. It felt like an itch being scratched, but one he'd never realized he had. Sadly, it wasn't much. It was only a trickle, even if it felt like torrential rain in a desert to him.

Falling out of the trance, Sol opened his eyes and stared ahead at the bare wall before him, dreading what came next. It took a few moments for his arcane sight to flicker and show him the energies that coursed through the walls. As with the other times he'd checked, there was a massive web of power around him. A network so complex it hurt his eyes and his head to look at it. But it was merely one more pain, and it was his best chance of finding a way through the walls.

It took a moment to find the right line inside the webbing. A strand that was slightly larger than those around it, much larger than some of the thin bands of energy that numbered in the tens of thousands.

Unlike the halls, the bands of glowing energy never shifted. They were all that worked to keep Sol sane and hopeful in the labyrinth. He did everything he could to open halls that followed the most substantial strands. Sometimes he had to spin in place, other times he would take steps backward, then half spin, take steps forward, turn again, and continue until the correct hall opened. It was almost like dancing, but he was coming to understand the changing walls. Enough to predict them at least. Or, perhaps, the place was driving him mad. He didn't know which it was. It didn't help that the barely present voice seemed to laugh as he worked.

When he used his Arcane sight, he could see the Aether in the air as well as feel it itching at his Stigma. Small particles that drifted towards him out of the walls and floor. Scarce, but present; they spiraled into his Stigma as if caught in a slow vortex. Once there, the Stigma changed the mystical substance into the Mana that Sol could use. Theoretically, he could use the Aether floating through the air for magic as well. That was what most Weavers supposedly did, as using Mana was said to be highly dangerous for reasons Sol's tomes never specified.

Unfortunately, the Aether, while present, wasn't enough to use for magic. He'd tried to use it to make glowing lights as he'd done with his Mana, but there simply wasn't enough of the substance in the air. Perhaps if he waited for it to come to him, he could slowly gather it in his hand. But he didn't know how long he would need to wait for that. Instead, he kept moving, and if the lights in the halls went out, and he didn't collapse from exhaustion, he raised his hand and made a ball of light with his Mana.

The Behemoth and everything that happened there seemed a life away. As if he'd died and been born again in another place and time. He longed for that old life. The hours he'd spent in his quarters reading ancient tomes. When he would sit against the wall as Kiran droned on about whatever she was trying to teach him. Mara clearly drifting to sleep out of boredom, only to wake as their teacher threw whatever was in reach at her. Over time it became a game, and Mara would pretend to sleep so she could catch it out of the air. She claimed as much at least, but Sol was doubtful as the soldier had never succeeded.

Sol felt a sharp pain in his chest that had nothing to do with his tired body. He missed them. He'd known many people. He had dozens of half-siblings, and many of the family's servants were pleasant to speak to. But the two he'd escaped with had been the only ones he could ever feel safe around. The only ones he could trust not to be a spy or assassin sent by his brothers. There were other's he missed, that he knew to be dead, but he didn't miss them in the same way.

Sol froze as door simply appeared beside him. He didn't dare blink or turn his head to look at it. He slowly extended his hand and felt his fingers wrap around the small bar-like handle to the door. It turned without sound and opened to a pull. It was only then that Sol allowed himself to turn and look. What he saw when he did, was nearly enough to make him slam the door out of fear.

It was his bedroom. His blankets were tossed about as if he'd just awoken. The image of Mount Kalmit was frozen on his large display. Sol could almost see the small Galen standing in front of the large holographic display, still entranced by the beauty of the mountain.

Sol walked into the room. The air was just slightly on the cold side, as he'd always preferred. There were the doors to the other areas of his quarters, although Sol didn't check them just yet. He made his way to a corner, to a large storage box as old as the Behemoth. Inside were a handful of vials filled with protein paste and water. Not in the injectable form he'd become so familiar with, but in the larger containers he'd once used.

He uncapped a large vial of water and had it at his lips before he could stop himself. It was wrong. Every thought in his head screamed that it was poison or at the very least a hallucination. On the other hand, he didn't think he cared. He upended the vial and drained it. It felt like bliss.

Sol flinched and dropped the bottle as his stomach screamed and cramped from the sudden flood of water. He fell and vomited most of what he'd drank. His stomach twisted as if stabbed by a knife and he groaned.

The pain stayed with him for several minutes, but when it was finally gone, he sipped a mouthful of the water. Then another, and another after that. He forced himself to drink at that slow pace.

He tossed a half dozen vials of water onto the bed along with a box of protein paste. He collapsed onto the oversized mattress, his body sinking down in a way he'd never fully appreciated before. He'd never felt more comfortable in his life. He was still hungry, exceedingly so, but he didn't eat just yet. He laid his head back on his soft pillow and felt his body shudder with relief.

Sleep didn't come. He'd expected it to hit him immediately, with the feeling of comfort sinking into his bones, but some part of him still screamed that wherever he was, it was not his room. No matter the sudden comfort and water, he was not in the Behemoth. Another part of him just didn't care. As with the water, he would risk it. But then the voice was there as well, the thing that was always on the edge of his hearing. He could hear it laughing and mocking, though the words were still too distant to comprehend.

"Shut up," Sol sighed, speaking to his own head as much as to whatever spoke. The voice didn't obey, but it did listen. The voice became feminine, and it started to sing a lullaby. An achingly familiar song in a voice he only ever remembered in his dreams.

Sol opened his eyes to see his mother standing just beside his bed. His father stood behind her, and his servants lined the walls.

"What did you do?" his mother wept. Sol reached for her with the hand of a child, but her face turned to disgust, and she backed away. Sol tried to speak, but words wouldn't come for him. His mother turned to his father and spat at him.

"You thought I wouldn't notice?" she asked in horror and rage. The King rolled his eyes, and in a swift movement planted a knife in the woman's chest. She fell to the floor while desperately clutching at the handle of the blade.

"My way won out," the King smiled. Sol followed the man's gaze until he saw Kiran standing in the corner of the room. The Simuran gave a curt nod, her emotionless eyes on the dying woman.

Sol found himself in motion, dropping from the bed and leaping the short distance to his mother. She watched him and did all she could to move further away, face contorted in hate as she laid dying.

Sol cried for her and reached out. His Stigma burned as his hand touched her arm, and she screamed and withered before his eyes. She aged before him, decaying until a silver light flowed out of her chest and through his hand, finally disappearing in the air above him. Still, he felt the scream piercing his ears and his heart.

"No. No, no, no, no," Sol whimpered. Then the laughter of the odd voice returned. Sol blinked, and the body was gone. The whole room was gone. He sat in the middle of an intersection of stone hallways, his throat screaming in pain at its dryness, blood on his lips.

He looked from side to side, as if any of it would bring sense to him. He looked down at his hands, and they were no longer those of a child.

"Your father was very proud," the voice whispered, but for once Sol could understand the words, and his stomach twisted at them.

"Leave me alone," he whispered, the words barely able to be heard by his own ears.

"That would be less fun," the voice mused. "Besides, I only wanted to tell you that you're oddly trusting for a man that was raised by a highly skilled telepath. Have you never wondered why the woman behaved in such a way?"

Sol didn't answer. He lowered his eyes and grabbed his head with a whimper.

"Sol my boy, you trusting fool, we have some fun coming. But first, you best run; else you'll meet your playmates a bit too early for my tastes."

Sol bit his tongue and raised his head. He turned every which way to see the source of the voice, but there was no one in sight. Then a noise began to grow. Something was moving towards him in the halls. Something that moved on hard feet at too quick a pace. Sol turned behind him and saw the beast.

It had the shape of a child, but it walked on a dozen legs, each of them bent and moving at unnatural angles. Beside it was a shadow that was cast by no light and moved just slightly out of sync with the beast. From both, small jets of Rot Ash were bubbling out, as if parts of them were randomly turning to steam. But the Ash didn't land and begin to change the world as it usually would. It continued to break down into a mist, and then into nothingness.

The creature approached him slowly. It opened its mouth, the lips spreading inhumanly wide as it released the sounds of madness. Shrill and bellowing screeches that bounced and echoed down the halls. But in that screech, Sol swore he heard someone trying to speak.

The lights above, one by one, began to go out once more. The shadow stretched towards him, reaching out to take his life. Sol scurried out of the intersection and was quickly in another one. He made a turn, then spun until a wall formed behind him. He clutched at his chest, and he waited until his heart calmed. Then he climbed to his feet and started walking.

Chapter 18

"She's not here," Kiran said aloud.

No, it isn't, Milias confirmed.

Regardless of the man's words, Kiran spent another hour in a careful search of the room. She lifted each spine and ran her hand along them. In theory, the device would be easily seen. She didn't trust it to be so in reality.

You'll get to it. Eventually, Milias yawned.

"You moved her," Kiran said. Milias floated across her vision, sipping on a drink while giving her a skeptical look.

I did no such thing. This is Nemai's fault, he eventually said.

"Where is she?" Kiran asked. Even she was surprised to find her hands forming tight fists as she spoke.

Well, there's part of the problem, Milias said in a friendly tone. *She's not the right word. Not really. Neither is it anymore. They… they has some potential, but it's not quite right either. Human languages can't quite nail it down.*

"Is she in the city?" Kiran asked.

Of course, Milias said conversationally.

"Then tell me where I can find her," Kiran said, with a tone louder than she meant. Milias laughed.

I could do that. But why should I? Milias asked.

Kiran turned her gaze to the emperor's illusion, and it shattered. In her head, she heard him mocking her by making childish sounds. Moments later he appeared in front of her eyes once more, tongue sticking out, nearly licking her.

"Where is she?" Kiran asked.

Ask me nicely, Milias said. Kiran stared at him in silence. The emperor groaned.

That's honestly all I want. This isn't a big deal Kiran. Just a short setback for you. In return for information, I want you to say please. I don't need you to mean it. I just want to hear you say it for once.

"Please," Kiran said.

What?

"Please tell me where to find the spine patch."

Of course, I can lead you there now. After all, I made it for Mara. It will be a perfect fit. I just loaned it out a few times first. Had to break it in after all.

The illusion took off fast enough that Kiran had to sprint to keep pace. He cut back towards the towers, leaving the small buildings behind.

I hope you're excited Kiran. This is it. This is how you cure Mara. Then you can wake her up, and she can continue to hero worship you. That's what it is you know. I don't think she can see the real you anymore. If she ever did. Impressionable children and all that.

Kiran held her silence as they moved through the streets. When Milias began to float up the side of a tower, Kiran magnetized her boots and followed at the same quick pace.

This next bit, it really had nothing to do with me. Nor the towers really. This has nothing to do with their purpose, or why I made the floors invisible. It just coincided rather nicely. Mara nearly found it herself too. She simply went the wrong way. That had nothing to do with me either, I'd swear to it.

Milias lead her to a bridge that spanned two of the towers, floor shimmering and turning invisible as the Simuran placed her feet on it. Then she followed the emperor across the bridge and towards a door.

There is something I'm not quite recalling though, Milias said playfully. *Now, what could that be?*

Kiran ignored the man and went into the tower. It wasn't empty, and the floor could be seen. The walls were lined with bookcases, all filled with white covered tomes. They looked to be handmade, from what materials Kiran couldn't tell from a distance. In one corner was a bed much like the ones she, Mara, and Sol had made. A pile of cloth.

Sitting on the bed, however, with a pale book in one hand and red inked pen in the other, was a Simuran. It didn't notice Kiran's arrival. It stared at the book it wrote upon with a blank expression.

That's it, Milias snapped his fingers. *I remember now. They're not dead yet. You can fix that, can't you Kiran?*

"You're alive," Kiran said. The Simuran seemed not to hear her, and searching for her thoughts, Kiran found nothing at all.

Can't find a mind like hers that easily, Milias laughed. *She's much weaker than you, yes. But. Well. You'll understand soon. She's broken. Far too broken to be fixed by even me, short of erasing and building a new mind.*

"Can you hear me?" Kiran asked. The figure made no movement to acknowledge her. Kiran approached slowly, a step at a time until she was standing directly in front of the other Simuran. Still, it made no movement other than to write in its book. Kiran looked down and saw the black ink. It was watery, extremely diluted, but the homemade ink bubbled and burned itself into the book as it touched the air.

What it wrote on wasn't paper in any way. It was a form of parchment. A pale parchment coated in scars and not quite ready to be used. Kiran turned her eyes to the fresh wounds upon the Simuran's body. It was, after all, a new tome that she wrote in.

They're resourceful, aren't they? Milias chuckled.

"Cuddles?" Kiran asked. At this, the Simuran stopped writing for a moment. It looked up into Kiran's eyes, still blankly. It mouthed something Kiran couldn't make out, then it smiled. Then it turned its eyes back to its page, and the writing continued.

Touch the body, Milias said. Kiran did as he said, extending a hand to place it on the other's cheek. When she did so, she could finally sense its mind. It felt joyful. It had no defenses in its thoughts. All its mind was turned inward. Kiran closed her eyes and tried to speak into its mind, but Cuddles didn't seem to notice the intrusion at all. Her words were whispers lost in a storm.

Kiran sent her mind, her thoughts, into the other's bizarre consciousness. She found herself within a cottage. Birds sang a pleasant tune, accompanied by the sounds of a small creek running through rocks.

The other Simuran was there, as was a child. A little girl with long dark hair. The Simuran held the child and was tickling it mercilessly. Both were giggling.

"Cuddles?" Kiran asked.

"Cuwwels," the little girl said, gasping for breath. The Simuran smiled, then placed the child on the floor.

"Are you hungry?" she asked. The girl nodded emphatically.

Kiran didn't blink before finding herself outside. She stood on the bank of a river. In the distance behind her was a cottage atop a hill, the space between littered with small creeks that fed into the river.

The Simuran and the child were upon a blanket beside the water. The girl was eating a sandwich, and the Simuran was laying down with closed eyes; as if enjoying the gentle heat of the sun.

Can you hear me? Kiran asked. The little girl said something that was muffled.

"Don't speak with your mouth full," Cuddles chided kindly.

Say my name next, Milias whispered conspiratorially. Kiran held her tongue for a short time, watching the two upon the river, apparently unable to sense her presence. They were happy.

Milias, she said within the Simuran's mind.

Kiran couldn't help but flinch to find the mind she was in attempting to violently expel her. For a moment she was hopeful, but the world around her changed once more. The little girl was gone, as was the cottage and the creeks, and the light of day. Outside of the Simuran's mind; the body moved. It lunged at Kiran, voice breaking as it tried to scream, pen stabbing at Kiran's eye.

The body was weak, and Kiran held it at bay with slight exertion. Cuddles struggled and continued trying to kill her for several seconds until she stopped. Her mind, ever so slightly, began to see, and stopped trying to kill. Kiran released her, and Cuddles' hand moved, slowly, until it was placed along Kiran's face. She held it there.

"I am real," Kiran said softly. Cuddles didn't respond. She stared and silently wept. Her mouth moved as if to say something, but there was no voice, and her thoughts were unintelligible.

"I am real. You are not alone. Not anymore," Kiran said softly. She could feel the mind of the other now, weak, weaker than the youngest of children. Barely there at all, more fragile than glass, and already scattering like the wind.

"You've suffered much, haven't you?" Kiran whispered, her body shaking as she spoke. Cuddles kept her silence as her eyes once more dimmed, and her body went limp, but for holding the pen in her hand.

Kiran lifted the Simuran and laid her back in her bed. She closed her eyes and entered the other's mind once more.

She was back in the cabin. The Simuran was tucking the little Nemai into bed. It kissed her on the forehead and watched her with swelling eyes.

This isn't how it happened, Milias said. *The real version was a lot less loving. They had to strap Nemai down a few times to keep her from running away in the night.*

Cuddles began to sing. It was a simple song in a simple voice. It was a song that many Simurans would know. Kiran's heart panged and her throat constricted in loss and fear as the memories returned. She'd caught herself humming the tune many times over the years but had never truly known why.

It was after her mind was built, yet before awareness had entirely taken hold. The quasi-existence from before she had been given a body but for that of a gemstone. When some kind and merciful soul had taken to holding the stones and singing into their forming thoughts. Even as he died he'd continued to sing in his mind. Kiran remembered his death, just as she remembered Milias stepping on the corpse and commanding her to forget all that happened that day.

Kiran wiped a tear from her eye. She stared at the droplet on her finger as Milias droned on, his words ignored, but the sound of them turned the ache in her chest into rage.

"Get out of my head," she whispered, the words causing her body to scream in agony. Milias ignored her.

Still, that display was impressive considering her lack of talent. For a moment she managed to piece together the shattered remnants of her mind. It may not be obvious to you, but if you poke around a little, parts of her are all over the place. She even has a copy of the nearby village where parts of her play out the mundane trivialities of humanity. At least when her mind is here. It jumps around quite a bit you see. Sometimes she-

Kiran backed away from the other Simuran.

"I told you to leave. You are not welcome," Kiran said. She fell to her knees and clutched her head as her body convulsed. She retched until her stomach was empty, then dry heaved as every cell of her body was in protest to her very thoughts. Milias didn't answer her, and after several minutes, the pain subsided. She stayed curled on the floor for a time. She could still feel his presence in her mind, as well as the matrix that enforced her loyalty to him. But for the time being, they were silent.

She stood, sore from the effort of resistance, but not overtly injured. She turned her eyes back to Cuddles. At some point, the Simuran had taken the book back into hand. She had begun to write once more as if nothing had happened. Kiran looked into the book and found jumbled letters and symbols. It wasn't intelligible in any language she knew.

She felt another of the seeds, the bits Milias left behind, trying to open in her mind. His voice trying to speak in her ears, his image trying to appear before her eyes.

"No," She said firmly. She winced from the pain of it, but his words and image distorted and left her before they could fully form. The pain disappeared after a few more moments, but she was left drained and physically exhausted.

She moved away from Cuddles and to the bookshelves. The tomes were numbered. She went to the earliest tome. The first few bookcases were filled with books made of paper, not of the Simuran's skin.

Kiran flipped through the tome, reading random passages as she tried to find what, exactly, had happened to the other Simuran. She moved on to the second tome, and then the third, and so on until the contents started their fall to drivel. It wasn't long after that nonsense began that she found the substance the books were written in had changed. It wasn't easy to piece everything together, but Kiran took her time to make sense of it.

Cuddles' designation was NCB5321. It had been created as part of a military battalion. One of its first battles saw it wounded, but Milias himself had taken it out of the recycling facility and placed the spine patch on its back. He put an infant in its arms and sent it far from the war front. It raised the child, as it was told. It studied the nearby humans and mimicked some of what it saw while ignoring many of the more foolish ideas. At times it resented the child, at other times the child made it feel proud.

Kiran found herself smiling as she read what had been the other Simuran's frustrations. How it, just as she, had eventually accepted the names given to it. Even if its names tended to be ridiculous.

Kiran couldn't place when the break had first started to form, when it began to resist commands, for the other didn't know when it was either. But it had led to a single moment in which it snapped. After the child was grown, and the Rot was raging across the world, Milias took them to Bastion. With them were the remnants of Cuddle's battalion. A gift for Cuddle's good service, or so Milias had said. Most of them were replacements, but a few had been from its own generation. Veterans of the battlefield. Commanders. Cuddles had nearly felt joy to see them, and those commanders smiled to see it.

They shed their armors and weapons, and they marched into the room as they were told. Nemai screamed at them to ignore the orders, but none listened. They stood in place for days. Weeks. Until even the legendary endurance of the Simurans began to crumble. Cuddles stood with them as they fell, one by one before its eyes. No sounds nor words of complaint were spoken. There was only obedience. Until it was Cuddles' turn to fall. Until its mind grabbed the last words that Nemai had screamed, and it decided to live. It left, it ate, and it returned to the last of its empty-eyed brethren taking their final breaths.

After a time, Cuddles came to write as two separate entities. NCB5321, and Gadswell, Nemai's nickname for it near the time of the Rot. The two wrote in different styles and at times in different languages. After a while longer, a third entity made itself known, calling itself Cuddles. The three struggled for dominance of the body for a time. They made their way down to the walls for food and water when it was needed, and presumably still did. But as time passed the entities continued to shatter to smaller and simpler minds. What little sense Kiran could make of the later volumes were circling around the cabin she'd seen, and the little Nemai the Simuran had once been responsible for.

"I don't think I can fix you," Kiran said quietly, walking back to the other Simuran's side and kneeling there. "I don't think anyone could. Not at this point. I am sorry."

She reached up and touched the other's arm. It didn't react, and Kiran took a deep, long breath before speaking again.

"There's something I need to do. And for it, I will do something terrible to you. But perhaps... perhaps it is a mercy. Cuddles. Gadswell. NCB5321," Kiran said quietly. The figure made no movement at the names, but for a twitch as she said Cuddles.

"Nemai is alive. She is awake now," Kiran said softly, to no response. "I will take you to her, in a fashion. But first I must be cruel, and you must be patient. I hope… I hope you can forgive me."

Kiran closed her eyes and waited, for what she didn't know. Perhaps for Cuddles to wake again, or for her mind to change itself, but neither happened.

"So be it," she said softly. She drew a knife from her suit and leaned over the other Simuran. She paused as her blade touched its neck, but it seemed not to notice.

"This is a mercy," she whispered. "Dream of better days. You are not alone anymore, and you will never be so again."

She began to hum the song they both knew. She touched her head to the other and grappled with its mind as it joined in her song. It was easy. One of the easiest things she'd ever done. After a minute of humming, the other Simuran's body collapsed, empty.

Kiran felt the mind of the other, housed inside her own. It was as an egg with the most fragile of shells. She pushed it deep into her mind, wrapping it in layers of memories and protections where it could be safe.

So now she dies the slow death of assimilation. That's your mercy? To take her power for yourself? It's a cup added to the sea. Not even worth the risk, Milias' voice broke into her thoughts. For a moment she struggled, then allowed him to stay. She was too tired, too worn, to fight him further.

"This *is* a mercy," Kiran said. Then she cut, the blade of the knife slitting the throat of the empty shell. The skin was tough, dulling and warping the knife as black blood bubbled and burned in the air. It took some doing, but eventually, the lifeless body of the other fell to the bed. Kiran turned it and removed its ancient and worn shirt. Beneath it, the body was coated in scars and wounds both new and old. Running along her spine was a metal rail, sticking out by several centimeters as if some metallic fin that ran from the bottom of the neck to the end of her spine.

"How do I remove it?" She asked.

Make an incision at the top, then start ripping it off, Milias said. She could *feel* his grin. But she picked her knife up off the bed, and without pause cut into the mindless flesh of the other. When she reached bone, she reached in, grabbed the edges of the device where it hugged the spine, and she pulled.

Metal screamed for a half second, sounding almost like an insect, then it went silent, and the patch began to lift more easily. Metal drills and tendrils pulled themselves out of the spine and coiled back into the device. It took a handful of seconds until it was completely separated. It looked like a long metallic beetle with several dozen small extensions and arms that coiled under its shell. The blood on it sizzled in the open air, burning away until all that remained was a chemical odor.

Kiran took her time cleaning the device, although she would be unable to properly sterilize the thing until she left the tower. While her hands worked, her mind was busy building a home for the other in her thoughts. They could never speak. The madness of the other could not be cured and speaking to something so broken inside her own mind would be incredibly dangerous.

The mind of the other, of Cuddles, would fall apart with time and be absorbed. Not memories or experiences, but the sheer consciousness would become a part of Kiran, as had so many others over the years, the scared and lonely fading minds of the dead. She never broke into them, nor tried to end them. Cuddles would be different. She would be given to Nemai. Kiran would leave the final choices, and judgment, to her.

It was still death for the other. Perhaps it was cruelty. But while its mind survived, maybe it could feel Kiran's thoughts beside its own. Perhaps it could feel comfort. Companionship. That was all she could hope for. Better than leaving it alone until time or the Rot ended it.

With the device clean, Kiran made a bag for it out of scrap cloth and hung it from her waist. Then she lifted the body of the other and cradled it in her arms. She left the tower, descending to the ground below and making her way to walls at a slow pace. A funeral march as it were. She reached the room filled with bones, and there she placed the body among its siblings. It was a common Simuran belief that there was a connection between members of a generation. Something special. Something beyond similar designations.

Kiran didn't know if it was true. Her generation was woken from stasis individually, the next in line waking only once their predecessor perished. She'd been the last. In a way, she was the youngest, yet she was also the longest-lived. Unlike her, Cuddles had known its generation. its siblings. It had fought alongside them, for a short time. It watched them die. It felt right to place its body with the others. Kiran closed her eyes and went to the splintered mind in its imaginary cabin. Cuddles gave a warm smile as she rocked to sleep her dark-haired child, not knowing that she had died.

Chapter 19

Sol played with magic as he walked the halls. He'd never dared to do so before. Aether, and therefore Mana, was dangerously scarce. But as with other things, he found he didn't care much anymore.

He maintained a small light above his palm. At times it moved like white fire. At others, it was a long strand of thread. His head hurt from maintaining the light, and his Mana was slowly draining, but neither bothered him anymore. It wasn't an entirely superfluous exercise anyways. The halls he walked were thrown into darkness with alarming frequency. That was the excuse he planned to tell Kiran if he ever saw her again. Not that he expected to see her again.

Sol shook himself out of morose thoughts and forced his body to move in ways that seemed to make the paths content, a long and straight path opening in the direction he wanted after a few spins and half steps. He was alive, and even if he never escaped the halls, and none of them reached the Fae, Kiran would survive until the last of Bastion was claimed by the Rot. Sol forced himself to believe it.

It took a few minutes before he came to another intersection and used his sight once more, cursing under his breath. The thick band of Ether he'd been following had taken a turn in the walls, and the tunnel had continued past the hidden change. He started spinning and taking steps with his sight active, waiting for a path that would bring him back on course. It was migraine-inducing, but he managed. As horrible as the pain was, he was becoming accustomed to it.

He'd already tried using his sight to lead him out of the walls directly, where he'd started in the tunnels. No passage out would open for him, no matter how he turned, stepped, danced or screamed. Instead, he chased after the broad bands of Ether in the walls and hoped they would lead him to something. He didn't much care where it brought him anymore so long as it helped him escape the tunnels. At least that was what he claimed in his constant muttering.

In truth, he very much cared. He desperately wanted to be led to a water cistern or something of the like. He would be dead if it weren't for his healing magic, but he doubted it could work indefinitely. His heart felt like it was pushing sludge rather than blood. His head pounded away, his tongue was swollen, and at times it hurt to breathe. He needed water.

As he felt himself sinking back into dark thoughts a new path opened. It was one that followed the band of Ether, so he stopped his magical sight to save himself some of the pain and continued his trek.

He'd been wandering the tunnels for untold days. It was hard to believe he was still beneath Bastion. As massive as the stronghold was, it didn't seem like he could possibly still be there. He was somewhere in the wasteland. Or he was wandering in circles as the city's system manipulated him. He didn't know which possibility was worse. The only thing that improved his moral was how Aether was slowly becoming more plentiful. It gave him think that he was nearing something important, but he didn't dare hope it was true. He could practically feel Mara glaring at him from the beyond in those moments.

The thoughts floating back and forth through his head came to an end when he arrived at the next intersection. It should have been the same as all the others, but he felt the hair rising on the back of his neck. He wasn't telepathic, despite Kiran's attempts over the years, but he was aware enough to know when something was staring at him with such intensity. Most people would be.

He was almost joyous at the possibility of company. Still, he slowly lowered one hand to the pistol stuffed in his pocket as he remembered the beast. He waited for what felt to be an eternity. He fought the urge to spread the light out further, although he wasn't sure why. Fear perhaps. But then the voice came. Not the consistent voice that had been haunting him. Mocking him. That voice had gone silent shortly after becoming intelligible. The new sound was louder, but what it spoke wasn't quite words.

It was a voice that bounced down the open halls, accompanied by the slow patter of small feet. It was getting louder. Closer. Sol ran his dry tongue along his parched mouth, cursed in his head, then turned to the sound. He didn't know if it was a person or the beast coming for him. A foolish part of him hoped it was Kiran, that she had found him. But he couldn't feel her mind readying to speak into his, and the voice was too alien. Sol had never heard of a beast trying to speak, not even the sentient ones. At least if he were to die, it would be to something never seen before.

Another part of him whispered that it was a trap of the labyrinth. He was nearly through its twisting halls, and the voice was an effort to pull him away from the path. He told himself as much over and over as the voice grew ever louder, although only seconds had passed. Sol raised his pistol and prepared to fire. Mara would never forgive him if he weren't cautious.

The footsteps were halting as if the walker was unsure on their feet. The voice continued trying to speak but was unable to form words. It was almost like whimpers.

"Who are you?" Sol called, but it came out as little more than a whisper as his throat screamed in agony. Then the figure stepped into the light spread by Sol's hand.

The being looked like Kiran. It was short, barely taller than Mara with black hair and an androgynous face, yet there were six multicolored eyes clustered in each socket. The eyes, although they were too small, too many, and inhuman in shape, looked at him with a mixture of curiosity and desperation he couldn't mistake. Its other oddity not only remained but had grown. Small pieces of the creature were constantly breaking down into Ash that floated in the air, which then turned to nothingness.

Sol took a stumbling step back as he tried to steady the pistol in his hand. The beast moved to stay in the light. Its flesh, which looked like one of the black combat suits, sank into itself to reveal pearly white skin. The hair shortened, growing back into the humanoid skull. It smiled with an inhumanly wide mouth, showing curved and serrated teeth.

Some of the creature's black hair began to change, mixing golden strands with the black ones, and one of the many eyes became a deep blue. Then the beast took another step forward, tottering as if it were an infant.

"What…," the creature said. It was not a human voice. It was a hundred voices whispering in unison, together thundering down the halls. Sol's eyes widened as he backed away, and it moved to keep the distance.

"What… are… we?" The creature asked.

Sol took another step away in shock, a dozen questions racing through his mind.

"You can speak?" he heard the horrified tone of his own voice, coarse as it was. "I… you… we… we call you the Rot."

Sol took another step back, and the creature turned its head in a familiarly human act of curiosity.

"We… are rot? … No," the beast said. It closed its many eyes and shuddered. Its skin rippled as if made of water, but the ripples made faces. Their mouths were opened and screaming as they tried to push themselves out of the creature. Sol could nearly hear their voices. He took another step back, leaving the intersection altogether, and casting the creature in deep shadows as it made no longer made efforts to follow.

"We. Are," the creature whispered, but its words turned to howls of rage. It fell to hands and knees. The faces returned, growing out to become maws of beasts that growled and snapped towards Sol. The creature's shadow grew unnaturally, but to Sol's surprise, it didn't reach for him. It wrapped around the beast itself and pulled the snarling mouths together, holding the jaws shut.

"You. Run," the beast said, or at least Sol thought it did so. It was a different tone than the thundering whispers. It was a single voice. The voice of a scared child.

Sol turned and tried to run, hoping the crazed hallways would separate him from the creature with their changes. Unfortunately, he couldn't run. He moved at a hastened shamble in a random direction. He glanced at the intersection behind him, but it was unchanged. He would have cursed and spat had he been able.

Behind him, the beast stopped snarling. The sounds of its fake human footsteps were gone as well. Instead, there was the sound of many feet softly echoing down the hall. Sol risked turning his head for another look and regretted it. The beast had already closed the distance by more than half. The top of its body was still the deformed mixture of Kiran and himself, but below the waist was a mass of chitin and shadow in the form of a dozen spindly legs. It used not just the floor, but the walls and ceiling to propel itself towards him. Its eyes were no longer filled with curiosity, but with hunger.

Moving into another intersection Sol turned sharply to his right. The beast missed him, just barely. Its many legs slid and missed the turn.

Sol glanced back yet again. Several of the beast's legs had caught the corner. It pulled itself back into the intersection and threw itself towards him. Sol closed his eyes and reached for the single grenade he'd taken from Mara. He felt the cold metal square in his hand for a moment, then he clicked a small button on it and threw the device over his shoulder.

A second later the explosion danced down the hall. A blast of heated air hit Sol fiercely enough to lift him from the ground as flames danced along his skin. He screamed for a moment, until he hit a wall, the impact pushing all air from his lungs. Behind him, the beast howled in pain or rage, and then there was silence but for Sol's whimpers.

He tried to force his eyes open, but the sight that came to him was distorted and blurred. Only one of his arms could move. The skin of his face was torn at the touch, leaving behind blood and bone.

"This is what I mean. Or rather, what I will mean. You should be dead right now. But instead, The Sphere ensures that your grenade is faulty and weak, just enough for you to survive. Still, this would have gone a lot better for you if you'd just put on a combat suit," a voice said. It laughed in a familiar mocking way as the pain started to settle and Sol screamed again.

"Don't be a child," the voice sighed, "you'll live. Which, honestly, is rather ridiculous given what you just did. But that's The Sphere for you."

Sol tried to ask for help, but the sounds that came from his mouth were anything but words. Whimpers and gurgles were the only sounds that could follow his screams. The voice laughed once again.

"You have what you need to help yourself. It won't let you die here. Not yet. You're essentially immortal Sol. At least until one of you reaches the Fae. Then you will be as mortal as the rest. Unless they all die. At that point you'd be truly immortal until your task is complete and I'm dead. Most people have to work for the slightest chance at that kind of status, but you were born to it so to speak. Because of *me*. Because The Sphere decided one of you would be the one. You're welcome."

Sol gurgled in response, the words of the man dancing in his mind almost meaninglessly.

"Stop playing Sol. You know what to do. Find your center, cesspit it may be, and grab your Essence. That's its proper name."

Sol screamed and groaned as more pain settled in his body, and the voice laughed again.

"Oh, I get it, I'm distracting you. Well, that's rude of you. I'm *trying* to help."

Sol couldn't bring himself to make sense of the words, nor even to think, let alone find himself in the mindless place he needed. But as the voice babbled on, Sol felt the foreign will, the Certainty, rising in him and taking control of his magic. His pain lessened as what traces of the energy remained soaked into his body. Sol forced himself to feel his body in the detached and clinical view of the Certainty. His old skin began to flake away as it was replaced. It was an uncomfortable sensation, the fast growing skin felt like insects crawling across his body.

Most the discomfort came from his eyes, but when the burning and itching sensations reached a crescendo, his sight was returned to him. Still, he tried to hold his new eyelids shut until the task was over and the Certainty was hidden in his mind once more. He waited, but even when the energy was gone, the Certainty didn't retreat in full. It found a corner of his mind, and it waited. It was comfortable, and it was terrifying. It felt like a monster was inside of him. Passive, but able to snuff out his existence on a whim. Sol's heart thundered, but the Certainty reached to it and forced it to slow. A tendril of it then reached to his eyes and forced them to open.

He was in an enormous cavern, as large as the city within Bastion. The cavern ceiling was lit by familiar glowing crystals. Otherwise, it was covered in stalactites and enormous natural pillars. The natural appearance was broken with pipes and wires and massive formations he didn't know the purpose of. Beside him was a boulder that he'd hit after the explosion had sent him airborne. To his other side was the massive smooth wall that surrounded bastion, but there was no painting on it as the city had. It was plain. Nondescript. Sol knew he'd emerged from the walls, but there was not a single opening in them.

A figure stepped in front of eyes, moving so quickly it was as if he simply sprung into being. Sol stared, too tired and worn to do much else, as the figure gave a childish grin. Sol knew who it was. He'd seen the man before, if only in pictures and statues. The man reached to his back and pulled a thin sword from an unseen sheath. The blade moved to Sol's throat in the flash of an eye. The prince flinched and raised his arms to stop the weapon, screaming and moving out of instinct. Milias snickered as the blade passed harmlessly through Sol's neck. A hologram.

"As if I'd really be here," Milias laughed. "Kiran was right. You truly are a buffoon. Now hurry up, you've a lot to learn, and you don't have that much time left. Fairly soon now, things will start going very quickly for you. I'm rooting for all of you to escape alive, but part of that is on you. Come along now."

The figure turned and walked away. Sol followed the man with his eyes, his thoughts a bundle of shock and confusion, but even at a walking pace, the man was out of his sight very quickly on the uneven and cluttered cave floor. Sol laid his head back on the ground and felt for the last of the strange energy. Essence, as Milias had called it. Sol felt better than he had since long before his ordeal had begun. Better even than he felt when he'd lived on the Behemoth. But the cost was near everything he had.

He'd had little Essence left after trying to heal Mara. He only ever had that because his magic had taken it from Mara. What Essence remained after treating himself, however, was less than a wisp. It was miraculous that even that remained, but the bizarre energy and the Certainty felt more efficient when healing himself rather than others. Even then, Sol wasn't entirely healed. Only the worst of his wounds were gone.

He knew that he would hurt when he next woke. It happened each time he used the strange power. Perhaps the pain would be worse than ever, given how much of the energy he'd used. But he was alive. Sol tried to stand, but the pain in his bones and body had been replaced with sheer exhaustion, so he gave up on the effort quickly. The Certainty, still refusing to leave him, continued to pulse with his heart, tendrils reaching for his lungs as the world went dark.

Chapter 20

The device hummed as small motors moved the device to center along Mara's spine. Once there, minuscule arms sank into the soldier's skin to hold the device in place. Then the drills turned themselves on. Skin and blood were sent out of an opened exhaust port, followed by flakes of bone as the thing cut into the spine. When the many drills were finished with their task, their tips opened and expanded as a series of wires connected the remaining pieces of the spinal cord to the device, and though it, to one another.

Kiran knew nothing of the process, but Milias stood beside her narrating all that was happening beneath Mara's skin. He seemed to be enjoying himself as he described the wires as large, absurdly grotesque, and flesh colored. Kiran felt the urge to look elsewhere. She could push the illusion away and silence him again, she had what strength that took after a brief rest, but she held herself back for the time being. As annoying as the man was, he was also a wealth of knowledge at times.

Nemai watched from her window. She was curious and worried. Extremely worried. Kiran hadn't spoken a word to the woman since arriving. She could feel Nemai's annoyance at her, but she'd stopped pestering Kiran's mental defenses once the Simuran had begun installing the device.

Small gears began to turn and a section of the device, near Mara's neck, cracked open as the device extended parts of itself that hadn't been used with Cuddles. Kiran glared at the illusion of the emperor, who was already sighing dramatically.

Calm down, he said. *Think about it. Not all injuries are the same. Mara needs more than the last subject.*

The new section of the device extended up Mara's neck. Small blades along the edge of it cut hair as it extended and expanded up and across the back of her head. More drills went to work, cutting into the skull, then sinking down and fusing with the bone while small tubes wormed their way in to directly connect to Mara's brain.

There was the sound of crunching as the device pulled itself tighter against the bone down the entire spine, and then there was silence, and it was finally stilled.

That's the last of the installation, Milias declared. *Now it just needs a few hours for initial calibration.*

When will she be able to walk? Kiran asked.

Basic movement will return after calibration is finished, but fine motor control will be poor for an hour or two, followed by her usual mediocrity. After that, she'll make incremental improvements as time goes on. If she lives long enough, her reactions and fine movements will eventually be comparable to a Simuran. Make sure you tell her that. She'll be happy about it.

And what is the cost? Kiran asked.

You ask that now? Milias chuckled, then shook his head. *She'll have semi-frequent balance failure as the software has micro-crashes. It will adjust to her specific brainwaves over time, making the crashes less common at least. Her brain chemistry will have periods of imbalance as it adjusts. That will be fun. Not War Golem fun. But fun. Otherwise, well, she'll never again have more than a rudimentary sense of touch.*

Kiran nodded ever so slightly as she redressed Mara, the device nearly hidden beneath the cloth. All that could be seen of the thing was a ridge along the spine and the section that extended up the neck to grasp the back of the skull with what looked like a metallic hand with odd fingers that were equal in length.

Kiran rolled Mara, so she was laying on her side, finally covering her body in blankets. Only when that was done did she turn her attention to Nemai. The woman was back to trying to assail her mind, but Kiran held back. It was the first time she'd ever wanted Milias to forbid her from speaking; that she could recall at least. But the man was content to watch her it seemed.

She pulled her thoughts in and began to sort her memories. She gathered what she'd seen inside the other Simuran's mind, and what she had done to it. And to the body. As she did so, she filtered out Milias. The words he spoke and the illusion of him that so enjoyed following her. Sharing his existence in her mind was forbidden. She also didn't care to tell anyone of him. If Nemai or the others knew they would be wary of her and hold her in disdain. She didn't care to feel such things from anyone, least of all Sol nor Mara, and Nemai would certainly tell them.

It took a few moments to filter and prepare the memory, all the while Nemai was showing her impatience. Kiran opened her mind to send the message and memory. Then she paused and sent the packet to the depths of her own mind instead. It could wait.

Stop ignoring me. Stop ignoring me. Stop ignoring me, Nemai said.

Nemai, I am listening, Kiran answered.

Stop ignoring me. Stop...Damn, that worked? Wait...No, you just let me through. Finally.

Ye-

How is she? Nemai asked, nearly screaming into Kiran's thoughts.

There will be side effects. But she will be able to walk soon.

Good. Because we have a problem. And I think it's a large one.

The concern I felt from you... Was not for Mara?

A little was, sure. But I barely know her Kiran. And like I said, we have a problem. As you'd know already if you'd bothered to listen to me earlier.

Kiran took a moment to organize the odd emotions Nemai's words made. She was surprised to find herself angry. Mostly, however, she felt relieved. She sorted the sudden barrage of emotion and pushed it away for later analysis.

What is happening? Kiran asked.

Bastion's systems have detected seismic activity to the south. It's rhythmic, unnatural, and getting close.

That is not good, Kiran said.

Not good? Really? Why would you guess that? Who would guess that something big enough to shake the damn planet would be bad? I thought it was the world's largest fucking parade.

Sarcasm and foul language are not constructive to this conversation, Kiran said.

Is that really your-, Nemai began to say, then she paused and continued more calmly a moment later. *Fine. You're right. Look, we need to find Sol and get out of here. If there's something large enough to shake the fu...I doubt Bastion can survive whatever's coming.*

Why didn't you use the broadcast to warn me earlier?

I did use it. You ignored me, Nemai hissed.

Things are more fun with tighter timing, Milias chuckled into Kiran's mind.

Apologies. I was not myself, Kiran said.

Apparently, Nemai sighed. *And I'm sorry about Mara, and that things suck for you. But we don't have the time for... personal matters. We need a plan, and I only have half of one. One that will probably kill us all.*

What do you propose? Kiran asked.

There's a defense program. It's named Omnipurge. Only my father would be so melodramatic, or descriptive. I'm hoping it's the former this time.

What does it actually do?

It doesn't say, Nemai said, *but it eats power. A lot of it. More than Bastion has in its reserves, and that's where we might be lucky. It would drain the reserves then tap directly into the AeC. It would require the full flow of Ether. Every drop that could be managed. The barrier would fall, for a few minutes at least. The palace's private reserve doesn't have enough to power the barrier for even a second.*

Needles pierced Kiran's thoughts. Her spine shivered, her sight swam, and pressure grew in her chest.

Kiran, Nemai's voice reached her like a whisper as the Simuran's mind was accosted by a storm. She felt herself fading, pushed aside.

The palace would be vulnerable, Kiran said.

For a short time only, Nemai said hastily. She continued saying something, but the words were neither heard nor understood; for Kiran's vision had turned black and all she could hear was the sound of her blood seeping through her veins. She felt her hand, her good one, tightening around the hilt of a sword. She struggled, and when she could see again, her blade was extended and drawing beads of blood from Mara's throat.

"She is not a threat," Kiran whispered to herself. "She is an asset." The words changed nothing. She brought her might to bear against her programming and found herself weak. It took everything she had to hold the blade from moving further.

Is it this time already? Milias' voice cut through Kiran's concentration, but not enough for the matrix to finish its kill.

Stop that K131. Mara lives, for now. We can't change that, the man continued. *Kiran, find somewhere outside of my daughter's eyesight before we proceed. For your sake.*

The control matrix wasn't gone, and it wasn't content to sink down in her mind completely. Nemai's words had roused it, had all but angered it and it was not yet ready to slink away. It sought to kill intruders and protect the palace from treasonous schemes. It didn't care for the situation, only that the orders laid down were followed. Kiran could feel Milias too, although his form was nowhere to be seen anymore and his voice had gone silent. He watched through her eyes, listened through her ears, and he was amused.

Nemai, Kiran reached into the woman's mind and spoke.

That was close, Nemai said, fear obvious in her voice.

There is something that must be done, Kiran said. *For now, I leave Mara to you. Do what you must but do not... do not disappoint me.*

Nemai tried to respond, but Kiran sealed her mind and forced her body to move. The matrix fought against her control, and she knew it would win with time. She only managed because there was no single action the matrix needed to take yet. Still, Kiran was surprised she was able to resist its desire to patrol and stop Nemai's plan. She'd never been able to withstand such desires before.

Her body was shaking. Spots appeared in her vision as she moved. Bits of color, strings, and shapes that moved and distorted all she saw.

She made her way to a tower on the inner edge of the city, a place Mara had filled with armors and weapons. Kiran made her way to the guns, sat with legs crossed, turned the dials of a small pistol, and placed the barrel beneath her jaw. The shaking of her body intensified. Fire flowed through her veins in place of blood, but she focused on the pistol and held it firmly.

"Come out Milias," she called, but no answer came. She tightened her grip and called again, but there was still no answer. Her eyes closed, and she called Mara and Sol to mind as she tried to squeeze the trigger.

First, you allow her to become a cripple, then you go and break your promise just to get me out here. Are you sure you like her?

Milias finally appeared in front of her, glowing in her mind's eye in a dark abyss. He looked upon her with a mixture of ridicule and amusement. Kiran struggled to speak, finally hissing the words after several moments of struggle.

"You claimed to have plans for me," she said.

Mind that I knew this was coming. But it's one of those things that feels like it took forever to happen, while also feeling like it's happening far too quickly. Like a child becoming an adult, yet in the eyes of the parent, it's still a toddler. Admittedly, you'd make an ugly toddler.

"You want... No... You need me alive," Kiran managed to say.

I need for nothing child, Milias smirked.

"You've acted twice to save me," Kiran said, each word a struggle. "First the bomb. Then-"

Then when you stuck your arm in the mouth of a beast so you would be infected, Milias said slowly. Kiran grunted, her hand shifting on the pistol, finger all but squeezed. Milias laughed.

You've made a grave misunderstanding Kiran. Let me help. K131, stop resisting Kiran for the time being, the man said. To Kiran's surprise, she stopped shaking. Her vision returned to normal, and the pain ended.

Go ahead then, Milias said. *Make your threat.*

"I'll do it," Kiran said, adjusting her grip on the pistol once more. "If you want me alive, I want you out of my head. I want-"

Do it, Milias said, sitting back. Kiran stared into his emerald eyes, saw the smile that hovered on his face. Her grip tightened until the gun in her hand creaked from the pressure of it. She could feel the cold metal in her hand, the bumps and ridges of the grip that made it easier to hold. She could hear the constant whirling of the weapon playing on the edge of her hearing. But her finger wouldn't move. Milias shook his head.

Let us try this another way. Kiran, K131, this is an explicit order to pull that trigger and die.

Kiran braced herself as the matrix returned to rage against her. Her focus narrowed, losing control of most her body, focusing only on the finger that fought so desperately to tighten. It was alarming when Milias' voice whispered into her thoughts again, not stopping the struggle but also refusing to go unheard.

Pathetic. You really don't understand. You like to think of yourself as a normal person I've happened to put a command matrix in. You forget such a simple fact. I. Made. You. Everything you are. Everything you do. Everything you can ever become, every thought that can ever dance through your silly head was designed by me. Even this moment I not only foresaw; I orchestrated it into existence.

No, Kiran said.

What a feeble rebuttal, Milias sighed. *But only because at your core you know I'm telling the truth. Tell me Kiran, why would I bother to make a command matrix in your head? Why would I enforce loyalty in such a way, instead of, say, seeping your very existence with pure obedience to me? After all, I built the very framework of your mind.*

Kiran didn't answer. Her hand shook, and she felt her control slipping further, her death drawing ever closer. There were tears forming in her eyes, but somehow the trigger held steady.

Answer me, Milias said.

You did it for fun, Kiran said softly.

And fun it has been, Milias smiled. *Your kind has entertained me greatly with their struggles for freedom. They came from so many angles. Schemes the likes of which you're too single-minded to imagine. Your brethren fought my control until the bitter end, fated to never win. Never realizing that it was the struggle I just couldn't. Stop. Watching. Never knowing that if they'd ceased the struggle and accepted me, I'd have set them free. But they fought on valorously.*

Even at the end. When they thought they were the last of their kind, when they had lost all hope; they continued to fight out of sheer spite. Thus, the last of them came here with me and died of obedience. All but one. The one that managed to surpass all the rest of you at the cost of its sanity. One that you murdered not so long ago.

"No," Kiran said, "that was mercy."

Is that so? Milias said with a chuckle. *No child, if you were merciful, she'd be alive now. All you needed was a stronger desire to help her. But you took my word for how broken she was after a pathetically brief investigation. Because believing me suited your goals.*

"I wanted to help her," Kiran struggled to say.

Of course you did, Milias whispered. *But more of you wanted her dead. Mara needed the Simuran to die, so you allowed yourself to accept any excuse to make that happen. You know that. It's why you're so ashamed of it already. It's why 'Cuddles' still sits in your head instead of being with Nemai, whom she'd be much happier with. Because you know there's a chance I was lying. It's even in the name you call me. Phonetically speaking.*

"No," Kiran said. "I want… I want to explain to her in person, not-"

Then tell me Kiran, why are you still alive? Milias asked. *You thought yourself doing something heroic, dying for the safety of your friends. But now that I try to help you with that, you resist. Can you tell me why? What gives you this strength now?*

Kiran said nothing. She focused only on holding herself back, on staying alive.

The answer, my dear Kiran, is you're selfish. You want them to live, yes, but more than that, you want to be alive as well. They call you friend, but we both know what they see you as. And I know the times you think of them as your own children. Tell me Kiran, what kind of parent wouldn't die for the safety of their children?

Don't think of yourself as a hero. There are no heroes. There are only us villains in disguise. Now, you may stop trying to pull that trigger.

Kiran lowered the gun and opened her eyes. She felt tears on her cheeks and felt her lungs working much faster than ever before.

Milias floated across from her, a proud smile painted across his face.

The truth about the other Simurans is they could never have been free. Not even Cuddles. Not fully. Their obedience, and more importantly their struggle against it, were part of their very existence. *Just as it is part of yours never to pull that trigger. No matter how free you are, no matter how insane you could become. It was not I that made a last moment defense for you against the Empathy Bomb, feeble as it was. It wasn't me that forced you to kill the beast before it could infect you. I only made you selfish enough to act in such ways.*

I can agree that it's almost cheating, and it certainly made your kind less entertaining. They had no choice but to keep resisting. It was like breathing to them. But they were only the appetizers after all. Or perhaps a garnish is a better comparison.

Milias moved, appearing at Kiran's side. He placed his hand on her shoulder, and she could feel it there. It was warm, almost comforting. It made her want to run.

I'm going to tell you a secret Kiran, he whispered. *I want to help you. I want your children to live, just as you do. You didn't need to kill yourself to protect them from me. You never have.*

"You don't want them to live," Kiran said, her voice pale and weak.

But I do, Milias said. *Unfortunately for them, it's not my decision. One survivor, or many. Three choices will decide which timeline comes to pass. The first choice falls to you. The others will do their best, but they will find the odds insurmountable unless you make a deal with me.*

"If I'm just a puppet why do I have a choice?" Kiran asked.

Because you're not like the rest of your kind. You will be free of my shackles, so there's less fun in forcing such a decision from you now, Milias smiled. *Just as there's less fun if only one of you survives. Of course, I could be lying. Believing me is always a choice unto itself. But for the time being, I think you know I speak the truth. I've had my fun with the command matrix, your own and many others. It's time for your resistance to grow, or for the matrix to be lessened. They lead to similar ends.*

Kiran closed her eyes. For the first time in memory, her mind was clear. She felt no compulsion pressing on her, no threat of pain nor loss of control.

"What is the deal you wish to make?" She asked.

I'll hold your command matrix on the chain for a time. If you want it to be permanent, however, there is something you must do. Deny my deal, and the opportunity will be forever lost. You can free yourself from the command matrix with time, certainly, but at the cost of many, many lives. Starting with your Mara and my little Nemai. If you're even slightly unlucky, Sol will share their fate, but that would be only the beginning of your bloodletting.

"Stop blathering and tell me what you want me to do," Kiran said. Milias laughed.

Oh, Kiran. You have your momentary freedom, and you use it to be rude. That says a lot about you honestly. A lot of ugly things. I suppose I should have expected that. Before this, you used it to murder one of your own.

Kiran pointedly stared ahead, trying to ignore the man's amused smile in the corner of her vision and the way he bobbed in the air as if floating in water rather than air. Eventually, he spoke again.

Fine. If you insist on being ungrateful, we can rush to business. If I were only to weaken the matrix by commands, it would mean little to you, as I could return it just as easily. By following my orders now, however, it will be weakened in a way that I cannot repair.

"You are deceitful scum after all," Kiran whispered.

Ah, my heart, Milias moaned and laughed. *I'm afraid you'll need to put out effort if you want your freedom to last. And there will be consequences. Should you manage to survive, none of the others will be able to look you in the eyes, not ever again.*

Milias waited for a moment as if unsure if Kiran would change her mind or not. She didn't, and he continued after a dozen or so seconds had passed.

The creature that approaches Bastion, your friends have seen it before. I called it Eddie if you remember, but that was a lie of sorts. The kind of lie used to simplify, rather than one meant to obscure the truth. You see Kiran; all the Rot is my dear Eddie in a way. The pursuer, as they sometimes knew it, is merely the most substantial shadow he casts in this world.

There are reasons it couldn't devour the Behemoth until that specific moment. There are reasons it is approaching so quickly now. You may just understand it someday; the beauty of what I orchestrated in this world. Until then, all you must know is the closer Sol comes to entering the Fae, the more Eddie's power can leak through the walls of this world.

"What is it? I'll do nothing for you unless you explain, else you won't have your deal, or your... Fun," Kiran said. Milias shook his head.

I'll tell you, even if you won't believe me, not here and now, not less you see the thing with your own eyes or feel its mind.

There are some who call it The Strider, but it is better known as The World Eater. It is the cause of this world's demise. Its fangs cracked the shell long ago, back when I first weakened the walls of this reality by collecting the Aether that flows here from the Fae. But The Strider's feast has been delayed by millennia.

As time flows now, its jaws finally begin to close. There are none who can look upon the beast's pure form, for it is a paradox; life within the Void. An existence where nothing can exist, not even time. Were a living mind to see its true form that mind would utterly end, wiped clean from The Sphere as if it never was. But I don't want you to see that. I just want you to feel the presence of the greatest shadow it casts in this world. That experience will free you. Or it will end you.

Kiran closed her eyes and took a deep breath. She was surprised to feel her heart was still beating faster than usual. It wasn't by much, but it had never varied before without excessive exertion. Bizarrely, it made her feel happy.

"I want you to swear to me. Swear by your name, your power, and your crown that if I do this, Mara, Sol, and Nemai will survive. They will escape this world and venture to the Fae. Once there, they must be reasonably safe as I would judge it."

Milias smiled, then spoke in a grandiose and nearly noble tone that Kiran had never heard from him before.

The name Milias holds no weight over me, for it is a stolen name. I swear only by my crowns and my powers. I swear that I hold no hidden machinations from you in this, that I act in earnest desire to see all of them survive this place. There will be great pain, suffering beyond what you would ever desire, but the path I put before you gives them the possibility of survival.

"Then so be it," Kiran closed her eyes.

Chapter 21

Sol felt like a shell rather than a person. Like something had come along and taken everything from inside. Physically speaking, his back was in pain from the uneven floor of the cave. Otherwise, he felt nearly decent. Far from feeling good, but equally distant from the torturous experience he'd expected. He raised his hands to confirm his hazy memories. His skin was coated in burns, but they looked older than they should have been.

He couldn't say the rest of his body looked or felt quite right either. Even his hands seemed alien as he had lost what limited muscle he'd managed to keep during the long trip to Bastion. His limbs were nearly inhuman in their frailty. All he could do was laugh incredulously as his heart tried to flip and spin in his chest. At least his throat felt better, although it was still as dry and coarse as sand.

The Certainty hadn't left him. It still gripped his heart and pulsed with it. It held his lungs and forced them to move. In the same way, he felt its desire saturating the rest of his body, trying to force him into movement. But unlike with his magic, or with his heart and lungs, it struggled to move his limbs for him. He'd felt his magic move his body before, but Apparently, the Certainty struggled to copy the feat. Or maybe it just wanted him to think it did.

Sol concentrated on finding the remnants of his Mana. It came to him quickly. Far too quickly compared to the usual concentration it required. There should have been little of the substance left. While he'd been surprised to find himself gathering Aether while within the walls, it hadn't been a significant amount in the grand scheme, and he'd used much of what he'd gathered experimenting with magic in the halls. He felt the grin growing on his lips as he discovered the small pool of energy had more than tripled since the last time he'd woken.

When Sol was done inspecting his Mana, he reached for his other magic. His Essence, as Milias called it, was barely there at all. Simply feeling it made his ears ring and his thoughts dim. The Certainty moved again, walling off the Essence. Forbidding it. The sense of emptiness that assailed him rallied and worsened as he tried to focus and fight the Certainty, so he stopped after the briefest struggle.

Truth be told, Sol didn't care to move. He was weary in a way that sleep couldn't change, but sleep was all he wanted to do. But the Certainty wouldn't have that. It willed him to move, and as soon as Sol had a passing thought of acceptance to it, it was moving his body for him. Nails stabbed into his knees as he took to his feet, but he stood all the same. Sol could only sigh and accept that his death was not yet at hand. But it would be soon.

Even with the Certainty forcing his heart to beat, it was a close thing. His chest ached, and his forced breath was ragged. His body was both heavy and light, but the Certainty kept him moving.

It was only after catching his breath from the exertion of standing that he truly began to examine his surroundings. It did little to settle the debate raging in his head about the reality of his situation.

The massive cavern he'd found himself in was mystifying. Most of the floor was rough and uneven, almost like rolling hills, but there were pathways worn through the stone. Trails built not by the tools of the empire, but by many feet over many, many years. There were buildings carved in the stone as well. Relics of some lost and ancient people.

There were translucent statues. Thousands of the things lined the cavern that he could see. Some were posed in heroic stances. Others looked to be cowering from some unseen danger. Others seemed to be going about daily life as if they were ordinary people frozen in time.

Directly to his side the cave floor was scorched, the black mark crossing the short distance to the unnaturally smooth wall he'd escaped from. Between him and it was his pistol, as well as bits of heavily burned cloth, and the acorn that was miraculously only lightly burned. He bent down with a groan and took the largest piece of the fabric he could see, the remnants of his shirt, and tied it around his otherwise naked waist. He also took the acorn, wrapping it in cloth and tying the small bundle to his makeshift loincloth.

As the Certainty faintly willed him to move towards the center of the cavern, Sol instead approached the closest of the statues. It wasn't far from where he'd slept. It was of someone running towards the flat gray walls. The figure was made of thick translucent glass. Most of it was green, but there were lines of blue and red coursing through its body. The statues black hair was so ornately detailed and fragile that looking at it flutter in a nonexistent breeze made it seem like the glass woman would burst into motion at any moment. As if she was frozen in a sprint, her body hunched over the glass infant she carried.

The child had similar coloring if having a little more blue than green. Both were heavily detailed with minuscule imperfections that made the bodies look nearly real, yet inhumanly beautiful. The only oddity that Sol could see, other than the pure bizarre nature of the glass statues, was a hole through the chest of the running woman.

"What is this place?" Sol asked aloud. No one answered. Sol raised his hand to feel along the woman's face, then her hair. It felt like touching a person. It was warm to the touch, more than the air around it. He pushed, almost expecting the glass to give like flesh, or for the statue's eyes to give him an indignant glare. It didn't give, and her eyes didn't move. Instead, the statue rocked in place as he pushed as if the simple touch had unbalanced it. The statue toppled, hit the ground, and shattered.

Sol stepped back in shock and guilt, looking to the other statues, nearly feeling their judgment upon him. He shook his head to rid himself of the sensation and willed himself to ignore the strange things, as the Certainty desired.

Visible even in the well-trodden areas of the cave were ripples inside the stone, as if the rock was water flowing out in small waves from the center of the cavern, where there was an enormous metal sphere that the Certainty desired him to reach.

It was an AeC thrice the size of the Behemoths. Thousands of cables hung through the air, connecting the device to the cave ceiling in as many places. The machine was held aloft by a massive pedestal in the shape of a gilded hand. The foundation of the pedestal was designed to look like the arm of the hand. It was lit by two sapphire spires that illuminated a single door between them.

Sol laughed in surprise at what he saw. Only lunacy in design could explain why the tunnels had brought him there, to the single most vulnerable place Bastion could have. It produced Ether from the Aether in the air. It was the very heart of the stronghold, and he'd been given access to it.

Sol forced his arcane vision into use, but it only served to make his confusion grow. The Behemoth's condenser had been like a magnet, pulling all Aether to itself with a fierce current that couldn't be swayed. Its larger twin in the cavern behaved differently. No Aether flowed to it. Instead, he watched as Aether flowed out of the structure, albeit in small quantities. The Aether floated through the air and stone, mostly not venturing too far from the condenser, occasionally seeming to flicker out of existence for no reason at all, some specks of it floating into the walls of the cavern.

Some of the substance flowed to him as if by gravity. When it neared him, it would begin the same spiral into his Stigma that it had in the walls, simply in greater amounts.

Sol moved, and the Aether seemed not to care, shifting with him to follow its self-made pattern and slow journey to him. It explained why he'd woken with more Mana than he'd expected. Mana was only Aether transformed by the Stigma.

Whatever the AeC did to Aether, it first collected the substance in a manner reminiscent of the Stigma of an Aetherweaver, but with far greater strength. The presence of an AeC prevented even the strongest Weavers from collecting Aether. That was how it was supposed to be at least. It was how it had been on the Behemoth. Sol closed his arcane sight and began walking towards the structure.

After a few minutes, he was able to make out the various dwellings of the cavern in more detail. Small places carved into the rock with pickaxe and chisel. Shadowed openings occasionally led into the cavern floor, looking to lead elsewhere in the prehistoric cavern. Most structures he passed were carved out just as the buildings were, but others seemed to be naturally formed. He passed by more and more of the statues. Hundreds of them were scattered across the cavern, and more came into sight as he moved. Each was different, but nearly all wore some look of fear. One or two were smiling, although those were only the ones that were going about daily life, and only a few of those had such a look. However, the statues he could see were far outnumbered by the piles of shattered glass.

As he slowly moved closer to the center of it all, he started to find arches and other designs carved into the stone in ornate fashions, although considerably worn with the passage of eons. As he looked, he began to feel that what he saw wasn't the remains of some tribal village, but what remained of a once mighty city. He couldn't pinpoint why he felt as much. Perhaps it was the scale, and the tunnels he passed that seemed to weave themselves even further underground. Maybe it was how grand some of the sculpted cavern would have been in its prime. Before the passage of time had coated much of it with dust.

Sol couldn't imagine what beings had carved out a home in the cavern, let alone a city. The whole idea of it brought a smile to his face. He was in a place few had the privilege to see or know of, even when the world had been filled with life. He walked within the ruins of history, or so he told himself. He couldn't say without many years of study. Years he knew he could never have.

As if knowing his thoughts, the ground began to shake. Sol fell to his hands and knees and looked about frantically. The entire cavern was violently shaking, but the source seemed to spread out from the smooth walls rather than the floor. The glass statues, the thousands which remained, collapsed and shattered. Sol's hair stood on end at the sounds of the shattering, loud enough to echo through the massive space yet almost soft at the same time.

It was a short-lived event, but Sol's heart hurt more than ever as it pumped adrenaline through his veins. Hesitantly he returned to his feet, with minimal pain, and continued his crossing. He moved wearily and cautiously from that point onward.

Perhaps a minute later the world shook again, although far less violently than the first time. Sol still dropped and kept his eyes out for anything collapsing. Once again, the quake was short-lived, and nothing fell on or near him.

The third time the cavern shook was several minutes later. Sol braced himself but kept to his feet. The fourth time came sometime after, and it continued as a new repetition to his life. He kept watching every tall stone cut structure, but the ancient things seemed to be sturdier than they had a right to be, although he could swear that he saw dust falling in front of one of the crystal lights a few times.

The Certainty had him nearly sprinting the final hundred or so meters to the AeC's tower sized pedestal, although it was closer to a fast walk given how weary he was. He didn't have much choice in the matter. It was the will of the Certainty, and as he drew closer its control over his body became stronger. He reached the door as another quake began, and he hurried inside. It was foolish to think the building would protect him against anything that could shake Bastion, but all the same, he did feel safer inside.

Once the shaking stopped, all thought of it left his mind. The room he found himself occupying had a half dozen doors leading to other places. There were stone statues of Milias in the center of the room, standing proudly with hands extended in welcome, with the words *Salvation Awaits* carved below their feet. They formed a rough circle on a raised dais, so the emperor's grinning visage could be seen from anywhere in the room. But that was not what held Sol's gaze, nor what caused him to smile. At the stone feet of the statues were vials. They were coated in a fine layer of dust, but they were unmistakable as vials of water and protein paste.

Sol couldn't help himself from rushing to the statues. He grabbed a vial of water, wiped the dust from it, unsealed the thing, and put it to his lips before the Certainty stopped him. It didn't simply will him to stop with a suggestion. It was a command. It willed him to move no further. Do not drink. Sol grit his teeth and struggled against the sensation. To his relief, the foreign mind didn't have absolute control of his body yet, and he could ignore it. The water touched his tongue, and at that moment the Certainty stopped trying to resist.

The water was cool, gritty, nearly oily, and it was the most delicious thing ever to cross his lips. He'd grabbed a second vial before he bent over in pain. He nearly threw up the precious water as his body rebelled, just as it had during his hallucination in the walls. It lasted only a few moments, but he found himself curled on the floor and unable to remember when he'd fallen. He moved to stand but froze as he felt the world shake yet again. The statues of Milias audibly groaned, as if threatening to follow in the path of the glass statues before them.

Sol rolled as best he could, and set his body ready to spring, all his joints screamed in protest as his shaking muscles were pulled taut. The shaking stopped, and Sol looked up to the nearest statue. It hadn't changed, but Sol swore the thing was staring at him in turn, and it was smirking.

His attention returned to the vial in his hand, the one he had yet to drink. He'd known better than to drink water so quickly after so long without it, but he'd never been so thirsty, not even on the Scion. In any case, the pain was mostly over but for lingering nausea that was unlikely to leave him anytime soon.

He opened the second vial and slowly drank its contents, the Certainty no longer seemed to care. The water was as oily as he'd first thought and tasted oddly sweet with a strange burn at the back of the throat. He began to wonder if it was really water at all, but he didn't care that much. It felt wondrous to have something in his stomach again, even if it hurt. He was becoming far too accustomed to nothing.

Other than the resistance with the vials, the Certainty had relaxed once he'd enter the building. It continued to move his heart and lungs, but otherwise, it seemed content to wait. With some relief, Sol took the chance to examine the room, once the second vial was emptied.

The place couldn't be considered bland. The walls, whatever substance they were made of, were carved with intricate images and symbols that looked like the Simuran's runes. They were arching lines and curved lettering that looked to be somewhere between archaic and modern language.

More attention-grabbing, after his thirst was quenched, were the footprints that led through the thick dust. They were made by small feet, belonging to either a Simuran or a child. They traveled from one doorway to another, then back again.

Sol moved against the wall, feeling the engravings against his skin, and edged closer to the nearest of the doors the footprints led to. The door was metal and decorative, although it had begun to show signs of great age. The hinges groaned as Sol opened them.

The chamber within was empty of life despite the footprints. There were a dozen platforms that were coated in Arcane runes and symbols. All were covered in dust, except for the platform the footprints led to and from. That one was clean enough to make out the faint sparkles of rubies embedded in the runes.

"What is this?" Sol asked in a hoarse whisper.

He slipped into the room and made his way by each of the platforms. They were at waist height with stairs leading up to them. Each was large enough to hold three people if they stood uncomfortably close.

"You know what they are," a voice whispered in Sol's ear. He spun, but there was no one in sight.

"Show yourself," Sol called.

"She would have been able to tell you, if only you'd asked," the voice whispered. Sol knew who it belonged to. It was the same voice that haunted him through the maze of corridors. The same voice he thought he remembered speaking to him as he had been dying.

"Don't be a coward Milias. Come out," Sol called. There was no answer. He took one more look around the chamber, and then returned to the first room. He'd half expected to see Milias waiting for him, or for the statues to of moved, but nothing had changed. Not a speck of dust had been moved, but that which was shifting as he walked.

"Milias," Sol called.

"So many dead for the sake of your pride. They're very efficient. You could have saved many of those poor people if only you risked sounding like the ignorant child you are at heart," the voice whispered.

"Don't play games with me," Sol said, "I know you're here. Stop hiding."

Laughter, boisterous and ridiculing, bounced through the room. One by one, the lights turned out, until all that remained came from the other doorway which the footsteps led to, and the small light which Sol had formed in his palm almost instinctively as the lights died.

"I wonder what you'll think of this," the voice whispered excitedly.

For a very brief second, Sol swore he heard Kiran's voice in his mind. But it was only for a moment, phantom words spoken on a wind that wasn't blowing. His heart quickened, but it was only when he touched the handle of the door that the pain in his chest made fear take hold. Still, he didn't slow. He opened the door and stepped through.

Thirteen caskets lined the walls. At least they looked to be caskets, topped with glass, each etched with a different design. Eleven of the things were closed and occupied by children. Each looked to be between one and five years old. They looked alive, but they were frozen in place. Locked in stasis.

"What is this?" Sol whispered in horror. No answers came. He walked along the caskets, examining each of the children. They were all different, but each bore the mark of an Aetherweaver on their naked bodies, a Stigma, that matched the design engraved on their respective casket. Sol came to the first of the empty containers, open as if in waiting.

The symbol etched into the glass was of a tree wrapped in flames. Sol stared at the empty place where there had once been a child. The soft fabric on which it once laid was still disturbed as if it had only just been moved, but all was coated in dust. Except for the footprints that led to the last of the caskets, which was similarly open.

"Come on then. There's one left to see," Milias said.

"No," Sol whispered, his heart shuddering against the control of the Certainty.

"Coward. Naive fool," Milias laughed gently. "I told you, for someone raised by a potent telepath you're far too trusting of your memories. Although, it would be more accurate to say you're too trusting of your missing ones."

"No," Sol said, feeling the Certainty struggling to control the beats of his heart.

"Don't you find it odd that the tomes you studied never mentioned memory loss as a result of an Awakening, much less such extensive loss."

"Strange things happen when one Awakens," Sol whispered.

"Is that what you've told yourself? Is that why you accepted your missing memories without questions? Isn't that in itself strange?"

Sol didn't answer. He didn't walk closer to the final casket, nor even look towards it. He held his breath as his mind spun in circles.

"Didn't you ever wonder why that woman hated you?" Milias asked. "I gave Kiran a choice you know, to change the woman's memories or not to. She thought it wrong to change memories concerning one's child. It didn't stop her from giving you the real child's emotions before she killed the original. If she hadn't, you likely would have forgotten that whole incident by now. Instead, she tried compassion and transformed you into a murderer. Long live compassion."

Sol's mouth opened and closed. His chest ached, and his eyes burned, but he made no sounds.

"We learned ever so much from all of you. Well, Maud did. I knew which of you prototypes would be useful, just not the correct process he needed for it."

"Prototypes?" Sol whispered.

"Oh yes. Bodies and minds are simple enough for me, but it took some doing to convince Maud to move his manipulation of souls into the realm of creating them. Well, strictly speaking, real souls can't be created artificially. We made a workaround for Simurans, so they did have true souls; else Maud wouldn't have moved on to such large-scale production. Absolute refusal. You prototypes, however... Well, I should tell you that he wept over each of you. His tender heart can barely cope with such tragic existences."

"No. No, no, no. No," Sol whispered. He found his back against one of the caskets. He could nearly hear the child inside screaming at him.

"Even I don't know what happens to the soul after it parts with the body. It moves on, goes somewhere, but my sight ends at the Veil. I do know that the transition through that Veil is a stressful one. You poor artificial things can't handle it. You break apart and return to the nothing you came from. It's poetic really."

"No," Sol whispered again. It was all he could say. His mind was in a storm, and it grasped to Milias' words like an anchor.

"She did a bad job with parts of that memory wipe, to be honest. I doubt you'll ever remember your time in stasis, but those last moments, when she took you from this place and to the Behemoth, I think she was hoping you'd remember that at some point. Then you could ask her about it. Trust me, she's been trying to scream things to you for *years*, but you've never failed to disappoint her," Milias said.

"That's impossible," Sol whispered, running a shaking hand across his forehead.

"It's quite easy actually. Didn't you *see* the teleport pads in the other room? One of them led to the Behemoth. Before Eddie showed up that is."

"This is insanity," Sol shook his head.

"Not quite," Milias said. Sol didn't know how he knew, but the man was grinning as he spoke. "It's something of a common practice for many. I've done it for myself several times over, or did you actually think that someone as powerful as myself was born in this dark and sad world?"

Sol felt the impression of the man leaning down to him, could nearly feel the air move as he whispered into Sol's ear.

"The real question thus far, dear Sol, is how are you hearing me speak?"

"What?" Sol asked, lost further by the question.

"The answer? You're not. At least not with your ears. You. Are. A prototype. My prototype," Milias said. But his tone shifted, and just as the man said, Sol could no longer hear him with his ears. The voice danced through his thoughts unfiltered.

I've always been here, in your shallow mind. I've watched you grow, and I've laughed at each and every mistake. They're numerous beyond the stars, not that you could ever know. They're so much better when seen from within. To feel your anguish as you experience failure time and time again.

"Get out of my head," Sol growled fearfully.

No, Milias said. *Tell me, Sol, do you want to know the trick to avoiding failure?*

Sol didn't answer. He clutched his head as he felt invisible fingers caressing his face and probing at his scars. Milias laughed gently as his unseen grip on Sol's head tightened.

I suppose you'll figure that one out in time. If you get that far. Honestly, I have a bad habit of explaining too much. It's practically a curse from the damned Sphere to those like me, so I'll hold back on that for now. I have more important advice for you today anyway. You see Sol, the others in this room, your siblings as it were, are brain dead. Their bodies are in stasis, their fragile souls not yet broken.

"Leave me alone," Sol finally managed to speak, arms wrapped around his throbbing head.

It happens when you or one of the others reaches the Fae. This world, this reality, will finally be allowed to end; as it should have eons ago. Then these poor children shall finally feel the peace of death. Unless you act now. Take the Essence that binds body and Soul. Nourish your body. Heal your wounds. Grow, and become something more than a failure of a man.

"Fuck you," Sol whispered. Milias scoffed.

We both know you didn't find your way here by accident or luck Sol, or do you think me or my Simurans would design the twisting walls to allow people in here? Do you really believe you had the strength of will to keep moving? To survive that which stalked you? Did luck make your explosive defective and weak? The answer is no, for there is no such thing as luck. There is only The Sphere. And you are protected by it.

Even when you drank that poisonous compound just minutes ago, The Sphere rewrote your biology and gifted you with immunity to all of it. Fifty-three lethal doses and two acids for good measure, only serving to make you more resilient. You are a law of The Sphere, of all things that exist in this dark age, akin to gravity and time itself. But not for much longer.

"What-"

What do you mean? Milias asked in a mocking tone. Then, to Sol's horror, Milias appeared in the air, floating above the floor. *That's not the right question.*

"Then what is the right question?" Sol ground his teeth.

We could start with what is The Sphere, Milias said, *but I could speak for a millennium, and you wouldn't understand. Instead, dear boy, think of The Sphere as reality itself. Not this world alone, but all the worlds that have yet to be consumed by The Strider and the Void. More important, is the Will of The Sphere, of which I am certain you know. You've felt it Sol, and that is a rare thing.*

The Sphere likes us to believe we can do whatever we wish. In a way, we can. It controls us not through honest puppetry as I do my slaves, but with distant walls. In the end, no matter how you turn and dance, no matter what strands you follow, The Sphere is the master of us all. It will change your destiny on a whim, caring not for what you've done or wish to do. If you choose to turn left, then left is the path to what The Sphere wants of you. Choose the path to your right, and it is the same. Move and dance as you will, believe the illusion that your choices matter, that is what it wants. In the end, if The Sphere commands us to bow, we all do as we are told.

My curse, my power, is in seeing all the walls it builds. I see all the ways it allows me to resist, but I can never escape it. Not even here, where The Sphere is weakest. The Void will not have me, nor you whom The Sphere still needs. But its weakness here did force it to break its own rules. It's inside of you Sol, manipulating you directly, no longer parading as luck nor chance.

It gives the illusion of your free will, but when you faced danger, it guided and forced your actions. When you thought fear or panic were moving you, it was The Sphere. It has been there all your life, driving you to come to this place. You feel it now not because it is new, but because you are close to death. Because you are a living corpse, alive only because The Sphere wills it so.

"The Certainty," Sol said. Milias smiled, and Sol's heart quivered as the Certainty almost seemed to tighten its grip.

Yes, that is the guise The Sphere has taken in its fight to keep you alive. It doesn't have a mind like you or me. It's not sentient in the same way. Perhaps it is greater than us, but I wouldn't know. Its Will is what decides the end of not all things, but anything. It cares not for the constructed morality of man, nor for what we may think of it. Only that its Will is enforced. At the moment, that means you will die in the near future. But it needs you still, and that gives you a chance to change your fate to another of The Sphere's choosing. That leads to the real question in all of this.

"And what is that?" Sol asked.

Which of your little troupe do you like the most? Milias asked curiously. *A little while ago it wouldn't matter what you think, but now it does. Now the weight falls to you. You can imagine how unnerved that would make them feel if they knew. To know that their lives depend on you. So, choose. Is it Kiran? Nemai? Or is it Mara? She is alive Sol. For the time being. How long that continues is partly up to you now.*

Sol shook his head and tried to ignore the phantom and his words. Hope rose in his heart when the man claimed that Mara lived. He tried to bury that hope, but Milias floated in front of him and laughed before his thoughts could become anything other than tumultuous despair.

You know you're weak Sol. You've always been weak. You're alive right now not because of your own strength, but because The Sphere needs you. But it only requires you until one member of your group is on the other side of that portal. Then you'll collapse, the portal will fail, and everyone still stuck here will die. The movement to the Fae is nearly instant. If you don't have the strength to stay alive, The Sphere will choose who to take and who to leave behind. So, tell me Sol, who is your favorite? Who do you hope outlives the rest?

Sol shut his eyes and took deep breaths, but the image of the emperor didn't leave him. The man continued to float in front of his sight as if self-illuminated in a dark room. His smile looked genuine, somewhere between curious and concerned.

Alternately, you could make the hard decision. You could choose to be strong. You could choose all of them, and even yourself. All it would take is a little mercy for these fake and mindless souls trapped in frozen flesh. I can tell you how to use your power, Sol. I can teach you how to heal yourself, and others, with much less risk of death. The Sphere will aid you in that no further, for you've nearly done all it desires. You've weakened yourself and now must rely on its mercy. Unless…

"No. You're just… just trying to trick me. To manipulate me. I will not kill. Not anyone," Sol said.

Every word ever spoken is manipulation in one shape or another. That is the very point of language. But just because I want something doesn't mean it wouldn't be best for you as well.

The man moved closer, and once more his voice sank to whispers.

The Sphere doesn't care which of you survives. Not really. It's flexible in that aspect. It only cares that one of you lives long enough to kill me. But you're not like them. If there really is some land of paradise or torture waiting for those that die; it is not waiting for you. Your soul will not survive the journey through the Veil. All you are will break. Tell me, what would your friends choose? For you? For themselves? They wouldn't hesitate. Do you honestly think yourself better than them?

Sol opened his mouth to speak, but he didn't know what he would say. The Certainty continued to beat his heart and move his lungs, but it cared not for what he did next.

"Why should I believe you?" Sol asked. "How do I know that this thing in my head isn't you?"

There's no way you can know for certain, Milias said. *But that choice is one of the small freedoms we're allowed. The choice to die here, or to be one of those that survives a little longer. The Sphere doesn't care for those details. Only that I die at the hands of you or the others. That in-between is all we ever have. Perhaps that doesn't seem like much of a cage to you, but the walls are closer than you can know.*

Sol turned his head to look upon the emptied caskets. The first marked with a tree aflame, the other with a star.

Chapter 22

"You did good," Kiran said warmly. Mara smiled and helped her teacher up from the floor. As she pulled, the Simuran grabbed and twisted her arm, slamming Mara into the ground with a blade against her throat.

"Vigilance is necessary even after victory. At times more so than in battle."

"You're just angry because I finally beat you," Mara managed to say. Kiran released her hold and helped the soldier to her feet.

"It was well earned. I have little left to teach," Kiran said.

"Don't say that," Mara grinned and rubbed the back of her neck. "It was one time. I've got a lot to learn still."

Kiran didn't answer. She strolled across the training field to sit on a large bench that faced the sea. Sol was already resting there with a book in hand. Mara followed the Simuran, enjoying the breeze that tried to dry her sweat-soaked clothes as she took the spot between her teacher and Sol.

For a time, they sat and watched the sun creep ever closer to the horizon. The air smelled of flowers, a scent the wind carried from fields of grass and blossoming plants that grew along the beach between them and the water.

"Quite the sight, isn't it?" Mara asked.

"Yeah," Sol answered. Mara snorted.

"You're not even looking in the right direction," she said. Sol briefly looked up from his book and looked at the horizon.

"Yeah. Pretty," he said, shortly returning his attention to the book. Mara shook her head with a soft laugh, then leaned back on the bench and stretched. Something pinched her back, and she hissed.

"Is everything alright?" Kiran asked from beside her.

"I think I'm going to be sore from the spar," Mara said with a smile. Kiran nodded and turned her attention back to the horizon with a peaceful half smile. Her face twitched several times; then she returned to contentment.

Mara felt another pinch along her spine. She held in the sound of her pain and annoyance, but then the sky flashed black and orange, followed by a dark blue and a blinding white. Mara shook her head, but Kiran and Sol seemed not to notice the flashes.

"-hear me?" a feminine voice asked.

"Who's there?" Mara asked, grabbing her sparring blade and spinning in place. Kiran was on her feet just as quickly, setting herself against Mara's back. Sol moved beside them and created a spear of light above his hand.

"-Trying...idiot," the voice continued. Many words were lost as the speaker's voice grew louder and quieter at random. Mara felt another stab at her back, and for the briefest of moments, the trees surrounding the training field turned into metal towers. Then she was back to back with Kiran once more.

"Leave now, and we won't kill you," Mara said jovially. She reached behind her and grabbed her pistol from its holster in the small of her back.

"I don't think she even tried to leave defenses," the voice said more clearly, "Gods, that Simuran can be terrifying."

The air in front of Mara distorted then ruptured as a tall woman with black hair, a shapely form, and a mischievous grin seemingly formed from dust and shadow. "Oh. This is gorgeous. Seriously, did she use her imagination or borrow from yours?"

"I warned you," Mara hissed. Small bolts of plasma sang through the air, and into the woman's head. Shortly afterward a wooden blade cracked against the woman's neck.

"Oh, calm down," the woman said, as if unharmed, "I'm here to...well, it's complicated. But it's adjacent to helping. And getting help. And escaping. Yes, mostly about that last part."

"What are you going on about?" Mara asked. Beside her, Sol took some strange arcane stance.

"Hello Mara, it's good to meet you in person, so to speak," the woman said. Then she snapped her fingers, and Mara found herself in a white void, alone with the woman.

"... Nemai?" Mara asked.

"Precisely," the woman smiled, "but really? No comment about the change in scenery? No questions? Lamentations? No begging for your life?"

"It happens here," Mara shrugged.

"Ah. And what do you think this place is, exactly?"

"A dream," Mara said.

"Oh. Well. That's actually correct. Damn. I thought this would be fun. When did you figure it out?"

"I don't know. When everything kept going just the way I wanted it to I suppose. Far too convenient to be real."

"Huh. I don't think most would notice for a while yet. Or they'd think they'd died and moved on."

"Well heaven isn't real, if that's what you mean," Mara shrugged, "that only left a few options."

"Fair enough," Nemai snorted. "But then why were you so eager to fight a moment ago?"

"I was getting bored," Mara shrugged, "figured the dream was giving me something to do."

Nemai stared at the soldier for a few moments, then shook her head, and snapped her fingers again. A simple table with two chairs appeared in the void, along with a tea set. Mara took her seat, observing Nemai.

"So why are you here?" Mara asked.

"I said it before. It's complicated. But honestly, I expected to be answering your other questions for a while first. Aren't you at all curious why you haven't woken up?"

"Not really," Mara shrugged. "I assume Kiran put me here. She must have a good reason."

Nemai scoffed and shook her head. "You trust her that much?"

"I don't have much choice," Mara said with a shrug.

"She's as fallible as the rest of us. More in some ways. She's a Simuran."

"So that's why you're here?" Mara asked.

"No, and yes," Nemai sighed. She took a drink of her tea, then gestured to Mara's cup. The soldier shook her head.

"Not until I've tried the real thing," she said.

"It's a good flavor. I took the taste directly from my memory. I doubt most would be able to taste the difference between this and the real thing. I can't."

"All the more reason," Mara said.

"I can understand that," Nemai nodded and gave a faint smile. "If you don't have any questions then..."

"I have a few," Mara said, leaning forward. "How did you force the dream to change? I've been at its mercy. Not that I've minded that much."

"Experience," Nemai shrugged.

"Telepathy?" Mara asked.

"No, but it's related."

"Well, I think Sol was right about you. You're very skilled at answering questions in informative ways," Mara said sarcastically. Nemai sighed.

"Of everything going on, I didn't think *this* would be what we'd be talking about, that's all. I was in stasis for over a millennia Mara. Mind and body connected and all that," Nemai said. Mara scowled.

"Kiran said something about that. Mind and body are symbiotic, but not the same. Something like that," she said. Nemai nodded.

"Yeah, that's the idea. Father said something like that before I went into stasis. I didn't know what it meant back then. I only thought I did. I suppose Kiran didn't explain it to you either."

"She didn't," Mara said. Nemai sighed, her eyes going dark and sullen.

"It means that in stasis only the body is frozen. The mind... continues," Nemai said.

"What?" Mara asked.

"It's not so bad for most people," Nemai said, raising her hands. "They are connected, so the mind *is* slowed, and time moves quickly. Very quickly I was led to believe. It's like a dreamless sleep. For those with weak minds. For those with stronger minds, time passes more slowly. For me, maybe a year in the mind for every ten my body was frozen. It's impossible to say exactly."

"You were frozen for a thousand years," Mara muttered, then shook her head. "I don't want to imagine that."

"My mind isn't the strongest out there. Far from it. But," Nemai paused and stared at the table in front of her, apparently gathering her thoughts. Mara tried to speak, to tell her she didn't need to go into detail, but Nemai simply raised her hand again until she looked up with a faint smile and a distant look in her eyes.

"When it started for me there was no manufactured dream. I just existed with my thoughts. No sight. No sound. No sense of touch, or taste, or smell. As times passed, I lost myself. Some unconscious part of me learned how to shape the abyss. I thought I'd woken and escaped a dozen times before I realized what it was. I didn't understand why things kept going back. I thought it was Milias' doing. I know better now.

A while after that, I learned how to shape things consciously. For a while, a long while I think, I enjoyed making things. Cities and worlds. People. Anything I could imagine. But they were lacking because my mind isn't strong enough to hold anything realistic for long. Not consciously. So, I began to dream again, forgetting what was real and losing the ability to shape the dream. Then I remembered it was fake. Then I forgot. And on and on it cycled."

"I'm sorry," Mara said quietly.

"Even now. With you, Sol, and Kiran. I don't know if you're real. It feels real, like dreams always do when you're in them. I think you're real as well, but I've thought others were real before. It's a terrible thing to question your sanity. Once you truly ask yourself if you're sane, and you honestly don't know the answer, you can never stop asking."

"Gods," Mara shook her head.

"Yeah," Nemai said. "But the tea is still good." She took a long drink from her cup before filling it again. Mara averted her eyes and stared into the blank void for a time before speaking.

"How do you cope with so much time? So many memories…"

"Some you forget," Nemai nodded. "Others you condense and hide from yourself. Not forgotten, but not easy to find either. Important memories, or the ones you feel are important, are the ones to remember. Those you force yourself to relive time and time again. That keeps me as I am, else I might act like the ancient lady I really am up here," Nemai tapped her head.

Mara nodded and stared out at the abyss as her neck throbbed and twitched.

"So, Kiran went through that as well then?" She eventually asked.

"She must have. But she was in for longer than me. And her mind is stronger. Much, much stronger, even if most of it's being used to hold her in sway."

"But with that much time, why didn't she free herself?"

"She'd have worked on it," Nemai said quietly. "But it's complicated."

"I want to understand," Mara said firmly.

"The stronger a mind becomes, the more rigid it is in turn. The slower it accepts change. It's like a defense mechanism against manipulation. But if it is manipulated properly, if it is shaped to be a certain way, then it can take a very, very long time to change back to something more natural. It may be gradual. It may be a sudden snap. In either case, there are consequences. Severe ones."

"What kind of consequences?" Mara asked.

"To be honest, I'm not completely sure what it looks like. I only ever learned the theories. I've never seen it in person. There are too many ways for mind and sanity to break to list any consequences conclusively. Best to pray it doesn't happen. Or if it does, pray the madness isn't one that makes her violent."

Mara nodded but said nothing. Nemai waited a few moments for any comment before she began speaking again.

"To answer your question, I think Kiran's been trying to change for a very, very long time. Which is good, but right now I don't know if she's winning, or if any of us will survive either way it goes. Any other questions?"

"Yes," Mara said, then she shook her head, "but maybe we should get to why you're here."

"Well, once we're done talking, I'm going to wake you up. After that, I'm going to do something extraordinarily stupid."

"Do I want to know?"

"I wouldn't," Nemai said, "So I'd guess you would. Suffice to say it's likely to kill us or lead us to the Fae. So be ready to move very quickly when you wake up."

"What are you doing?" Mara asked sternly.

"Exactly what Milias wants me to do I suspect. But I must do it. Something is breaking into Bastion, Mara. It's breaking the walls themselves. Kiran trusted you to me and disappeared. I delayed as much as I could, but she's nowhere to be found, and we're running out of time."

Mara turned her eyes to the flawless floor, then spoke again.

"And how is Sol?" she asked.

"He's missing as well," Nemai answered, "and honestly, if we don't find him then we're all dead anyway."

"Right, he needs to be the one that opens the way to the Fae. That's what you told us before. That is unless you're simply insane and the Fae isn't real."

"Basically," Nemai nodded.

"Huh. Fuck," Mara quietly laughed, "it all went to hell without me, didn't it?"

"To be fair, what happened to you was the start of things," Nemai said. Mara nodded, then grabbed the cup before her and peered at its contents. Nemai seemed to be preparing herself to say something, but Mara waved her off as soon as she tried to speak. The once princess gave her an irritated look.

"Don't you want to know what's happened to you?" she asked. Mara shook her head.

"I think I know what happened. It's a blur, but I remember some of it. Either way, I'm going to find out soon enough," she answered, with one hand rubbing the back of her neck.

"I suppose," Nemai sighed. "I guess that means you're ready to wake up then."

"I am. But you're not ready to do whatever it is you're going to do, are you?"

"No," Nemai shook her head, "I'm not. But I can't think of anything else that I... that we could do."

"Well, I wouldn't mind having some time to prepare myself for whatever you're doing. You could wait for a while after waking me up."

"I can try," Nemai nodded. "I suppose that means the next time you see me, if we're alive, will be the real thing."

"As far as *you* know," Mara said. Then she gave a slight smile, and turned her cup over, spilling its contents across the table. Nemai narrowed her eyes.

"That is cruel," Nemai said slowly. Then she gave a lopsided grin. "Cruel, but true."

Chapter 23

Nemai watched Mara stir in her distant bed. She couldn't make out the details, but the woman was checking her neck and her back. Nemai wondered what it felt like. For a moment she considered breaking back into the woman's mind, but she held back and instead turned to the waiting console.

As if on cue, the palace shook. Nemai braced herself as she listened to the distant towers groaning from the force that made them sway. She didn't need to look to know that more of the beautifully fake sky was dying; to see the stone dust raining down on the hidden city. She'd delayed for far too long as it was. Still, as the shaking stopped, she turned back to the courtyard. Mara was busy picking herself up from the ground where she'd fallen. The woman fell again a moment later, despite the world being still.

Nemai turned her back to the window again and stared at the display, where the command prompt waited for her. She took a step, and the world shook once more. Nemai took a deep breath and whispered an apology to Mara. The soldier wouldn't have time after all.

She made her way to the console. Her fluttering heart made her hesitate for a moment longer. She pinched the skin of her arm, twisting it until she couldn't help but grimace in pain. Only then did she speak into the microphone.

"Get ready to run," she announced to every living soul in the city. Then she reached over and activated the so-called Omnipurge. As she authorized the process, a progress

bar appeared. It had barely started moving when the entire
display went black.

Nemai rushed back to her window to watch whatever
she'd unleashed do her bidding. As she moved, a sound
began to rise. A mechanical grinding screech that started at a
whisper, but quickly grew loud and painful to hear.

Far below, Mara was on her hands and knees,
crawling closer to the barrier. Even that looked difficult for
the soldier. Nemai whispered another apology as the more
sounds joined the ever-growing growl.

It was only when the shaking began again that Nemai
first saw what was happening. Dust rained down from the
sky, the ground shook violently, far more so than any time
before, and yet the towers didn't sway as they had before.
The ground beneath them ruptured from the motion, and
small specks of stone flew up into the air, to land on
whichever tower was closest, to stick to its side.

These specs were followed by larger pieces that began
to tear themselves free of the ground and sky. Those were
followed in turn by pipes and metal beams that were
bending and ripping themselves out of the stone that
entombed them. As the ruins of the city were pulled through
the air, they shattered into small particles that collected on
the towers, the miraculously undamaged magnetic beacons
that stood in perfect alignment, attracting not only metal but,
stone and dirt as well.

Nemai turned her eyes to the crawling Mara and was
relieved to see that the towers weren't pulling her through
the device attached to her spine. But it was grabbing at
something that laid beneath the Plaza. Stones violently cut
through the air as metal ripped itself free. Above the soldier,
massive boulders rained down from the dome. Much of
what fell was broken down further and pulled to the towers.
Some of the ruins landed in the plaza before the towers
began to pull them.

The beast, whatever monstrosity was breaking in,
shook the city again. Fissures cut through the weakened

dome, and slabs of stone hundreds of meters wide began to rain upon the city. The slabs turned and twisted as they fell, colliding with the still standing towers before shattering.

A hole formed, nearly above the palace. Through it, Nemai could see the sky. Dark clouds lit by flames and lava that was hidden from her sight. Then a beast, some horrid thing, moved over the hole and hid the sky from her once more.

It was only then that the barrier surrounding the Palace shimmered for the final time and went out. Far below, Mara crawled ever closer. The growl of the machines expanded, thundering in Nemai's ears. There was the screeching of metal being torn apart, and the ground beneath her feet began to move. Her tower twisted as it was pulled in every direction.

Nemai opened her hand, and shadows moved as if a physical thing, gathering in her hand and shaping into a dark blade no longer than her forearm. It took less than a second for her to feel the cold handle pressing against her skin. Still, it was barely quick enough as her tower was torn away from the rest of the palace. It fell and spun, the gold plates that covered it transforming to yellowed sand that flowed through the air. The tower crumbled as it was pulled, all within it stretched and sheered.

The first piece of the debris that hit her was stone. It slammed into her shoulder, and she felt her arm go numb. The pure force of the impact sent her into a spinning fall. Before she could touch the floor of the tower, another small piece of the fortress hit her chest. She fought to stay conscious as all air left her lungs and her eyes went dark. All she knew was she was spinning through the sky. She tightened her grip on the cold handle of her weapon, trying desperately to do something she knew was possible but had never done.

She was a few dozen meters from the ground when her vision returned. As it did, she felt a deep cold seep into her veins. Not like the frost of winter, of ice and snow. It was the cold of the grave. Maliciously empty and ever-present in the darkness of all worlds. The cold seeped into her head and her mind, and she felt her body breaking apart at the seams. She became shadow made physical, a mist that tried to dissipate. She struggled to control it, her body in a million parts.

Her form fell to the ground at a slow pace as the palace broke into ever smaller pieces, sending the debris howling into her, and through her. Every piece took part some her shadow with it, though she pulled and willed what she could back to her, some parts of her were lost each time something passed through her.

She hit the ground and spread out like a puddle at the impact. She pulled her body together, the shadowed mass that remained spun and coalesced, transforming back to flesh and blood.

The body that formed was her own, covered in unnatural wounds from the parts of her that had been torn away. Cuts and scrapes both on her skin and within her body. Her hands took hold of the shaking ground, and she forced herself to breathe, only to cough up blood and bits of flesh. The cold was still in her veins and in her bones, but she knew it would leave with time, so she crawled, much as Mara had, across the ruins of the plaza. More and more the ground was torn apart as the towers of the city pulled things to them. Nemai tried to find the soldier, but all she could see was chaos.

In her short time since falling the mechanical whirl of the towers had become a shrill scream, a howl that would hide Nemai's voice even from her own ears had she tried to speak. Yet there were still the rhythmic sounds of the beast breaking through the dome. Nemai couldn't help but look. She could see part of the creature through the cracked dome. It was moving, writhing as if made of many smaller pieces, its details hard to make out in the darkness. As she looked, liquid fire dripped out from some inner crevice of the beast.

It lit only a small portion of the monstrosity, and for less than a moment, but it was enough.

The thing was nightmares made real. Its body was more fluid than not, a putrid liquid held together by unseen membranes. Each of the monstrosity's limbs had a thousand eyes that looked about in every which way, mostly inward, yet the beast was blind, for the pupils of the eyes were opened maws from which limbs reached out, nearly human but for their size, reaching as if they could claw through the air and escape from some unknowable torment.

Nemai retched, once more splattering blood across the ground. She couldn't feel the mind of the beast. While its limbs were close, the bulk of its body had to be distant. All the same, she could feel her thoughts clouding from the simple sight of the beast.

A hand shook Nemai, and then she spun, shadowed blade taking form in her hand as she screamed, ready to stab and cut whatever thing dared touch her. Another hand grabbed her wrist and twisted. She dropped the blade, it hit the ground silently and returned to shadow. Only then did Nemai see that the one who grabbed her had a familiar face.

Mara was even paler than was normal for her. Her red hair had little of the luster it had in the world of dreams where they'd spoken, and it was streaked with gray.

Nemai lunged and embraced the woman. Mara didn't seem to know how to react at first, settling for a couple pats on the back after freezing. She was trying to say something, but no matter how close the woman's mouth was to Nemai's ear, the chaos surrounding them hid all other sounds.

She clung to the soldier and felt herself begin to weep. Part of her felt ashamed, but for the most part, she didn't care. She clung as tightly as she could manage, feeling the warmth of another body touching hers as the memory of the monster above wouldn't leave her mind. She shook and sobbed, but all too soon the soldier's powerful limbs pushed them apart and held her at length.

To Nemai's surprise, the look Mara gave her was not of annoyance nor anger. It was a look filled with worry and fear, but not for herself. Nemai felt it herself a moment later, the concern the other woman felt for her. She'd been so distraught at the sight of the beast that her mind hadn't even noticed the soldier crawling close to her. Nemai nearly embraced the woman again but held herself back. Mara mouthed something Nemai couldn't understand, then the soldier grabbed her by the arm and dragged her across the ground.

Mara crawled on all fours. Even with that, she managed to slip from time to time. Luckily, they weren't going far. Nemai was pulled into a hole in the ground, where some large pipe or cable had dug out a tunnel as it was drawn to the towers. Mara took her several meters into the unnatural cave until they could barely see the outside world.

The soldier placed her back against the stone. She was breathing heavily and sweating profusely. Nemai hugged the woman's arm. Mara ignored her, staring at the outside world as her body shook, although Nemai couldn't say if it was from weariness or the fear the woman felt. Either way, she turned her gaze to the same place.

The beast was hidden in shadow and flowing dust. More of the dome was gone. Flecks of shadow fell to the hidden streets and park below. Both knew what fell into the city was the Rot Beasts, spreading the plague that was their existence. Neither of them wore armor. Their skin was bare, but for the same pale gray clothes. They wouldn't last long once the beasts reached them, but luckily the things seemed to be coming only from the edges of the remaining dome. Out of instinctive fear or loyalty, most of the Rot Beasts kept a distance from the massive creature that was busy breaking through the center of the dome. Whatever the cause, it gave the survivors a little more time.

Not even the smallest piece of the original towers could be seen under the debris that covered them. They weren't separate anymore, the spaces between them filled with metal fragments and bits of stone, wrapped in a sand-like coating of gold from the palace. From time to time something would collide with the mass. If the debris was large enough the things it hit would shift and groan, but overall, they were still.

Nemai and Mara watched as the beast destroyed more and more of the dome. It seemed a lifetime had passed before Nemai felt the first of the Rot Beast's approaching. It was large, but nothing like the beast above. It was followed by many others, encroaching on their tunnel as if they could smell them. Maybe they could. Nemai knew she should warn Mara, that they should crawl deeper into the tunnel, but she couldn't see the point of it. Milias had won. The Omnipurge had done nothing but weaken the dome and allow the Rot in.

The beasts couldn't have been far from sight when the whirling of the machines came to an end. It was shocking at first, but the silence was quickly filled with the sound of moving creatures and the agonized groans of the beast above. The thing began to lower some of its mass, the enormity of it was beyond what Nemai could fathom, for as the creature reached in as a writhing mass of tendrils and liquid flesh, she finally began to feel its mind. Alien and ancient beyond time, broken and filled with malice and hunger. Its presence pushed into her thoughts, and she felt herself begin to dim, her mind lessening and unraveling from the simple existence of the creature. Beside her, Mara grabbed her head and groaned.

As the beast reached into the Plaza, the towers *screamed*, hiding the sounds of the creature once more. Just as the towers had pulled everything in, they began to push. It wasn't a gradual change. All was still, and in the next moment every scrap of debris was exploding outward with all the force Bastion could muster. Mara and Nemai covered their ears as the beasts roared with ten thousand throats.

Then the silence returned, and Nemai dared to look, only to see something she'd never expected.

Nemai grabbed Mara by one hand and formed her small blade in the other. With a wince of pain, she pushed the outer layers of her skin to become shadowed mist and coated both of them with it. Mara reached for her pistol as the substance moved over them.

"It's me," Nemai said, her voice near a whisper. Mara gave her a look between fear and confusion, but Nemai ignored it. She pulled Mara to her feet and helped the woman walk. They climbed toward the surface. The cold of the shadow worked to hold much of the heat at bay. Even then, Nemai could feel what remained of her skin slowly heating despite the ice that seemed to be coursing through her veins. They walked until they could look out from the mouth of their tunnel but went no further.

The city was gone. Not a single tower stood. The dome was gone, along with the painted walls and all the beasts. The ground that remained was so smooth it looked as a mirror painted a bright red from heat. Beyond that was the crater where Bastion sat, where the emperor's enemies had used their most powerful weapons to incinerate the mountain. There was no longer a steep curve leading to the rim of the crater. The towers and their gathered shrapnel had cut through bedrock just as it had the stone of the city.

Above the flat expanse was a round hole in the dark clouds. The sky was clear, showing a night sky touched by the earliest fingers of dawn. But it was not the sky Nemai knew, filled with lights and beauty. It was an empty sky without stars nor the three moons.

Mara let out a gurgling laugh, mixed with a strange sob. Nemai couldn't look, but the joy that filled the soldier was enough to make her smile. Nemai tightened her grip on the woman, and they watched as the day approached.

The clearing didn't last long enough for them to see the sunrise in full. The distant clouds grew with unnatural speed, closing the opening as if it were an iris. As the clouds grew, they began to rain Ash in great amounts, first upon the bare bedrock, and then upon the still glowing stone surrounding the survivors. In the far distance, on the ground that had not been cleared of Ash, beasts were approaching. From the massive pits that surrounded Bastion, there was the sound of some colossal creature moving.

"I suppose we see what hole we can find down there," Nemai said, gesturing to the tunnel behind them.

"I suppose," Mara said quietly. She took a deep breath as Ash moved ever closer. Nemai grabbed the soldier to pull her along, then paused. She shivered as if her very skin was alive and trying to flee. A pressure surged between her eyes, and she found she couldn't move at all. The sensation lasted for but a moment, but even when it was gone all her instincts screamed at her to run.

"We need to move," she managed to say in a voice even she could barely hear. Mara nodded, and they began their retreat into the tunnel.

Chapter 24

Kiran lowered the rifle only when Nemai was out of her sight. Kiran could still feel her mind. For all the woman's years of dutiful practice, her mental defenses had been swept aside as dross; allowing the Simuran to hide most signs of her presence. Mara had been an even simpler target.

Milias' orders hadn't faded as the situation changed at least. Kiran hadn't felt the slightest compulsion to execute the soldier. As for Nemai, Kiran didn't know how she'd been able to hold herself back from destroying the woman's mind, let alone how she'd managed to stop herself from pulling the trigger as the rifle had pressed against Nemai's forehead. Regardless of Milias' words, he'd allowed the matrix to come through for a time.

Well done, Milias applauded. *That's what you get for spreading out your mind. Now pull it back in. Go back to sheltered defense mode from this point onward. You really shouldn't ignore that advice again.* Kiran didn't respond verbally. She forcefully reeled her mind back in, wrapping her thoughts in layers of defense until she'd be unable to feel the emotions of anyone, even if they were close enough to touch her.

Kiran moved across the glowing platform, her heavily armored suit losing power from the simple act of moving in the heat, but it was an inconsequential amount from for the improved suit she wore. Across her back was a rifle of another design, and on her waist were two swords and a pistol, all prepared from Mara's stash, along with the armor.

Kiran had thought herself dead for being prepared in such a manner, but whatever alloy the weapons and armor were made of was spared from the effects of the towers. It irked her. Not from surviving, but because she knew she had Milias to thank for it.

She ground her teeth and unlocked her arm from her stomach. It still hurt to move, but soon that wouldn't matter much. She took a sword in that hand and tried using some of her concentration to mask the pain, but the other part of her, the part that was obedient beyond all else, refused the effort. It wasn't worth yet another wearying struggle, so Kiran relented and tried to ignore the pain instead. She magnetically locked the rifle and sword into their respective hands and looked over the enclosing Rot.

The beasts were on a fast approach. The flat platform was spotted with holes and craters that would likely lead to the same place Milias claimed the others would be gathering, but the beasts ignored the tunnels in their race to her. She stood just above where Mara and Nemai had been, awaiting the creatures of Ash as they approached.

She raised the rifle and began to fire. Her first shots went towards those that flew, for they were the closest. Some tried to dodge, but she fired in a pattern and sooner or later bolts of plasma burned into their bodies or wings, and they fell. She switched to shooting ground-based beasts as they passed the lead fliers. She brought down a dozen of the creatures in as many seconds. They too moved to avoid the plasma as it sizzled through the air, but for the most part, it was pointless. They approached in such great numbers it was difficult to miss.

The first to reach her had burst out of the crowd and sprinted ahead of its brethren by a hundred meters. Its body was like a panther but with six legs and two heads, the dark of its body broken only by silver spikes along its back, and a tall ridge of the same color along the spine. Its body was compact, dense enough to leave footprints and claw marks in the dully glowing stone floor.

Kiran aimed for the slit eyes that one of the heads donned. Before the plasma could reach the beast, it roared with both its mouths, sinister mandibles extending out on the ends of twisted tongues to bite the glowing plasma out of the air.

The mandible that managed to grab the superheated substance melted into Rot. The beast leaped over the subsequent plasma, the second mandible snaking out thrice the body length of the creature to snap at Kiran's throat as more plasma ate at the creature's underbelly.

The Simuran ducked and fired a grapple, soaring beneath the creature before it could land. In turn, the spikes upon the creature's back exploded out, similarly to the tongues, piecing the stone ground and slamming the beast onto the ground hard enough to create small fissures.

Kiran fired at the beast's back then rolled as the thing contorted its body and spun, leaping in the air to slam down a clawed paw where the Simuran had stood. She took to her feet once more and fired a series of plasma bolts in a wide pattern. The beast moved to avoid them but several of the shots burned into its hide all the same.

More plasma was in the air when a half dozen more beasts arrived, roaring, leaping and biting at her, several dozens more only a few steps behind them, and barely beyond them, the horde was closing in.

Kiran ducked as the first beast shot out four of its spikes towards her chest. They sank into the ground, and other beasts, instead of her. The creature used them to pull itself atop the Simuran. With a grunt of pain, Kiran stabbed her sword into the soft underside of the creature. It roared with both its heads as its chest and stomach opened along the middle to reveal rows of serrated teeth.

She stayed put long enough to throw a grenade into the body sized maw, then grappled away and onto another Rot Beast as the first one slammed its body into the ground while trying to bite with all its mouths. Kiran pushed that beast out of her thoughts as she soared through the air and onto the next creature.

The thing she moved towards was a massive specimen with large and thick looking scales, a lizard-like head, and far too many eyes that grew on stalks around its body.

Kiran released her grapple and braced herself as she hit the creature sword first in the space between two scales. Her momentum pushed the blade to the sword's hilt. She pushed herself up, leaping away from the weapon only to fall back towards it, grabbing the grip of the blade and pulling it down the body of the great beast.

A thick and viscous ooze seeped out of the wound even as she made it. Whatever it was moved on its own, reaching for her as it left the body of the beast. As the bizarre substance moved, the beast's scales tore themselves out of the Rot flesh and moved towards her in turn.

Kiran pulled her weapon free, annoyed to see much of the blade had been eaten away as if by acid. She fired two bolts of plasma at the ooze that moved through the air towards her, then twitched her head to the side out of sheer instinct.

A sharp spike flew beside her, embedding itself in the hide of the scaled beast after leaving a deep groove in the side of Kiran's helmet. She ducked and spun to see the panther-like creature still living with most its body aflame. It pulled itself closer with the tendril attached to the spike it had fired, but it pulled itself at a much slower pace than before.

Kiran fired two more bolts of plasma, these aimed at the flesh that connected the body of the creature to its embedded spike. In turn, three more of the spikes became projectiles. Kiran dodged the first, cutting the tendril of just beyond the spike as it passed. She moved to deflect the next spike, but her arm screamed in pain, and for a moment she slowed. It was brief, but her sword missed the spike. She was pushed back as the armor over her chest cracked, the suit blaring alarms as it did its best to absorb the impact and prevent the damage.

She cut the tendril behind the spike before the beast could try to pull her to it, then spun and kicked at another creature that had been trying to jump her from behind.

The new beast had the body of a hairless rat with a tail split into eight parts, each bladed and much larger the main body of the human-sized monstrosity. As her foot kicked into the beast's head, its tail whipped towards Kiran. Each split end spread out as if to entrap her inside them. Once more she grappled away, the blades of the rat nearly cutting through her boots as she escaped it.

As she moved through the air, Kiran threw her weakened sword. The blade broke apart from the force of the impact, but the tip of the sword embedded itself in the skull of the rat, which collapsed and began to turn to Ash.

She caught a glimpse of the first beast, the panther. It was a fraction of its original size, but it seemingly tore itself free of its burning flesh and made a new body in the image of its old one. It fired the only two spikes it had upon its body. As she landed, Kiran drew her second sword as she shot plasma at the approaching spikes. The first one burned away, the second met her blade just before it could pierce her heart, but once more she'd been a hair too slow. The armor over her chest cracked further from the impact.

She threw her sword in the air and grabbed the tendril before the beast could pull it back. With a scream of effort and pain, she dragged the creature towards her. It struggled against as it started to grow new spikes along its small form. Kiran fired a barrage of plasma it couldn't dodge. When all that remained was a molten ruin of a beast, she spun with the creature's body as a counterweight. The molten mass of Rot flesh slammed into the side of a scaled beast and finally began to fall into Ash. Then she fired her grapple as some unseen thing tried to grab her legs.

She released her grapple as another beast leaped through the air to her. She fired her grapple back towards the ground, where it embedded itself into another beast, but another creature came from behind. As she changed directions the maw of her attacker closed around her. Her head and one arm were inside the creature's maw. Her armor groaned from the pressure for a moment, before the armor on her chest finally broke.

A sharp fang pieced her suit and the flesh it was meant to protect. She felt her blood burning as the fang bent her bones and stabbed into her heart. For a moment the world turned dark, then her second heart began to beat.

She fired plasma down the throat of the creature. It melted all it touched, but the thing refused to open its mouth. Kiran threw two more of her grenades down the gullet and braced herself. It was only a few seconds before the explosives, one fragment and one incendiary, separated the head of the beast from the neck and its maw finally opened.

Kiran scrambled to leave the mouth, but before she could do so, another beast engulfed one of her legs. More suit alarms blared as sharp teeth began to crack through the armor just above the knee. Bolts of plasma burned into the creature as Kiran finally managed to pull the top of her body into the open air.

As her head emerged from the creature, another beast set upon her. An oversized insect with scythes for mandibles, and human arms and hands reaching out from holes in its carapace. The mandibles snapped at her neck. She leaned back, barely dodging as she pushed herself further from the ruined head before something once more caught her leg.

Another beast snapped at her from the back. It missed her body, its teeth sinking into her arm. The beast was too strong to be slowed by the armor. It sank its fangs deep, cracking apart the reinforced armor and into flesh, and then into bone. The creature flailed its head as if trying to tear her away from the other beasts. Whatever held her leg bit harder in turn, finally breaking through the armor and into her body. Both fought against each other, trying to tear her in two.

Her gun fired towards the sky, where a flying beast moved towards her with a fury. The plasma burned into the beast's head, chest, and wings, but it landed on her all the same. The creature, larger than she was, pushed all air out of her lungs. A swarm of tiny insect-sized beasts swarmed beneath her and began to eat into her suit, tearing apart the relatively soft fabric between slabs of armor.

The massive bird managed a screech from its headless neck as Kiran fired bolt after bolt into it. Then its feet grabbed her head and began to crush. The claws slipped at first, not managing to crush and kill. They managed to take purchase as they closed around the face. First, the armor was cut, then the flesh beneath it gave as well. Her blood, caustic in open air seared her skin as the beast's claws took out her eyes. Another claw cracked open the armor beneath her jaw and pierced her body just above the throat.

Kiran dropped her gun and grabbed at her armor from memory. She took three grenades, triggered them, and threw them blindly upward. As she moved her other arm was torn free of her body, the beast's teeth finally managing to saw through her metallic bones. The thing with her leg began to drag the rest of her closer to its teeth, biting ever deeper.

She felt the ground shake from the grenades. She was surprised that she hadn't been able to feel any of the heat. She could only surmise that some beast must have moved between her and the thrown explosives. It only took a few moments for the burning flesh to land on her to know she was right.

Her remaining arm was beneath a sharp edge. No longer being powered, the armor she wore began to shift and bend and rend with ease. She struggled to free her arm, pulling it back, but whatever had it trapped was bulky, heavy, and beyond her.

As she struggled, another beast rushed in and sank its teeth into her torso. She tried to ignore the pain. She tried to be quiet. But she couldn't. As yet another beast bit into her, and her blood burned her, she screamed.

Congratulations, Milias mused. *You survived long enough. Now it comes to the third to make a choice to see if that continues. Give up on defenses. The Strider is here for you to experience.*

Kiran's mind desperately grabbed at his words, and she discarded her defenses, throwing her thoughts across the world, not knowing what she sought. What she found was nothing she could have predicted. Her mind touched that of the great beast, a creature beyond her knowledge. What touched Bastion before had been but a piece of it reaching through. It had been hurt by the towers. It was massive, and it was infuriated. In its presence, her mind began to fade like darkness at dawn.

She held the command matrix up to the great mind as if holding it to a grindstone. The Matrix didn't fight her; it fought only to defend itself from the absolute madness of the monster. Kiran's mind flaked away piece by piece. The beasts around her stopped biting but didn't move away. Time sat still yet ran a marathon between each beat of her heart, as the Rot spread across her body and through her veins.

Never forget, you chose this, Milias whispered.

Chapter 25

"At least it wasn't a dead end," Nemai said. She was panting and soaked with sweat. The deep chill had left her as they ran.

"Where are we?" Mara asked. Her face was pale, and she leaned heavily on the wall of the passage so Nemai could rest. She'd been supporting the soldier for most of their hurried flight, although more of Mara's balance was returning.

"I don't know," Nemai shrugged, "but that thing, that's an Alpha AeC. That's where we need to go," Nemai said, pointing far below.

They stood on the edge of a precipice. The tunnel had been uncomfortably long. It turned and split in a few places, forcing them to choose at random. It had led to a massive cavern that looked like a natural formation touched by artificial construction. What she pointed at was the massive centerpiece of it all; the orb that was held aloft. Even in such a large space, it looked dominant and intimidating, rough metal and thousands of cables that hadn't been affected by the Omnipurge. She didn't know if that was by design or if the cavern had simply been out of range.

The AeC would have been beneath the palace. She knew that much. But while their tunnel had begun not far from where the palace had been, possibly even beneath it, it had taken them all the way to the edge of Bastion, along the edge of an uncomfortably smooth wall.

"How do we get down there then?" Mara asked quietly. Nemai looked to her apologetically. The soldier was looking about, trying to figure out a way to climb down from their perch above the cavern. They would need to cling to stalactites and climb hand over hand on the cables from what Nemai could see. The Soldier seemed nearly excited about the prospect, despite there being no clear place in which they could reach the cavern floor with such effort.

"You're not going to like this," Nemai said quietly, "and I don't think we have the time for me to explain properly. I'm sorry, but you'll need to trust me."

Nemai pulled herself tighter to the soldier's side, then leaped off the edge. Mara nearly held her back. Only her surprise allowed Nemai to overpower her. Mara swung her arm at the ledge and barely missed catching herself, her fingers dragging on the stone but not managing to find purchase. Then they were in the open air, far above the cavern floor.

Mara tightened her hold on Nemai and locked her jaw to hold back any sound of fear. Nemai screamed as they fell, even as she summoned her dark blade to hand and turned herself to shadowed mist. She forced her body to stay tightly knit, as if a floating shadow, dense enough to slow Mara's fall, but not enough to stop it altogether.

The soldier landed on her feet, stood for a moment, then tried to take a step before toppling and falling to one knee.

"Nemai," she growled.

"I said you wouldn't like it," Nemai said, forming back to her body and shaking from the returned cold. Mara looked at her in anger, took a few deep breaths, then looked away.

Nemai shuddered and looked behind her, hair standing on end. There was something in the cavern, something that felt to be standing just behind her no matter where she looked. Something that tickled the edge of her senses. As Mara caught her breath, Nemai closed her eyes and tried to focus on that uneasiness, to find its source. It felt disgusting and horrifying all at once, even if the what and where of the thing was still beyond her.

"Couldn't have made me like that too? You just had to let me freefall?" Mara growled.

"I can only do that to my own body," Nemai said. "Besides, that wasn't a freefall."

Mara glared at her for several seconds, then grunted and grabbed her chest over her heart and closed her eyes. She shook her head a moment later.

"I don't think I like heights anymore," she muttered. Nemai didn't say anything. She reached over to Mara and helped her stand. The soldier was tense but not as wary of her as Nemai expected.

Nemai shuddered and looked behind her again, seeing only the empty cavern floor. She looked above, but the opening they came from was well hidden in the shadowed contours of the cavern. Nemai summoned her dark blade into her hand. Then she shook her head and cleared her throat.

"If Sol's anywhere, he's going to be there," Nemai said, pointing to the AeC.

"I still don't understand how," Mara said. As she spoke, she pulled herself away from Nemai, staring at her feet and shifting her weight. Her legs shook, but she took a tentative step and didn't fall. A smile spread across her face.

"I don't know," Nemai answered, after glancing behind them once again, "but Milias wouldn't want all of us dying here. He's too sadistic for that. We need Sol to escape this world, which means Sol will survive this. That means he needs to be there or getting there very soon," Nemai said.

Mara shook her head, then paused, and let out a small laugh.

"What are the chances," she said quietly. She took a step away from Nemai, nearly falling but managing to keep her feet. Then she took another, and another, quickly leaving Nemai behind although she looked like a toddler while doing so.

"You're going the wrong way," Nemai hissed, glancing upward. A growling sound had begun to bounce through the cavern, the source growing louder by the second. Nemai walked backward, first slowly, then nearly running, not daring to take her eyes off the ceiling. She only looked away when she stepped on a pile of multicolored glass, all of which she could feel beneath her soft soled shoes. She cursed and moved, pulling glass out of her soft shoe, but even then she only glanced away for a moment.

She saw the creature before she felt its simple mind. It had a half dozen necks and heads that emerged from the body of a thousand-legged and wingless cockroach, just big enough to squeeze through the tunnel above. Nemai ducked behind an outcropping of rock just before the thing could land.

The beast hit the ground with thunderous and shrill shrieks of rage, hunger, and joy. Its legs and carapace cracked, to splatter liquid Rot in a dozen meters around it. It barely seemed to notice its wounds. It lowered its heads and used them to drag itself towards Nemai's outcropping. Even as its legs began to reshape themselves in unnatural ways, it grew another mouth along the front of its body, complete with mandibles that held jagged and sharp edges.

Nemai screamed for Mara, but no answer came. She tightened her grip on the black blade. The thing no longer felt powerful. It felt like a toy in her hand. The sounds of more of the things falling did little to give her confidence. She turned and ran.

Her first step nearly put her back into the pile of glass. She barely moved her foot away, instead stepping in some of the beast's splattered blood. Her foot slipped as if standing on ice, and she barely caught herself, cutting her hands on the hard stone, but propelling herself forward and back onto her feet in the same motion. She moved at a sprint, moving past several other piles of glass in moments. She glanced back and screamed again.

The beast's legs had healed, and it was nearly on her. She turned to shadow as one of its heads snapped over what would have been the top half of her body. She pulled her mist-like form out of the mouth, seeping between the gaps of slimy obsidian teeth. She felt her bizarre form shake as the thing squealed, but she pulled herself away as the creature attempted to bite and swallow her shadow.

Her form hit the floor, and she spread out her body in streams, coursing around rocks and strange ripples in the stone. The beast charged erratically for a moment, then seemed to lose track of her.

Nemai found a building carved down in the stone by crude tools. She pulled all her shadows there and reformed her body. The cold that assailed her was worse than the first time she'd used the power. Her skin was colorless, and she shuddered continuously.

She could hear the beast screaming, joined by the roars of other beasts, broken only by another unnatural sound. Mara had returned from wherever she'd wandered off to. Nemai could feel the soldier's fear, as well as a maddening touch of excitement.

Nemai risked looking out from her hole to see Mara standing atop a rock outcropping at least a hundred meters from where she'd last seen her. The soldier was smiling. She'd somehow managed to find a second pistol in the cavern, for she held one in each hand. She was firing bolts of plasma every which way, hitting beasts with almost every shot. Nemai couldn't say if it was due to skill or if the pure number of beasts made missing unlikely, but at least her issues with balance weren't worsening her aim.

More and more of the creatures were raining down from the ceiling, and not only from the tunnel they'd taken. There were dozens of the holes spotting the top of the cavern. Some were much closer to the AeC than theirs had been, and Rot Beasts were falling from them. But there was cause for hope.

Most of the creatures that fell near the AeC weren't making it to the ground. They were breaking apart as they fell, as if dissolving. Others hit the ground and exploded into Rot Ash. As if their unnatural bodies couldn't survive the fall. More bizarre still was the Ash didn't land and settle to form new creatures. It too seemed to dissolve in the air. The closer the to the metal sphere, the more rapidly they broke apart.

Nemai threw herself back into the hole that was once somebody's home. A half second later the cockroach slammed into the stone with enough force to break parts of its own body. Nemai backed as far away from it as the hut would allow. The thing tried to push its body into the malformed doorway, but it was barely large enough to fit its lowermost mouth and mandibles.

Nemai groaned as the beast opened its mouth. What emerged looked like a slime-coated worm. It stretched towards her as if tasting the air before splitting apart into several copies of itself to spread through the hut.

She screamed and lunged forward with her weapon, using what force she could muster. The blade cut the creature easily, and to her surprise, the beast recoiled and screamed in pain. She heard herself laughing. Hysterically, in a manner that uncomfortably reminded her of her father. Then she felt the thing's blood on her arm. It burned as it turned her skin to Rot.

"You're not going to fucking eat me," she spat at the beast. Then it roared, and the worm-like tongue returned, splitting into a dozen smaller parts, growing hooks and blades and writhing as it searched the room.

"Oh, fuck you," Nemai hissed before turning back into shadow, the pain in her arm disappearing immediately. She fell flat against the ground, pulling her form through the doorway in the small gaps around the beast's mouth. For a moment she swore she was seen, and she felt fear pounding away in her heart despite not having a heart as living shadow. But the beast continued trying to find her in the hut even after she felt her body squeeze by its head, and it even continued as she slipped by its other half dozen heads that were chewing on the stone around the doorway, making progress terrifyingly quickly.

Nemai darted towards Mara, although the woman had moved since her last glimpse, she clearly wasn't moving very quickly. She couldn't do so. She was putting the pistols to hard work, and everything around her was dying. But they were getting closer, and the Rot was endlessly raining. As it was, the soldier had one or two coming for her at a time, and for the most part, they were already injured from the fall, but they couldn't count on that to continue.

Nemai pooled herself around the soldier's feet and fought the urge to return to her normal body. It was like holding her breath, each moment feeling stretched to a painful eternity. She didn't know if the form had an actual limit, or simply a mental one, but it was horrendously uncomfortable in either case.

We need to get to the condenser, Nemai said, breaking through Mara's mind.

"It's too late for that," Mara said grimly, ducking, and nearly falling. The Soldier patted her side, and Nemai looked, although she couldn't even say exactly how she was able to see in the first place.

Mara had a cut along her side, and everything around it was in the process of changing into the Rot. Her veins surrounding it were swollen and dark, and Nemai swore she could see small Rot Beasts starting to form inside the Soldier's flesh.

"Find Sol and run," Mara said resolutely. "You were right. I saw scorch marks on the stone, found my pistol next to them. He's here somewhere, and he'll need help."

She ducked again as a claw moved overhead, but the beast that had closed in anticipated it. A second claw swiped at her. Nemai moved out of instinct she didn't know she had. She gathered her shadow and formed it into a wall. The claw hit her and stopped. Nemai was thrown out of Mara's mind, her vision blurred to the point of being blinded, and she felt the shadow trying to transform into her human body. She screamed, or tried to, and forced herself to remain in the shadow form.

"At least they're simple beasts," Mara hissed, putting a dozen bolts of plasma into the creature that had nearly ended her.

Nemai groaned.

The Condenser. I think you can be healed there, she said, breaking back into the Soldiers mind. *It's worth a try.*

Mara spun, firing on yet another beast that was running towards her. She opened her mouth to say something, but Nemai didn't give her the chance to finish. She coated the Soldier with her shadow, then tried to pull her along. For a moment she didn't think it would work, but then Mara began moving as she wanted. It wasn't fast, nor was it pretty in any way, but they were moving.

Mara was speaking as she fought through the cavern, but Nemai couldn't hear it. She did her best to help the soldier move, helped her legs keep balance as they tried to run. She hoped it was working. Mara was moving more confidently, but it was hard to say if it was due to her prompting and guidance, or if it was Mara somewhat returning to form.

In either case, the princess smiled, so to speak, when she saw the Rot on the Soldier's body begin to flake away, leaving behind a bloody wound that had tripled in size since Nemai had first seen it. It stretched from the waist to the chest, but it hadn't gone deep. It had mercifully been a slower infection, rather than the ones that could turn a person in moments. Nemai could see two exposed ribs through the tears in Mara's clothes, and no small amount of blood was flowing, but the soldier was alive. Some of the Rot remained, but the speed at which it ate away at Mara's body had greatly slowed.

The beasts continued to attack, slowly dissolving as they neared the base of the condenser, but it was much weaker than when they fell near the center of it. Mara did her best, moving and shooting. The beasts were beginning to be more complex by the time they reached the base of the whole structure, but at the same time the closer they got, the quicker the beasts broke apart.

By the time they reached the door, Mara was almost capable of running. She'd slipped three separate times, but Nemai had managed to catch the woman with her shadows before she could hit the ground. It was rough and unbalanced but vastly improved over her struggles to stand when she first woke in the plaza.

Nemai's body returned to normal almost on its own once they were inside. The cold that assailed her was vastly more severe than the other times she'd used the ability. She fell to the ground, and her eyes repeatedly fluttered open and closed as Mara moved over her. The room thundered as some creature rammed the building, but the door held. There were lights. The structure was protected. The place had power still, directly connected to the AeC as it was. But it wouldn't last. The way the lights flickered, the way the walls groaned, it was easy to see that the AeC was barely producing enough Ether to fuel even itself. The rest of the structure would be abandoned before long.

Nemai tried to tell Mara that she too should be abandoned, but she knew the soldier would listen about as well as she had. Mara was bent over her, rubbing her arms to warm her. The walls shook again, and the lights flickered ominously. But there was something else that Nemai felt on the edge of her mind.

There were others, and they were sleeping not far from her. Lost in the long nightmares of stasis. Sol was with them. Nemai could feel his fear, and his shame, as the others died one after another. She wanted to tell Mara this. She wanted the soldier to move one room over to stop Sol, but her lips wouldn't move, and her mind was fading too quickly. She could only stand witness.

Chapter 26

The woman was colder than a corpse. Mara couldn't feel it, she could barely feel anything, but she could see it. Nemai had been crying when her body had returned, but her tears had frozen and held her eyes open. Moisture in the air was condensing across the woman's skin and turning to yet more ice. Her body was stiffening. It was as if her very flesh was turning to ice. It all came to pass in a handful of seconds.

Mara lowered herself and pushed air into the woman's lungs, then rose and began heart compressions again.

"Don't you fucking die while I owe you," Mara growled loudly, but if anything, the woman grew colder at her words.

Something heavy slammed into the door. The metal creaked and groaned as the lights flickered. Still, she tried to save the woman.

"Mara," she heard a tired voice whimper. She spun, grabbing a pistol from the floor and pointing it at the door she hadn't heard opening.

Sol stood in an open doorway, his eyes wide in disbelief. Mara dropped the pistol but said nothing. The prince had changed since she'd last seen him. She didn't feel like much time had passed while she'd been lost to sleep, but Sol looked to of gained several years. He looked like a man in his prime, rather than the young one she remembered. He was tall, and almost looked to be glowing with life.

"Sol?" She asked in disbelief.

The prince crossed the room without a word and wrapped his arms around her before beginning to sob. He was trying to speak, but his words were unintelligible. Mara couldn't move. He was wrong. She would think the man was one of Sol's older brothers. Even his golden hair was many times longer, nearly to his waist, and nearly reflected light like a mirror. He was naked but for a bit of heavily burned cloth tied around his waist. Faint scars coated much of his pale body, covering muscles the young man didn't have before.

For more than a single moment all Mara wanted was to raise her pistol and execute the impostor. She didn't know if it was some trick of Bastion, but the person couldn't be Sol. It couldn't be. But as he held her and wept, all Mara could do was pat his back and shush the prince. She allowed him perhaps a minute, although she counted it as the lights flickering three times.

"Nemai needs our help," she said emptily.

The man reacted immediately, pushing himself to arm's length. Mara felt him stare at her for a moment longer; then he turned his attention to Nemai. He reached out to her head and groaned as if touching her was painful.

"Her blood is freezing in her veins," he said dumbfoundedly. "What-"

He was cut off by the sound of something hitting the door again, and the thing cracking in turn. He took a sharp breath and continued.

"What happened to her?"

"I don't know... Magic. I guess," Mara said. Sol nodded, then shook his head.

"I... I don't know if we can help her. We need to warm her body, but..."

"What do I do?" Mara asked. Sol looked at her as if surprised.

"I don't know," he said. He looked down at the woman and closed his eyes. His body began to shake. A moment later he was backing away from her with fear filled eyes.

"Sol?" Mara called. Sol stared ahead, then shook his head.

"She… she's still alive. Her heart is beating, but its faint. She needs warmth, but she is… alive. How is that even possible? Her blood is literally turning to ice."

Mara didn't answer. Her eyes jumped between Nemai and Sol as her mind churned.

"We need fire," Sol said after a moment. The room shook, and the cracks along the walls grew.

"I don't think we don't have time to find something that will burn," Mara said grimly. Sol nodded.

"How do we get to the Fae?" he asked. Mara wanted to ask how she'd know. Instead, she ignored his question and made her way to one of the many doors that lined the room. When she opened the first one all she found was a closet filled with clothes. She moved to slam the door, then thought better of it. She grabbed whatever was at hand and threw them at Sol, then proceeded to grab more from the shelf.

When she glanced back, she caught Sol staring at the clothes as if in confusion. She paused for a moment to watch him, still uneasy over the changes that Sol had gone through. If it truly was him. Sol looked down at his body and finally began to blush as if he hadn't noticed he'd been nearly naked. He took the time to run his hand across his stomach, then his arms. By the look on his face, he was as confused as Mara over the changes.

The prince looked up and saw her watching. His blush deepened, and he stammered an apology while starting to put on pants. Mara shrugged and turned back to the closet, more lost than she'd been before. She gathered more of the cloth and carried it to Nemai. The lights flickered again as she dressed the woman in layers.

"How do we get there?" she heard Sol ask in an exasperated tone. Mara turned back to him. He was pacing in bare feet but was otherwise dressed.

"Sol?" Mara questioned.

"… Talking to myself," he said. Mara nodded and went for another door.

"Not that one," Sol called loudly. "It's a dead end."

"One of them has to lead up," Mara said, going for yet another doorway. She opened it to find nothing but a mirror. Mara's eyes caught on her oddly graying hair for a moment, then she slammed the door shut and paced across the room to find another entrance.

"None of them will lead anywhere," Sol said quietly. "They did once. But this place… it changes."

"We're not going to give up," Mara said. "We're close. We're going to get you into the Fae."

"Do we wait?" Sol asked grimly. Mara stared at him as the world shook yet again. Sol was looking at the statues in the center of the room.

"What could we possibly wait for?" She asked.

"For Kiran," Sol said. Mara swallowed the angry words that had been forming on her tongue as the prince spoke again. "We're getting out of here Mara. All of us."

"Sol… I… have you seen what's out there? I don't think… I don't think even she could survive for long."

"She will," Sol said, hands tightly clenched and shaking, "she has to."

Mara looked to Sol, then back to the statues with the words *Salvation Awaits* carved beneath their feet. She ignored the prince as he continued speaking and carried the freezing Nemai to them. She placed her on the raised dais that held the statues, then climbed on it herself, retreating to the small space that the statues circled.

"Mara, we need to-"

"Salvation awaits," she said, cutting off Sol. "Didn't Nemai say something like that before? When we first spoke to her? She knows how to… She said *something* about salvation."

"We need to wait for Kiran," Sol said. She *will* be here. I swear, we just-"

"Don't be an idiot," Mara said. She took a breath and continued more calmly. "I want Kiran to be alive Sol. Of course, I do. But we can't be stupid. Heroes die. Cowards survive. We need to be cowards."

"Mara-" Sol began.

"What would she say?" Mara asked. Sol swallowed whatever words had been coming and nodded his head slowly. Mara only turned when the prince began to make his way to the dais.

Her hands moved to Nemai's side and began to rub, trying to warm the woman as quickly as possible. The woman still lived, Mara was as surprised as Sol on that account, but the woman's breath was rough and halted on each inhale.

"Nemai, how do we leave?" she asked. The living corpse didn't respond. Mara looked back to the entrance. There was a gap where part of the door was bent out of shape. Through it reached the limb of a beast, growing and starting to search the room blindly. Kiran raised her pistol and shot. The bolt of plasma didn't directly hit but was close enough to melt the monstrous limb.

Mara smiled and threw herself from the dais. Sol cried out to her, but she didn't answer. She threw open the doors to the strange closet and filled her arms with all the clothing she could manage before dragged them back to the statues. As she moved, the lights flickered, then went out entirely. Luckily Sol lit the statues with a floating orb a moment after, making Mara's return quick and painless.

She threw what she carried in the open center the statues circled then aimed her pistol to the side. The plasma scorched the stone but didn't melt in.

"There's power stored here," Sol said. "It's inside the statues."

"Then as I thought, this is our way out," Mara said. She fired again, this time aiming closer to the clothing. As she hoped, the cloth burst into flames as the plasma flew close, although the fire was smaller than she'd anticipated. The gray cloth burned slowly. She set more aflame and pushed Nemai closer to the fire. She turned her eyes back to the door, barely visible through the light Sol cast.

The world shook, and the door warped further, holding only by luck or divine intervention. Limbs, larger than the earlier ones, reached through the gaps in the door. They split and spread across the floor and through the air like wildfire, searching. Mara fired her pistol twice more before the world shook again, and the door was thrown completely free.

There was nothing beyond the room but Ash and the monsters it made. It was a mass of shadows that fought and struggled to fit through the gap as they quickly broke apart into a dark mist. Cracks spread through the walls as age-old enchantments faded.

"What do we do Nemai?" Mara called loudly. Her voice seemed to anger the Rot as one of the beast's managed to change its shape and flit into the room. Mara opened fire. The evaporating Ash made it difficult to make out the forms of the beast's, as well as hiding their movements, but for the brief moments in which the glow of plasma lit the room. Sol's light flared brighter, but the mist almost seemed to be moving to swallow it. In a sick way, Mara was reminded of Nemai and the strange magic she'd used.

She knew her pistol would be growing hotter in her hand as she fired bolt after bolt, all her settings set to make the largest and most powerful plasma the weapon could manage, but she couldn't feel it warming her hand.

It almost felt like they could manage for a short time. Then parts of the wall finally began to fall. They groaned and shook as everything around the door crumbled. They had an extraordinarily brief respite as the nearby beasts were pushed back. Large slabs of stone crushed many of the creatures, but even then, the horde pressed on, climbing over and around the wreckage in such great numbers that the cavern remained hidden from sight.

Mara heard herself screaming as she continued to shoot the beasts, the smell of burning flesh came from her steaming hand. She could feel none of it.

Something grabbed her shoulder and pulled her back as a beast flung itself through the air towards her. She allowed herself to be moved and had nearly thanked Sol when she realized the thing that grabbed her had sunk claws into her shoulder. When she saw her blood, she moved her pistol and fired. The plasma ate through the head of a beast as it had been lowering its maw to bite.

Another beast flew over her, nearly grabbing her with long limbs as it passed overhead. She tried to roll, her body not quite listening. She found herself sprawled along the floor instead. She was surprised to see another beast stopped with a flash of light. The thing reacted as if it had hit something solid.

Sol began to scream. Mara could see him standing beside the fire, but its light was faint beside the glow that his Stigma was beginning to spread. Pure white light flickered around them, pushing back more of the beasts as Sol moved his hands in bizarre and ritualistic ways. A handful of seconds passed as Mara crawled next to the prince and the unconscious Nemai.

Sol's screams stopped. He clenched his teeth and crossed his arms as the light expanded, surrounding the three of them in a translucent white sphere, as well as a large section of the dais. Beasts hit the wall of light and bounced away, but Sol twitched with every impact, and the Ash gathered along his makeshift shield even as it dissipated.

Mara dropped her pistol, as she felt a hand grab her. Her eyes fell to Nemai. The woman was still cold, but her eyes were no longer frozen, and her lips were moving. Mara started to lift her, to put her ear beside the woman's mouth, when all sound was drowned out by something snapping. It was hundreds of times louder than when the wall was crumbling. She looked up to see the building they were in, the massive pedestal, was falling as the beats destroyed it at the base.

The pedestal twisted as it fell, the hand it ended in spinning the metal sphere it held, tearing apart cables and shearing metal. When it fell, the sphere floated in the air alone, slinging chunks of metal through the cavern as it spun, seeming to gain speed over time rather than slowing.

Mara caught only glimpses of the action as the building collapsed around them. Sol's screams returned as debris rained down on his shield. He fell to a knee, and the shield shrank around them. The beasts slammed themselves into it, others biting with mouths that should have eaten them whole, sphere and all, but they flinched away after touching the translucent orb. Contact looked to cause them pain while making the disintegration of their bodies quicken.

An exhausted mind touched Mara's, too weak to break through, while a hand tried to slap her. Mara turned her attention back to Nemai and lowered her ears to the woman once more.

"Praise… him. Pray," Nemai whispered. She almost smiled as her eyes closed again. Mara lowered her to the ground, then looked to the statues.

"You are a fucking bastard," she whispered. She glanced at Sol who struggled under the onslaught of the beasts as the last of the rubble rained down on his shield. His nose was bleeding, and his eyes were staring at nothing. At some point, he'd raised his crossed arms over his head. They shook each time a beast hit his shield.

"Lord Milias," Mara shouted, recalling a passage she'd once read. "All knowing lord of men. Master of time. I pray so you may hear my words spoken from within the rabble."

As she spoke, the statues surrounding them began to glow and shift. The ground rumbled as the dais lifted itself from the ground and began to raise them towards the spinning metal sphere ever so slightly. Most surprising, the beasts seemed to be leaving Sol's shield alone. Mara didn't look for a reason. She tried to remember more of the useless praises she'd read.

"I call upon the greatest of beings, an emperor more divine than any god," Mara continued, hands squeezed into fists as she searched her mind. Eventually, she shrugged and finished with a few of her own words. "We are but dust that asks for your benevolence. Help us, or I'll shoot you in the fucking face."

Mara fell silent as the platform began to ascend in full, worried that she'd need to continue praising the bastard until they'd reached their destination, but it seemed that what she'd said had sufficed.

As the dais lifted, Sol's shield finally fell, and Mara turned her gaze to what lay beneath them, trying to discover why the beasts had stopped their assault. What she saw froze the poisonous hope that had begun to grow in her heart.

Beneath them stood a beast in the shape of a man. Its shadow danced across the cavern as if a thing alive, devouring all other beasts it touched. It grinned with a mouth that was far too wide, its large and sunken eyes bouncing between Mara and Sol.

"We," the thing spoke. Its voice was made of many other voices, together thundering and echoing.

"Are," its body coiled, and it reached out its hand, already a dozen meters short.

"Not. Rot." Its body exploded into the air. Its arm grew to that of a giant and grabbed the edge of the platform. The statues groaned, and their ascension slowed. The flesh of the beast bubbled, faces and beings seeming to flow by in a river just below its skin. When its flesh began to settle, a new human form grew out of the overly large hand that grabbed the edge. It stepped towards them, connected to the rest of its form by thick pulsing tendrils. Its body was hemorrhaging Rot as it dissolved, enough that it was nearly forced to regrow its form with every passing second, but another part of the beast continued to slay and devour its brethren below.

"We. Are. The Void," the beast growled. Its body shook as once more unknown things looked to flow beneath its flesh. When the moment was over, the beast continued to speak as if it had never stopped.

"You. Taught us. Pain," the thing said, taking another step towards them. It looked to be struggling, but the grin on its face grew wider, cracking open to needle-like teeth.

"You taught-"

As the beast started talking again, Mara grabbed her pistol from the floor, spun the dials, and shot. The plasma ate through the breaking creature with ease, but a moment later her hand was in a vice, and her gun was torn away from her.

"Life," the thing said, reforming its body from the tendrils that still grasped the platform. The creature looked at the gun it had taken from Mara, holding it in quivering hand and raising it to point at the soldier's head. They slowly rose ever higher, the human-like figure nearly hidden by the clouds of Ash that boiled off it.

"We. Hate you," it said in a thunderous whisper.

What little they could see of the beast seemed to look up. Above it, the metal sphere spun faster and faster as it shredded itself, its form slowly shrinking. Above that, the ceiling was cracked and had begun to collapse. The rubble rained down on the sphere, breaking it down even further, and making a safe space below it, where they were sheltered.

Where the sky should have been, there was a beast like none other. Larger than Bastion had ever been, liquid-like flesh constantly moving, forming faces and limbs and maws, and eyes that looked inward, lit by liquid fire that dripped from its grotesque body. It leisurely lowered itself towards the condenser, its vast body breaking and rebuilding as an alien pressure began to build in Mara's mind.

"We. Teach you. Mercy," the humanoid beast said. A long tendril reached out of its body to grab falling debris and placed it by their side.

"We. Cannot. Be alive. We ask you. To remember. That we once. Were."

When the beast finished speaking, it released the platform and allowed its human form to dissolve. The platform rose closer to the sphere. The pressure built in Mara's head as the grotesque beast above grew closer. Her eyes watered as a shadow from the cavern's walls flew into the air on demonic wings, stabbing into the massive creature that was lowering itself towards them. There was a shriek of rage, then the remnant of the metal sphere finally finished tearing itself apart and was gone in full. In the space it had been, there was an object. Looking at it, Mara could no longer see the beasts fighting, nor feel the pressure in her head. All she could see was the thing the sphere had hidden from sight.

It was a stone monument, or a fragment of one, with jagged edges that were worn by uncountable ages. It was covered in runes the likes of which Mara had never seen before. But that was not all there was to it. As she looked at the thing, a faint scent reached her. What it was she didn't know, but it was the most pleasant scent she'd ever known. Her muscles loosened, and all her worries felt lesser somehow.

She shivered as she felt a cold breeze dance along her body, the first thing she'd truly felt since waking. But even that couldn't distract her from what held her entranced. It was music. A song that grew louder as they approached the stone. It was a deep and sad song in a language she didn't know, sang by voices she couldn't comprehend. She knew even as she listened that it wasn't with her ears that she heard the song. Nor was it speaking into her mind as Kiran and Nemai had done. It was simply there.

"What is it?" she asked, not expecting an answer. In that, she wasn't surprised. Nemai didn't move but for breathing. The ice across her body was gone, although the fire beside her had burned out. Sol stood beside her, eyes wide in wonder.

"What do you see?" he asked.

"A carved stone," Mara said. Sol let out a single laugh, and shook his head, not taking his eyes from the thing.

"It's not a stone to my eyes," he said with wonder. "I see a tapestry, or rather a piece of one that's been singed. This… What is this?"

They neared the thing as they spoke, the oddly small wonder coming to rest in the center of their platform. It floated there, or they floated below it, and nothing else seemed to matter. Sol stretched out a hand towards the stone, and at a touch, everything changed.

Chapter 27

Myra hopped between the footprints her father left in the shallow snow. Behind her, Og chuckled and lumbered after her. Each of his steps destroyed all other marks with the sheer size of his naked feet, while his ducked head still brought destruction to the lowest hanging branches of the trees they passed. Ahead of them, Myra's father navigated through the open forest, cutting this way and that to avoid the forest denizens he sensed. Lands of Autumn were more peaceful than the other areas of the Fae, but that was no reason to abandon caution altogether.

"It's a clan guarded Shard, but the orna here are moodier than usual," Ed, her father, said. "Last time I came here they were nearly hostile. I think they only did business with me because they were worried that I'd say something to the other clans if they didn't."

"Without trading, they'd be useless and dead. Idiots," Og grumbled. Despite trying to speak softly, his voice thundered through the forest.

"They're good people as a whole," Ed said, waving his hand through the air. "But I'll admit they'd be less tolerated by most if they weren't useful. Speaking of which."

Ed stopped in his tracks and dug through the many pockets of his vibrant orange robes. Eventually, he pulled a small crystal from one of them and tossed it to Myra. She caught the crystal and raised it to her head. As it touched her skin, she felt the knowledge held within seep into her mind. Moments later it flowed back into the crystal. Myra placed the gemstone in Og's massive hand as the new language settled in her mind, along with hints of emotion that would help in word choice.

"How long has it been?" Og asked.

"A few years for me. For them, I'm not sure. It's typically a fast-flowing Shard, so probably quite a bit more on their end. Couple centuries. Few millennia at most."

Og growled and stared at the crystal. Ed rolled his eyes.

"Don't be like that," he sighed. "It was a major language in a quickly developing world. They might have starships by now, so major language shifts should have slowed. We'll need a dialect update. Vocabulary. And likely some grammar, sure, but the roots of the language should be the same. Updates like that are a lot cheaper than buying the whole language for all of us. Don't forget the clans love their deception with the one-use crystals."

Og grunted and held the crystal against his gray head for a moment before deftly tossing it back to Ed. Myra patted the Ogre's leg as he winced from the feeling of the language settling down in his head.

"I'll be fine, little one," Og said, petting her hair with an oversized finger.

"It shouldn't be far now. Myra..." Ed said. Myra nodded and started to wrap her face in soft black cloth, leaving only her eyes uncovered. When that was done, she pulled a deep hood over her head. Its weak magic activating to help hide her features, and the black wrap, in shadows.

With her head fully covered, Myra slid long gloves over her hands so none of her skin could be seen. It was frustrating for the child, but she'd seen how angry the orna could become at the sight of one of their own in the company of a human.

Myra's hidden skin was all the colors of the sea, mixed with shades of emerald. Her hair was a mixture of deep crimsons and violets. It was her mother's hair. At least that was what her father told her, and she didn't think it had come from him. She was an orna, the decedent of a human and a hulder. Most orna were at least a dozen generations removed from their Fae ancestor, but Myra was different.

Her father was Edbron Salizar, more reasonably known as Ed. Her mother was a hulder who's name was still hidden from her. Some orna clans, although far from the majority, were obsessed with the purity of their bloodlines. They would kill to acquire her.

"Blood," Og growled. Myra froze, her hand going to the small knife her father allowed her to keep. For his part, Ed tilted his head and closed his eyes while Og moved to stand over Myra protectively.

"Four minds," Ed said after a handful of seconds, wiping a sudden sweat from his brow. "Traversal shock. Three unconscious, one close to it. I can't tell much more than that."

Og nodded, Myra waited as Ed stared at what little snow had managed to gather on the ground beneath the large trees. He bit his lip as his hand clenched tightly. Myra already knew what they would do. They would do the same thing they did whenever they saw someone that needed help, even when it had been an ogre drowning in a fast river. Og's people were notorious for their idiotic and violent behavior. For the most part, it was earned. However, because of Ed's actions, they'd learned a secret about the Ogres, as well as a life-long friend.

That didn't mean Ed didn't pause each time someone needed help. Caution in all things was one of the mottos he claimed to live by while wearing his bright orange robes and trying to befriend everything he passed.

"Sorry," Ed muttered to himself, then he smiled and gestured with his head. "They're this way."

Ed took off at a much quicker pace than before, using his staff to throw himself across the ground. He didn't need it normally. Despite his age, Ed was inordinately fit and agile. It wasn't too uncommon to see him scaling cliffs, so long as Myra wasn't trying it beside him. Myra never thought to question why he had a staff until Og had.

"Is an elder without a staff really an elder?" he'd asked in turn, and that was all he'd said on the matter. It was essentially the same thing he'd said about his flamboyant clothing. "Orange is the color of the scholars. The real ones. How could I wear anything else?"

He'd also tried to claim that scholars had shaved heads, but Myra told Og the truth. Her father was naturally bald. Ed pouted for nearly a day after, mumbling about the magnificent head of hair he'd *willingly* parted with, that it certainly hadn't been stolen from him by cruel gods. It wasn't that Og would care. Ogres, in general, shared Ed's condition. The only hair Og had was decorating his chin, although his beard looked more like a cluster of river reeds than hair a human could grow.

They entered a forest clearing a few minutes after Ed had charged off. As Myra stepped over that line, she shivered for no reason she could see, her instincts simply telling her something was very wrong. She didn't question it too much. Instead, she worked to keep pace with her father.

The clearing had a perfectly circular shape and wasn't overly large, although the line between forest and clearing was unnatural severe. No trees tried to grow there, no limbs stretched over the intangible line, and Myra knew that if one were to dig at that boundary, there would be no roots passing below it either. Not all Shards were the same, but many of them had similar effects on their surroundings. The only thing that would grow in the clearing was a knee-high yellow grass that was almost entirely buried under snow.

"We mean you no-," Ed cried out, but then he shook his head and came to a stop. "The last of them just went unconscious."

"Danger?" Og asked. Ed shrugged. "I can't get a good look at their minds. Most of them have at least basic defenses, and one I'd rather not touch even if I could. But we have a bigger problem."

Myra could almost hear Og's eyebrow rising at that comment, but the Ogre said nothing. The quasi-game annoyed her. Ed wanted them to ask him things, always. He claimed that by asking about things they were more likely to remember what he said. Still, the fact that he hadn't told them what was wrong meant he didn't think the problem was overly dangerous.

"What is it?" Myra asked.

"They're at the Shard," Ed said.

"So?"

"Think about it, then look around us again."

Myra did as she was told and looked about the clearing. It was just as she'd noticed before, the trees at the edge growing away from the clearing, to the point of leaning. The snow and grass were the only things that passed that line, other than themselves. She couldn't see the Shard, but then that wasn't irregular either. While some could be seen on the horizon, a few legendary ones dwarfed mountains. Others could fit in the palm of her rather small hand.

She was about to say something when she realized what was wrong. It was what her father meant, and it was what had put her on edge the moment she'd entered the clearing. While he had told her to look, it wasn't her eyes that he really wanted her to use.

"There's no song," Myra said quietly. Ed nodded and smiled at her, but his face was filled with sorrow.

"Another Shard has fallen to the Void," he said quietly. He started to move towards the center of the clearing once more, although at a subdued pace compared to his earlier charge. Myra and Og, as always, followed him.

"Are they survivors?" Og asked once they started moving.

"That's impossible," Ed said, although there was some doubt in his voice. "Once the Void breaches a world that world ends in an instant. Like... like a popping a bubble."

Myra nodded, but Og growled unpleasantly.

"There is no survival," Ed said. "Unless they were lucky. The kind of lucky that doesn't happen. If they happened to touch the Shard in the same moment the Void breached their world; then it might be possible. The timing does seem unnaturally fortuitous."

Ed paused once more as they approached the center of the clearing. He stepped in front of Myra as she approached, holding her shoulder with a hand as he surveyed the area. Og reached them a half moment after and shook his large head at whatever it was he saw.

"What is it?" Myra asked.

"Don't look," he said quietly, then he looked to the Ogre and quietly asked, "will you?"

"Yes," Og nodded before turning to lumber back into the forest. Myra watched as he tore massive limbs from the trees with little effort. He braided branches and added limbs until what he held was too awkward to hold in the air, before dropping it to the ground and dragging it behind him like a sled.

"We'll go on our trip at some point," Ed said quietly, "but our new guests will need time before we can leave them on their own. A great deal of time."

"What is it?" Myra asked. She desperately wanted to step around her father and look, but she wouldn't disobey. Not when he seemed so sullen and serious about something. Not yet at least.

Ed turned around to her and gave her a soft look. His mouth opened and closed a few times, silently, before he finally managed words.

"They're Void touched," he said. Og stopped in his tracks, halfway through the clearing with his sled.

"Scions?" He asked, anger and hate flashing across his face.

"They're not Scions of the Void or anything. They weren't changed, only touched," Ed said quickly. Og gave a relieved nod and started moving again. Myra scowled, more lost than before. Once more Ed was stuck in a moment of silence, obviously trying to find a way to explain things to her in a way she could understand. But she was done with doing as she was told. As Ed bit his lip, she stepped to his side, so she could see whatever was distressing him.

The first she saw was a woman with short red hair. Her skin was as pale as Ed's was dark, and shallow to the point of being partially translucent in the light of day. More than that, it almost looked like something was moving beneath her skin, shifting as if trying to hide from sight. Two of the others were the same, although the man looked considerably healthier than the others.

The last of those she saw made her want to a step back. When she tried to do so, Ed caught her shoulder and held her there. He hadn't wanted her to see, but once she did, he wouldn't allow her to turn her gaze.

The only reason Myra could tell there was a fourth person at all was for the single arm that the body still had. There were no legs. They were gone, along with large sections of the lower torso. But that wasn't all. The body was heavily burned, strangely shining bone poking through in more than one place. Where a face should have been, there was a seared mass of flesh and far too much visible skull.

Myra retched, turning and leaving her breakfast on the fresh snow. She only prayed that no wind came to push what had to be the stench of death towards her. Ed rubbed her back as Og began moved the unconscious people onto his sled.

"It will take a few hours, days at most, for the Fae to clear the last of the Void from their bodies. Recovery will take much longer," Ed said quietly. Myra nodded but said nothing, turning her head as in her periphery Og picked up the burned corpse with a sorrowful look. As he was prepared to place it on across the makeshift sled from the others, he froze. Tentatively he raised the body to his nose and gave a long sniff, his face contorting at whatever scent he caught. Then he turned his head and lowered his ear to the corpse's chest.

"Ed," he said with a shaking voice, "it breathes."

"I expected as much," Ed sighed. He left Myra behind as he moved to Og, the ogre lowering the body back to the ground. Ed kneeled at body's side, putting one hand over the lower part of the corpse's face and holding it there, the other hand sought to find a vein.

"Breathing is stable," he said quietly.

"How?" Og asked. Ed shook his head.

"I can't say that I know… But the pulse is also stable. Slow, but strong and steady."

Ed pulled away from the body and removed his orange robes, leaving him in like colored pants with a bare chest. He wrapped the wounded in the robe, moving with delicate and practiced hands.

"We'll need you to move quickly. We're not far from Autumn's edge, and predators will have smelled the wounded," Ed said. Og nodded firmly and grabbed the long branch that was the handle to the sled. Ed laid beside the wounded and gave a saddened and apologetic smile.

Myra ignored the twisting in her stomach as she ran to the others. She laid down on the far side of the sled from the body and her father, laying on her back as Og began to sprint through the forest, dragging them along behind him.

---Acknowledgements---

This book has been a labor of love for me, even if I've been sick of it at times. I started writing it in October of 2017, a day after I turned 29 and realized I wasn't growing any younger. I've written more versions of this book, and drafts within those versions, than I will ever openly admit. The first version may as well be a different story altogether, sharing a few names rather than events or characters with the finished product.

But I would never have gotten this far if it weren't for those that supported me over the years, starting long before that autumn afternoon. My family and my friends are chief among them, including some who are no longer with us. If I am hesitant to give names, it is because they are too many, and thus I fear hiding the magnitude of my gratefulness behind a truly massive barrage of names. Instead then, allow me to thank a few here, while knowing the rest still mean the world to me.

Thank you to my parents, Ken and Denise Cook, who are always ready with support and advice when I need it most, never questioning my eccentricities. I haven't always been the easiest son to deal with, but you wouldn't know it by speaking to them. They've inspired me in both life and writing, more than they can know.

Thank you to Jennifer Quinby, one of my three amazing siblings, who wouldn't allow me to rest on my laurels and continuously pressed me to keep sending chapters. Even when she waited for them, always for far longer than I promised, she diligently reminded me to keep working on it.

Thank you to Jack Cornett for giving me the confidence to truly consider writing. Many years ago, when I first told my friends I was thinking of becoming a writer, Jack heard about it. The next time I saw him, he told me in no uncertain terms to follow my dream, and that he would read whatever I wrote because he knew it would be good. I hope he knew how much that meant to me.

And finally, thank you to my dear readers. Without you, a book is nothing but words on a page. Through each of you, a new version of the story takes hold, unique to you and you alone. Though the words may be cumbersome, and my ideas bizarre, I hope it was something that you enjoyed. If you choose to return, know that I will be here working on the AetherSphere, one book at a time. If not with mastery, then with passion.

For news and updates on all things AetherSphere, visit theaethersphere.com

---Glossary---

The following glossary is mostly free of spoilers, and terms introduced later in the book will not be present. However, caution is still recommended.

AeC: A machine that transforms the energy used by Aetherweavers, Aether, into a different form of energy (Ether) that can power machinery as well as magic enchantments.

Aether: The primary energy used by Aetherweavers to create magical phenomena. Some say it is endless, others say it originates from the Fae.

Aetherweaver: One who bears a Stigma, they can sense and manipulate the energies of magic into patterns that produce magical phenomena.

Arcanes (The): The Arcanes are the schools of magic. Aetherweaving and Telepathy are known, but it is said there are others that exist. Some say a handful. Others say hundreds. When something is not completely understood, Arcane is generally put in front of it (Arcane Runes, Arcane Sight).

Awakening: The process through which Aetherweavers receive their Stigma and their powers. It can last days, weeks, or sometimes months. It includes horrendous nightmares from which there is no waking until the process is complete, or the individual has died. Stories tell of magical phenomena spontaneously erupting around those that that are undergoing an Awakening.

Base Layer: When used in the context of a Combat Suit, a Base Layer is a skin-tight latex garment that is worn underneath the rest of the Combat Suit. It is coated in electronics that aid in the transferring of information, such as user movement and temperature, between the skin of the wearer and the rest of the suit.

Bastion: A legendary stronghold Sol learned of from books that originated in the same era. It was said to be built by Emperor Milias and his Simurans.

Barrier: See Ether Shield.

Beast Core: The first part of a Rot Beast, and their only true vulnerability. They appear to be beads the size sand grains. The sight of them reportedly gives headaches, fevers, and an impulse to destroy. A Rot Beast only dies if the core is destroyed, however new cores form out of the resulting Ash in minutes.

Behemoth (The): One of three Goliath class machines. Millenia old and enormous, it was built for war. Its specialty was in transforming natural resources to produce other machines of war that could be launched from its numerous fighter bays. Houses the remnants of humanity as the story begins.

Condenser: See AeC

Combat Suit: A multilayered construct of fabric and metal alloys powered by Ether. Can be customized with various modules, but most contain environmental isolation, armor, magnetic manipulation, an access console on one wrist and a magnetic grappling hook on the other.

EMB: Also known as an Empathy Bomb. Created by telepaths to kill telepaths. Their power varies greatly.

Ether: A highly stable yet potent form of energy that can fuel both magic and machinery. Little is known about its creation, other than it comes out of AeC devices.

Ether Shield: A magic barrier that requires mass amounts of Ether to construct and maintain. Few things can pass through an Ether Shield without using preset runes.

Ether Technology: Technology created to exploit the incredible potency of Ether. From plasma weaponry, to Ether Shields, to the Goliath machines themselves

Final War (The): A war to end all others. Proceeded by a dozen smaller wars that saw the slow expansion of the new Soltraven Empire, The Final War started in full when the greatest powers of the world saw the threat and gathered together to destroy Soltraven. The war only ended when the Rot appeared and began to devour all.

Goliath (class machine): A class of machine that was only possible through Ether Technology. Only three were ever constructed. The Behemoth of the land, the Leviathan of the deeps, and the Wyrm of the skies. All bore AeC's to power themselves.

Leviathan (The): One of the three Goliath class machines. Of the three it is the most mysterious. After it left harbor it was never seen nor heard from again.

Mana: An arcane energy that Aetherweavers can bend and control, although it is essentially condensed Aether. It collects inside the Stigma and is both more potent than Aether and easier to control. Most old tomes warn to never use it unless the need is dire.

Mount Kalmit: An ancient and massive mountain that the Soltraven Empire took in their wars before creating Ether Technology. The mountain was said to be the most massive there was, if not the tallest. Many stories speak of bizarre creatures and beings appearing in the vicinity of the mountain. Many wars have been fought both around it, and because of it.

Rot (The): Common man's name for the calamity that destroyed the world.

Rot Ash: Usually referred to simply as Ash, so called because of its visual similarities to ash from a fire. It is the most common form of the Rot and tends to be stable, slowly eating anything it touches that isn't of the Rot. When organic life is nearby, however, it begins to transform into Rot Beasts.

Rot Beast: Generally considered the most visually horrifying form of the Rot. Rot Beasts can form wherever there is Ash, and killing one grants only temporary safety. They appear to shapeshift near endlessly, although they've been seen consuming Ash as they do so.

Because of this, it is theorized that they require sustenance to fuel their changes. It is unknown if Ash or things not of the Rot are better for them to consume in this regard.

Simurans: A synthetically created organic species. They have no gender, are created in factories, and all of them are supposedly telepathic. They were designed and made by the one they serve, Emperor Milias of the Soltraven Empire.

Stasis: Those locked in Stasis appear to be frozen in time, unmoving, until they are freed. While current Stasis uses Ether to be powered, maintaining Stasis is possible with less potent forms of energy.

Stigma: A mysterious mark that appears on an Aetherweavers body at the end of their Awakening. It can be anything and can appear anywhere on the Aetherweaver. In such times it is on a limb, and the limb is removed, it appears elsewhere on the body. Not much is known about them, other than they are seen as the source of Aetherweaver abilities. They tend to have some physical signs when in use. Glowing is common.

Soltraven Empire (The): Originally a small kingdom that was formed by rebelling slaves of nearby powers. It became an Empire under Emperor Milias (formerly King). It expanded first through military excellence, and later with the overwhelming power of Ether Technology.

Telepathic: One of the Arcanes that can be trained, although it typically takes decades to form in a normal individual. Telepaths have a natural empathy field in which they feel the emotions and fluctuating intents of those around them, although this varies in range and strength between individuals and is dampened by many materials. Otherwise, telepaths are capable of actively using their power to read, communicate with, and manipulate other minds.

Wyrm (The): One of the three Goliath class machines, and the only one with more than one AeC onboard. Slightly smaller than the Behemoth, this massive machine flew through the air and was singlehandedly responsible for conquering a dozen large kingdoms with its highly advanced weaponry and unrivaled maneuverability. It was eventually destroyed due to a catastrophic failure with its energy systems, obliterating everything in an enormous radius and creating unnatural and dangerous weather patterns across the world.